I0582394

INK & CROWN

INK & CROWN

T.S. CURTIS

FIRST EDITION PAPERBACK

ISBN 978-1-7779995-1-3

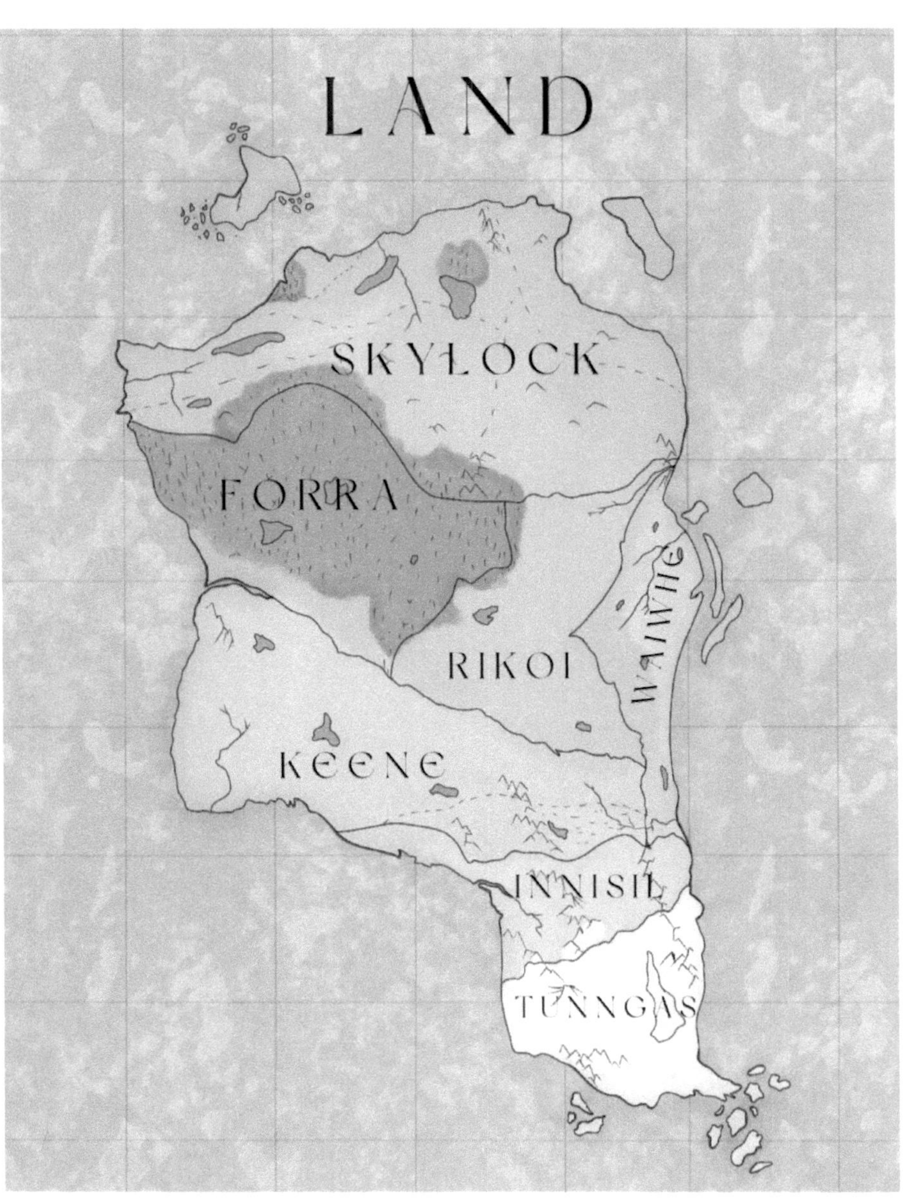

LAND
SKYLOCK
FORRA
RIKOI
WAIWIE
KEENE
INNISIL
TUNNGAS

Trigger Warnings
This work contains mentions of attempted sexual assault/unwanted advances, and death (including death of sibling, and death of unknowns).
This work contains depictions of depression, grief, anxiety, injury, blood, hospitalization, weapons, death, violence, and war.

- LISTEN IN -

Immerse yourself in the dreamy world of *Ink & Crown* with the
Ink & Crown: In Sound playlist

This book is dedicated
To every little one who has struggled to decide whether
To be a Princess
Or a Warrior
Let this be your reminder that
No matter what life throws at you
You can be *both* if you choose

And, like so much else in my life,
This book is dedicated to Sarah
Who helped me back to a place where I could find my crown,
And raise my sword

Autumn

- CHAPTER I -

The doors to the small morning room flew open, the royal family looking up from their breakfast. Grey daylight poured in through the windows as the sun rose behind the thick, grey clouds, a streak of light falling on the single empty chair between the King and the Princess, a long scratch on the one arm. An attendant stepped through the doors, panting heavily like they had just sprinted through the halls, their eyes darting around the room at the family as they all waited quietly.

The attendant gulped, resisting the urge to pull at their castle-issued tie, the colour matched to their assigned wing. "Sire?" they asked, hands clasped in front of their chest. The King waved the attendant over, each one of their steps falling heavy over the quiet room. They paused, finally leaning over to murmur something to the King.

He rested a hand on his beard, which had not been trimmed in a while, nodding slowly. "Alright…thank you." The attendant stood, bowing rapidly to the rest of the family before scurrying back out the door. The King looked out across the table, his family slowly lowering spoons, waiting, watching. He was quiet for another moment, tapping a finger against his chin, finally standing. His large, ornate chair screeched a little behind him, one of the servers dashing to keep it from tipping over. He met his daughter's eyes, the two of them studying each other and she could see the lines between his eyes deepen as she swallowed hard.

Clearing his throat, his eyes still on the Princess, he announced, "The Writer has arrived."

- CHAPTER II -

Theodore Crawford bounced on his toes as he waited in the huge foyer, which was unlike anything he had ever seen before. The hall at his university paled in the grandness that surrounded him, and the holes in his socks were suddenly painfully evident inside his mostly-polished shoes. He held his case tightly, slowly turning in a circle as he admired the high ceilings, feeling his feet against the white and dark-grey marble floors. Three young women bustling across the other end of the foyer caught his eye, disappearing down a hallway even more swiftly than they had appeared. Theo craned his neck as he leaned forward, trying to see where they were rushing off to.

"Theodore!" the King called, his voice echoey in the hall, walking towards Theo. Theo set his case down, brushing out his vest, reaching to shake the hand extended to him. The King's handshake was firm, almost jarring, as he gripped Theo's hand. "Welcome to our home! Thank you so much for coming."

Theo bowed, trying to remember the list of things his editor had mentioned hurriedly before shoving him out of the office that morning. "Thank you for having me, your majesty."

"I have business to attend to and they're waiting on me, but my aid, Voghen, will show you the palace and answer questions about your stay…I'm sure there are many."

"Thank you again, your majesty."

"And if you need anything, please, don't hesitate to ask, or send a note through the messengers to me. Sometimes they're the only ones who manage to track me down," the King laughed, a warm, inviting sound that filled the foyer.

Theo smiled. "I will, your majesty."

"Alright, well! Welcome, and enjoy the tour! Voghen, he's all yours." The short man behind the King stepped forward, bowing slightly to the King as he walked down one of the hallways.

"Welcome, Mr. Crawford–"

"–uh, Theo's fine, or Teddy, or–"

The aid cleared his throat, his mouth pinched together in repugnance. "Mr. Crawford. I'm certain you understand the privilege that comes with living in the palace, and the access you will have to the royal family. This evening, the King will bestow an honourable title upon you, meaning you will be more than just Theodore Crawford. So no, *Theo* or *Teddy* are not fine. Your life is about to change, and you would be best not to forget it. So, if you will follow me," he clapped his hands together, spinning on his heel, "the tour."

Voghen gestured around the pale coloured room, Skylock's grey daylight streaming in the windows high above their heads, rendering the beautiful candle chandeliers almost completely unnecessary. "This here is the main hall, as you probably guessed, where guests and visitors are welcomed into the palace, much like yourself. From now on, should you want to leave, you will need to inform both the family and the guard, as you are under the castle's protection and act at their will." Theo looked up, admiring the largest of the chandeliers high above him, the painted ceiling beyond it almost dancing in the late morning daylight. He recognized the faces and colours of Skylock's twelve deities, surrounded by stars and clouds and fruit trees. Out of the corner of his eye he noticed a balcony, almost out of sight, a flash of pink at the bannister.

It was quick, but he would recognize her anywhere.

He stared up at her, squinting a little, starting to smile. Princess Amair stared down at the young journalist, raising her chin a little as she caught him noticing her. Even from far away, she seemed intimidating.

"Follow me, Mr. Crawford!" the aid called, halfway across the hall towards the grand staircase. Theo scrambled to grab his case, glancing up at the now-empty balcony, and jogged after the stout man.

Theo tried to build a mental map as Voghen led him down corridor after corridor, up dozens of stairs. They passed through colourful hallways, filled with brilliant wallpapers and what had to be hundreds of paintings. Every window let the grey light spill in, glinting off golden frames. Every door had a deities' symbol carved over them and Theo tried to listen to Voghen and recognize each one as they nearly jogged through the halls.

"The Queen insisted you have a room in the guest wing, instead of with the staff, against all good conscience if I do say so myself, and you must be mindful as these are among the nicest of our rooms. Everything in them is of great value, so *please*, Mr. Crawford, do not damage them. This is also where any important guests and visitors will stay, and you will be courteous with them but do *not* interact unless given permission from the King, the Queen, or the Oighre.

"You will have a valet and two chamber attendants who will take care of your dressing and grooming while you are here. After all," the aid slowed for a moment, looking Theo up and down distastefully, "you are the most honoured guest of the royal family now. Practically one of them. Your valet will be in charge of ordering every new outfit. You will of course have input, but please…just allow him to do his job, as it *is* his job. He knows what is needed for the life you will have now. You will meet him and the attendants later. If there is anything you need you have a button there which calls a member of your staff and they will use one of the servant staircases to come to your aid, regardless of the time. Your valet will also assure you are up on time and sent where you need to be when you are needed. These men will also be good resources for you if you need help learning the customs of the palace.

"You will take meals in the morning room and the dining room with the family. Every meal will require you to be properly dressed. You can expect to change clothes at least twice a day, three or four if there are any important events taking place. If you find yourself hungry between meals, call for your valet and request a snack. There are hidden doors along all of the hallways and in some of the drawing rooms which make it easier for the staff to come and go from the staff quarters, the kitchens, the working part of the castle. Your room, and all the other rooms, are fitted with bells you can ring whenever you need assistance.

"You are welcome to go out into the gardens and see the grounds, your valet will be able to help you find the correct doors. As I said earlier, going beyond the gates will require permission from the King, or in your case preferably the Princess.

"You are also free to use many of the rooms throughout the palace, however some wings and rooms will be locked to you, such as the family's private quarters, unless you are specifically invited.

"The Princess is...delicate, and in quite a state at the moment." Theo furrowed his brow at the aid, opening his mouth to stop him but the aid pressed on, "How much contact you have with her is dictated by her. Please do not go about pressing her. You are here as a journalist, we all understand that, but I believe the King and Queen are hoping she may be able to find some kind of friend in you, given what happened. But, still, allow her to come to you and dictate this relationship as she wishes."

"Um..."

"Good. Here we are." He pushed open the door they had stopped in front of and Theo's eyes widened. The walls were covered in pale blue wallpaper with tiny, gold foiled details across them. A small chandelier hung in the middle of the room, dark wooden furniture and a lush rug making everything inviting.

"You can set your case here and if you follow me, I will show you some of the rooms you *will* have access to, as well as, and more importantly, a few you are expressly forbidden from entering."

Theo was still looking around the room, trying to take in every inch of the luxurious walls and the bedspread on the square, canopied bed, looking towards the bookshelf and the vanity, and–

He realised the aid was clicking down the hall and tossed his case on the bed, running to catch up with the guide who evidently had not even realised he had left Theo behind.

***

"What is this place?" Theo asked in awe, turning slowly as the dim light from the clouded sky streamed in the glass roof, brilliantly hitting the hundreds of picture frames around him.

"The Hall of Memories…seventy years' worth of the best moments the royal photographers have captured." Voghen tucked his hand behind his back, standing a little taller. "A good place to start, I would say, if the Princess is not ready to speak with you."

They slowed as he walked through the room, recognizing dozens of faces of the recent sovereigns and their families, older photos with the whispers of movement around the subjects melting into slightly less grainy photographs and he noticed the Late Prince Layton's stoic smile start to fill the frames. Theo paused at the arched doorway, squinting a little at a black and white photo of three girls standing on the castle steps. He recognized the Princess, standing between a girl in a headscarf and a girl with her hair in intricate braids, all three of them with matching grins like they had been about to melt into laughter. He grinned to himself, trying to remember the last time a photo had been published of anyone in the royal family with smiles on their faces. He cautiously pulled his notebook from the pocket of his vest, writing down the number on the card below the frame, adding a star and reminding himself to ask the Princess about the girls – and if she remembered what they had been laughing about.

Theo was about to follow Voghen out of the hall but paused at two frames next to each other, the Late Oighre smiling, a man with a proud smile next to him in the further of the two. He leaned a little closer, noticing Princess Amair at the edge of both photos, arms crossed protectively over herself, smiling from the shadows. Theo stepped back, realising he could spot the edge of a dress, or a sneak of her hands in the back of nearly every frame that held Layton's life. He went to examine a few of them closer when Voghen's sharp voice calling his name spurred him towards the exit, forcing him to leave the whispers of royal memories for another time.

"Keep up, please," Voghen clipped, his mouth twitching. "Now, this corridor leads to the Family Wing, where their majesties and their royal highnesses reside. It is strictly off limits to you unless you receive an explicit invitation to enter. While the whole of the castle is their house, the Family Wing is their *home*. There are only a few staff allowed there, and the family."

"Seems like a fairly straight forward concept." Voghen narrowed his eyes and Theo bit his lip, turning away and pretending to be extremely interested in the painting on the wall.

"Follow me."

Theo kept his eyes turned away as the aid led him down the family hallway. "Should we?"

"It's a tour, Mr. Crawford," Voghen turned his head to look the writer up and down, "you should know where things are, and this is where you would find the family. In the rare event you are summoned, *I* don't want to be accused of getting you lost." Voghen rattled down the list of names, pointing out rooms and studies for the members of the family. "This is…" He cleared his throat "this…*was*, the Late Prince Layton's room, may the gods hold his soul. Officially, it is the Oighre's suite, but no one has been able to coax the Princess to move in…." He cleared his throat again, shaking his head a little. "Yes, well…anyway, over here," Voghen walked on, "is the Princess' room." Voghen met Theo's gaze and squinted at him. "Under no circumstance should you *ever* enter into this room."

Theo shrugged until he noticed Voghen's pointed look. He stood a little straighter. "Yes sir."

"Don't forget."

They were both silent as Voghen led him back out of the Family Wing, taking a flight of stairs up, rendering Theo lost again.

"Ah, Sir Ephenezer!" Voghen called down the hall. A broad-shouldered man turned and smiled, but his smile turned from kind to forced as his eyes shifted from Theo to the aide.

"Voghen."

"Mr. Crawford, this is the Knight General Sir Moritz Ephenezer. He sees to the Royal Guard and the Knights, and coordinates the protection of the Sovereign. Sir Ephenezer, Mr. Theodore Crawford. The Writer."

"It's very nice to meet you, Theodore."

Theo pulled a hand out from behind his back. "Likewise, Knight General."

"Just Moritz is fine." Voghen lifted his chin a little, glaring at the Knight General, who ignored him. Theo almost would not have recognized the Knight General without the top position's signature gold-plated armour that was present in all his portraits, official and otherwise. He looked just like a man, his structured, light blue shirt complimenting his salt and pepper hair. He had rolled the sleeves up to just below the elbows and, for a split second, he looked tired.

"So," Moritz's voice pulled Theo from glancing at the short sword that was at his hip, even in casual dress, "you're the one who's going to be sharing the story of our beautiful Princess."

"Sounds like it."

"I've known her her whole life. She's like a daughter to me." Moritz smiled, but Theo caught the slight warning as the Knight General tightened his fingers on the sword at his hip. "Please go easy on her. She's…well, she's adapting."

"I'm not here for some hard-hitting exposé, General," Theo said assuredly. "I just want to help the people learn more about our future Queen."

Moritz smiled. "I'm glad to hear it. I think you'll fit in here nicely." Moritz patted Theo's shoulder, glancing at Voghen. "Well, Theodore, I shall see you at the investiture ceremony this evening."

"Yes. Ah…thank you," Theo stuttered a little. Moritz chuckled, waving, as Voghen ushered Theo down the hall, murmuring *off limits* every time he pointed to a door.

***

"This here is one of the libraries. The Queen has–" Theo heard slow clicking behind them and Voghen stopped, spinning on his heel. Theo turned, slower, watching as Voghen straightened his cravat, pushing his shoulders back, clearing his throat.

"May I present to you, her royal highness, reigning Oighre, Princess Amair Skylock."

"Your highness." Theo bowed deeply, a hand crossed over his chest, the way he remembered his school teaching them when the King had ridden through on a tour. He glanced up at her from where he stood leaned over.

People from across the realms recognized Amair. She had been blessed with the generations of her family's beauty. Her warm chestnut hair with a small, striking section that was almost black. The section peeked through in all her updos, woven in like a dark ribbon. Her eyes were the same blue as every Skylock ruler that had come before her, the blue colour in her right eye interrupted with one little section of dark brown. Stories had circulated of her being blessed by a witch, her marks remnants of a spell.

She pressed her lips together and he could see how she composed herself, swallowing a little. "Welcome, Sir Crawford."

"Actually, it's still Mr. Crawford," Voghen reminded her.

"Right. Of course." The two strangers peered at each other, cautious.

Theo remembered a photo of the Princess from when she was young. Younger, he reminded himself, looking at the nearly seventeen-year-old. His mother had set the photo down on their table, smiling and pointing at the picture of the girl with her messy hair down her back, a lopsided flower crown on her head as she spun and grinned in what looked like a field, the warm light of a setting sun lighting up her pale face and the wildflowers around her. "*That is our beautiful Princess,*" his mother had told him.

Theo took a breath, hoping she would not notice him composing himself the same way she had. "I am…so, incredibly excited to be here, Princess." She bowed her head a little, running a hand over the bodice of her dress.

"Voghen, may I…may I have a moment with Mr. Crawford?"

"Of course, your highness." He bowed and stepped away, hovering by the doorway. Theo caught the biting look Voghen shot at him.

Amair stepped closer to Theo, glancing up at him but averting her eyes back to her hands.

"I appreciate why you are here, Sir…*Mr.* Crawford. I won't lie to you, it was not…" She looked up, trying to find the words, "I didn't choose to have you here."

Theo licked his lips, trying to make out the look on her face. "I'm just here to get to know you."

She narrowed her eyes a little as she studied him, and he could see her biting the inside of her cheek. The Princess tipped her head a little, the tulle sleeves of her off-white gown shuddering a little in the light breeze. "Then I guess we both have a lot to learn."

***

"And with that, we have come full circle back to your chambers." Voghen clasped his hands. "And your staff should have arrived, so." He pointed a hand towards the door, waiting for Theo to open it. Theo took a slow breath, almost afraid of what was on the other side, and pushed inside, Voghen right behind him. "Ah, good, you're here!" Theo heard him say.

He took a deep breath, shook his head and his anxiety, and followed Voghen inside. "Everyone, this is Mr. Crawford."

"I thought he was styled as Sir Crawford?" the blond with a childish face quipped. Voghen narrowed his eyes at him, making the two men in attendants' uniforms cower slightly.

"*Not* until *after* the ceremony." Voghen turned his nose up, not looking any of them in their face. Theo noticed the young man in the valet's uniform trying not to laugh. "Now. *Mr.* Crawford, these three young men will be your staff. Despite our vast numbers of highly skilled and long serving employees, the Queen insisted you have...*buddies*." At that, Theo nearly lost his cool, biting his tongue.

"Gaelen here is your valet. He is in charge of everything you need, and will be in charge of instructing your attendants for their daily tasks. You may discuss how you would like your day and things to be organised. Gaelen will also be in charge of all your personal and professional communication. If you need to send something, he will deliver it personally, or send it through the necessary channels. The attendants are mainly in charge of cleaning and some basic alteration. Your attendants are Hammanich and Ivan. You are expected at the ceremony this evening. Gaelen...ensure he gets there."

"Yes, Sir Voghen." Galen bobbed his head, catching Theo's eye again as they both tried to keep from laughing.

"Very well then. Good day, *Mr.* Crawford." Voghen spun on his heel, his heavy footsteps passing through the door and down the hall. Theo finally let out an anxious laugh, the other three young men following suit. Theo bent over, catching his breath, undoing his tie as he stood back up.

"Well, I'm glad that's over," he breathed, shaking his head.

Gaelen chuckled. "Sir Voghen can be a lot," he agreed, hands still tucked behind his back.

"So, which one is Hammanich and which one–"

"–I'm Ivan," the blonde one raised his hand a little. "That's Hammanich. He doesn't talk much, though…" Hammanich smiled, bobbing his head at Theo. "Nice to meet ya', *Mr.* Crawford."

"Please," he reached to shake Gaelen's hand, "just Theo, is fine."

Gaelen nodded, smiling as Theo shook hands with the two attendants. "Theo it is. We're very happy to have you here. I believe the family is too."

"Thank you." Theo rubbed his brow. "I um...would it be inconvenient to you if I unpacked myself?"

"But we can do—"

"—you can certainly," Gaelen cut Ivan off, "unpack your bags, though I will ask you to leave everything *out,* so that we can put it away in a way we can find it."

"What um...sorry, what exactly do you *do*?"

"I will help you dress, and undress. Like Voghen said, I will deal with your communications, so whenever you need something sent, just pass it off to me. I'll help organise your schedule, organise a whole new wardrobe, fit you for clothing. A few other things, as we see fit. Most valets start showers, help with basic grooming, shaving. These two will take care of replacing hygiene products, cleaning and tidying, making the bed, um...basic alterations and repairs, if needed. They'll bring you the papers every morning, keep the snacks prepped, bring meals, when you want to work in the room. They'll be in charge of your laundry. And like I said...whatever else we, as a team, decide you'll need."

"I don't know what I'll need. Can't say I've ever had *staff.*"

"And we can help with that too. Hammanich was raised in the castle, and I've been here for two years."

"How old are you?"

"Nineteen. Same as you."

"And you've already been here for two years?"

"Six months as a kitchen hand, six months as an attendant. This last year I've been a junior guests' valet. You're my first permanent assignment."

"We'll see how permanent I am after the first interview."

"I have a feeling you'll be great," Gaelen assured him.

"Would it be...I don't know, rude to sit in your presence?"

"Only if we were her highness," Ivan snorted, earning a raised eyebrow from Gaelen. He looked back as Theo flopped onto the bed, trying not to gasp at the soft mattress as he sank into it.

"Nice?"

"I've been sleeping on little more than slats since I started at the paper," Theo laughed, pressing his cheek into the duvet, hearing the three young men chuckle. "Oh," Theo sat up, "I'm sorry, you sleep in the staff quarters...that was probably inconsiderate–"

"–oh, no, our beds are pretty comfortable."

"More comfortable than the farm I grew up on," Ivan agreed.

"They try to take care of us, here. But, enough about us. Ivan, Hammanich...off with you." They bowed slightly, bumping shoulders as they fought to get out the door first.

Gaelen let out a breath, chuckling slightly. "They call the twin princes Wee Terrors…" He smirked. "Though, I'd say Hammanich and Ivan give even them a run for their money."

"They seem nice."

"They are. Good workers, too. They've offered Hammanich any number of high positions, since he grew up in the palace and palace kids technically get first choice in assignments, if they choose to stay here. But...he likes the routine of being a lad's attendant. Once we fix your schedule, I'll be able to assign him a concrete list of daily tasks."

"Hm."

"I'll let you unpack," Gaelen grinned, tucking his hands behind his back again, "and I'll come back later, in time to dress you for the ceremony. I can get you a bit to eat, you missed breakfast and the family luncheon."

"I'm um...I think I'm still too nervous to eat. Still feeling a little nauseous."

"Very well. Welcome to the palace, Writer."

- CHAPTER III -

There was a knock at Theo's door as he sat on the lush carpet, holding his silver pen between his teeth, a notepad in hand. "Oh, uh, am I…can I just say 'come in' or…is there a procedure–"

"–no procedure," someone chuckled, pushing open the door. "Theodore, right?"

"That's me, but usually it's just Theo," Theo smiled at the young man, tossing his notepad aside and pushing himself to his feet. The boy reached a hand out, a lopsided smile on his face.

"Jasper."

Something clicked and Theo's eyes widened, stumbling. "Oh!" He fumbled into something that did not count as a bow. "Oh, your high–"

"–just Jasper is fine." The Prince and the writer shook hands, almost matching grins on their faces. Prince Jasper ran a hand through his fluffy hair, glancing around at the two cases half-emptied on the bed. "Getting settled in?"

"I think so. I had to send the…*valet* and attendants away. They were a little…"

"Much?"

"Yeah," Theo chuckled. "It's uh, a pretty big change from everything I've had before."

Jasper nodded, his eyes running over the stack of books waiting to be shelved. "You lived in town, yeah?"

"For a few months. Just a tiny little place, this...it's my first job. I spent most of my life in the office, though, so I didn't need much, just a bed, a brown blanket and a window. Oh, and a very little stove."

"Oh, so yeah, this is just a *bit* of a change."

Theo laughed. "Exactly."

"Are you from here?"

"No, Glenn. I moved to Carening to take journalism at college, and then managed to get a job at the paper in the Royal Village, so I moved here. Lots of homes."

"Hm. Have a favourite?"

Theo bit his lip, glancing out the window, the clock tower at the town's event hall just barely visible in the distance, shrouded in grey fog. "Here's shaping up to be pretty cool."

"If you want to change anything, to make the room feel more like yours, go ahead. Just ask your valet. If they quibble, tell them the Prince told you to." Jasper grinned.

"I'll remember that."

"So," Jasper sat on the edge of Theo's bed, "what did you have to do to land this assignment?"

"I batted my eyelashes and smiled a little at my editor," Theo chuckled, making Jasper snort, which only made Theo laugh some more. "No, the castle requested someone young. They thought it would give the Princess someone who is a little more…relatable, I guess. And I'm the youngest so...I'm thanking whatever fates made that happen."

"You feeling ready, though?"

"For?"

"The job…and my sister."

Theo picked up one of the shirts from his case, focusing on a thread fraying on one of the dull buttons. "I think so. I mean...it's...a lot. I'm uh, apparently being *knighted* tonight."

"Ah, yes. I heard. Don't worry, Ama's only stabbed the candidate twice." Theo whipped his head up from his case, raising an eyebrow but Jasper laughed. "I'm totally kidding. She's the only one of us who's actually any good with a sword. And I'll be there cheering for you. Plus the rest of the boys. And Amair supports you too. She's just...y'know. *Amair*."

Theo chuckled, rolling his eyes a little at the Prince. "What...what's she like?" Theo asked, his face shifting a little, gripping the shirt tightly between his fingers.

"She's...a lot of things. Smart as a whip. Words that could cut you before her sword ever does. She used to be a lot of fun," Jasper shook his head a little, thinking about his family. "She was bright. Always keeping everyone smiling. She's the only person who can...could? I don't know. But the only one who could get our brother Kylo to put his guard down."

"The accident changed her."

Jasper raised an eyebrow at Theo's certainty. "More than I ever would have expected. She's always been...quiet, at least outside the sibling bubble. Reserved. But it's more...angry, now." He stopped, thinking for a second. "I don't know if it was his death...or becoming Oighre, becoming...the next Sovereign."

"Or maybe both?"

"Yeah. She likes the shadows. She likes...behind the scenes stuff. I don't think being so in the public eye has helped. This is all new to her. And she doesn't have him. Or their friends. And the two of them might have been best friends, but Layton and Ama're...*were* total opposite. And yet, she *keeps* comparing herself to him. Which is super frustrating cause like...if she let herself just be herself, she'd be really, really good at this in her own way. Instead, she's haunted."

"I can't even imagine how hard it is..." Theo tipped his head a little. "For any of you."

"This is gonna sound harsh...and if you write it down, I'll deny it...but...Kylo and the twins, and me, we weren't really affected. Even our parents weren't, really. Not in the same way, I guess. It was the two of them that were close. But Layton...don't get me wrong, he was a great brother. We loved him. But...he wasn't really close with us. Too focused on other things. He sort of...chose one sibling and let the rest of us be. By the time I was born, then Kylo was born, and then the twins...Layton was already halfway to being King, and Amair was always there, right behind him. We went off and did our thing, the two of them did theirs. *Their* bond was special. It's only in the last...year that Amair got close with Kylo and I, because Layton was starting to take meetings she wasn't allowed to go to."

Jasper shook his head a little. "I think part of why dad is doing this – inviting you – is to try and...get some of her sunshine back.

"But she's never liked talking about herself. Or talking all that much in general, it...it may take her a bit to...get on with you."

"I get it. A journalist showing up isn't easy, in any case."

"It was easy for Layton. There's a reason all the papers and magazines had a story about him almost every week. He was–"

"–the Golden Boy," Theo murmured, nodding a little.

"Yeah." Jasper sighed. "The Amair I love...she's in there but she's..." he coughed, "she's under a couple sad layers at the moment."

"Mr. Crawford?" a messenger called from the door. Theo jumped a little, both boys swinging their heads to him, forcing smiles.

"Yes?"

"The King has arranged for you and the Princess to have your first interview. It will take place in thirty minutes, in the White Parlour."

"Oh! Alright. I'll be there."

"Very good. I will let her know." The messenger bowed a little to Jasper and turned back into the hallway.

"I should go," Jasper said, glancing at the clock behind Theo, hands on his thighs as he pushed off Theo's bed. "Let you finish unpacking. Find something to wear for your *first interview.*"

"Oh. Yeah, sure thing. I should probably find..." he glanced suspiciously at the half-empty wardrobe, "something appropriate."

"In a couple days, they'll have you completely outfitted. It'll be like you lived in the castle your whole life. I heard my mom talking about fabrics and buttons with your valet yesterday."

"Oh boy."

Jasper snorted. "Welcome to the castle! I'll see you...tonight."

"Yeah! See you then!" Theo smiled as Jasper went to leave.

He paused in the doorway, turning back slightly to Theo. "Hey Theodore?"

"Yeah?"

"Don't let her intimidate you," Jasper smirked, slipping out of Theo's room.

- CHAPTER IV -

Theo took a deep breath, staring at the tall door to the White Parlour, thankful for the directions the guard in the guest hall had given.

"Come in," a girl's voice called, and Theo nodded to himself once, pushing forward.

"Sorry, Princess, they seem to have lost my guidebook," he tried not to wince at the awkwardness in his voice, "I wasn't sure if I should…I don't know, announce myself or not, or…"

"It's fine," she looked up at him, closing what looked like a notebook. "I've never really been one for procedure…anyways, I forgot to have an attendant outside to wait for you, so that's partly on me."

"Mhm." Theo nodded, giving himself a split second to take in the White Parlour, its tall windows and cosy looking fireplace, one of the walls covered in a giant, painted mural of two narwhals emerging from the water, skylarks nesting on the end of their crossed horns.

"There's tea…just black tea, but there's milk and sugar."

"Oh, great." Theo tucked his hands behind his back, turning his head from the room to study her for a second.

She looked up from the table, her intense blue eyes and their dark spot matching his gaze. "You can sit." She looked him up and down, pulling her eyes away to stare into her teacup. "I don't bite." She barely murmured it, but Theo caught her words, trying to push back his smile. He cleared his throat a little, pulling the other chair out, laying out his notepad and his favourite, slightly dented pen.

"You alright to do this?" Theo asked, watching the grey light cast shadows through the windows, making the pattern on Amair's dress almost look as though it was moving.

"I…" She took a breath, looking around the parlour, sitting straighter. "Yes."

"Alright. Stop me if you need a break – there's no pressure. You can…avoid a question, or tell me to shove off. Whatever you need." He noticed Amair flash the quickest smile, but her face settled immediately. "Um, alrighty. Let's start easy then. What is your name?"

"Amair…Amair Daniella Skylock."

"Title?"

"Princess of…um…Oighre Princess of Skylock."

"Age?"

She squinted a little at him. "Do…do people really want to know these things?"

"I thought we'd start with more of a…profile. Let people get to know you. Before we let them in on any of your secrets."

Amair chewed the inside of her cheek, studying Theo's face. "How about a trade."

"A trade for what?"

"I'll give you an answer, if you give me one." Theo raised an eyebrow. Amair tipped her head a little, her eyes steady on Theo's. "I want to know who's writing about me."

Theo leaned back a little and tapping the end of his pen against the table. The two watched each other, the pen the only noise in the room. "Okay. Deal."

"Fine. Name?" Amair asked.

"Theodore Ritten Crawford."

"*Title*?" she raised an eyebrow, studying him, smirking ever so slightly.

Theo smiled. "Journalist."

"And *Sir*," Amair reminded him.

"Title pending." He smiled. "Age?

"Nearly seventeen. You?"

"Nearly nineteen. Favourite colour?"

She blinked, almost shocked by the question. "Um…blue."

"Skylock blue?"

She didn't say anything, but the corner of her mouth managed a knowing half smile. "Favourite colour?" she shot back, her face settling again.

"Blue."

"Just blue?"

He tried to avoid studying her eyes, brilliant blue, almost brighter against the dark spot in her right eye. "Um...that sort of...dusty purple blue." He smiled, keeping his eyes on hers. "Like the flowers that grow in the fields through Glenn and Glasslight and Flora." Theo raised his chin a little, still unable to look away from her. "Kind of like your eyes." She squinted at him again, but turned her eyes down to her hands in her lap and he watched her throat tighten for a moment.

"Next question," she murmured.

"Favourite food?"

"Is this really just...are all of these going to be about my favourite things?"

"Yup."

"Huh..."

"Favourite food?"

"Pancakes. The super fluffy kind."

"There's this really awesome little food stand when you go through Beatha, in Carening." Theo smiled as he remembered, finishing numbering his page and turning to the next one, looking up at her again. "Right near the university. They serve breakfast, and by far the *best* fluffy pancakes. You can get them regular size, or a cup full of these little one-bite ones."

He caught the tiniest hint of a smile as her eyes widened. "That sounds amazing."

"It really is."

"Your turn."

"Biscuits and gravy," Theo laughed. "Apparently we both like comfort food."

"It rains more than two hundred days a year. Comfort food is very much called for in Skylock. There's a reason our national dish is cream of potato soup."

He saw the corners of her mouth turn up, softening for a moment. He took a deep breath, glancing at his notebook. "Your best day?"

"That's happened or could happen?"

"Whichever."

Amair thought for a second, pulling on one of her fingers. "Cup of tea and a window seat. On a grey day. With Lupa nearby – that's my dog. Layton…mmm, *someone* playing the piano."

Theo didn't write it down, but he noticed the slip, remembering a photograph in a magazine of Layton practising on the keys, Amair hanging on his shoulder.

Amair cleared her throat a little, "What's your best day?"

"A picnic," Theo grinned.

"Really?"

"They're my favourite memories from home. All the way back to when I was a kid. We'd pack a basket and go sit out near the lochs. I'd get flowers to bring home and we'd just…enjoy the day."

"That sounds really nice."

"It was. It is. I did it all through university. A piece of home."

"Have you had the chance to recently?"

"Not since I started at the paper in town. If I have free time, I work on research to try and get a bigger article."

"Oh. Right, yeah."

"What do you do with your free time?"

"These days I don't have much."

"Fair enough."

"But in those quiet moments…I get outside. Whenever I can, no matter if it's raining or not." She tipped her head a couple times. "I actually like the rain. Makes me feel…alive. When it falls on my skin. And I read. And when I can I…um, I train."

"Train?"

"Swords. Knives. Tried a battle axe a couple weeks ago. Archery. A…well-placed punch to the nose."

"Ah, right. The star of the games."

"Sometimes."

Theo chuckled, scribbling a couple notes for himself. "Alright. Next question…favourite class?"

- CHAPTER V -

"How did your first day with the Writer go?"

Amair watched the King from across his desk. "Um…I don't…I don't like talking about myself."

"I know hon. I'm sorry you've been thrown in so fast." They were both quiet for a second, Amair chewing her cheek.

She looked down at her feet. "Am I meant to be the distraction?"

"Amair…"

"I heard you and Moritz. That people are…they're starting to ask questions about the accident, about Layton, and Johanna, and Dylan." She looked up at her dad, eyes bright. "It makes sense. My brother…my best friend, and our best friends. Deaths that…even I know don't add up. Questions we don't have answers to."

He peered at her. "There have been some…questions. But this *isn't* about distraction. It's about them getting to *know* you. You are *the* heir now. It's time you came out of the shadows."

"I don't know if I can do it, dad."

"Hon–"

"–I'm not ready!"

"Amair," her father said, his tone warning.

"Daddy–" She shook her head. "I'm not…I'm not ready! I've been…I've been out of bed for, like, three weeks, I can't…I don't know…"

"Amair, you must. The country needs…they need hope. You have to be that hope."

"I don't know if I *can be*." She took a deep breath. "I don't know if I have *any left*!"

He shook his head, his eyes down. He took her shoulders carefully, looking up from the ground. "Amair…I know this is not something you asked for. But I believe in you."

***

"Sweet Amair," the priest smiled, his green robes twirling around his feet as he brushed across the floor towards the Princess.

"Hi," she managed to smile, reaching towards him as he stretched out his hands and took hers gently.

"How are you?" She watched the priest's eyes studying her carefully.

Amair didn't say anything, watching him back. The words tumbled out of her mouth before she could stop them, "I don't want to be Queen. I can't be"

He smiled sadly, letting go of one of her hands to wrap his arm around her, leading her further into the temple. "I know that it was not the path...you planned."

"Planned? This wasn't even in my purview. My brother was going to be King – he was going to be a *great* King!" A single tear slipped down her cheek as they stopped in front of the fountain and she stared into the falling water. "I was going to watch, and be proud."

The priest was quiet for a moment, letting Amair calm down with the water. The priest jerked straight suddenly, looking around. "There's someone here with us." Amair glanced at the priest, and then around the room. She stood, the only noise the falling water, letting the priest take whatever message he was being given.

"Amair," he let his arm fall from around her, turning to face her, "there are generations of Sovereigns before you, that *believe* you can do this."

"Mhm."

"Do you remember what the High Priestess and I told you at the funeral?" Amair was quiet for a second, squinting at the priest a little. "Fate sets out our paths…but sometimes there are blips in the plan that even it cannot catch. Sometimes, *life* takes over."

"I don't…" She paused, chewing her lip. "I feel lost."

He smiled a little, looking around them. "You watched your brother for years. He trusted you," the priest looked into the open space around them, like he was listening to someone else, "you were his hands, his eyes. His heart. He knew your potential." Amair felt a chill run over her spine, inadvertently squeezing the priest's hands. "He saw in you great potential. And a fearlessness unlike any other." The priest broke his concentration, smiling back down at Amair. "Your ancestors believe in you. The *gods* believe in you, Amair…Sitwell and Endra are keeping their eyes on you." The priest chuckled. "And from what I hear…your people do too."

"What if I let them down?"

"Do you love your people?"

Amair didn't hesitate, "Very much."

"Then you have everything you need." A breeze whistled through one of the chimes behind her, wrapped around her and for a moment she swore it felt like an embrace, and slipped quietly out the other side.

- CHAPTER VI -

His valet fixed the collar of Theo's jacket again as Theo watched in the mirror.

"I think it's fine, Gaelen," Theo chuckled, easing away from the gloved hands. "Pretty sure it was straight three tries ago."

"Apologies, Mr. Crawford." Gaelen shook out his hands. "I just want everything to be perfect for you tonight."

"With you in charge of me, I think my days of mediocrity are over." Theo looked himself up and down in the mirror. The jacket felt heavier than anything he had put on before, the light blue velvet trimmed with gold pressing into him.

"I'll have a regular evening jacket and cravat for after the ceremony, so you can change quickly before dinner. More comfortable."

"Right."

"The King or the Oighre – or maybe both – will ask you a series of questions. Pledges." Gaelen fixed another button on Theo's shoulder, catching Theo's eye. "The correct response is *I do swear*."

"I do swear," Theo murmured to himself, shifting as an attendant knelt to fix his shoes.

"The King is very kind. So is the Oighre, she's just quiet. Particularly in recent weeks. It should be easy tonight. And then the castle's head photographer will instruct you on posing, for records and such. I can retrieve copies in a few days, should you want one or want to send them to anyone."

"Yeah, that would be great…I'm sure my mom will want one."

"It will likely end up in a newspaper, also. All investiture ceremonies do. To keep the castle open to the people."

"Right…" Theo took a slow breath, catching a glimpse of himself in the mirror and for a moment it was someone completely new looking back. "It'll be strange to be in the paper and not be the byline." Gaelen chuckled, doing up the gold buttons on the coat.

"Alright. I believe that's everything. Let's get you to the grand hall."

***

Theo couldn't help turning as he walked, head tilted back to take in every inch of the ornate room, with its tall windows and arched ceiling. It was unlike anything he had ever seen. The King and Voghen stood at the front, murmuring as two attendants set out boxes and fixed the carpet on the platform. Theo heard footsteps behind him, stumbling to the side as he turned to see a group filing into the room, staff and members of the royal family amongst them. Amair walked in, on the arm of one of her brothers, the young twin princes running in after them. A man chased after them, arms out as he tried to grab for them, the boys always just out of reach. Theo chuckled, watching one of the youngest princes dropping to the floor and crawling through the legs of an attendant, who jumped, trying not to step on the boy.

Amair and her middle brother whose name always escaped Theo walked towards the platform, talking quietly. They both bowed to the King, who smiled as the Prince left Amair, retreating to stand next to the Queen. Moritz, the Knight General, was next to her in his golden armour this time, Jasper off to the side.

"Psst," someone whispered, and Theo spun to find a young attendant watching him. "You need to stand at the doors. So the King can call you forth." Theo nodded, sticking to the wall as he slinked back to the doors, hands behind his back.

The King looked up, noticing the visitor in the doorway and smiled. He brushed his fingers against Amair's arm. She stood taller, straightening her shoulders. Theo watched her for a moment, the way her face hardened as it focused, her perfectly straight collarbones in line. She looked to her father, folding her hands in front of her, and he nodded. She looked back to Theo, their eyes connecting, and he straightened under her gaze.

"Come forth, Writer," she called down the room to him. A final, perfect hush fell over the room Theo nodded, his hands in fists as he stood as tall as he could, and took a step forward. The crowd parted as he walked down the light blue carpet, keeping his eyes on the Princess. He stopped at the two young guards with their spears crossed, just in front of the steps. The King raised his chin, putting his hands behind his back as he glanced between his daughter and the Writer.

"Come forth and kneel, Theodore Ritten Crawford, before your King and Oighre." Theodore swallowed hard as the guards stepped to the side. He felt himself nod, bending to one knee. "Do you acknowledge us as your Sovereigns?"

"Yes. I-I do." Theo tried no to wince at the nerves in his voice.

"It is the intention of this house to raise you by virtue of honour, loyalty, valour, and skill, to bestow upon you the honourable title of Man of Letters, and Creator of Words. Do you recognize the great power that words hold?"

"I do."

"It is a power that cannot be taught. It is something special, to craft words and share them. Do you swear to use your words for good, of the Kingdom and its people?"

"I do swear." One of the attendants opened an intricately carved box, presenting it to the Princess. She turned with the box, opening it to present to her father but he shook his head. Everyone watched in silence as she breathed, slowly but too harshly to be calmly, glancing down at the box. After a moment she turned back to the attendant, setting it back in their hands, and opened the lid, staring at the contents. She flexed her hands and Theo wondered if everything was about to be cancelled right there as he knelt at her mercy.

Finally, she withdrew a badge. She took a step forward, carefully pushing the pin of the badge through the breast of Theo's dress jacket. She turned and pulled a beautiful silver pen from the box, vines and flowers carved into the side, a Skylock thistle painted near the top.

"Do you swear to use The Pen to the best of your abilities, to uphold the honour of this household?" Her voice, for some reason, caught him off guard.

"I do swear," Theo nodded a little. Amair bit her lip, opening her palm. Theo didn't move but she took his hand, gently wrapping her fingers around his. He jumped a little, offering his open palm and she gently laid the pen in it, closing his fingers around the pen. She moved his hand to his chest, flicking the quickest smile as he glanced up. The second attendant opened the longer carved box, the inside lined with soft looking velvet that matched the carpet beneath them. Amair took a breath, turning and carefully withdrawing the ornamental sword.

He bowed his head, suddenly feeling extremely vulnerable as a swish of cool air rushed across the back of his neck, the collar of his jacket shifting. The weight of the sword rested against his first shoulder, and he glanced up, watching Amair lift the sword over his head and rest it against his other shoulder.

"Then I, Princess Amir Daniella Skylock, O…" she choked on the word for a moment, "Oighre of Skylock, dub thee *Sir* Theodore Crawford, Man of Letters, Creator of Words…Writer." Theo noticed the King nod his head in quiet pride at his daughter as she spoke. "Rise, Sir Crawford, and wield this pen with as much caution as a sword." Theo smiled, surprised at his exhilaration and rose, rolling the carved pen around in his hand. Behind him he heard a few people clap, glancing over to see Jasper and the second prince standing with the Queen, a few attendants and guards clapping with them.

"If not more," she added, quieter, just enough for him to hear her, his smile faltered but he nodded to her solemnly.

"Alright. Now for dinner!" the King exclaimed, making the small audience laugh and nod. The second prince offered his arm to his mother, the two of them turning out the door, following the castle staff.

"Sorry, would the three of you mind staying for one moment?" a young woman waved a hand, catching Amair's eye. "Just to get the official shots?"

"Of course."

She raised the camera as Theo glanced to the side, trying to decide where to put his hands, trying to emulate the King, finally getting into position, hearing the click of the camera.

"Sire? Would it be possible to get one of the Oighre and her guest?"

"Ah, yes," the King bobbed his head, slinking back and the Queen walked up to him. The two grabbed hands, turning to chat. Theo noticed the Queen's eyes on them, her head tipped as she watched, talking to her husband at the same time.

"Would the two of you mind stepping just a little closer?" the photographer called, waving her hand. Amair glanced over to Theo, waiting. Theo watched her chest rise and fall once and she looked down, swallowing hard. She picked up her skirts and rustled closer to him. Theo sucked in a breath, glancing down at Amair as she settled next to him. One of the attendants popped over to her, straightening her skirt, and disappeared off to the side again. Amair turned her head and for a moment, it was quiet.

The noise of the guests and staff in the room dissipated, the two of them breathing in sync. Theo felt her lean against his arm ever so slightly. She was warm, her skin just brushing against his, hovering near him and he wanted to press closer. He felt her turn her head just enough so she could slide her eyes towards where the zap of heat passed between them.

The noise returned as the photographer called for them to look into her camera. They stayed still as she pulled on the cord, the bulb flashing and Theo had to force himself not to blink as the photographer called out a reminder to stay still until the shot had finished. It felt like minutes, standing there in front of everyone as they kept their eyes open, before she called to them again and Amair leaned away. Theo let out his breath, keeping his eyes forwards for a moment. "I'll get the film developed first thing, your highness."

"Thank you."

"Alright, *now* it's time for dinner," the King chuckled, an arm around the Queen as the doors were pushed open into the corridor.

***

Gaelen straightened the lapel of Theo's grey jacket. Theo noticed the valet smiling, reaching to fix his hair. "I'll pin your badge on, to have it through supper. Just so you can wear it a bit longer," the Valet grinned, placing it. "You'll wear the badge on any official occasion. Alanmas celebrations. The Princess' birthday."

"Right. Of course."

"Don't worry. The attendants and I will be here to remind you when to put it on."

"Thank you."

"Alright, you're ready. You know your way to the family dining room?"

"I...believe so."

"Any of the attendants will point you along the way, if you're lost. I will see you when you retire for the night."

"Theo?"

"Yes?" Theo paused in the middle of the corridor, fussing with the cuff the valet had just finished with.

"There was...with the Princess, you and her..." Gaelen hesitated, looking the Writer up and down and finally shook his head. "Good work tonight."

- CHAPTER VII -

Theo looked down at the badge as he waited in the hall, running his fingers over the light blue velvet. He stopped, noticing three small gold symbols embroidered in a line near the bottom.

"Quinnm'on, Rowenea, and Noabhail," he heard Amair's voice say, looking up to find her in the doorway with her hands behind her back. "The Goddess of Wisdom and Education, the Deity of Music and Art, and the God of Messengers, Travelers, and Adventurers." She walked up to the table, resting her hands on the back of her chair. "Everyone's investiture ceremony is created for them, individually. Each badge crafted for them, individually. Having their symbols with you is a call on the deities that protect your service. Usually it's two, though when they asked for my input on this one, I believed you needed the three of them. Writing… journalism…those aren't just one thing. They're special crafts. They take knowledge – wisdom – and much learning, but my father was right, it's not something that is taught. You're an artist. You craft something from nothing. Create narratives, and pictures in the mind. And you are a messenger, of course. That's why you're here, after all. So, to me, they all felt necessary. Plus," the smallest hint of a smirk edged onto her face, "you're dealing with the royal family. You need all the protection you can get."

"Noabhail was the patron deity given to me at birth. But Caraoidhtce is my second, because of my Winter birthday."

"Endra and Sloane are mine," she murmured, her eyes on his badge. "The sky and…warriors?"

She nodded, peering at him a little. "I always wanted it to be Noabhail. Travellers and adventurers…those words felt like me, then. But every Oighre…every Sovereign has Endra. She's the Kingdom's patron…she must stay with its Sovereign. And Sloane…well, warrior did make sense, actually. My Aunt Elena, she used to remind me about how you don't have to follow the path of your deities set out for you at birth…she's big on carving your own path."

Theo chuckled a little but furrowed his brow again. His face changed, watching her for a moment, remembering. "Weren't…weren't Prince Layton's deities Latarix and Quinnm'on?"

Amair nodded, raising an eyebrow. She looked up into Theo's eyes. "Apparently the universe knew something we didn't." Cold ran over Theo's back and he resisted the urge to shiver.

"Apologies!" the King exclaimed at the doors, the Queen on his arm, "I'm not as limber as I once was!" Three of the young Princes followed behind them, the attendants setting up their station at the side of the room turning to bow as everyone entered. "And getting out of that jacket is not as easy as it once was." He laughed, a warm, full body laugh that could be heard halfway down the hall.

"I had been planning on stealing a roll to munch on, but Sir Crawford here foiled my plan." There was a flash of that smirk again. The family found their seats, attendants helping with the King and Queen's thrones. An attendant tapped Theo on the shoulder, discreetly pointing to a chair next to one of the second prince. Theo nodded, mouthing a thank you and the attendant winked. The Prince bobbed his head at Theo and averted his eyes back to his book. The twin princes across the opening in the table grinned at him before turning back to each other. Jasper rushed in, fixing his tie and jacket, winking at Theo as he passed, sitting on the other side of the younger Prince.

An attendant pulled out the other chair at the head of the table and Amair sat, thanking the attendant and glancing at her brother. "Nice of you to join us, Jasper." He just grinned as the soup was set in front of them.

"Has everyone had the chance to meet Sir Crawford properly?" the King asked, jabbing at his soup.

"I did!" Jasper raised his hand a little, leaning forward to look at Theo.

"I haven't met the other Princes, yet," Theo looked around at them. "It's been…a bit of a busy day."

"Well, Sir Crawford, you're next to Prince Kylo, there, and across from you are our twins," the Queen smiled at them as they glanced up, "Princes Alec and Evander."

"Careful around them," Amair smiled slightly, glancing at her youngest brothers.

"They bite," Kylo snorted. The two of them glanced at each other as Theo noticed the mischievous grins growing on their faces.

"And we haven't had the pleasure yet either, Sir Crawford," the Queen smiled, her spoon in her soup.

"But I would know you anywhere, your majesty," Theo said, making her smile. "And I'm happy to just be Theodore, or Theo." Amair looked up at him, swiping her spoon around her bowl as she studied him.

"Are you settling in alright, Theodore?" the Queen smiled down the table, sipping her soup off her spoon. Theodore nodded slowly, setting his spoon aside.

"My valet and attendants have been…wonderfully helpful. Thank you so much for arranging that. And I've gotten lost a few times, but yes, I think so."

"Well, that's nice to hear. The attendants know this place better than anyone, so please, lean on them, they'll get you used to this place in no time. The boys…" The Queen glanced at them, smirking. "If the twins give you directions, you may end up stuck in one of the passageways with them. Amair has been okay, thus far?" Theo glanced at Amair, who stopped, her spoon halfway to her mouth, waiting for his response. He smiled, looking back to the Queen.

"We're finding our footing," he assured. "It's going somewhere good, though, I think." Out of the corner of his eye, he saw Amair's chest decompress.

"Well, that's…a good step." Amair felt her mother give her a pointed look, not looking up from her soup. "So. Anything interesting happening across the rest of the castle?"

"I read a book about the impact of the FarmStart program," Kylo offered, Amair's four brothers keeping their eyes on her. Even the twins stopped bouncing in their seats. "I've gotta write a paper about it for this month's assignment."

"You should sit down with your sister and get some details," the King told him, glancing at his daughter, and Amair tried to ignore the weight of everyone's eyes. "We've put her in charge of the program."

"Oh! That's cool."

"Yeah," Amair looked up, smiling weakly at her brother. "It's a good program." Her mouth twitched a little. "Lots of paperwork, though."

"Fair enough."

"What part of the program are you learning about, Ky?" the Queen asked.

"The economic side. How putting the money out leads to prosperity. Or at least, that's my hypothesis."

"A strong one, too, my smart boy."

"Thanks, mom."

"Alec? Evander?" The Queen looked to the young twins.

"We…went for a swim," Alec grinned as Evander snorted.

"Do I want to know?"

"Probably not." Evander matched his brother's grin.

"Are your tutors going to come and inform me otherwise?" The Queen raised her eyebrow at her youngest boys. Amair smirked, watching the twins decide.

"Um…not the tutors."

"Not quite the answer I was hoping for," the Queen sighed, sitting back in her chair but letting it go.

"They're fine, Kier," the King chuckled. "If it were really bad, we would have heard by now."

"Fair enough." Evander caught Amair's eye, flashing a goofy grin and she covered her mouth, trying to stifle a laugh.

"Jasper? Anything from you?"

"Not really. I went out to the garden. Did some homework. Met our guest."

"Amair?" Amair swallowed, looking up at her parents. She turned her eyes to Theo, the two of them studying each other for a second.

"I…I met with Sir Crawford. We…like he said, we're learning to work with the other. I um, I wrote a letter to Elena. And…" she thought for a moment, "oh and spent some time with the seamstresses…they're testing a new way of creating printed tulle."

"I sat and watched them work for a while…watching the way their hands work is incredible." Theo raised an eyebrow, watching Amair light up for a second, Jasper reaching out to stop her hand from flinging her soup off the table. The King and Queen shared a quick look, a flash of a smile, looking back at their daughter.

"Sounds fascinating," the Queen smiled. Amair settled a little, but the little smile lingered. When their dinner had ended one of the attendants opened the door for the family and their guest to leave. Amair's fluffy white dog and the King's giant, shaggy hound ran up, Amair tossing bites of rabbit to them. She dropped her hands to her side, her white dog tapping her nose to Amair's hand, earning a pat on the head. Amair glided down the hall, disappearing around a corner.

- CHAPTER VIII -

It was a quiet morning, teacups balanced shakily in their hands as Theo tried to reach into the Princess for more than one-word answers. He watched her hand shake as his questions deepened, her mouth tightening as more words spilled from her lips.

Theo scribbled Amair's answer into his notebook, the depth of the notepad starting to shorten as he reached the final page, wondering to himself where he had stashed his extras. He took a deep breath, peering up at her, thinking. "What do you dream about?" he asked, his pen poised above his paper.

She thought for a moment, wrapping a chestnut curl around her finger. "Before my brother died...magic." For a second Theo wished his pen could capture the look of wonder on her face, the little smile as she stared into space. "Magical lands and magical people and…adventures in new lands. Magic." Her face darkened again. "Now it's just nightmares. About the night Layton and our friends died." Theo's pen stopped moving, looking up at her, taking in how old she suddenly looked. He kept forgetting how young both of them really were.

"That's the only thing on your mind, isn't it?"

"Yes," she nodded slowly. "That, and sometimes running through the things I will need to know to be Queen."

"Being Queen is on your mind?"

"Of course it is," she looked at him incredulously. "Every second of every day."

***

The days came and went, Theo lying in his grand, soft bed as he searched for questions that pushed the boundary just enough, knocking away at the protective walls Amair had built around herself.

He drank through pots upon pots of coffee, Gaelen appearing to refill his cup and help him change for the many various meetings and meals he was called to. He read over his notes again and again, from the moment he left an interview until late into the night, the stars often shrouded by the grey, Skylish clouds. He tried to get inside her head, picturing the way her blue eyes snapped at him with every new question. She sipped her tea, ending the interviews as soon as the questions pushed a little too hard, whisking out of whatever room he had been summoned to that day

"Do you know much about Skylock's history?"

"Not as well as my brother did." She shrugged. "Layton was interested in history and politics. Jasper is, too. And I think Kylo is starting to. Though, he's actually really good with numbers. I spend more time with...plants. And swords. And...arrows." Amair laughed a little. "And now policy documents. But I'm learning. Trying to, at least. Dad thinks every good politician, every good King..." She swallowed, seeming to remember her own part in all of it. "Every good *Sovereign,* understands the history."

"Do you think he's right?"

"I think understanding where we came from…how we got here…is important to understanding my people. We've made mistakes, I don't want to be the Queen who makes them again."

"What about the idea that history will repeat itself?"

"I think history will repeat itself whether we like it or not." She leaned back in her chair, running a finger over the gold rim of her teacup.

"Why's that?"

She shrugged. "From what I *have* read of history…" She smirked a little. "People don't have the best track record."

"Hm."

"Hm?" she mimicked.

"Nothing," he mused, watching the way she watched him, waiting to confirm his opinion of her answer. "So, do you have a favourite story? Or fact?"

"Mmm…Princess Hermia, youngest child of the Third King, Sovereign King Euan. She convinced her brother, the future King Diarmad, to invest in agriculture in Skylock. And she's the reason there is no draft or mandatory guard or knight service. She thought it was barbaric, to force people to participate in war, even if it was *potential* war."

"Interesting."

"The draft was quashed within a few months. She married her attendant Christina, and the two of them lived out their days in the castle, both of them acting as advisors to the future King Diarmad."

"Strong Skylock women."

"As are all of them," Amair shot back.

"Touché." He chuckled, writing down her words. "You should meet my mother."

"What does your mother do?"

"Oh, Princess I'm…I'm sorry, I'm…you don't want to hear—"

"—I do, though." Amair shrugged. "I thought I was allowed to ask you questions. That was the deal."

He raised an eyebrow as she sipped her tea. "I guess I just did not realize that extended past that first day." He shrugged this time. "You haven't asked a question for a couple weeks."

"I had nothing to ask you."

"Alright then."

"So. Your mom."

"She was a farmer's wife – my dad was an herb farmer, and also co-owned a sheep farm."

"In Glasslight."

"Glenn."

"Glenn, right. Sorry." She looked up, slowly committing it to memory.

"It's alright. But yes, on the outer border of Glenn. Once I started school, my mother took up a position as the librarian at the school in the village."

"Is that why you said that's why I should meet her?"

"I just meant on the strong Skylish woman part…she definitely lives up to that name," he chuckled. "Most of the students were afraid of her. *Loved her*, but were afraid of her…she has this thing, where all she has to do is raise an eyebrow and the whole place would go completely silent." Amair smiled, trying to picture his mom.

"Were you the first in your family to go to university?"

"I was. They were very proud."

"I can imagine."

"Mom read a lot, she's super smart, but nothing formal after high school. The university was far away, she was the only child of a farmer, she stayed home to help take care of it. Met my dad at a market…rest is history. He talked about going back, getting a Masters of Agriculture when the Mature Degrees program started, but he died before he made it happen."

"I'm so sorry, Theodore." She tipped her head. "Do you think you would like your Master's Degree?"

Somehow, Theo let himself go a little, letting down a barrier he had never realized he had, slipping into conversation with her he had never let himself say out loud. "You know…someday, I think…"

- CHAPTER IX -

Theo managed to get the door to his room open, trying to balance the teacup of coffee on top of the stack of books with his chin, another book under his arm, and stumbled into his room. Waddling over to his desk, he carefully pulled the thin volume from under his arm, laying it on the edge of the desk, when he noticed the neatly folded daily paper Hammanich had expertly placed in the very centre of the desk.

Blowing a curl out of his eyes, he picked up the cup and the books all tumbled towards the ground, one of them nicking the toe of his dress shoes. He stared at the strewn books, holding the teacup near his face and sighed. With one foot, he shoved them off to the side, sipping his coffee and picking up the paper.

It unfolded and he nearly dropped the teacup onto the books, eyes widening.

Introducing the Man of Letters: The Castle's New Correspondent

Theo placed the teacup on the edge of his desk, grabbing at the other edge of the newspaper, pulling it close to his face. A photo in full colour of him standing next to the Princess filled the bottom corner, the short announcement of his title next to it. The Princess looked gracefully into the camera, her eyes with the intense thoughtfulness he had come to know, to appreciate, a soft smile pulling at her lips, hands folded in front of herself. His eyes were averted, and he followed them to look back at Amair, his smile excited and warm. He noticed the point in the photo where her shoulder brushed against his and he could almost feel where it had been on his arm, his arm vibrating and warm.

Theo tossed the paper onto the desk, rifling through the desk drawers, mumbling to himself as he searched, finally emerging with a pair of golden scissors he knew he had seen when Gaelen had forced him to only be allowed to watch the attendants unpack his things.

He plopped into the chair and, ignoring whatever his colleague had written on page two, sliced into the front page. He cut carefully into the soft newsprint, trying to keep the edges sharp. He pulled the square away from the rest of the paper, smiling, rifling through his desk again. He emerged with sticky paper, putting the roll between his knees, using one hand to rip off a small piece.

He tossed the roll aside, keeping the sticky paper on the tip of his finger and pushing his chair back with his foot. He leaned over his desk, pressing his hips into the edge of wood as he reached up, rolling the sticky paper and pushing it into the wall, putting the newsprint over it.

He took a step back, admiring the photo of him looking at Amair in the middle of the space above his desk. He heard the door click open behind him, the tap of Gaelen's well-polished shoes pulling Theo to look over his shoulder.

"Good afternoon, Sir Crawford."

"Hey, Gaelen." The valet slowed, glancing at Theo's wall, a knowing smile on his face.

"I do have an order in for photos." Gaelen set down the clothes in his hand, watching Theo look back at the photo.

"We can send a few to my mom, but..."

"You're partial to that one?"

Theo blushed. "I think so."

Gaelen chuckled, glancing at the newsprint photo. "Fair enough."

***

Theo wandered down the halls, lost again, peeking in the open doors to try and orient himself. The giddiness of his official title in the paper coursed through him, picturing his mother unfolding it to find the photograph of her son and the Oighre looking so official. Adding a copy to the newsroom at her library, and taking it to gush at her weekly tea with her friends.

A warm light radiated out from one of the open doors ahead of him, picking up his pace to peek inside, recognizing the soft curls pulled into a loose bun.

"Hey, you," he called, slipping into the room. She didn't reply, legs tucked under herself, just staring into the fireplace. "You're up late."

She snapped out of her trance, blinking a few times, looking up at him, her eyes and the tip of her nose red, jarring Theo as he finally put together that she had been crying. "Sorry, did you need something? Were we…were we supposed to meet?"

He smiled softly, lowering into the chair next to her. "We can take a break this week. A story about…" He hesitated. "About The Lost Ones is being featured because of the final memorial going up soon." He watched her nod slowly, staring back into the fire. "So, what's going on in that head of yours?"

She was quiet for a moment, the crack of the fire filling their ears. "Mulayah brought me a photo of the memorial garden," she whispered, her voice strained. "It's funny," she murmured, and Theo noticed the tear rolling down her cheek, gripping her mug of cocoa with both hands. "They're gone…but *I'm* the one who feels lost."

- CHAPTER X -

"Eenie meenie minie moe, catch a skywolf by the toe, if it howls let it go, eenie meenie minie…moe! You're it!" a young Amair squealed, already running away from a boy with golden brown hair that was just a little brighter than her own.

"Not fair! You were counting!" Prince Layton shrieked, taking off after his sister as she ran across the field, the sound of waves crashing far below at the bottom of the Skylock cliffs. A pair of golden eagles were squawking in the distance as Layton changed courses, turning on his toes to go after Dylan who shrieked, realizing the Oighre had turned his sights on him and he had not been planning to run.

"No! No! Oi! Go for your sister!" he yelled with a laugh. Johanna was already at the forest line, jumping for one of the trees and hoisting herself up onto the first limb, leaning out to watch the two boys dancing around each other. Amair jumped,

"Push off the big root, there, Ama!" Johanna crouched a little to point.

"You lose!" Amair called to Dylan.

"Next time," he leaned onto his knees, "I," he raised a finger, still catching his breath, "I get to choose whose it."

"Oh, please," Johanna snorted, jumping down off the branch, Amair a second behind her, "Amair would have caught you before you could say Rivvens." Dylan rolled his eyes but was smiling, glancing at Ama, who was watching Johanna with wide eyes and a smile.

"You're probably right," Dylan finally admitted, the edge of his words cold as air came back to his lungs. Johanna looped her arm through Amair's, flinging one over the Oighre's

"That's what best friends are for." They all laughed, walking back out of the woods, eyes on the gardens that were starting to fill with the afternoon shift. A few of the outdoor hands recognized the four best friends even from afar and waved to them. Amair

and Layton standing a little taller as they were caught. Layton waved in return, putting on his winning smile his sister teased him he must practise in the mornings to get that perfect.

He would never admit that she was right. He was going to be King and he needed everything to feel right.

They got to their favourite nook in the garden, near the castle wall, green vines twisting up the stone and surrounded by tall, leafy hedges so that people had to be at the right angle to spot them. There was tall grass scattered with little blue wildflowers, some of Amair's favourites, that they could sprawl out in, lay on top of each other and watch the rolling clouds on nice days or play games that they were trapped by enemies on particularly dreary ones. The perfect, playful hiding spot.

"Should I go and say hello to the Head Gardener? Word will spread that we're out here and I wouldn't want to be rude—"

"Oh, look at me," Johanna pulled her dark hair back, trying to make herself look boyish as she mocked the Prince, Dylan and Amair stretching in the tall grasses and laughing, "Prince Layton, Golden Boy of the Wooooooorld!" The three kids squealed with laughter and even Layton couldn't help the laugh that escaped his lips. He pulled his short sword from his hip, challenging Johanna.

"Treasonous girl," he said, trying to keep a straight face, "mocking your future King."

"Who is just so mockable." She started to pull on her own sword, Layton immediately hesitating and putting his sword back in its sheath.

"Smart move, dude," Dylan chuckled. Johanna turned, bowing mockingly to all of them.

"Layton!" the King called from a balcony just off from where they thought they were so perfectly hidden, the four kids pausing, turning towards him. "I'm sorry son. This is not play time anymore…" Squinting into the unusual sun, they could all see the pained smile on the King's face. "We have a Council meeting…you have your first Council meeting."

Layton swiped at his bright hair, glancing back at his best friends. Johanna was already reaching for Amair, assuring her that she was not being abandoned.

"You and I can go practice in the ring."

"I'll come watch," Dylan offered. "Even if Dylan wants me to be his secretary, can't actually do it til he's allowed to induct a Circle."

"I'm sorry," Layton sighed, "my duty comes first…"

"Maybe I lost him the day he was called into his first Council meeting…maybe it's the job that killed him. Not an accident."

"Princess…"

"What's it called to write down a memory?" she asked quietly, looking back into the fireplace. Theo stared at her for a moment, squeezing the arms of his chair and trying not to let the tear escape him as he watched her. She looked back at him. "Is that allowed?"

"I…y-yes, your highness."

"Then I'll leave you with that." She turned her head again and something in her face, in the move, told him it was also her goodnight. He wanted to reach out and squeeze her hand and tell her grief got easier or that he was there for her but a part of his brain reminded him he was no match for the future Queen. It wasn't him that she needed. He stood and bowed sloppily, in a daze, squeezing the pen he kept in his pocket, and found his way into the hall, his cheeks hot from the flames and the weight of Amair's old memories.

- CHAPTER XI -

"Princess Amair!" Ebberon, the head painter grinned, reaching his arms out. "Long time no see!"

"You'll have plenty of time to see me for my official portrait," Amair smiled, cradling her notebook to her chest.

"Mulayah mentioned you had an idea for another portrait?"

"I…I do. My father – and the Council – offered to me that I should…I should come up with some kind of memorial. And I have the sculptors working on something for the public but…"

"You want something here," he smiled kindly.

"Right." Amair nodded a little, playing with the edges of her notebook. "So…I'm hoping to put a fairly sizeable portrait of them up in the gallery hall."

"Absolutely." The elderly artist settled in his chair. "I'm guessing you have some ideas in that book you're holding onto so tightly?"

Amair nodded, smiling shyly, pulling on the ribbon so that that book fell open. "I have found tons of photos from their last year…as references…since…since they can't be here. But um…they were such a perfect little group, y'know? All four of us. It felt perfect. But um…for the painting…I want Layton, front and centre. He was going to be King. He was going to be…" tears welled in her eyes, "a great King. And he was…the one that pulled us together. So, I thought him in the middle. Maybe sitting…in what would have been his throne. Or something like it. And Johanna and Dylan on either side of him. His support system…*our* support system." She glanced to the side, watching Mulayah writing on a piece of paper. She examined it, finally handing it over to Ebberon.

"I think I see what you're picturing," the artist smiled, adjusting his glasses to read over the page. "Mulayah and I will start on some sketches to run past you."

"Actually…could you keep it a surprise? I trust you, I…I leave this in your hands." Mulayah grinned, glancing at the Ebberon.

"I think that will be fine, Princess."

"Okay." Amair felt the warm tears that always appeared when she thought about her friends. The pain and happiness of memory. "Thank you."

- CHAPTER XII -

Theo stretched his fingers, staring at the blank pages in front of him, the inkpot off to the side. He slowly picked up the quill from his graduation, turning his eyes to the pages of notes he had been keeping for the first few weeks as he tried to focus on Amair's words. The questions, the dreamy stares out windows as she tried to find her words.

The way her lips moved when she practised her answers in her head.

He sighed, setting his quill down again and getting up to pace back and forth in front of his desk. He felt himself sigh, and then sigh again, trying to focus on the words he needed.

He slowed his pacing, staring at the collection of photos he had asked Ivan tape up over the desk. His mom smiling at the gate when she sent him off to university. His mom beaming at his graduation. His first roommate. His first university newspaper team.

His first headline.

Amair's shoulder brushing against his.

The tiny crook of her smile.

He grinned to himself, plopping back into his chair excitedly, licking the tip of his quill.

Ink & Crown Theo scratched into the top of the page, smiling to himself, a dribble of ink spurting next to the title. He watched the sharp tip of the quill drag across the soft paper, the words finding themselves. He crossed out words, making sure everything was spelled perfectly, and that the story held the truths it needed to.

***

"Gaelen?"

"Yes, sir?"

"Could you have this delivered to my paper as fast as possible? We have a deadline." Theo grinned, holding out the large envelope to his valet.

"Of course, sir. What is it, may I ask?"

"The first edition of the serial."

Gaelen smiled, something sparking in his eyes. "You've finished."

"I think so."

"And it feels right?"

Theo bit his lip, nodding. "It feels perfect."

"If you should allow me, I will deliver this personally to your editor. Precious cargo, after all."

Theo chuckled. "Sounds great."

"I will be back in time to dress you for dinner."

Ink & Crown:
The Princess Serial

by Sir Theodore Crawford

I arrived at the castle, pen in my pocket, with no idea that the story I was asked to cover would turn out to be so much more than anything I had covered before.

In the few weeks I have been here, I have watched the airs in the castle start to shift.

My reception was mixed, and some of the sentiments were cooler than others. An outsider, inside a grieving palace inside a grieving kingdom. But there is a kind of warmth beginning to grow, and I get to be both within the circles, and without, and because of that I can bring you the inside scoop - but also, and perhaps more importantly, I want to bring you the view from the outside. The *Princess* is a bright young woman, for whom my ink and this page will never have the chance to truly capture into a few folds. Instead, I want to bring you as many pieces of her as I can discover.

Dear readers, dear Skylish people, this is the Ink & Crown, The Princess Serial: An Introduction to Her Royal Highness.

While I have learned many things about *Princess Amair* over the past few weeks, I feel the best way to introduce you to her is from the inside -

in her own words.

I spent the first day easing into getting to know The Princess. No good interview comes from discomfort.

So, I had the Princess tell me all of her favourites.

I was most shocked by the fact that her favourite season is, despite many beautiful choices, Winter. In a very Skylockian move, she 'likes the torrential rain' over the 'disappointing drizzle of the others'.

What are some other things that make the *Princess* the young woman she is?

She loves the colour 'dusty blue'.

Her favourite food is pancakes - but only the very fluffy kind.

Despite her very large, fluffy, beloved dog that follows her everywhere she goes, she thinks she may actually prefers cats.

She is skilled in the bow and arrow, but her true skill lies in anything with a blade - swords, throwing knives, and daggers.

She is a skilled horse rider. You can often find her reading, both in the library, but also in some strange tucked away places. I have found two of these secret nooks she has taken to reading in, but I am told there are at least nine more that I have to keep an eye out for.

She thinks her eyesight is her strongest sense - but also mentioned that she always knows when and where an attack is coming from, even when she cannot see it.

She prefers coffee to tea, but prefers to drink from either a tea cup or wine glass.

She is very happy when it rains, and loves to be outside in it. On the rare sunny days we do have, she usually drags her brothers out into the garden with her.

Despite everyone's best efforts, she does not play any instruments.

Her name was supposed to be Annis, but a smudge in her grandmother's letter was interpreted to be *Amair*, instead.

She has the messiest penmanship I have ever seen in my life. I should really just refuse to read any note she sends.

Though her training has led to her having "many dumb injuries and scars", she things the worst and "most ridiculous" to date is a scar on her back - though I have to "work for the rest of that story".

She has a favourite person..but to keep the peace, she has asked me not to print their name.

So, welcome to the palace, dear readers. Follow along every week as we all get to know *Her Royal Highness, Oighre Princess Amair Skylock*: the girl behind the crown.

- Sir Theodore Crawford, Staff Writer, Special Liaison Reporter to The Palace, Man of Letters

- CHAPTER XIII -

"Oh, Ama!" her mom smiled, holding the folded paper in one hand, her coffee in the other. The kids waited, watching her read. "The first serial has been published! Oh, Theodore," the Queen looked towards him, "it is so wonderful to see your name here."

"Thank you, your majesty," Theo bowed his head, making one of the twins snicker as he popped his last bite of his toast into his mouth.

"All good things, hopefully," Amair muttered, staring into the omelette on her plate.

"I look forward to reading it!" the King exclaimed, patting Amair's shoulder. She nodded again, picking up her fork slowly and poking at her food. She looked down the table at Theo, sipping her tea, raising an eyebrow ever so slightly at him.

"So, big plans today, anyone?" the King asked, stabbing at a fennel sausage. Theo heard Kylo discussing an idea he had for a school project, explaining a diorama of a water system, the words of the royal family meshing together as he studied Amair eating her colourful omelette.

"And you, Theo?"

Theo snapped his head towards the Queen, blinking a few times. "Sorry?"

The Queen smiled softly, reaching for her tea. "Any plans for your day?"

"Oh! Oh, um…" He glanced back at Amair, her eyes down, reading something that had been passed to her. "I think I'll just do some exploring,

I'm still managing to get lost, it's almost embarrassing at this point." He grinned at the twins as he heard them snort.

"That sounds lovely…it doesn't look like the rain will be too heavy today, it will be a nice day. Perhaps a good day to explore the gardens, or the rest of the grounds. Amair's favourite places are a bit further out…" He caught the way the Queen raised an eyebrow, trying to catch Amair's eye but the Princess would not meet it. "Anyway. I hope you find some joy in exploring our beautiful space…we are very blessed here, and you're welcome to as much of it as you would like."

***

Theo thanked the guard as they opened the exterior door for him, looking up into a stone awning and stepping through the stone arch, blinking through the grey light. He turned, slowly, smiling as the scent of thousands of plants hit him. The fresh smell of grasses and trees and the hedge that turned the sprawling gardens into a maze. Theo cautiously stepped through each of the green arches that turned the one end of the gardens' twisting maze, certain he was about to walk into one of the twins' booby traps. He kept one hand on the green hedge, holding himself steady and remembering some old tale about finding your way out of a maze like that, the leaves seeming to twist and hold on to his fingers, not wanting to let go until he pulled on it and for a moment, he had to remind himself it was simply his mind playing tricks on him.

He was pretty sure.

He took another turn, grumbling as he realised he had stepped out of the hedges into a large circle and there was just a collection of rocks in the middle. He turned, intending to find his way back out but something in his gut stopped him, looking back over his shoulder at the rocks. They looked familiar, somehow, almost as high as his hip, round at the top and wider at the bottom.

Burial stones.

Something hot caught in his throat and his feet had a mind of their own, stepping closer to them and he could see words carved into the three stones, alike in shape, though different heights and colours. The first was blue-grey and he recognized it as the rock of the cliffs near the back edge of the property, and it was the tallest.

HERE LIES LAYTON ERRAN SKYLOCK
PRINCE AND OIGHRE OF SKYLOCK
SON ~ BROTHER ~ FRIEND
MAY BASIGÀN BRING HIM TO REST

Theo brushed a layer of decaying paper butterflies away, noticing the smaller words *The Lost Ones* carved along the bottom of the stone. Theo swung his legs over, shuffling over to the neighbouring stone. It was more a reddish grey with dark spots like a sprinkling of freckles.

HERE LIES JOHANNA ALINE MOORES

Theo couldn't bring himself to read the rest but spotted *The Lost Ones* carved on the bottom of the stone. With a gulp, he leaned to shuffle on his knees again, swallowing hard as he spotted the third one, the darkest of the three, like the rocks he used to try and climb at home with his friends and the words on this one had been filled with a slight sheen of paint to be able to be read properly. Theo did not need to read the name to know it belonged to Dylan.

Theo brushed his fingers along the decaying paper butterflies left to carry their souls back to the Goddess of Death. Some of the butterflies were perfectly crafted while others were messy and Theo pictured the royal children working together on them, from Amair's perfectly steady hand, to the twins, tears ruining the tissue before they ever even made it into the rain.

It was a Basigàn loop that he had walked through, a memorial meant to invoke thoughtfulness as mourners walked towards the middle. It had not occurred to him that it was more than a maze as the only one he had ever seen had been made of pebbles, drawn out on the ground to get to the burial ground near his mother's home.

Theo decided to stay there, for a while, and see if he could hold on to any piece of The Lost Ones that was still tormenting every member of the castle except him.

***

"Theo!"

"Hey, Jasper," Theo waved a little at Jasper halfway down the hall. Jasper raised his hands, and Theo was just able to catch the outline of two glasses.

"Up for a drink?"

Theo grinned. "Absolutely." He padded quietly down the hall, dark from the moonless night sky and slipped into yet another random study he had not yet stumbled upon. The room was almost completely filled with half-melted candles, small golden plates catching the hot wax, the hundreds of small flames casting enough flickering light it almost made up for the dark grey afternoon.

Jasper passed him, the warm scent of imported Innisillian cinnamon liqueur wafting up into Theo's face. "The first sip is a bit of a bite," Jasper warned, taking a sip of his. Theo took a deep breath and took a sip. Jasper laughed as the look on the Writer's face passed from shock to excitement, taking another sip as he sat on the chair behind him, pulling his legs up to sit cross legged. Theo sat across the small table from him, taking another sip.

"What is in this?"

"Layton was the one interested in drinks, I however know just that it tastes good or not good. But I figured this one would be warm, after I spotted you in the garden out in the rain."

"We're Skylish. Pretty sure we're made of rain at this point, I barely noticed." They both laughed, sipping their drinks. Theo looked into his glass, swirling the warm liqueur in his mouth that finished with a sweetness as he swallowed. "Hey, Jasper?"

"Mhm?"

"I saw Layton's grave today."

Jasper paused, a mix of emotions on his face. He sighed a little, a sad smile on his face. "So you finally stumbled into the cemetery."

"It wasn't exactly on the royal tour."

"No…no," was all he said and despite all Jasper's words to console his own grief, Theo noticed the pull of anguish in the Prince's voice.

"Shouldn't he be buried on the Forgotten Isle?"

Jasper leaned back in his chair, drumming his fingers against the small table between them. "Ama *begged* for him to be buried with the Old Sovereigns on the Isle of Ilona." He shrugged a little, the light from the dozens of candles not enough to illuminate whatever expression was deep on his face. "But the law states what it states…and he was never King. He doesn't get the…" he choked on the words a little, his mouth twitching a little, "the *honour*. We tried our best…at least this way, all three of them are together. The stones for Dylan and Jo were donated by their traditional clans to tie them to their ancestors, and then a piece of them was taken to return to their ancestral lands as well, to balance. Ama is still hurt that all three of them aren't on Ilona. She…she still blames herself, or hates herself for not being there."

Theo opened his mouth, but Jasper hurried to say more. "Theo?"

"Hm?" he asked, tapping his half empty glass against his chin.

"Please don't…please don't ask Ama about this…she…she hasn't been to see them. Not since the funeral."

"Oh."

"Arthur and I were taking turns replacing the butterflies, but it fell off after a while. I don't think *any* of our parents have gone out there, I," Jasper shrugged, "Evander and Alec helped make the butterflies, but Evander would end up crying and the tissue paper would start to disintegrate before we put them out. I think uh…I think it's just the groundskeepers replacing flowers, now."

Theo swallowed hard, taking a sip of his drink, picturing the decaying white and red tissue butterflies, the only physical piece left of Amair's grief.

- CHAPTER XIV -

Amair felt her feet hitting the floor, listened to the way they echoed as she escaped down the hall before any of the counsellors noticed she had bowed out. She technically did have somewhere to be, even if it was not for another fifteen minutes and she was making a pit stop at the photo studio.

"Good morning, Princess," the young woman smiled, bowing her head a little.

"Good morning Jinnalye," Amair smiled, glancing around the studio. "You've been busy," she mused, noticing the prints hanging across every inch of the main studio.

"Always busy, your highness," she chuckled. "With five royal children and now the Writer, there is so much for us to capture."

"As always, I appreciate you and your team greatly for it."

"Except when you're on that side of my camera," she smirked. "Were you looking for something today?"

"Mostly an escape," Amair laughed quietly. "Council meetings may be the death of me."

"Luckily you're in for many, many more," the photographer laughed. Amair stopped suddenly, staring at a photo hanging to dry.

"Are these from the ceremony?"

"Yes, Sir Crawford's," Jinnalye smiled, glancing up from her notepad. "They came out very nicely. He's quite beautiful."

"He is," Amair murmured, her eyes flitting across the line of photographs. Theo alone, Theo and Amair, the two of them and her father. One of him kneeling in front of her, the sword resting on his shoulder. The two of them, arms brushing against each other and she thought about the way it had felt like a zap of electricity when he touched her. She had convinced herself it was simply a static shock from his lush, velvet dress jacket but she knew in her heart that was not the case.

Jinnalye lowered her notepad, a hand on her hip as she watched Amair study the photos. She glanced down at the counter, grabbing something, walking up beside Amair and handing it to her.

Amair looked down, two photographs held out to her, just larger than Jinnalye's hand. "Here. Keepsake."

"Oh…oh I wasn't…I–"

"–I insist, Princess. I printed them the wrong size for the slide inventory anyways. I wouldn't want them to go to waste." Amair peered at the photos, Theo's playful smile in portrait of him alone, and the one of him standing with Amair.

"Th-thank you."

"Certainly, Princess." Amair caught the smirk Jinnalye shot her, but she ignored it, her eyes still on the photographs.

"I must go. The tutor will start to wonder if I got lost on the way back from the Council room."

"Certainly. Have a great day, Princess…I'm always here if you need something." Jinnalye paused. "Photos or…or just someone's ear."

"Thank you," Amair murmured, slipping out the door, not looking up from the photos. She walked up the stairs, slipping around the corner into the Family Wing. She crept past the twins' playroom, hearing a crash somewhere inside and knowing it was better to not investigate. She pressed into her bedroom, a breeze coming in the open window. Amair leaned against the table, staring at the photos. At the soft smile on her face, her arm grazing against Theo's jacket.

"Lydia?" Amair called, and her lady's attendant stepped out of the bathroom.

"Good afternoon, my lady."

Amair tucked the photos behind her back, turning to look at Lydia. The young woman was her age with a kind face and sharp eyes that were always studying the Princess' face, her blonde hair intricately braided at the back of her head to keep it out of her face. "Do we have any empty frames kicking around?"

"Ah, yes, we do," Lydia walked over to one of the wardrobes. She pulled open one of the drawers, peering into it for a second, finally pulling out a dark brown wooden frame. "Here we are. I started stashing the extras. You do like your photos." Amair smiled, taking it from her. Her sharp eyes were already working. "Did you find a new one?"

"Just a…just a nice test shot from the grounds," Amair lied, holding the photographs closer to her back, looking up at Lydia. She avoided eye contact, hoping her attendant was not looking straight through the lie. As she waited, glancing at the waiting picture frames, she knew that Lydia was just still being overly nice, not ready for a rampage yet.

Lydia's face softened into a pleasant smile. "I need to run and pick up the refill of your shampoo and conditioner, is there anything you need?"

"No, no, go ahead, I'm fine for now."

"Alright my lady," Lydia smiled. "I'll see you later."

"Mhm." Amair pushed off the table, laying the frame and the two photographs out. She studied them again, picking all the details apart, finally shaking her head, opening the back of the frame. She carefully placed one of the photos down, putting the frame together and carrying it to the small dresser beside the storage closet door, already littered with frames. Amair ran her thumb across the glass as she got it to sit steady, over her face, and then Theo's. She looked next to the new frame, the photo of her standing and grinning next to a laughing Layton, taken at her seventeenth birthday party. Her eyes flitted between Layton and Theodore, back and forth, shaking her head after a second and turning to look for the visiting tutor.

- CHAPTER XV -

Some days in the castle were a bore and any one that began with math, in Jasper's opinion, were a bore. As he wandered back to the family quarters late one night, wondering if Theo was around somewhere for a drink or just a conversation, he noticed Amair's door ajar.

"Ama?" he asked, peeking in. She sat on the edge of the bed, gripping the edge of her cover. "Ama!" he exclaimed, noticing her face pinched, hung over her chest. He closed the door, kneeling in front of her, taking her cheeks in his hands, feeling the tears that streamed down her cheeks, fluttering through his fingers. "What's happened?"

"I finally convinced myself to read the first serial." Her voice was stained with tears. "I can't do this, Jasper."

"Hey, you can! You *have* been!"

"It was supposed to be *him*. He was our golden boy, he…" Tears cut her off. "*He's* front-page news, he was…I can't *be* him."

He sat next to her on the bed, wrapping an arm around her as he tried to calm her down. She tumbled into his side, her skin clammy as she cried, her bare shoulders shaking. He held her, letting her cry, whispering little words into her sadness.

"I never asked you," Amair murmured, sitting up a little.

"Hm?"

Tears streamed down her cheeks, too tired to swipe at them. "I never asked you if you were okay. After Layton died." She looked up at Jasper. "Everyone was there for me…but I'm your big sister. I…I fell apart when the four of you needed me."

"Ama." He tucked his fingers into her hair, biting his lip, trying to find the right words. "We…we weren't *affected*, the same way."

"It's still so traumatic–"

"–the most traumatic part was watching you and mom fall apart." She paused, her red face looking up at him, brows pulled together. He rubbed her head a little. "I can count how many times I spent time with Layton. And you…you lost Jo, *and* Dylan. We were hit, Ama but…it was…*different*."

"Jasper…"

"I was sad, don't get me wrong, and I *miss them*. But the person Kylo and I, and the twins, were close to was *you*." He took a deep breath, watching how she tried to process what he was trying to tell her. "I just want to see you be okay again. The person *we* miss is our sister."

He had never said it aloud, not like that, and never intended for his sister to be the one to hear it. She had enough, a whole country waiting to rest on her shoulders. She gripped fistfuls of the bedspread, not looking up at him.

"I…I miss you…" They were, somehow, the only words he could manage.

- CHAPTER XVI -

It was a quiet morning at the castle, a few tensions still hanging on from a few days past.

Until Amair spotted her best friend.

"Denna!" Amair called, running down the hall towards the young woman.

"Hello your highness," Denna grinned, pulling her skirt aside to curtsy.

"Don't even start that," Amair rolled her eyes with a laugh. "I didn't realize you were back."

"I would have sent word but I…well, I wasn't sure if you were…out of bed or not…" Denna trailed off, her brilliant eyes searching Amair's face for an answer as she fiddled with her headscarf. Amair managed to keep her smile on her face.

"Lupa and Jasper coaxed me out with the promise of butter cake." Denna smiled and Amair tried to ignore how forced it looked. "Jasper remains a jerk at times who has yet to learn to hold his tongue–"

"–and you have yet to learn that sometimes the people around you are the ones who know you best." Denna quirked up an eyebrow, knowing she was one of the few people who could call the Princess out on it without a hint of consequence.

Amair paused but nodded after a long moment. "I've missed you. It's too quiet, when you're gone."

"I missed you too. But I hear the Writer arrived while I was gone?"

"You heard correctly," Amair nodded a little, staring at the floor.

"So? How is he?"

"Um…he's very nice. Really, he…he doesn't want to barge in. He's trying to do the serial without stepping on my toes too much."

"Uh-huh."

"He's incredibly good-looking," Amair giggled, rolling her eyes at herself. Denna raised an eyebrow, smirking.

"Oh yeah?"

Amair laughed again. "I know I should be giving him more. But it…it's…"

"Hard," Denna finished for the Princess who nodded. Amair stopped walking, sighing, looking at Denna intently.

"Tell me what to do, Denna." Denna didn't say anything, hands behind her back, watching the Princess thoughtfully. "I need to talk to him. I love my people, I…I always have. That's not why I don't feel like I'm meant to be Queen." Amair swallowed hard. "I was never meant to be Queen."

"Let him in, Amair." Amair looked into Denna's eyes, the nervous quivers running through her slowing. "You're right. You were never meant to be Queen. But you will be…and I believe you will be a great one." Denna took a deep breath, watching her friend. "You have spent your life being amazing in the background, in the shadows of a great Oighre, and a great King. Let them know you."

Amair nodded slowly at Denna, looking down. "How long are you back for this time?"

"Two weeks."

"I'll have to make the most of that, then." Amair smiled. Denna grinned, nodding. "I have to go. I have a Council meeting."

"Ah yes, the glamorous part of your life."

Amair managed to grin, nodding. "Oh, you know it."

"Till later, your highness."

"Bye, Denna." Amair slowed, watching Denna keep on down the hall, and took a deep breath. She turned back the way she had come, letting her hands swing by her sides a little, a skip in her step that was enough to make the castle employees stop and watch the Princess in a way they had not seen her in what felt like a very long time.

- CHAPTER XVII -

"I remember a photo of you," Theo smiled at her, leaning back in her chair, the new week of interviews having started and something new around Amair making her seem just slightly more at ease.

"Oh?"

"You must have been six, maybe seven. In a field."

"Oh gosh," she laughed. "Yes, I remember. There's probably a dozen of them around rooms in the castle. It was an accidental photo – a tutor may have taken it." She shook her head, smiling. "I think every home in the Kingdom was sent one."

"Really?" Theo asked, laughing.

"I think so. It…honestly, it may have been Layton that convinced everyone to send out the photo."

"Yeah?" Theo laughed.

"He would have been about eleven. Just started royal training with dad and the advisors, and sitting in on Council meetings. I think it was that he wanted that to be his first act as Oighre or something." Amair rested her hands in her lap, thinking. "I remember telling Layton I felt bad for the people who worked the printing presses since that was a lot of ink and cutting, just for a photo of some girl."

He smiled, trying to picture her as just some girl. Trying to picture her seeing herself as just some girl. "What did he say?"

"That he would import the ink from every corner of Land if he had to." Theo laughed, the way that made his shoulders shake. "He wanted everyone to know his sister."

"I came home to my mom holding the photo," Theo chuckled. Amair leaned on her hand. "She had me sit down and showed me this picture of this little girl, and I was probably ten, just sort of understanding our world, and my mom looked at me and grinned and pointed at your smiling face and said 'Theodore, *that* is our Princess'. It's probably still in a drawer in my mother's house somewhere."

Amair was giggling, one of her hands over her mouth. "It wasn't until I was about nine that I started to understand the…the *public* aspect of who I was. It was the same time that Layton was starting to be more involved with the political side of things. I saw myself in the newspaper for the first time…a week later, I showed up in one of those teen magazines. It claimed to be an interview with the Princess, but I had never given an interview. I had…a full-blown panic attack and hid in my room for thirteen hours."

"Oh dear…"

"Layton convinced one of my attendants to sneak him in through the passageways. He and my dad sat down with me and they…they *explained* why people were interested.

"That was the day that I told them I didn't want to be in the public. Didn't want to be a Princess. And that if I was, it was only to be on my own terms. Layton took it upon himself to keep me out of the press. No one was allowed to publish about me except in a very few circumstances – like the Skylock Games, they were allowed to share when I started competing, since I…well, I started winning."

"You did start making some more public appearances, didn't you?"

"When I joined the Circle – I mean, it was part of the transparency of the Kingdom, they had to share all the names of the Oighre's Circle. And yeah, I started *appearing* in public…I was slightly more comfortable, but I still wasn't allowed to be the spotlight. A magazine a couple years ago wanted to do an interview with Johanna and I – we were up and coming warriors…role models to girls, they said. But…I just couldn't. I made her do it by herself.

"I've always felt a little bit bad, not…showing up, that way." Amair looked down at her hands as she pulled at her fingers. "Especially now that…now that we're…where we are." Theo smiled a little sadly, his pen off to the side as he watched the Princess. She looked up at him, her eyes a little shiny. "I love the Skylish people, Theodore. I love my Kingdom. The land, the people."

"They love you too, Amair." Theo smiled. "You forget I'm one of them. I know you've hidden yourself away but…we did know you, to some degree." Amair raised an eyebrow, tipping her head a little. "And I'm here because…we want to know you more, so we can love you more." Amair didn't respond, raising her teacup, still watching him. He pressed on, "Can I ask you something?"

"Always."

"You were against me coming here."

"I don't think that's a question." Theo just smiled, waiting for her answer. She sighed. "No. I didn't want you here. I didn't want anyone here…*especially* not so soon after…the accident."

Theo nodded, opening his mouth but she stopped him, a hand up in front of her. "But…you're growing on me."

- CHAPTER XVIII -

Theo bowed as he spotted the Princess walking towards him one dreary morning.

"Hello, Princess," Theo smiled, still half in his bow. "Busy day ahead?"

"Unfortunately, yes, you'll have to do without me this afternoon."

"I'll find something to amuse myself. What are you up to?"

"Receiving a diplomat," she told him, gripping the arm of the guard escorting her a little tighter. "Very..." she pursed her lips, "official."

He smiled, his eyes trailing down her dark dress, grinning at the way it glittered as she moved, crescent shapes sprinkled throughout, a heavy, navy velvet cape attached at her shoulders. "It looks like the night sky sneezed on you," Theo grinned. The Princess blinked a few times, her lips curling and a giggle bubbling out of her mouth. Her fingers absentmindedly dragged over a few of the delicate silver stars on her bodice. Theo sucked in a breath, realising it was the first time he had earned a full laugh from her.

"I'll see you later, Writer." She was still giggling.

"Keep the dress on!" he called after her. She looked over her shoulder as she followed the guard down the stairs, an eyebrow raised. Theo shrugged. "For today's interview. It...it suits you." He caught her biting her lip as she swung her head, the twirling staircase taking her away and the velvet cape swishing out beside her.

- CHAPTER XIX -

Sun was breaking through the clouds, lighting up the pink hall adorned with ancient looking paintings. The hallway that Theo was, once again, lost in.

"Hey, Theo!" Jasper called, patting the young guard next to him on the shoulder, and jogging down the hallway towards the writer.

"Hey, Jasp."

"You busy?"

"No, not really, I was just heading to read or something. I can't find your sister so I'm calling it a day off. Why? You wanna do something?"

"I can't, I have to go write a test for mathematics, I am *this close* to testing out of it. But, uh, you should head over to the stables. And… quickly."

Theo blinked a few times. "I…I'm sorry?"

"And um…if Ama asks…*Evander's* the one who told you."

Jasper waved, and Theo's brow furrowed, watching him disappear out into another hallway. Theo shook his head, glancing back down at his notebook, chewing the inside of his cheek as he thought. He stood, grabbing one of his coats by the door and rushing into the hall, trying to slide by the attendants cleaning the walls.

"Pardon me!" he called to a young attendant rushing down the middle of the hall, making her jump. "Sorry! Didn't mean to spook you!"

"It's fine, Sir Crawford," she laughed, picking up the pillows she had dropped. "I thought you were out."

"What's your name?" Theo asked, leaning up against the wall.

"Imogene, sir."

"Well, just Theo works for me."

"Pleased to finally make your acquaintance, just Theo."

Theo snorted, glancing out the window. "I was hoping you could point me in the direction of the stables?" She raised an eyebrow, and he watched a knowing smirk spreading across her face.

"Easy, follow me." She bobbed for him to follow with her head, leaving the pillows on one of the windowsills. "I'll open up the door on the end of the hall. Take the staircase down and hang a left. Once you're in the yard you can't miss the stables." She turned her head, looking him up and down. "Can't miss *her*, either." Theo didn't respond, trying to hide his smile.

"Thank you so much for this."

"Takes some getting used to, this castle. Keep being nice," she winked, "and the attendants can show you all our shortcuts."

"Now I just need a map," he muttered, and she laughed, shrugging.

"It's one of the places my photographic memory comes in handy."

"Maybe I should suggest they just make you the Castle Tour Guide."

"They usually leave that to Sir Voghen."

"Well," Theo shrugged, "that's clearly been *very helpful*." Imogene snorted, reaching for the dead end of the hall and pressing gently, the wall popping open.

"Have fun, just Theo."

"Thank you again for your help!" he called, taking the steps two by two. Imogene grinned, watching him go, and pulled on the door to let it swing closed. The shadows of the staircase fell over Theo, letting the faint lights guide him and trying to avoid tripping down the long, shallow stairs. He recognized the outline a door and pushed on it. It swung open easily and he emerged into the daylight, the sun peeking through a few spots in the grey clouds. He took in the yard, the gardens off to the side, wild and tamed Skylish plants whispering back and forth in the breeze. He could hear the faint crash of the waves at the bottom of the cliffs far off to his right.

Theo's eyes fell on the stables, warm light flooding out the windows and wide, open doors. Theo walked towards it cautiously, footsteps falling quietly over the cobbled ground, running his finger over the binding of his notebook. He spotted an older man with a warm smile leaning against a rail, talking to someone. Shifting his weight, Theo spotted Amair lifting a saddle onto an ink black horse, smiling and chatting, keeping one of her hands on the horse's side. The horse shook its head, nudging it against Amair and making her laugh. There was a strand of white in the middle of the horse's black mane, white dots like a constellation over the bridge of the horse's nose.

He watched her for a second, almost out of place in her dark brown pants and heeled riding boots, adjusting a dark brown jacket. No skirts and heels in sight. Intricate little braids kept her hair out of her face, the rest of her long, ever-so-slightly curly hair running down her back. Amair turned her head slightly, noticing movement in the yard, and turned to peer at the guest, a hand on her hip.

"Hello, Theodore." Her smile softened, looking at him. She seemed confused, but intrigued more than anything. "What are you doing here?"

"Oh, just...out for a walk," Theo lied, smiling. Amair squinted at him a little, glancing at the man next to her. He smiled, nodding, and Amair looked back at Theo.

"Was it Jasper or Kylo?"

"Uh, E-Evander," Theo fumbled, forcing a smile as she rolled her eyes at him.

"Uh-huh." She rolled her eyes. "Are you busy?"

"Not at all. Why?"

"Can you ride?"

"Ah..." Theo chuckled uneasily, glancing at the horse, "sort of." Amair snorted, patting her horse's side.

"Would you like to come?"

Theo looked between her and the horse again, nodding slowly. "Please." She grinned, pleased, turning to one of the stable hands.

"Would you get Sir Crawford a horse?"

"Right away, your highness." He bowed a little, disappearing down the line of stalls.

"Do you like riding?" Theo asked, walking closer to her.

"Quite a lot. Learned to ride sitting with Layton, arms around his waist. We'd go on trail rides," she laughed thinking back, "though eventually it progressed to races and long-distance adventures." She watched Theo stare at her "His name's Elleban."

"Hello, Elleban," Theo smiled, his hands still behind his back.

"You can pet him...if you're comfortable."

"Oh I...I'm not sure I should, I..." Amair reached out to Theo, taking his arm, her fingers wrapped gently around him, and carefully raised it towards Elleban's neck. Theo bit back his breath as his fingers brushed the horse's coat and he started a bit.

"Good boy," Amair murmured, watching Theo pet her horse slowly.

"Thank you!"

"I was talking to the horse," she laughed, looking up at him. They kept their eyes on each other, Theo petting Elleban. Amair shook her head, pulling her eyes away as the clopping of hooves sounded behind them and the groom led a cream-coloured horse towards them.

"I tacked Mexifiah for him, your highness."

"Perfect, thank you Javon." Amair looked back up at Theo. "Alright. Ready to do this?"

"What are we doing?"

"We're going to fly," she grinned as Theo spotted the small wagon being attached to another horse, a tall man with short hair shaking the hand of one of the grooms, adjusting the heavy tarp. "Come on. Mexifiah's waiting for you."

The horses were led into the courtyard and legs were thrown over the great animals and before Theo knew it, the castle was starting to disappear behind them.

They rode through the trees, Theo thankful for the riding class he had taken at school. He heard Amair laugh as she veered off the centre path, jumping over a thick fallen log.

Theo was mostly concentrating on not falling off.

They rode through the thick trees, dodging low hanging branches, Amair and one of the guards taking every jump they could. A fluttering light appeared in front of them, seeming to bounce at the end of the trees, Theo realizing it was him that was bouncing.

Amair broke through the edge of the trees first, her guard close behind. Theo shielded his face, holding the reins in one hand as he slipped through the narrow exit. Warm light flushed over him, and he lifted his head to see the sun setting over the ocean as far as he could see, a cliff at the end of the grassy clearing, a small pool off the side.

Amair slipped off her horse, her long, flowing jacket picking up in the wind. Theo let the guard come over and hold his horse's bridle, cautiously getting off, leaning over to crack his back and groan. Amair laughed, the wind whipping her hair around her, the sound of the guard helping the man pulling the wagon unload it behind them.

"Here you are, Princess." Theo turned, watching the man place a shiny brown bird, talons wrapping onto the leather band on Amair's forearm.

"Oh my gods," he whispered to himself, grinning.

"Hello Breagha," she smiled, cautiously reaching over to pet the bird's sharp head, its watchful yellow eyes landing on Theo. There was a moment of silence, the crashing waves and the wind whispering around them. The bird squawked suddenly, making Amair jump, the rest of them laughing.

"Ready?" the Falconer asked her. She smiled at the bird, eyes sliding to look at Theo.

"*Ready?*" she asked. He nodded slightly, eyes still on the bird.

Theo's eyes widened, watching the bird jump into the sky, twirling in the golden sunset. It dove down the side of the cliff, and Theo resisted the urge to dive towards the edge after it.

After a few quiet seconds, it shot back up into the sky, drawing Theo's eyes up as he hollered in excitement, eyes following the bird. Its call echoed over the cliffs, Amair watching Theo as he watched the bird in complete awe. The bird circled back around, gliding through the air, the wind pricking at each feather like something out of a dream, winding circles around them in the air. Amair snapped her eyes away from Theo, fixing her fitted leather armband and grabbing a treat from the bag at her waist.

"What if she doesn't come back?" Theo asked over his shoulder, nearly bent in half as he looked up at the warming skies.

Amair smiled, whistling once, sharp and loud. and the bird found her way back to settle on the Princess' arm. "Good girl, Breagha," Amair smiled, reaching one finger out to brush gently against the bird's neck. Theo would have sworn the bird smiled.

"Jeremy?" she turned to the attendant that had come with them. "Could you grab an extra glove for Sir Crawford?"

"Of course, your highness."

"Princess...I don't...I don't know..." He glanced at the bird and then more warily at the bird's talons as the attendant pulled the glove onto him.

"Breagha," Amair said and the bird snapped to attention, "switch." The bird chirped slightly, a bright sound, and flapped her wings once for more of a hop than a flight to Theo's outstretched arm, supported by the attendant. Theo gasped as the weight settled on him, almost closing his eyes but his eyes found Amair's face instead. She was smiling, her eyes on her bird but for a split second, her eyes found his and even in the pink light, he could see her blush.

"And when you're ready, you can loose her."

"What if she doesn't come back?"

"Then..." She took a deep breath. "I don't deserve her." She glanced at the bird with a smile. "She's not a very good hunter though," Amair tapped the bag on her hip, "so I'm guessing dinner will entice her even more than whatever bond I've spent three years crafting."

With a deep breath, and the help of the attendant's skilled hands, Theo lifted his arm to launch the bird into the air and he could not explain the laugh that bubbled through him again, catching as it passed to Amair this time, the two of them watching Breagha glide through the sunset together. Theo did not catch her lower her chin to look at him, the brilliant, adoring smile that she was so desperately fighting as the breeze whipped up her loose hair.

***

"Was I right?" Jasper asked, arms crossed and leaning against the doorway of Theo's room as the Writer tiredly made his way back.

Theo couldn't find his words for a second, looking up and shaking as he tried to explain it. "It...that was amazing. The bird..."

"Breagha."

"What does it mean? I don't...know the old language," Theo admitted sheepishly. "Just know it when I hear it."

"Heck, none of us really know it. Ama's just extra and keeps trying to learn it. But it means something along the lines of like...beautiful."

"Fitting because...what an *incredible* animal. Watching her fly...gliding through the sunset...oh my *gods*."

"She hasn't done it in forever. Not since Layton died." Jasper looked him up and down. "I think you're a good influence on her."

Theo snorted, walking past Jasper. "That's the first time anyone's said *that* to me."

"That…I am *not* surprised by."

The boys laughed, Theo flopping onto his bed. "I'm gonna be pretty sore tomorrow, hey?"

"Oh yeah," Jasper snorted. "Especially if you were keeping up with Ama."

"Mhm."

"Have a hot shower and sleep. There will be more stories for you tomorrow."

"Night, Jasper."

"Goodnight, Theo."

- CHAPTER XX -

Amair tapped her spoon against her teacup.

Teo raised his head. "Can I ask you a question?"

"Pretty sure that's why you're here."

Theo snorted at her dryness. "Funny." Theo tipped his head a little. "It's a super random one, not even…really serial material."

"Oh, well then…absolutely not." Her mouth twitched as she laughed at herself.

"How many staff do you have? Or does the…the castle have?"

Amair raised her eyebrows. "The…castle is the largest employer in the Kingdom. I wish I knew every single person's…name and story and position. I know a lot of them. But we have a really high turnover rate because we have a lot of young employees. If you work for the castle for two years, we pay for… well, two years of education, on top of the country's free two years. On top of their pay. Which I love, because a lot of them come back and work over school breaks and tell me stories of their classes, and their friends, and their professors, and all the university experiences they're having. I sort of live vicariously through them.

"But numbers um…whew, I don't think I know *all* of them. I have a head attendant who bosses around my three lady's attendants. Each of the boys has a valet and 2 lad's attendants, like you. Plus another half dozen who are always on call for when we have guests. My mom has the three ladies' in waiting and a couple of lady's attendants, my dad has two valets and three lad's attendants. The family has a butler, and the other parts of the castle have a butler and an under butler. Then we have…I think fifteen tutors across us five kids?

"There's…sixty-five dining room servers and attendants, three head chefs, a head baker, and I believe a hundred kitchen hands, including five dish washers. Plus a few apprentices who are hired by the chefs and bakers.

"Then there's…about fifty stable hands and grooms who are overseen by two trainers, three head gardeners who oversee five hundred outdoor maintenance staff and outdoor attendants. Six interior designers. The butlers oversee…gods, I think three hundred cleaners? Including five people who only wash the windows. Another sixtyish people who work in the laundry. Twenty sewers. Twelve librarians.

"Not to mention the royal guard…there's gotta be almost two hundred of them. Then there's the two Criers. Their apprentice.

"Three falconers, a hundred and…six musicians, two painters, a carver. The photography staff. About a dozen nurses, and I believe three doctors. No…four doctors. My dad's Sovereign staff. My mother's secretariat.

"And every single one of them is overseen by Ms. Manell, the castle steward, who manages the whole castle, with the help of the butlers. She has an apprentice as well. I…I don't know, how many *is* that?"

Theo scribbled as fast as he could, trying to keep up.

"I don't know how interesting this is for the serial," Amair shrugged.

"Maybe not, but I live here now. It'd be nice to know who I live *with*." Amair smiled at him. "Can you name any of them?"

"A lot of them, I think."

"I can see the headline now: Oighre knows every castle employee."

"My dad said to Layton and me once that a good royal is able to say hello to every single person they meet. Greet them by name." She shrugged. "And I have a cheat sheet."

"Now that I need."

"Ooh, no, sir, you have to *earn* that. It's taken me years to compile."

"You put each name in individually?" Theo exclaimed.

"Well…now, yes. Every time I hear of a new employee, they get added. I mark who's retired or gone to school, or just moved on. But the original list…Layton stole Ms. Manell's ledger."

"Oh, so you did cheat!"

"I was nine! I had like, a thousand members to memorise!" Amair chuckled. "Layton would sneak into my room and we'd sit by candlelight and try to learn a page a night."

"So…share the knowledge?"

"Oh, hell no." She smirked, getting up and brushing out her skirt. "You're a good university lad…let's see how well you do."

"I already know one…Imogene."

"I like Imogene. She's nice. Seems loyal."

"And has a photographic memory."

Amair laughed. "Good to know." She tipped her head, thinking. "Useful skill…"

- CHAPTER XXI -

"Now, I know you like to find adrenaline wherever you can," Layton chuckled, *"but please, for me, make it to Keene in one piece."*

"I promise, Layton." Amair had rolled her eyes, bumping her shoulder against his arm.

"Hey!" Theodore called, with his little lopsided grin, pulling Amair from her memories on the cold morning. "What are you thinking about?"

"My last conversation with Layton." His eyebrows pulled together, and she could see him trying not to give her the pathetic look of pity most people couldn't keep off their face. "It's nothing special. This is the last place I said goodbye to him." She took a deep breath. "That day felt very far away this morning."

"Is that good or bad?"

"I'm not sure, really."

"Let me know if you figure it out?" He looked down to her and she met his eyes, nodding a little.

"You'll be the first."

- CHAPTER XXII -

Theo waved to Jilly, the receptionist at the paper, as he walked back to what had once been his shared office. People waved, reaching out to shake his hand every once in a while, and somehow it felt incredibly like home, like the thing he had been striving for since he had first put ink to paper. And yet something about the office no longer felt right. He tried to convince himself it was just because the story was not over.

"Theodore!" a warm voice boomed through the office. "Or should I be calling you Sir Crawford now?"

"In this office, you outrank me so…whatever is easiest to make fun of, I'd say." He reached a hand out to Jacobus Trint, the Editor in Chief of the paper, earning himself one of the firmest handshakes in the kingdom.

"How's life in the palace?"

"They prefer to call it the castle," Theo said, not even realizing he had said it at first and trying not to cringe. "It's decent. Everyone's been very kind."

"You're getting picked up left, right, and centre…it's bringing in tons of advertisement from in and out of the kingdom. Horrible circumstance, but the paper has never been in higher demand."

Theo's mouth twitched a little. "Glad to be of service, sir."

"In many ways, I am sure. Sorry, it's been a long morning, I am down a couple people right now."

"Any way I can help?"

"Keep doing what you're doing…what brings you in? Shouldn't you be in your *new home*?" Theo searched his boss' voice but the words were kind, not malicious in any way.

"Just a quieter morning. The Princess had a series of meetings, so she asked to meet later, and the Princes are all in lessons in the mornings. Grabbing a few old notebooks, things like that. Checking the junk drawers."

"Fair enough. Well, good luck with your day. Keep checking in…keep sending the great articles."

Theo wandered through the office, going through the remnants of the desk he had all but abandoned that first day, finding a few pens exactly like every other pen he owned, shoving scraps of old stories and pitches into his pockets.

He opened one of the junk drawers on his way out and paused, noticing an envelope with a title written in heavy black marker.

"Hello?" he whispered to himself.

***

"I found something for you," Theo smiled, plopping onto the ground next to Amair.

"What do you get a girl who has everything she needs?" Amair asked, raising an eyebrow, setting the papers she was holding onto the rug.

"I had to run into the office today. I found these in a pile of old photographs."

She furrowed her brows, reaching in to slowly pull out a medium sized black and white photograph. Amair covered her mouth with a hand, turning the envelope over to dump out a dozen photographs.

"Layton," she murmured, picking up a second photo, putting his stoic glance next to his silly grin.

"It was from some stock photoshoot, or maybe a test shoot. I thought they would be better here than sitting in a drawer in a news office."

Her face contorted, nodding a little, her bottom lip quivering. "Thank you," she whispered, running her fingers over the photo of Layton with the biggest smile on his face.

"He was special…to all of us. Almost every boy I knew looked up to him for some reason."

"I looked up to him for every reason." He could hear the tug of tears in her voice.

"He been on your mind lately?"

She shrugged, thinking for a second. "Off the record?" Amair asked. Theo raised an eyebrow, surprised, watching her let down her guard for the first time. He set his pen and notepad on the little table beside him.

"Absolutely."

"I have been content being Princess. I am no Queen. I was happy for my brother to be King, to rule. It wasn't what *I* wanted. The law of the land made me an heir, but never could anyone expect anything to happen that would make it come to be."

"What did you want?" Theo asked, a playful smile on his lips. Amair smiled back, squinting her eyes a little as her round cheeks pushed them closed.

"To travel. I wanted to see the world outside the castle walls. I mean, I *have* but…with a burden on me. To run through fields in the highlands, travel as far as the mountains to the east. Perhaps even further, though crossing the seas seems a little daunting."

"Ahh, so you planned to be an adventuress."

"You have no doubt heard stories of Skylock women." Amair grinned. "None of us like to settle." There was something in her stare that made him know she was one of those who did not.

- CHAPTER XXIII -

"Oof!" Amair looked up, smiling a little at Theo, who had grabbed her forearm to keep her from tumbling over. "My apologies, Sir Crawford."

"None needed, I should know better than to walk while trying to write."

"And *I* should know better than to walk and read." Denna rounded the corner, making eye contact with Amair. Denna grinned, slowly backing up into the side hallway, and Amair heard her bolt away.

"How are you today?"

"I um…I'm alright. Lydia wanted to try a new hairstyle…she's been practicing."

"I like the braiding."

"Yeah, it's uh, it's pretty. According to the Council, a Queen doesn't wear her hair down. Luckily I've always preferred it back anyways."

"Doesn't get in the way?"

"One boy pulling it in a sword match was all I needed to keep it out of the way." She licked her lips a little. "Are you um…are you finding ways to stay occupied around here?"

"Observing you is a very interesting pastime," Theo smirked, watching as Amair blushed. "I like sitting in the big library. I thought my university had a lot of books."

"We're a family of readers." She waved the book a little. "We like our books."

"Helps that you've had thirteen generations to collect them here."

"Plus, a flock of librarians to care for them," she smirked. "You know you're welcome to any of them. We bring in books from the other six Kingdoms, and have a copy of every book published in Skylock. The librarians can help you get any book you like, show you how to sign them out."

"Do you have a favourite?" He raised an eyebrow, and she matched the look.

"I do," she smiled slowly. Theo took a step closer to her, dropping his voice as he fixed a stray hair, tucking it under the intricate braids.

"And what is it?" She tried to hide it, but he felt the skip in her breath.

"I'm sure you'll figure it out," she smirked. Her dog rounded the corner, running past them, and Amair brushed past him, tucking her hands behind her back and swooshing down the hall.

- CHAPTER XXIV -

Theo opened his door at the incessant knocking and took a little step back, shaking his head, surprised at the gaggle of royal children standing there.

"We're going on a picnic," Amair wiggled the basket on her arm, trying to make her point.

"Wearing that?"

"I just got out of a meeting," she defended, glancing down at the layers of dark teal skirt, moving her shoulders and making the white sleeves swish. "We need to go, we don't get much sunshine. It's Skylock…the rain could return at literally any minute."

"Are you coming or not?" Evander asked, adjusting the huge blanket wrapped in his arms. Theo glanced between the boy and Amair, who was smiling softly.

"I'd never say no to a picnic," Theo grinned, reaching around the door and grabbing a coat. "Let's do it." The royal children grinned, Alec turning to push on the hidden staff door and slip inside.

"Do you know where you're going?" Theo asked, following the royals through the narrow door, Jasper pushing the door closed again. Their eyes adjusted to the light, and they followed after the twins.

"We used to play hide and seek," Amair told him. "Nothing off limits kind of hide and seek. And all the kids would get involved…not just us, but everyone. Staff children and all. Layton always played."

"Oh boy."

"One game took three days," Kylo snorted.

"What?" Theo exclaimed.

"Attendants would just leave plates of food on random tables so that we could sneak out and grab something and sneak back into our hiding spots."

"Did you…did you sleep?"

"Dylan was searching, and I don't think he did."

"I did, though," Jasper laughed.

"Same here," Amair agreed. "But we would hide in the staff staircases, we would change hiding spots, I think Kryla once managed to hide in the rafters of the kitchens."

"Wowza."

"We knew how to make our own fun."

"Yeah, when you have very little real adult supervision, things get crazy."

"*Real* adult supervision?" Theo laughed, stepping out into the sunlight as the twins held the door open.

"I mean…for us, our parents were King and Queen. They love us, they go out of their way to spend time with us…"

"But they still have huge jobs," Amair finished for Jasper. "We had…a few nannies amongst us, and tutors, and a series of attendants and stuff. The other castle kids…you know, their parents had shift work. Mostly we just all had each other. Layton and Johanna pretty much became a stand in mom and dad…for all of us."

"Some of the castle kids walked into town, for school, and I remember Layton and Johanna signing permission forms and stuff when they were forgotten," Jasper smiled.

"We were a good group." Amair's voice was wistful and far away, filled with some old memory.

"We should do it again," Kylo raised an eyebrow, glancing at his siblings.

"What?"

"Get all the castle kids, and the ones who grew up here together, for a big game of hide and seek."

"I'm so down," Jasper grinned. "Theo, you'll have to join"

"I'm not a castle kid."

"You're basically one of us now." Theo smiled at him, tipping his head a little.

"Okay, let's *go*," Alec called somewhere ahead of them. The older kids laughed, running down the steps as fast as they could. Alec and Evander pushed on the door and the staircase flooded with light, everyone shielding their eyes as they walked out, into the yard and stumbling towards the garden.

"Boys!" Amair called them back, a hand over her eyes, trying to shield from the sun that was so rare. The twins looked up, the blanket in their hands. "I think we should head further out into the field...maybe the runoff?"

"Let's go!" one of the boys called as he raced ahead.

"Here!" Amair called, staring around the small patch of woods, the sound of birds and the bubble of the stream whispering around them, the wind flowing through the grass and flowers.

"Sometimes I wonder if Skylock is even real," Theo murmured.

"Hm?"

"Oh, it's just…places like this." Theo took one of the corners of the blanket, helping the twins roll it out, flattening it against the soft ground. "There're places like this near the lochs in Glenn, too. And they're just…a little extra special. Magical, I guess."

Amair grinned, looking around them, turning to look up into the trees. "We are...very blessed." Amair stepped onto the grey blanket, setting the basket down and flipping up the top of it. Theo could immediately smell the warmth radiating out of it.

"It smells so good," Evander crooned, jumping to sit, clapping his hands a little. Alec sat with him, the rest of them following and eyeing the containers hungrily. Jasper reached up, Amair using his hand to sit with the boys, her dark teal skirts filling out the whole corner of the blanket.

"Well don't just stare at it," she smiled. The boys grinned, Kylo handing a plate to Amair as the twins pulled the containers out, passing them around their little circle. Theo opened the black container Evander passed him, taking a deep breath as the warm, aromatic steam hit him.

"This smells incredible," he exclaimed, dumping some of the potatoes in their orange sauce onto his plate.

"The cooks got a whole new shipment of spices and herbs from RiKoi and Innisil yesterday," Amair grinned, putting a little pink cake onto her plate. "You should go down just after lunch, during the week. It's when they practise and try new recipes. There are always plates of testers lying around."

"Is that where all this came from?" Theo asked, passing the potatoes and taking the little pot of what looked like cream sauce.

"Mmhm. I just asked Chef if we could take some of it, and she put a bunch into containers for me."

"Wowza." They chatted absentmindedly as they ate, everyone commenting and groaning in delight as they tried each of the new dishes.

"The kitchen is getting a raise," Amair murmured, stuffing a potato into her mouth, the others laughing. Theo snorted as the twins licked their plates, laughing harder as he noticed Amair using her finger to wipe the last of the sauces off hers, popping the finger into her mouth.

"What?" she demanded, but Kylo and Jasper laughing. Theo reached over and brushed sauce off her chin with his thumb, letting it linger on her skin for a moment before pulling away. She swallowed, settling her shoulders. "Th…thank you." He had to bite his lip not to smirk at her momentary stammer.

They all wiped the last dribbles with a cloth napkin stuffed in the bottom of the basket, and loaded everything back into it. Amair's brothers got up, running around in the sunshine, pushing each other and laughing.

"Don't poke out anyone's eyes!" Amair called, laughing.

"Thank you. For inviting me." Theo glanced at Amair, watching as she smiled out at her brothers rolling around in the grass, Evander almost toppling into the stream.

"You said that your ideal day was this." She turned to smile at him now. "We don't get much sunshine." The two watched each other now, studying faces carefully. A shriek from Alec pulled their attention back to the boys, laughing as they watched Jasper and Kylo pulling Alec out of the chilly stream.

"Oh, honey," Amair laughed, pushing herself to her feet. "At least it isn't ocean water."

"Good point," Jasper laughed.

"Here, let's wrap you in the blanket," Amair turned, waving her hand at Theo to get him to stand up. He scrambled to his feet, helping her pick up the large blanket. They wrapped it around a shivering Alec, Amair rubbing her hands up and down his arms. "Any better?"

"A bit."

"Let's head home. You can have a hot shower and warm up."

"O-o-okay," Alec nodded, teeth chattering. Jasper messed with Alec's hair as he passed, picking up the basket, grabbing the few pieces of cutlery that had somehow made their way out.

Theo watched the siblings gather together to walk, all in a line, arm in arm, Alec wrapped in a blanket, Amair's arm around his shoulders and holding him close, no doubt getting the side of her dress wet, but she did not seem to mind. Their matching hair, and the matching pop in their step as they leaned into each other to walk. The slight overcast that no matter how much laughter they managed to fit into their days, something felt off.

There was someone missing from their lineup. And always would be.

***

"How's Alec?" Theo asked, the notecard with Amair's messy writing folded into his hand as he pushed into the library. She was thanking an attendant for fixing a tray of biscuits.

"Cold and on the verge of grumpy. I passed him off to an attendant who promised to whisk him off to a hot shower. You think the twins are a menace now…you should see them when they are in any kind of bad mood and when *one* of them is, it manifests." She laughed. "You said earlier you still wanted the interview…I figured you would be sick of me, after spending the whole day with me."

"Hard to get sick of you, Princess."

She wondered, suddenly, if it was the words or how genuine they were, no trace of his smirk or his charm, that made her blush that time.

"I do have a question, though, and forgive me, just…seeing you with your brothers had me thinking."

"Hm?"

"Who are your friends?" Theo asked, holding his notebook while they walked through the corridors.

She thought for a second. "My brothers. I know it may seem lame, but...as royal children, we sort of had to band together.

Obviously...obviously Layton was my best friend. But Jasper and Kylo...they've become my best friends. Not just in the months since Lay's death, but that whole year leading to it, when Layton spent so much of his time training.

"Layton was always the more social of us...I liked to keep to myself, a few people at a time. He was the one who dragged me to events, made me meet people like those in the guard. Most of my friends came by accident. His friends became my friends, and they *were* my best friends.

"The castle kids were really the only people I had, most of the time, and who we made friends with." Amair shrugged. "Johanna was a knight's daughter, which is why she and Layton came to know each other. Her brother, Arthur – now one of our best knights – became my friend because every once in a while, she would drag *him* along. Dylan was an attendant's son who was just...kind, and kind of a jester, and just...*there*. Always, when you needed a person.

"And there were the other castle kids. The groom's daughter. The gardener's child. Moritz's son. We got together to play, when we could. It was fun, there were a ton of kids, most of them either older or younger than me, but still. Denna – now *Lady* Denna Raziel – is probably my best friend outside of my brothers. She was always good to me...I realised just how much so when Layton died.

"And some of the staff, especially the attendants, have become friends, I'd say. I like meeting the knights and guards in training...though usually they're too afraid of me to really pursue being my friend.

"I don't know, it's...it's hard to make friends when your existence is in the walls of the castle, and fate has given you a title you still don't know if you deserve."

"I could be your friend."

"The point of having a friend is having someone who won't write down everything you say," Amair returned, raising an eyebrow.

"So then...call..." Theo thought for a second. "'Friends'. Call 'friends.'"

"What?"

"Like...off the record. Call friends, and...I stop writing things down. It stays between us." Amair blinked a few times at Theo.

"I...I like that plan."

"Perfect." The two glanced at each other, the sly smile softening on Theo's face, matching Amair's. The two looked at each other a second, pulling their eyes to the floor as they continued to walk down the hall.

"Friends," he heard her murmur, glancing down at her smile.

- CHAPTER XXV -

Quiet days passed with some kind of routine, but routine at the castle was nothing like he was used to. Even their schedules seemed to move on an ever-shifting clock that he had yet to figure out. Sometimes, Theo needed a sense of old normalcy and he tucked himself into old, hidden corners and he could almost pretend it was his uni days again, studying in the lounges or dusty bookshelves or a cleverly hidden vase right before an exam.

Theo watched from his nook as Amair and Kylo walked by arm in arm, smiling and talking. Amair tossed her head back and laughed, pinching Kylo's side, making him laugh with her.

"So, how are things going? With the Writer?" Kylo asked. Amair sighed, rolling her hands together, Kylo nudging her gently with his shoulder.

"Oh, Kylo, I don't know..."

"The first few of the serial have been quite beautifully written. It feels like a painting..." He smiled thoughtfully. "Like he's painting a portrait of you. Sketching an outline, bringing it to life. Bringing you back to life."

"Maybe we should have made you the Writer," Amair laughed, brushing his cheek. "You always have had a way with words." Kylo laughed.

"Maybe...but he *is* bringing you back to life, Ama." He reached up, grabbing her hand at his cheek and squeezing it. "There's that...spark, in your eye, that makes you...you. I don't really...know how to describe it. But he's doing more than just...writing about you."

"There are those words again." Her voice was a whisper, hard and scared.

"Well, someone's going to have to be your speech writer someday."

"He...has been a nice addition."

"Very." Theo bit his lip, watching from his nook as Kylo smiled at Amair. "I'd say he's even becoming...a good friend?"

"May–....yes."

"More than a–"

"–no," Amair interrupted, but Theo caught the smile and blush. Kylo offered her his arm again, letting her take it as they turned back.

"School is good, though?" Amair asked. Theo wheeled further back into the bright nook, hiding behind the big plant as the royals passed him.

"Oh, my life hasn't really changed. I'm beating Jasper in history as always, and I'm catching up in mathematics. Nusiq and I have been sending our favourite maths problems to each other. Whoever can't answer one is supposed to go and spend a few days with each other but, uh..."

"You're both too smart for that?"

"It would seem so," Kylo laughed.

"Maybe we should just have Nusiq come."

"Maybe when things start to calm down a bit."

"Things don't calm, Kylo," she reminded him. "As soon as one crisis is quelled, another swallows it and grows in its place. Invite your boyfriend, any time, honest…Oighre's permission fully granted."

Kylo laughed and it was nervous but grateful.

"Is he going to come for my birthday in the Winter?"

"I asked him to, but it's their Kingdom Festival, and he's old enough to participate in their games now. He's put in so much practice...I got a photo of him in his new boat. It's beautifully painted, with so many bright colours."

"Has he named it?" Amair smirked.

"The Kyte." Kylo blushed a little. "With a 'y'."

"Oh, to be young and in love," she laughed. "If you want to go there for the games, I would understand–'

"–I want to celebrate you, Ama. We can find another time to see each other."

"If you're sure."

"You're my sister. And this family has...we've had some hardship."
Kylo nodded. "I'm sure, Ama." The two turned down another hallway,
their voices disappearing. Theo leaned against the window, writing a note
in the corner of his small book.

Her family are her friends. Friends are family. People mean everything to her.

- CHAPTER XXVI -

There was already something sour in the air when Amair arrived. She was still dressed, her hair slightly dishevelled, and Theo had heard whisperings of a marathon Council meeting that had taken its toll on all involved and from the look on the Princess' face, she had not left unscathed.

Theo glanced down at his notepad as he finished flipping the page to the questions he had pre-written for himself, having finally felt like he was through the shell she had so carefully built for herself.

"What are you most afraid of?" Theo looked up from his notebook, watching Amair think.

"The thing I was most afraid of already happened," Amair told him. "Losing my brother. And it crushed me even harder, because even in my worst nightmares, I never thought I would lose all three of them. So...nothing. I'm not afraid of anything, anymore."

There was a beat, her teacup halfway to her mouth.

"Come on, that's crap." Amair narrowed her eyes, biting the inside of her cheek. "You're terrified of people knowing you."

"I am n–"

"–and you cling on to your family like your life depends on it." An attendant stepped towards them, ready to put an end to their chat, but Amair put her hand up, stopping them in their tracks, eyeing Theo. Theo resisted the urge to gulp under her stare. "There's... there's power in letting yourself be afraid."

Her fingers curled slightly, letting her hand fall back into her lap. "Friends?"

"No."

"Theodore—"

"—Princess," he cut off her shock. "I'm here to present you to the public, and I will drag you kicking and screaming if I must. You are allowed to be *human*."

"That's not the problem!" she shot back. She huffed, eyes turning to the window, sucking on her tongue, thinking. "Follow me." Theo noticed the worried look that passed over the attendant's face. By the time he looked back, Amair was halfway to the door. He stuffed his notebook into the pocket on his vest and tore after her.

He watched her storm down the hall, hands balled into fists. She tore around corners, taking stairs two by two as Theo followed sheepishly. She passed through a small wooden door onto the dewy training grounds, the noise of afternoon training filling the air.

"Lenora!"

"Your royal highness."

"Clear the field."

The woman with dark skin, curly hair tied up with a Skylock blue ribbon, bobbed her head. Theo noticed the crest on her arm band, the trainees that lingered near her side with clipboards. Her eyes flicked to Theo stumbling across the grass. "Certainly, your highness." Theo caught up, catching the smirk on Lenora's face.

"Hup!" she yelled, and the trainees slowed in the exercises, wiping brows before turning to stand at attention. As they spotted the Princess, they stood a little taller. "Clear out!" Swords were returned to their sheaths, the sound of snapping bows slowing as the trainees fell back to the edge of the circle.

"Oof," Theo gasped as the hilt of the sword was pushed into his stomach. He barely had time to lift it when Amair crashed her sword into it. Her eyes were angry, hair slipping out of her lazy braid. Lenora grinned, arms crossed over her chest as she watched, amusement in her dark eyes. One of the guards, clipboard in hand, leaned over and whispered something to her that made her chuckle quietly.

Theo's eyes widened as she swung her sword again, moving his just in time to keep it from taking a chunk out of his cheek. The sound of their clashing swords filled the area. Some of the knights slowly joined the guards-in-training at the edge of the ring, eyes fixed on the tiny battle.

"Ahh!" Theo exclaimed, barely having time to clumsily raise his sword with both hands, Amair slashing at him and he wondered exactly how many years of training she had had and instead of the battle he had landed himself in, he instead found himself trying to remember their old interviews.

He ducked without thinking, fast enough for Amair to throw herself off balance but when she turned back, there were tears on her cheeks.

"You're right, okay?" She caught her breath. "I *am* afraid. Is that what you want to hear? I'm afraid of most things. I'm afraid of almost everything. When the only fear you had is crushed, when it comes to *be*...everything seems like a threat. I have always said that being Queen does not mean I have to stop being Amair. But I don't know who that *is* anymore." A few of the young guards whispered to each other, Amair finally pulled her sword back. "I'm afraid of everything, okay? For my family. And my people. But if I stop and let myself stay afraid, I will no longer be useful. So, I spend every day convincing myself that I am not afraid – not because I'm not, or don't need to be, or that I think it's weak, but because I am learning to live despite all the fears. I *have* to."

"Why...why the sword fight?" Theo huffed, leaning over still trying to catch his breath.

Amair shrugged. "I was mad." Lenora snorted, her arms crossed. "There. You have your damn serial." Amair turned, walking away briskly, pushing her sword handle into one of the guard's chests. She stumbled, grabbing it, trying to stay standing at attention as the Oighre brushed past.

"Back to work!" Amair yelled to the guards, leaving Theo in the rain.

"Maybe wait a few days after the next breakdown to poke the bear," he heard Lenora say beside him. Theo hesitated, having missed whatever breakdown she was referring to but he shook his head.

"No...I think we both just had a break*through*, actually." Theo grinned, heading back towards the castle.

Ink & Crown: The Princess Serial

by Sir Theodore Crawford

The royal Skylock family is well known for being that kind of family that so many wish to have – not for their abundance of beautiful children, but for the deep bonds they have Their lives always entwined around each one another, able to lean in and support each other even in the most difficult of times – as we have all seen through the tragedy of The Lost Ones. The importance of family root all the way back to the times of old, woven in to the stories that pre-date our Sovereign throne, when the Skylock clan, the smallest clan at that, were so deeply bonded the gods looked favourably upon them to bond us all together.

No one exemplifies this importance of family more than our Princess. For her, there is no difference between family, and friends, and to her they are all the same. She holds people close, confides in those she loves, and holds that deep, caring love that we all crave.

With her brother Prince Jasper, for example, it is the head butting that first comes to mind. As the closest to her in age, they are the most likely to spar in wits and, though I have yet to see it, I have heard there have been several facers exchanged. With Prince Kylo, the

Princess seems to relax. The two of them chat about things from love and friendship to learning and school, and he has the reassuring words whenever she needs them.

With the young twin princes, Evander and Alec, she fits somewhere between *motherly* and just as tricky as they are. They bring out a young side of the Princess we so rarely get to see due to her commitment to her new role.

I have yet to get a chance to truly see the Princess with her parents, but sources tell me she is close to them both. The Princess is lucky to have a large family that cares for and supports her, The Princess often notes that while the family she has that bear the Skylock name are important to her, so are the people she has "collected" over the years. Some of these found family are members of the staff who have become like second parents to her. The others are her friends, who "keep her in line" and "pick her up when I need it." She notes Lady Denna Raziel as being like the sister she never had, and Shehada Westfall who, though away at university, "taught [her] the ways of the world, even when [she] was not ready to hear some of it." She also notes Sir Arthur Moores, brother of the late Lady Johanna Moores, who has taken up his late-sister's mantle training to be the

Oighre's Knight and eventual
Knight General.

A member of the guard
speculated that, while the
Skylocks have always been
close, and have always been
known to bring in people from
the outside to make their
family feel larger, it is the
recent tragedy that truly
solidified the bonds of this
generation. I would agree, and
I see this in how the Princess
acts. She is at the forefront of
this loss. The people she
surrounds herself with are
part of her healing, but some
days, I wonder if they are
reminders of what she has
lost.

*- Sir Theodore Crawford, Staff
Writer, Special Liaison
Reporter to The Palace, Man of
Letters*

- CHAPTER XXVII -

Theo tapped his pen against his notepad, taking a sip of the delicious coffee. Every sip felt smooth and intense. He let his head tip to the side, his now-dry hair falling to the one side in soft, tangled curls. He glanced up as the night staff came in, chattering and warm, a couple of them waving at Theo as they walked by. He heard the stoves, and the fires start up again, smelled flour and yeast being thrown and measured in a way that turned the castle into something that was so much like a home.

He turned his head back to his paper when he noticed a figure out of the corner of his eye that he recognized, pulling a heavy black cape over her shoulders. "Ah…what are you doing?"

Amair whipped her head around, holding her large black hood halfway to her head. Her eyes were so wide Theo worried they would pop out of her face.

"W-wh-what…what are you doing down here?"

Theo raised his cup and his eyebrow. "Writing."

"Why?"

"I like it down here." Amair looked to the side, still holding the hood, glancing around as the staff tried to keep from watching them. Theo looked her up and down, furrowing his brow at the pale green linen skirt, white linen blouse tucked in. Worn down laced boots were on her feet, scuffs on the heels and toes, the laces fraying slightly. "Seriously, Amair, what are you doing?"

Amair dropped her hands from the hood, light from one of the fires flickering across her face, her eyes brightly reflecting it back. "It's Wednesday," she told him, pulling her hands inside the cloak, brushing her skirt. "It's the night market. In the village." Theo grinned, slowly starting to understand, but dropped his face again.

"Alone?"

"Uh…yeah?" she asked, pulling on leather gloves, fastening buttons just above her wrists.

"Amair!"

"What?" She knelt to pick up a wicker basket, fastening one side of the lid and settling the handle on her arm.

"Is there a guard—"

"—it's not the first time she's done this." A kitchenhand paused, firewood in her arm. Theo glanced at her, raising his eyebrows at the girl. She bit her lip, glancing at Amair and ducking her head, walking away. Theo looked back at Amair.

"I have to go before the guard rotation finishes and my window closes."

"You're literally sneaking out."

She huffed. "Friends?" Theo nodded reluctantly. "I wasn't always Oighre, Theodore," she lifted her chin, her hand reaching for the door. "So, are you coming?"

"What?"

"Well, you've already caught me. If you promise not to say anything…" He could see the little grin through the shadow of her hood. He put the cap on his pen and slipped it into the pocket of his vest. He stood, taking a sip of his coffee, not taking his eyes off of Amair's, still standing in the shadows of the kitchen, hand on the door.

"I'm coming."

"Good choice." She pulled her hand back, grabbing one of the heavy brown cloaks kept for the kitchen staff and tossing it to him, already pushing out the door. "Let's go, then."

Amair slinked across the courtyard, pressed into the shadow of the exterior wall. "I can't believe we're doing this."

"Shh," Amair shot back, pushing on the gate and slipping out into the night. Theo closed the gate behind himself, just as two guards appeared in the courtyard.

"Phew," Amair shook her head fixing her cape's hood, "you almost made me miss it."

"I can't believe I'm sneaking the Princess out of the castle," he shook his head.

"Technically, I think I'm sneaking the Writer out of the castle."

"I'm guessing that's *not* how your father will see it."

Amair chuckled, taking a sharp turn down a side path. "We can't go right through the main gates…there are knights posted and they might notice me."

"Like no one else will?"

"People don't see you when they don't know to look."

"I…what?"

"No one would really believe the Princess just casually walked into their market," Amair bit her lip as she smiled a little under her hood. "So they don't know to look."

"Hm." She told him to hush as the market stalls came into sight, candles in their holders making the square as bright as though it were day. It was a beautiful night, the moon and stars twinkling far above, clear from clouds for the first time in what felt like weeks. The lanterns cast a shadow across Amair's eyes, leaving just her kind smile for the citizens to smile back at.

They quietly went from stall to stall, smiling to the merchants but keeping the conversation minimal as she passed coins to them, overpaying every time. There were dolls for sale, and pots of stew with buns still steaming, beckoning them over despite feeling stuffed from the supper they had just had. Amair bought a doll, immediately turning to pass it to the first child who ran past them. The little one beamed, clutching it to their chest and running after their friend, making Amair laugh a little.

They stopped, Amair setting down her basket as they leaned against a fence to eat their stew, warm with some herb Theo could not quite place. "I lived down here, and *I* didn't know there was a night market…" Theo murmured, biting into the fluffy bun, the top brushed with something sweet.

"You now know something Layton did not." He could hear the smile in her voice. "I knew he would lose his mind."

"Did Johanna and Dylan?"

"They did." Amair shrugged. "Johanna sort of approved. Not entirely, but sort of. Dylan…he thought I should have my own life. More than anyone else. I…I think he…he wanted his own life, in a way. He found his calling and his friends here but…it could be hard, to be around Layton, sometimes." She tipped her cup to drain the last of her stew back into her mouth.

They wandered back into the market, buying a bushel of green and blue carrots, a head of the most brilliant pink cabbage Theo had ever seen. Amair turned on her heel as she spotted a corn vendor, and loaded two jars of her spiced corn compote into the basket, pausing to let the vendor give her a tip about putting it on day old scones or crispy potatoes for the best late evening snack.

They found a few packages of herbs, Amair raising a few of them and inhaling them deeply, a wide smile on her face, handing over coins as she overpacked her basket until the bottom threatened to give out. By the time they got to the cider vendor, there was not a centimetre left.

Theo helped her carry the packages that she could no longer stuff into her basket.

"Friends?" Amair asked as they walked away from one of the baker's stalls, a loaf of honey bread folded into her arm.

Theo nodded. "I'm pretty sure this…whole adventure is off the record," Theo laughed cautiously, glancing to the stalls they passed.

"Sneaking out was. I just…want to be sure." Theo felt a little knot in his stomach but tried to shake it off.

He nodded. "Friends."

"I'm serious, it would be…horrible if this suddenly appeared in the paper–"

"–Amair!" he interrupted her and she looked up at him, the shadow lifting and her eyes piercing his.

"I was never meant to be Queen," she told him, looking ahead again. "I've told you that before. Layton was Oighre. A strong, healthy heir. Beloved. He was going to be the King. And then he was going to produce an heir and that heir would be Oighre and I would…fade into the background. I'm barely a Princess." She paused. "I was never meant to be Queen. And then in one horrible moment, I lost him. I blinked, and he was suddenly gone, and I was suddenly Oighre. I didn't have time to grieve because I was suddenly the person the people were counting on." Amair shook her head. "I liked the background. And now…now I'm almost eighteen, and learning everything Layton got to spend his whole life learning, all while trying to learn to live without him, and our friends. And I'm alone. And terrified. And this…this feels like safety." Amair looked at the basket in her arms, then up to the clock at the top of the market square gate. "We should go. Guard change will be happening soon, and we need to sneak back in."

"What will we do with all the food?"

"We'll leave it with the stock order that would have been delivered this evening. The kitchen knows what I do…they just pretend not to." He stepped behind her as they returned to the path.

"You know you overpaid for every item here, right?"

"Why have money if you can't give it away? We do what we can for the people, but I have what I need, and then some. Might as well spend it back on my people." She stood on her toes, watching the guards leave shift and motioning to Theo. They silently walked across the courtyard, leaving their market finds with the deliveries, discarding capes as they rushed down the hall.

Amair giggled, turning back to Theo and reaching for his hand. "So? Did you enjoy my adventure?"

"I'd enjoy anything with you." He smirked, trying to play it off, but the feeling of her hand reaching and wrapping into his, pulling him along behind her, sent a wave of butterflies through him.

Her hood fell back and he noticed the blush, even in the dim evening candles. "Goodnight, Theodore."

"Goodnight, Princess." She walked backwards, keeping her eyes on him until she backed into the staircase that led to the Family Wing, turning to rush away, pulling on the tie of her cape and trying to stuff it into her basket.

- CHAPTER XXVIII -

She was in one of her faraway places that morning, twisting a little in the hallway that shimmered in the dark grey morning light.

"Have you noticed?" Amair asked, hands behind her back as she swished down the hallway with Theo. She watched her feet peeking out from under her dress.

"Noticed what?" Theo asked, biting into an apple. Amair side-stepped the spray as the first bite exploded a little.

"They're trying to get me to look like a Queen."

"What does *that* mean?"

"The dresses. They've gotten longer. The skirts are bigger. My sleeves are longer. Puffier. There's more glitz. My hair isn't supposed to be down, or in ribbons. I look so rigid." She shrugged. "I miss linen."

"The people didn't see you much before. That's why they got me, remember?"

"Oh...the people knew me," she grinned slyly. "They just didn't always know it was me."

"Fair enough." Her face got a little sad again.

"I used to be...soft. And...I don't know. Less...in your face. I always feel so...mmm...so...severe." Theo stopped walking, Amair turning to look at him, shifting her arms from behind to link her fingers together in front of her.

"You don't have to be."

"What?"

"You're going to be Queen. You could say tomorrow that you will only be dressing in a corset and petticoat from now on, and that is your right. It'd probably become a trend." He raised an eyebrow. "Be soft. Even if it's just within the confines of the walls of the castle. You can't be Queen if you aren't you." He reached out and tugged on her sleeve. "I wouldn't mind seeing that." The two smiled at each other a little, Theo rubbing the lace between his thumb and his finger. "I quite like this one though." Amair raised her chin, the smile growing a little bit, pulling her hand away and putting it against her chest.

"I'll see you later, Theo."

"Goodbye, Amair."

"I don't like goodbyes. Even before…before." She took a few steps backwards down the hall, the sly smile on her lips. "Just later." She grinned, turning and walking away, leaving Theo standing in the middle of the hallway.

- CHAPTER XXIX -

"Tell me about Lupa," Theo smiled, scratching the dog's ears as they sat lounged out on the carpets of one of the libraries.

"Well, I don't think I could really tell you what *type* of dog she is," Amair laughed, watching Theo murmur nothings to the dog in a high-pitched voice. "I've always believed she was a wolf, although I think she may be *too* fluffy for that. Layton found her scared and alone one day. I was thirteen, lonely… Layton hadn't started his Circle yet, so he was just off learning from our dad. He was always away. And Lupa," Amair ran her hand over the dog's head, "kept me company."

"And Lupa means…"

"Wolf. Well…" Amair shrugged, "she-wolf."

"Creative," Theo snorted.

"I was thirteen!" Amair defended, laughing. "I thought I was a genius."

"Fair enough." Theo patted Lupa again, her tongue sticking out of her mouth, almost smiling.

"She's a good dog," Amair smiled, watching as her dog's ears picked up. "Good company. One hell of a protector. Fast as hell, too." Amair let out a sad sigh, even through her smile. "And another connection left with Layton."

Theo smiled, matching Amair's sad smile.

"I have to work with the guard later…would you…I don't know, be interested in seeing–"

"–yes!" Theo nodded vigorously. "When and where?"

***

Theodore had met up with Jasper after getting lost again coming out of luncheon and the Prince had graciously acted as guide to the training ring.

"The last time I was out here, I was tripping over my feet following Amair," Theo had told Jasper.

"Sounds like my sister," he had laughed. "How've you been?"

"Busy…"

"That sounds nice, though."

Now, they were watching Amair, a sword in hand, as the trainees tried to win in their fight against her.

"Geezus," Theo's eyes widened, watching Amair bring the knight-in-training to his knees, holding her sword to his throat. The young man dropped his own sword, raising his hands in defeat, staring down the sword. Theo watched Amair's face go from concentrated to grinning, lowering her weapon. She held out a hand and helped him to his feet, laughing a little. The young man bowed to the Princess, and she gave him his out.

She turned to Theo and her brother standing on the side of the lawn, smiling at them, holding her sword at her side and curtsied, laughing as she walked towards them.

"You are quite the sight with that sword, Princess," Theo offered, looking down at the perfectly crafted weapon. She spun the hilt in her hand, grinning smugly.

"Gotta beat the Princess if you're gonna be a knight!" a young man called, walking up to them.

"You've got some work to do yet, Arthur."

"They also need to learn not to fight you like you're the Princess."

"That would also help." Amair glanced at Theo. "Writer, this is Arthur, Knight General in Training."

"Arthur."

"Sir Crawford."

"I'll be right back," Amair turned, murmuring to one of the young women hanging around the side of the ring.

"Arthur?" Theo whispered to Jasper.

"Johanna's younger brother."

Jasper looked down at his feet. Theo could see his throat tighten, his mouth pursing as he fought a wave of what the Writer guessed was the same gut-wrenching sadness all the Skylocks were struggling with.

"Jasper and I played while Amair, and Layton, Dylan, and my sister – sorry... *The Lost Ones*, were off being friends," Arthur told him. "But my sister taught me everything I know about being a knight. I planned to serve under her." The young man, still almost a boy, stood taller. "Now I get to honour her and help her live on."

"You're looking a bit confused, Writer," Arthur laughed.

"I just...Amair, and she..."

"A few years ago, we...or actually, *my sister*, realized the best way to test our knights was if they could go up against Amair. She's brutal with that sword...or just about any weapon you put in her hand."

"Who needs a sword?" Amair smirked.

"We want our knights in top fighting shape. They train all day, every day. If we'd be better off sending Amair out than them, they aren't ready yet." Amair smirked, glancing at Theo as she accepted a cup of water from one of the trainers.

"I think that's the last of them, Ama. For today at least...anyone else has been scared into more training before they try and challenge you."

"Fair enough. I've worked out any pent-up anger," she laughed, curtsying quickly to thank the attendant who filled her empty cup. She glanced over at Theo. "Walk me back to the castle?"

"Of course, Princess."

Theo was bouncing with questions as he walked alongside the sweating Princess. "Where did you learn to fight like that? Your brothers? Layton?"

"God, no." She shook her head, snickering a little. "Layton was no warrior. He was a politician. No, I taught Jasper and Kylo how to hold a sword. Started showing Evander how to use a bow." She shook her head, laughing. "No, Johanna, she taught me. She um...was the daughter of a knight." She was thinking, staring across the lawn. "Would have been the next Knight General."

"Johanna..." Theo could just barely picture her face.

"Arthur's older sister. My...one of my best friends. Our best friends. Died with Layton."

"You don't talk about him much, you know."

She thought for a second, sneaking a glance at him out of the corner of her eye. She chewed the inside of her lip, watching as they walked at random through the large castle halls.

"Layton and I were…really close. He was my best friend. He wanted a sibling so badly. I came five years after him. They all thought it was a miracle. That was, until my parents started making babies like rabbits." The two laughed. "Layton could barely hold a sword. He taught me to read. To love books. To paint – which I suck at, by the way. Showed me plants in the garden. He loved beautiful things. But," she lifted her skirt, reaching to steady herself with Theo's arm as they headed up a few steps, "Joanna showed me how to wield a sword. I was, like, eight and she and I would be going at it. There were four of us. Her, and me, and Layton, and Dylan. Then…they all died. I watched the three of them get into the carriage that day. Watched them get on the road." Amair looked up at him. "He didn't die alone. That…that's my consolation."

- CHAPTER XXX -

"Princess," a knock came at the door, an attendant peeking into her study where Amair and the Writer worked quietly.

"Develina, right?"

"Yes, your highness," she smiled, "I have a message that the singer, Ohrra, has arrived."

"Oh! Fantastic," she tapped her pen against her chin, "great. Lovely, I um...I have to finish this," she dragged out the words as she thought, "could someone bring her to her room and help her settle in?"

"Absolutely, your highness."

"I'm not entirely sure which of the halls...or ballrooms are being used for the performance tonight, but perhaps have one of the senior attendants show her around once we know which one is being used."

"Will do."

"I likely will not get a chance to see her before her prep for her performance, but please tell her I look forward to meeting her in person later this evening."

"Anything else?"

Amair took a deep breath, tipping her head, thinking. "No, no I think that is everything."

"Alright, I will pass this on."

"Thank you, Develina. Theo?" He looked up as the door clicked shut. "She has someone from your paper travelling with her for the duration of the tour. Would you mind going to greet them?"

"Oh, sure! Do you know who?"

"I don't even know what day it is. I forgot Ohrra was even here today."

He chuckled, stretching as he got up. "Fair enough. I'll head out now. How long are they here?"

"Just tonight, they're leaving after breakfast. She's going to I think 34 cities and villages? At least...and into all seven of the realms. It's a...a pretty big deal. Even Keene has asked her to perform."

"Wow."

"Yeah, so they have to get going. I thought the tour had already started, but apparently this is the first stop, and sort of the kickoff."

"Interesting."

"Very." She smiled. "Go, I'll meet up with you later, I want to get these letters done."

"Anything exciting?"

"Castle Scholarship awards. The program got passed to me last week." She smiled. "This round means more university students who get to pursue their research in," she glanced down at her notes, "biochemical sciences." She looked back up. "Political science and communications applications are up tomorrow."

"Atta girl." He smiled. "See you soon."

***

Chatter sounded around the theatre as the guests made their way in, Ohrra's reporter seated in the front row, the twins bouncing excitedly next to them under the watchful eye of two of their tutors. The King and Queen stood behind the curtain outside the theatre, their two older sons behind them, Amair and Theo squished at the back of the small, makeshift waiting room, able to peek out at the staff and guests from the village heading in excitedly to find seats.

Amair leaned against the cool stone wall, listening to the sound of people's voices mixing with the orchestra warming up, the wailing violins overtaking the other instruments. She smiled, hearing the brilliant, light laughs of their younger guests.

"Alright, your majesties, your highnesses...Writer," an attendant whispered, pulling back the curtain slightly. "Everyone is seated, are you ready for your entrance?"

"I've been looking forward to this for weeks!" the King beamed, leaning back as the curtain was pulled back, offering his arm to the Queen. They made their way out, Jasper and Kylo following, whispering to each other. Theo smiled, looking down at Amair and offering her his arm.

"Shall we?"

"I was hoping you would ask." She smiled, gently placing her fingers over his forearm, taking a small step closer to him. "Lead the way, Writer." He smiled, stepping out of the small curtained-off room, noticing the faces of the guests and visitors as they looked over their shoulders to grin in awe at the royal family walking. The King and Queen waved, the dim theatre lights washing over them as the crowd whispered, the young Princes on their heels.

Amair slowed, taking a deep breath, before letting Theo pull her through the door. The whispers grew, eyes running over the soft, layered dress nearly engulfing her, the bodice of wrapped tulle, a piece wrapped up over her chest and one shoulder. Under the layer, with the lights catching the detail sewn in, the guests could make out the shapes of music notes, the lines of a music staff wrapping from the bottom of her skirt, all the way up through the tulle running over her shoulder.

"That's the Princess!" she heard a young girl whisper, turning her head just enough to watch a little girl with two buns pull on her father's arm. He whispered something to her, noticing the Princess watching with a smile and nodding his head in a small bow. She bobbed hers back, glancing across the crowd as they followed her family down the centre aisle. The family took their seats in the front row, the King and Queen folding their arms together as they whispered, Theo holding Amair's hand as she sat and taking the aisle seat next to her. Amair kept her eyes on the stage, trying to make out some of the whispers behind her.

The Crier's apprentice walked onto the stage in front of the black velvet curtain bowing to the King. The King nodded back, the Crier's apprentice looking out over the crowd. "Your majesties, your royal highnesses, friends, guests, and beyond, welcome to the inaugural performance of Ohrra Verrante, the Glasslight voice taking Land by storm. She has graced the Sovereign and Oighre with her first performance as she begins her tour of Land, and the doors of the castle were opened today to make this performance a special celebration for you all.

"Without further ado I present to you, Ohrra." He bowed a little, heading off stage as the curtains pulled open, the crowd cheering. The lights appeared, revealing the red-haired woman in a deep blue dress, a huge skirt swallowing her bottom half, smiling out at the crowd, everyone cheering, making her laugh a little. She turned as well as the skirt would allow, curtsying deeply to the royal family who bowed their heads respectfully in return. The musicians around her sat straight, watching the shiny black music stands in front them. Amair noticed a few of them blushing, side glancing a few times at the large crowd.

"Thank you, thank you!" Ohrra exclaimed, folding her hands over her chest. "Thank you so much for having me as we begin this tour, and for allowing me to share the songs that have meant so much to me.

"I have assembled a beautiful, classical, and memorable selection of music for you today, some of which will follow along the length of this tour, and a few special pieces, just for this first performance.

"I would like to begin with a very special song that came all the way from the lowlands of RiKoi." She nodded to the musicians, the conductor lifting the baton, instruments rising. Ohrra took a deep breath. The crowd was quiet as they waited, a few leaning forwards in their seats. The twinkling voice and music notes filled the room, slow and soft, growing slowly until the notes turned into words in a language Amair could not make out. Somehow, the feeling of the words went from goosebumps to heat.

As the music built, vibrating in her chest, she felt fingers brush against hers.

She smiled nudging her fingers closer, twining into Theo's. She felt him inhale sharply, trying to suppress the smile that brought to her lips, keeping her eyes on Ohrra as the song slowed. The last of Ohrra's words turning back into notes. Ohrra bowed, the crowd clapping wildly.

"Thank you, wow, this is such a warm welcome. I have been training in classical music for over twenty years, since I was twelve years old. I have had the chance to study with the great masters of Skylock's music, and the chance to travel and train at different universities.

"Starting this tour at the castle means everything to me, not just for the chance to sing to the Sovereign and Oighre and their family, but because I was able to pursue my passion thanks to the programs and scholarships I was provided. My great love has been Skylish and Prophetic songs, so I will share a few of those next."

Amair couldn't focus on any of the words in the first song swaying its way through the crowd. She focused on the way his fingertips felt against hers, soft against her callouses. She didn't even notice the music die down, Ohrra's introduction of the next song lost on her, her words nothing more than heavy air as Amair's mind filled with thoughts of his fingers.

The first line of a new song pulled her attention, pulling her fingers back as she looked up at the stage.

> *Oh*
> *Land with the rolling*
> *Thunder*
> *Trees with the broken*
> *Eyes*
> *Hold on to the darkest mornings*
> *Just as the prophet said*

The song felt eerily familiar, picking out the clues as Ohrra sang about each of the realms of Land. The song carried on, descriptions as the soft music accompanying her grew like a wave under her voice, carrying over the audience, leaving goosebumps

Amair couldn't breathe, listening to the clapping as the singer introduced her next song, the words of prophecy ringing in Amair's ears, blinking a few times. The music started again, Amair trying to find her breath, but the pounding of the next prophetic song filled her ears. Theo noticed her hands gripped the arms of the seat, the deep blue velvet caving under her nails. He turned, trying to catch up with the words he had not been paying attention to.

> *A Kingdom of Sky*
> *For a thousand years*
> *Of good*
> *And great*
> *And prosperous days*

Not a King
Of golden thoughts
In the arms of friends
Under starless skies
White rain
In an undampened sea
It's alright to find a light here
For the end of a rules reign

There will come a girl
Of wild heart
And words like knives
With the eyes of a God
A Queen will she be

A Queen will she be

A horse seeped in night
Her brow kissed by Sloane
The skies will hold her
Keep her right
In the time
Of chaos
She'll leave the world
Dripping in gold

A girl of blue
Doused in the moon
Wrapped by the sun's fallen fate
She—

Amair could feel Theo staring at her, eyes wide, but she couldn't bring herself to move as more of Ohrra's words dripped with meaning she tried to push away. She could not distinguish the end of the song and the start of the clapping.

The clapping thundered in her ears, her eardrums popping as she tried to catch her breath. Ohrra turned to curtsy to a young boy who had stood up in his chair to clap and cheer for Ohrra, earning even more cheering from the audience behind him.

Amair slipped out of her chair as the crowd cheered, too enamoured to notice their Princess, walking past. Even her parents and brothers who barely noticed her as they clapped. She pushed open the side door, into the hallway as she sucked in a breath of the cool night air leaking in from the open window.

"You're in a prophecy?" Theo exclaimed, rushing out after her, Amair waving her hand to shush him. "You're in a prophecy?" he exclaimed, quieter.

"Prophecies are dumb and they mean nothing," she said, her voice tight as though out of breath.

"You're in a prophecy."

"No!" She flexed her hands as she caught her breath again. "Not…really," she muttered, running her hands up and down her arms, hearing the music come to a close as applause started, a few of the audience members cheering and whistling. "I have to meet and thank her, are you coming?"

"Princess!"

"Writer!" Her tone was sharp, and she bit her lip as she noticed it but refused to take it back. She folded her hands over her skirt, trying to steady her breath.

"The song got to you," he whispered with insistence, walking alongside her brisk pace as the first people started to leave the Theatre Hall.

Amair huffed. "Alan of Rin's twenty-seven prophecies were distributed to three of their most trusted Priestesses," she explained, nodding to the guard who opened the backstage door. "They each had a date on them and a province to distribute them to, apparently this one made its way into Ohrra's hands."

"Just so happened to pass into her hands, played to the second woman to be Oighre, ever?"

"Theo…"

"At the kickoff of her first tour?"

"Okay, so it's weird!" she whispered, spinning towards him, clenching her hands, listening to the chatter of more guests leaving the theatre. "But if it is a prophecy, and it is me, then that means that somewhere in that prophecy, the most important person in my life was meant to die, and I really cannot face that right now." Theo's face fell as he realised. Amair turned, smoothing her dress and straightening her shoulders. "Let's go."

He followed just behind her. She nodded to the guard at the second door. "Princess," the guard murmured as she bowed, pulling the door open. The backstage filled with warm light and Ohrra's face came into view. Theo took a short breath, her red hair and sharp face even more striking up close.

The singer noticed them, turning away from her aide.

"Princess," the singer kneeled, her dark blue skirts blossoming on the floor.

"Ohrra," Amair smiled, bobbing her head in return. "Please, please, rise. Your travels are well?"

"As well as they could be," Ohrra shrugged. "You enjoyed the show?"

"Oh, very much."

"Your dress…it's an incredible welcome, by the way."

"Thank you. When I saw a music note dress in last week's sketches…I couldn't resist."

"I'm sorry I won't get the chance to see anything quite so grand again soon."

"Well, I shall pull out all the stops for breakfast tomorrow."

"Actually, we have decided to leave tonight! I like to listen to the night bugs from the carriage."

"Oh! Are...are you certain? We're more than happy to have you–"

"–I go where the winds take me, Princess," she grinned, her wide, dark eyes on Amair's, "and I think they are calling me away."

"If...if you're sure."

"I passed off anything that was needed." Her smile was warm, but it sent a chill down Amair's back. "Thank you so, so much for having me."

"It was...absolutely amazing, we can't thank you enough."

"I will be back, and maybe then we will be able to share a meal." Her aide caught her eye, holding a bag in his hand at the back door.

"The carriage is ready, Miss Ohrra."

"Thank you!" She wrapped her fingers around Amair's cheeks, kissing her cheeks and pressing their noses together.

"Fair speed, little one." She let go, waving a little to Theo, and disappearing out the door. Amair blinked a few times, lunging for the door before it shut, peeking out as Ohrra and her aide flew down the short hill to a carriage waiting on the barely lit side path.

"She is so odd," Amair mused, watching as Ohrra shrank into the distance.

"Some would say the same of your aunt Elena." Theo smirked, the two of them pulling back into the building, the heavy door swinging shut. "Or you."

Amair shot a playful glare at Theo, shaking a loose curl over her shoulder. "It's not a bad thing, I don't mean that." The Princess squinted, thinking. "But there's something about her."

"I get it," Jasper said, appearing behind them, making Amair jump a little.

"I'm getting you a bell. Like the cats."

"There are cats?" Theo raised an eyebrow and the siblings looked up at him, raising an eyebrow.

"Three," Jasper told him.

"Four," Amair corrected.

"Oh…four. At the stables, and around the yard. They keep out the rats."

"I thought you were observant, Theo," Amair chuckled, nudging him with her shoulder. "Walk me home?"

"It would be my pleasure, Princess."

They walked through the dark halls, still alight with the chatter of those visiting from the royal village. The two slowed, watching Amair's people spill out the main doors onto the path back to the town that Theo had almost called home. Amair leaned onto the bridge's windowsill to peer out into the night, the hum of the lanterns in the misty night and he could see the twist of confusion and pain in her face but did not push it.

As the sound of the main gates creaked closed, the last of the guests disappearing down to the edge of the hill into the village, they turned and wandered back towards the end of the family corridor.

Theo watched Amair whistle, Lupa appearing next to her, pushing against her heavy skirts as she panted happily. "We should…meet up tomorrow."

"Don't we always?" he asked.

"I…like…your company."

Theo matched her smile, lifting his chin a little. "Of course, it would be my honour, your highness."

She rolled her eyes, still smiling as she pushed her door open. "And I think we can drop the titles, Theo."

"If you wish…*Amair*." She caught the mischievous little grin again.

- CHAPTER XXXI -

"Can I make you a cup of coffee?" Amair smiled at him, her eyes squinting a little as her warm cheeks pushed her eyes up.

"Sure! Did you want me to ring for it—"

"—no, no, I want to *make* you coffee." Amair smiled wider.

"To the kitchens, then." Theo offered her his arm and she gently took hold of him, the two of them heading for the bridge to a shortcut toward the kitchens.

"Can you…can you cook?"

"I can, actually," Amair grinned, looking out into the grey day. "But there's no real…fascinating story, I don't think. It's warm, in the kitchens. I used to…sneak down there, as a child. I would go running through the rain, and through the gardens, and the forest, and come in shivering, dragging mud behind me. The head baker, Lisell, started noticing.

"She scolded the first time she caught me. Then the next time I crept through, there were tea and scones waiting for me.

"The fifth time, I was actually coming in dry, clean, and wearing shoes, and I asked her to teach me how to make bread. From there, I got passed around through the bakers, and the chefs, and the apprentices, and the kitchen hands, learning little bits from everyone.

"At the time I figured…if I was going to be an adventuress, I would need to know how to cook." Amair smiled at the ground. "I stopped when I joined the Circle. There was so much going on, then. But yes, I *can* cook. I'm not nearly as good as the wonderful people who work here, though."

She winked at one of the kitchen hands who chuckled as they passed.

"If she's telling you I scolded her, I'll deny it," a plump woman in a white coat, the sleeves pushed up, strong arms beneath them, turned to them. "Hello, Princess." Amair laughed, reaching a hand to the woman with kind eyes.

"Hello, Lisell. I don't know, though, you were much more effective than the nanny."

"A fair point," Lisell laughed, rubbing Amair's arm. "Your skirts didn't take up nearly as much room, back then."

"Well, that's true."

"Did you need something, my lady?"

"I was just hoping to make Theo some coffee," Amair smiled. "I like to remind myself how, every once in a while."

"You are welcome in this kitchen any time. You know where everything is?"

"I do."

"I taught you well." Lisell bobbed her head, fixing her sleeve and turning back to the dough on the counter. "Have fun!"

"Thank you," Amair called, reaching behind her to grab Theo's arm, pulling him further into the kitchens.

"So that's Lisell."

"That's Lisell. The reason why on my birthday every year, one of the pastries is *troighean* – chocolate footprints pressed into pastry dough. She's also a language keeper. She's taught me a lot."

"Ah," Theo laughed, sitting on one of the stools Amair pointed him to. He watched as she pulled things from a cupboard, one of the kitchen hands stopping to light one of the large stove's burners for her. She thanked him, setting a kettle on the heat.

"Is there anything else you like to make?" Theo asked, watching Amair's hands as they worked, measuring out beans into a handheld grinder.

"I used to love helping knead and roll dough. I didn't even care what it was for...I just loved how it felt against my fingers," she laughed, turning the handle to grind the beans. "I have a few recipes that I know pretty well, but the most I have time to do these days is make tea and coffee."

"I see..."

"Mom always used to say she wished her mom had lived. Apparently, she was an amazing cook."

"She died a long time ago, didn't she?"

"Just before mom and dad got married," Amair told him, setting a filter in the hourglass shaped container, carefully dumping the coffee grounds into the filter. "Mom almost didn't go through with the wedding because of it...she thought it was some horrible sign from the deities."

"Oh...oh, wow..."

"Yeah. Dad was ready to give her an out, too."

"How...why did she stay?"

"Because grief works hard, but fate works harder," Amair smiled, leaning back against one of the wooden counters. "Mom actually left, to make the trek back to Torrent when she met a traveller, who apparently said something to her. Something clicked, she turned her horse around and they were married two days later."

"Wow!"

"Yeah." He watched Amair's thoughtful smile as the kettle started to squeal and she pulled it from the heat.

"Do you...do you know what the traveller said to her?"

"Not a clue. She's never told anyone, not even dad, apparently," she told him, pouring the water out of the long narrow spout, watching the way it dripped through the beans and filter.

"How did your parents meet?" Theo asked absent-mindedly, watching the steam from the water. "She wasn't a Chief's daughter, I know that, I just..."

"No, I get it. It is surprising, honestly...I mean, my past two birthdays have been about hosting potential matches. It's not like Oighres get to spend a lot of time meeting people."

"Did...did Layton have anyone? I know there were rumours that he and Johanna..."

"Ha!" Amair set the kettle down, looking at him. "Sorry I know...it's not that funny, I just...I just saw their relationship. Um...Johanna and *I* were more likely to end up together."

"Ah."

"Plus, she spent much more of her time at the training ground yelling at recruits with Moritz."

"And...Layton?"

Amair sighed a little, watching the water running through the filter. "Layton...wasn't interested. At all, really. Any time it was brought up...he didn't have any interest in romance, or more than that, or anything related. He was really just interested in his work, and his friends. People used to joke Jasper or I would have to give him an heir."

"Gotcha." Amair smiled, thinking about him, as she handed a cup of dark coffee to the Writer, stopping to sprinkle a bit of cinnamon over it. "Thank you."

"Enjoy."

"Oh! My original question," Theo reminded her, the warmth of the coffee sending a shiver down his arms, "how did your parents meet?"

"Oh! Right," Amair chuckled. "Dad was on a trip to Torrent province, to work with the Chief. He was twenty, had his Circle, and they were starting to be given more responsibility – same as Layton was, at that age."

"Same as you'll be?"

Her jaw set for a second. "My timeline's a little shorter. Anyway, he was staying at the Chief's home for a week of meetings.

"Mom had almost been engaged, actually. But her girlfriend died in an accident...I believe she drowned? Mom was working at the Chief's home at the time, interning with an events coordinator. She didn't want to take time off work, despite her grief. She was at work while dad was staying there.

"Mom was still very much grieving. Dad noticed. He took her aside to ask her if she was alright. He took lunch with her every day he was there, and she claims she felt better, having someone to help her try and feel like herself again, push the accident out of her mind.

"After dad left, he sent a messenger with a letter to her, just to see how she was coping with everything. They started sending letters back and forth, and they were...they became friends. The best of friends. He invited her to an event at the castle and she went. She says she didn't plan on accepting but something told her to. Guards went out to fetch her and bring her to the castle. He had the seamstresses dress her while she was here. Things started progressing..." Theo loved the way Amair smiled, looking up as she thought. "They were engaged a few months later."

"Beautiful."

"Yeah. I've always hoped for a love like theirs. No one gets to see them the way we do...obviously...but it's special. They're still best friends. I couldn't ask for more."

Ink & Crown:
The Princess Serial

by Sir Theodore Crawford

Your princess can cook. It's true, dear readers, Princess Amair Skylock has admitted to me that she can, and even enjoys, cooking, thanks in large part to head baker Lisell McDaglen. The Princess shared a few key secrets with me — like a sprinkle of cinnamon in a cup of dark coffee.

Or her favourite thing to bake — bread, because of its versatility, and she recalls kneading it around a countertop at a young age after sneaking in to the kitchens, and listening to stories from Lisell and the other bakers. They would give her a portion of the dough and let her have her way with it, creating shapes and designs, which as her interests grew, apparently "quickly turned into bread-swords, so she was passed to the kitchen hands to fight." So her first training was not in the chill of the outdoor ring, but in the inviting warmth of the kitchens. When she is not in with the bakers, she is happy to help and chat with the prep cooks, or work with anyone creating a purée, as long as spices are involved.

- Sir Theodore Crawford, Staff Writer, Special Liaison Reporter to The Palace, Man of Letters

- CHAPTER XXXII -

"My lady!" Lydia exclaimed, dropping the dress in horror as she looked at Theo standing in the doorway. Theo noticed the tiniest of smiles on Amair's lips.

"It's alright, Lydia. I'm sure it's nothing he hasn't seen before."

"Yes." She tugged at one of the hair pins she had attached to her double wrapped apron. "That is what worries me." Amair looked up at Theo, raising an eyebrow. He said nothing, but smirked glancing back at Lydia.

"I'll take the dress."

"You will not!"

Theo looked over to her, holding out a hand. "You've done the hard part."

"Sir Crawford, I–" Lydia gasped.

"Lydia," Amair looked to the girl, her face soft. "He's already seen me and I'm essentially decent, it's just the dress that needs to go on. I'm sure Th…Sir Crawford can lace up a dress. I can ring if we need an extra hand."

"Y-…yes, my lady." She looked between the two before her, her eyebrows so tight together Amair worried they'd get stuck. Finally, she picked up the dress and handed it to Theo, turning to leave, not taking her eyes off them until she had closed the doors. Theo and Amair looked at each other, Amair covering her mouth as the two burst into giggles, Theo holding the dress to his chest as he leaned over, laughing.

"The look on her face," Theo managed to say through his bursts of laughter. A jolt ran through his body when Amair grabbed his arm, leaning a little as she laughed. Theo smiled at her, the two of them standing straight again, looking at each other, Amair still holding his forearm. She smiled, pulling her arm back, holding her fingers as she smiled a little. Theo tightened his jaw a little to keep from shivering at her pointed stare, the little squint as she studied him.

"I should get that dress on," she smiled, nodding towards the fabric balled up in Theo's hands.

"Of course." He unravelled the dress, holding it by the sleeves and admiring it.

"I haven't seen this one yet."

Amair grinned. "There are a lot of my clothes you haven't seen."

"Though now I've seen your corset," he murmured into her ear and a shiver ran down her back as she bit back a smile.

"There are more of these, too."

Theo fought the grin, gathering the dress as she stood. "You look lovely in blue," Theo murmured, running his hand down the velvet arm of her dress.

"Well thank the gods for that, seeing as it's the family colour."

"Ah, that would explain the flags, and crests, and banners, and–"

She threw a shoe at him, making him laugh. "Point made."

"You look really beautiful," her looked down at her, the two locking eyes. He tucked a stray hair behind her ear. "And now you look perfect." He leaned forward, his lips on her ear. "As always."

She grinned, trying to purse her lips to hide it.

"Shall I escort you?"

"I'm sure I have a guard lurking around the corner to take me somewhere but…why not."

He opened the door for her. "You off to anything exciting?"

"Meeting someone in the Royal Village – a scholar, visiting from Torrent University, who preferred not to come to the castle. Just starting the trend that as Queen I'll be surrounded by people who are much smarter than I."

"From what I hear, you're pretty smart."

"Shush with the flattery." She shot him a playful glare. "That's one thing about this Kingdom. I don't actually make most of the decisions. So far, during the marathon cramming session I've had the past few months, I've watched my dad play mediator more than anything. Trying to get advisors to compromise or even just stop the screaming matches. Trying to stop representatives or chiefs from…well, killing each other. Literally." Theo laughed, scratching something down on his notepad. "I was in a meeting, where that happened. It…it wasn't pretty. Layton would have been so mad. He was big on order."

"And you?"

"I was trying really hard not to laugh. Or call for a fist fight."

"Why am I not surprised," Theo chuckled. "Layton liked order?"

"He was funny about that. He loved games, and jokes, and the silliness that came with all the…shenanigans the four of us got ourselves into. But inside his office, or the Council room…rules were everything to him. Procedure, rules…everything had an order, and a role, and you followed them. Followed him."

- CHAPTER XXXIII -

"Sir Crawford," Lydia murmured, glancing back over her shoulder.

"Morning," Theo smiled. "I just wanted to pick up…" Theo trailed off, looking at the concern written across Lydia's face.

"Sir Crawford, today…today's not a good day."

"Is…is Amair…okay?" Theo eyebrows knit together, trying to glance past Lydia, looking into Amair's dark room.

"She…" Lydia hesitated, looking away from Theodore. She took a deep breath, looking up at him, narrowing her eyes a little. "She has days, still. Where Layton is with her so strongly that…" Lydia trailed off, licking her lips. "She's not okay today. Cannot eat. Cannot get out of bed." Theo looked at the slit in the door again, his heart breaking.

"Let me help."

"Sir Crawford…I…Prince Jasper, Prince Kylo, their royal majesties…none of them have been able to help when she's in a spell like this."

"Please, Lydia?" The two stared each other down, Lydia finally letting out a huff. "I've seen this."

"The things I do," she shook her head, stepping out of the way, pulling the door open. Theo rushed past her into the dark room. All the blinds were drawn, shutting out the little bit of light outside.

Theo found his way to the edge of Amair's large bed, just enough light for him to make out the edges of her slender face.

"Hi," Theo whispered into the darkness. Her eyes were closed, and he brushed a piece of hair off her nose. Just as he started to pull his hand back, her fingers wrapped around his wrist.

"Hi," Theo whispered again. She didn't move. Didn't say anything. But her thin fingers gripped tighter around him. He wrapped his other hand over hers, gently pulling her hand towards him and brushing his lips against her fingers. They sat there and Theo lost track of time, holding Amair's hand and letting the sound of rain fill the room.

- CHAPTER XXXIV -

"Ama!"

"Go *away!*" her voice cracked as she whisked herself into the Gold Corridor.

"Ah…" Theo glanced down at Kylo. "What's going on?"

"Jasper…I don't know, I'm gonna say picked a fight."

"And?"

"Those two have had more than a couple blowouts," Kylo told him. Theo glanced up, noticing the King appear behind Kylo.

"I *just* want the real you back–"

"–that girl is gone!" Amair yelled at Jasper, whipping her skirts around with her, nearly swiping a table out from under an ancient looking vase.

"Amair–"

"–Layton was more than my brother!" Hearts broke as Amair's face contorted. "He…he was my best *friend*. In the *whole world*. A part of me *died* in that carriage with him! A big part…" Tears streamed down Amair's face. She looked at her hands, trembling, angry and crying, losing her breath as she started to hyperventilate. Theo took a step towards her, carefully raising his arms. She shook once more before her legs collapsed.

Theo jerked, grabbing her and pulling her in, the two of them sinking to the floor. Jasper opened his mouth, the King pulling him backwards as they watched Theo gently stroke her hair, head bent against hers as he whispered her back to safety.

- CHAPTER XXXV -

"What are you reading?" Theo asked.

"The newest Liza Belgrade novel," she chuckled, flashing the colourful, matte cover to her friend and he chuckled at the image of the couple embraced on a dance floor in dresses even larger than Amair's.

"I expected the Princess to be nose deep in classics."

"Even a Princess looks for some drama and romance in her life," she shrugged

"So far, from what I've seen, you have enough of that to last a lifetime." Amair snorted, grinning.

"Drama, certainly." She glanced up at him, sticking her finger into the book to keep her page. "Romance could use some work." Theo opened his mouth. "Nah!" she warned, pointing at him, trying to suppress a smile.

"Don't you usually work today?" he asked, flopping over into one of the chairs, making her giggle as the chair screeched sideways.

"My dad said to take a break, but I'm pretty sure it's the closest thing to a timeout you can give the eighteen-year-old heir to a Kingdom." She chewed on her lip, trying to catch his reaction. "So…do you have another group of questions for me, Writer?" She flipped the corner of her page, setting the book in her lap.

"Actually, no. This week's serial is set and ready, in Gaelen's expert hand on its way to my editor."

"Well done, and a day earlier than usual too."

"What can I say, I was inspired."

"Do I get a sneak peek?"

"No."

"Well, I can only hope and *pray* it was not about my…" she looked up, "meltdown."

"I'm not here to humiliate you, Amair." She pressed her lips together, nodding. "It did teach me something about you, though." She felt her arms turn cold. "You're growing."

Amair snorted, eyes widening as she thought about his words. "Growing away from the girl I was."

"You're nearly eighteen, Amair. You get to be whoever you want to be. And change however many times you need." They stared at each other for a moment, Amair smiling softly, chewing on her cheek. "Now! Are we reading, or what?"

"You want to…read?"

"Isn't that what you were doing? Unless…" He leaned forwards, grabbing at her book. "You want me to read to you–"

"–ab–" she grabbed it back, "–solutely not."

"More tea, your highness?" an attendant asked, picking up the empty pot.

"And another cup, if you could?" She didn't look away from Theo, watching him pull a random, red book off the shelf beside him. "For the Writer?"

She didn't see the smile on the attendant's face, looking between the two young people with books in their hands. "Right away, your highness."

- CHAPTER XXXVI -

"Auntie!" Evander exclaimed, rushing away from the group who had just come in from archery practice. Theo watched him go, the other boys following on his heels. There was yelling and laughter, the foyer suddenly exploding with noise. Attendants rushing around slowed, glancing over their shoulders to watch the commotion as the boys flung themselves at a woman with her hair in a twisty braid, dark leather riding pants hugging her and a series of blades tied down one leg.

Theo heard the rustle of a skirt behind him, glancing to the side as Amair passed him. "Aunt Elena," she smiled, arms out in front of her. Theo noticed her bare feet under her dress and smiled, trying to imagine what adventure she had just come from.

"Hello, my darling," the woman ran towards Amair, pulling her into a hug. "How are you?"

"Fairly well."

"Don't you dare 'fairly well' me, bug." They let go of each other, the woman looking her straight in the eye, squinting a little. "I know you too well."

Ama bit her lip and for a second, Theo thought he may cry. "Later."

"Fine." They stared at each other a second longer and Amair shook her head, looking back over her shoulder and pointing to Theo.

"Elena Skylock, I'd like to introduce you to the Writer," Amair looked him up and down, her eyes playful. "Theodore, my Aunt Elena."

"Or just Theo," he said as he bowed to her.

"Ooh, nope, no bowing necessary." She waved her hands. "I have no title, just a friendly wave works. I'll even take a hug, though don't let anyone in charge of protocol see." Something clicked in Theo's head as he placed the young woman's face, tipping his head back.

"You're the King's sister?"

"I am."

"You gave up your title."

"Great deduction skills." Theo smiled at her, watching her grin and look down at Amair, putting an arm around her niece's waist. "But every once in a while, I need to see my family."

"You should skip me for a week and have Elena as the subject for the serial," Amair suggested, nudging Elena with her shoulder.

"Oh, no no. I am having way too much fun reading about *you*, bug."

"How are *you* getting the paper—wait, where have you even been?"

"I have my ways," Elena grinned slyly.

"Auntie!" Alec complained, his hands on his hips, the four boys all staring.

"My darlings, you are all sprouting like weeds, Jasper will you *please* stop growing!" Elena exclaimed as she turned to them, squishing each of their faces.

"Coming in from an adventure?" Theo murmured to Amair as Elena put her attention onto the boys.

"I don't know what you're talking about." Amair kept her eyes on her aunt and her brothers, a tiny smirk on her lips. Theo grinned down at her, to where she pulled one of her feet back into the safety of her dress, an inch of dirt on the hem.

"Mhm." He touched her arm ever-so-gently. "Bring me with you next time." He noticed Amair's breath hitch in her chest for a second, licking her lips and shaking out her hair. She stepped away, glancing at Theo and drawing her eyes away again, focusing on her family.

"So, Elena! Did dad know you were coming?" Theo watched the family walking away, Amair's arm wrapped through Elena's, the twins hanging off their aunt, even Kylo standing taller and grinning. Theo chuckled to himself as they all walked in step, and turned back towards the long hallway. He walked slowly, finally pushing on the door he was looking for, stepping into the small library.

There was a small table in the middle of the circular room, a tall window on the side opposite the door, the walls lined with white bookshelves, full of white and black bound books. Theo glanced at the table, the atlas on its stand open to a colour map of the world. A second book on the other side showed the Skylock family tree. Theo ran his hand over the page, stopping at the small painting of Elena Skylock, the King's only sibling. She was young, in the painting, the unmistakable Skylock blue eyes shining. He pulled his pen from his pocket, noting her birthdate on his palm, walking over to the shelves and running his fingers along the spines. He searched for the date noted on his hand, pulling on one of the books, this one bound in white. He pulled it open, going over to drop it on the table.

Princess Elena Skylock. The 'Princess' had almost entirely been scratched from existence, the edges of the letters peeking over the ink lines. The painting of her from the family tree was under her former title, and he ran his finger over her page.

Elena was only thirty, not that much older than the King's children, born months after their father had died and King Niall had ascended to the throne. When she was eight, the year that Layton was born, the Queen mother left on her great adventures. There was a letter signed by the King and Queen on the next page, promising to care for Elena. Theo wondered what it was like, to be caught between child and sibling, and child and sibling of the ruler of a kingdom.

A few years later, when she was twelve, Elena chose to go and live with distant relatives in Tunngas. When she was fifteen, she gave up her royal title and, following in the footsteps of her recently passed mother, began travelling around Land.

Theo turned the page, running his hands over the tarnished paper of answers Elena had once filled in, her writing messy like Amair's.

"Someday I shall be an adventuress, and nothing will be able to hold me down." Theo smiled, flipping to the back, a recent, discoloured photograph of Elena on a horse, a bow tied next to a quiver of arrows on the saddle. There was something wild and strong and defiant in her face and crooked smile.

Just like her niece.

***

"Is your aunt why you wanted to be an adventuress?"

"Mhm…yes and no," Amair rubbed her finger on a big leaf as they passed a large plant that hung partially into the path. "I heard more stories about my grandmother than Elena. Her adventures were sort of just getting started when I was a kid."

"And you and Elena seem very close."

"She always got stuck at the kids table," Amair laughed, standing on her tiptoes to water another plant. "Even as she approached thirty, she was dropped with us. It was funny because when he turned sixteen, Layton had to sit with the adults. It was more him being Oighre than being a grown-up. But Elena was always with us. And actually, she's the one who taught me to shoot arrows."

"So, there's a bond."

"Yeah and…" she tipped her head, "and she's just…she always cared. She was who I went to with problems and thoughts. Even if it meant sending a letter and just kind of *hoping* it would eventually find her. The big sister I didn't have. The little sister she always wanted."

"That's sweet."

"Yeah," Amair shrugged. "It's just really nice to have her in my life." She lowered onto one of the stone benches, fiddling the leaves on a flower she had plucked along their walk. "Off the record?"

"Sure."

"The press treats her like the castle's dirty little secret. The Princess born after her father died. The Princess born to a widowed Queen. The Princess born ten years after her brother. The Princess who went away. The Princess who gave up her title. The Princess who's…more than a little eccentric." Amair took a breath. "I like that she's a little piece of…irregularity in this place." Theo smiled, slipping his notebook into his pocket, tucking his pen away.

He looked around them. "Is this where you were earlier? With your…" he laughed, "muddied feet?"

"No," she grinned, "I was chasing butterflies." Theo stopped watering, looking up at her.

"What?"

"I…was…chasing…butterflies?" she repeated, slower.

"Seriously?"

"Seriously…why are you…what?"

"It's, just…" he laughed, setting down the watering can, tipping his head at her. "Not what I was expecting." She grinned, biting her lip.

"It's near the end of Autumn. The Blue Shines…they're starting to emerge, and they…they glow. It's said they carry souls." She shrugged. "The twins used to just call them glowers. Little wisps of light, floating through the forests."

"You're something else, Princess," he laughed. She just laughed, leaning over to pull weeds out of one of the beds, the strings of light breaking through the clouds warming her hair. Theo watched her as she concentrated.

He did not see the woman hanging back at the edge of the garden, watching him, eyebrow raised as she smirked, knowing the look on his face all too well.

***

"Mr. Writer!" Elena's cool voice called, the sound of shoes on the floor echoing behind him.

"It's Theo," he laughed, bobbing his head at her. He raised an eyebrow looking over her. "They got you into a dress."

"Yeah well, even an ex-Princess wants to look pretty and fit in. Though I am amazed by how much Amair enjoys being in these things." She pulled at the bodice a little. "I keep tripping on the bottom. I have half a mind to cut three inches off of it." Theo laughed, nodding a little. "So."

"So?"

"My nephews tell me you've become quite the…hero," she smirked.

"Oh the…breakdown? I just…"

"Breakdown?"

"When I…held her? After her…breakdown?" He watched her confusion. "Isn't that…what you meant? Or the depressive episode…" Her squinted at her, watching her wheels spin.

"No, actually…but I'll add those to the list." She tossed her loose hair back over her shoulders. "I'm planning to sneak out tomorrow morning…I have to be back for her birthday in a few weeks, can't spend too long here. But…I don't disapprove."

"Disapprove of what?"

She grinned, tipping her head. "It was lovely to meet you, Writer."

- CHAPTER XXXVII -

"You need to be able to do this dance for the dance in Keene!" Layton laughed, trying to scold his sister as she flopped back over the edge of the couch in his study.

"No, I'm pretty sure you *need to know this dance," Amair shot back.*

"Ama!" He dragged out her name. "I promised dad we would both *learn it and by the gods, if we don't…" He blew air out, sitting on the ground and running his hands through his hair.*

"What's the big deal?" Amair raised her head a little, watching him stress. "It's just dinner and a quick wave to the man who likes to call himself an Emperor despite barely having an empire which is already such a shitty thing which I don't know why we keep showing up to endorse—"

"—protecting our *people from ending up* his *people."*

"Touché…what about all the other *people?"*

"Not the time. Ama." His fingers were pressed into his temples. "Not the time."

She could tell there was something else up. Something, for the first time, he was not telling her.

"Renn?" Amair asked the musician as she dragged herself off the couch. "Let's do this stupid Keenian dance again."

"On the record?"

Theo raised an eyebrow, catching up with her words. "What's up?" he asked, staring at the book in his hand.

"I'm ready to tell you about the accident." Theo whipped his head up, looking across the table at her. Amair's eyes were wide, cautious, but they weren't shining with tears.

"Okay." Theo tried to smile reassuringly but felt his stomach turn. He closed his book, reaching into his pocket and pulling out his pen. "Okay." Neither of them said anything, Theo setting himself up, flipping for an empty page in his notebook, Amair's eyes trained on his fingers moving each of the slightly yellow pages. Amair called for more tea.

He tapped his pen against his thumb, uncapping it and resting it to the page. He looked back up to Amair, their eyes locked. "Whenever you're ready, Princess." She took a deep breath and nodded.

"I wanted to go. We were four – Layton and Dylan, me, Johanna. We did everything together. But Layton had turned twenty-two. He was going to Keene for a meeting with Emperor Omnan because the Council wanted him stepping in more. Or…stepping out, in a way. He had a knack for words, and they thought he could help in the…*tense* situation, with Keene. So, they went. Dylan was part of his Inner Circle, so was Johanna, and she was about to officially be appointed Layton's knight, the one who is always with him, so she had to go."

"Weren't you part of Layton's inner circle?" Theo asked, looking up from his page.

"I was." She bit her lip a little. "Two royal children aren't supposed to travel outside the Kingdom together. In case." She shook her head to herself. "It sounds grim but it's law and…it's grim but it makes sense. So, Dylan went. I helped prepare everything before they left, and they would send a messenger back to us when they got there. Once they were safe, I would ride out with two Knights and meet them there.

"Do you…do you want the story in chronological order or…how I learned about it?"

"However you need to tell it."

"Mhm…" Amair leaned into her hand, running a finger over her lips, thinking. "The messenger should have reached us by supper. I was walking down, the note would be delivered to me…I was in his circle. My father asked but I said they may have stopped and made it a little bit later than planned. I sat down, and supper came and went. I spent the evening reading. My attendants got me ready for bed…and still there was nothing.

"By then I was worried." She took a deep breath. "I rang for my attendants, and my father, and Moritz, and two other Knights, and part of my brain said I was overreacting. There had been so many times where I had been told I was overreacting, but…it didn't feel like it… The guard at my door escorted me to one of the briefing rooms and we all realized something had to be wrong. A messenger was sent to go see the Emperor and see what Keene knew, Moritz and two Knights rode out behind.

"I wanted to go with them. I knew I'd be safe. Probably safer than any guard. But my dad said no. They had only been gone an hour, my mom, my dad, and I in my mom's sitting room, when they all came back. The messenger was back." Amair looked down at the table. "They told us we needed to come quickly, and we got on our horses…I was still in my nightgown. I just threw on a cloak, and…honestly, I don't even remember putting on my riding boots.

"We rode hard for what felt like hours. Apparently, it wasn't, but still. I just thought he was hurt. Thought *they* were hurt, that they needed help.

"I never…never could have expected what we arrived to."

Theo gulped. Stories of the accident had circled through the Kingdom, but no one really knew what had happened.

"I remember screaming, when we rode up to the crash site. I think my mother did, too, but honestly so much of that time has slipped away." He noticed her bite the inside of her cheek. "I slid off my horse and ran towards the crash. The carriage was overturned. It had been set on fire. Before I could reach it, Moritz grabbed me, held me back. I kept screaming. Moritz still has scars on the back of his hand from where I tried to claw away from him." Tears streamed down Amair's cheeks, her bottom lip trembling.

"We were there, just watching the smouldering wreckage. Every breath of wind pulled sparks out of the wreck. The Knights would switch off holding me, because I kept trying to run *towards* the coals. Looking back, it was dumb...but my brain kept telling me that I could still save them. Dad was holding mom. A water carriage arrived to douse the fire.

"The three of them died holding each other." A little sob escaped her. "Their bodies were found down the hill from the carriage." Amair swallowed hard. "I…I can stop or…or the next, this next part has to be kept quiet."

"Okay." Theo could feel tears running down his own cheeks, trying to keep his breathing even.

"Dylan must have been thrown from the carriage, because he had...a broken neck. Johanna and Layton had burns so they were in the carriage when the fire was started. They all had lots of broken bones.

"Layton and Johanna must have crawled down the hill to Dylan and...someone, um...someone had stabbed Dylan. We don't...we don't know who. Johanna had a stab wound, through her stomach.

"When the bodies were found...the Knight holding me lost his grip and I got away. Or honestly, maybe they just let me go. Layton and Johanna were on either side of Dylan, arms all wrapped together."

"Oh my gods, Amair..."

"Y'know some days...some days I wish I had died with them."

"Amair!"

"They were my best friends. It hurts every day...that I wasn't there with them." Theo slid out of his chair, kneeling in front of Amair.

"I...I for one, am *so glad* that you weren't." Theo looked into her red eyes as he squeezed her hand. "And I know I am not the only one."

She wiped at her tears. "I believe in journalistic integrity, Theo, I do, especially yours...I've wanted to scream this story from the tower since that very night, I want my people to *know*, they deserve to *know*. But...you have to run your article past the King's office. There are things...I don't know what they're keeping, for now. Until we...figure everything out..."

"I don't have to run it at all–"

"–it's time." Her voice was tight with tears but when she looked up, her eyes were ablaze. "It's time."

- CHAPTER XXXVIII -

Amair didn't look up from her book as she pushed her back against the door to the sewing room, waltzing in. "Princess!" someone yelled, and Amair started to look up, to find a bare-chested Theodore. Amair opened her mouth, dropping her book, hands flying to cover her eyes.

"I'm so sorry!" she exclaimed, standing there with her eyes covered, hearing one of the seamstresses' apprentices giggle as Theo laughed with them.

"It's fine, Amair."

"I've been told I need to learn to knock."

Theo's warm laugh filled her ears again. "It's *fine*, Amair." Amair dropped her hands slowly, one at a time, one of the seamstress' attendants swooping to pick up her book and hand it back to her. Amair brushed a couple threads off the cover, holding the book against her chest, still averting her eyes.

"Amair, there are two new sketches for you to see," the head seamstress told her, "we're going to head off for luncheon, but please stay as long as you need, and leave a note with any comments on the gowns."

"Of course, Metali."

"Julianna is just going to finish up with you, Sir Crawford, and then you can go."

"Thank you, Metali." Metali and three of her apprentices bowed their heads to the Princess, smiling, and scurried out the door.

"Here are the sketches, Princess," Julianna smiled, a pencil sticking out of the side of her bun.

"Thank you." Amair set her book down, settling into a chair, looking at the shading of the beautiful yellow fabric, the shape and details of the dresses. Her eyes trailed off the page, following to where Julianna stood on a stool, pulling a tape measure down Theo's back, turning her head sideways trying to read the number. Amair kept looking, suddenly realizing she was looking into a smirking Theo's eyes, pulling her head back to the sketches in front of her, trying to suppress a smile. Julianna disappeared into one of the side rooms, sticking her pencil back into her bun.

"What are the gowns for?" Theo asked, rubbing one of his arms, studying Amair.

"Every Sunday, designers from across the Kingdom put in designs for a new gown," Amair smiled. "Just to add to the collection. And every few months, we donate them out across the Kingdom, sometimes in their original form, sometimes remade into multiple dresses."

Julianna reappeared, holding a folded shirt, passing it to Theo. "The new shirts will be passed to your valet, Sir Crawford."

"Thanks, Julianna."

Julianna blushed, smiling. "You're welcome, Sir Crawford." Julianna stared at him, smiling for a second, finally turning her head away to smile at Amair. "Do you need anything, your highness?"

"No, Julianna," Amair smiled, glancing ever so quickly at Theo. "I'll be done in a moment, but I'll just leave these on Metali's desk."

"Alright, have a good day Princess." Julianna curtsied, grabbing her shawl and scurrying out of the sewing room. Theo and Amair were quiet, watching Julianna leave, their eyes drawing back together.

"So…new shirts?" Amair asked, finding a pencil on the head seamstress' desk.

"Yes. A few more formal ones – they had two more suits made for me which are both absolutely beautiful – but some slightly less stuffy ones too."

"Mhm?" Amair jotted a quick tiny note about the skirt on one of the sketches, dropping them on Metali's desk.

"Like…actually, exactly like this," Theo said, shaking out the folded shirt. Amair watched as he pulled on the loose tunic, tucking the front into his black pants, the neck wide enough that his collarbones peaked out, a small slit where the top of his chest poked through. "What do you think?"

Amair trailed her eyes across the white linen, pulling her eyes up to his face where Theo waited, smirking. She managed a tiny, sly smile back, squinting a little. "I quite like it." She looked around, grabbing a piece of black twine off one of the sewing desks, playing with it in her one hand, walking over slowly to Theo, still on the little pedestal. She stopped in front of him, looking up, their eyes trained on each other, Amair biting the inside of her cheek. After a second, she broke the gaze, reaching her hands up to meet his chest, weaving the twine through the little holes in the slit at the neckline. She pulled it through the six holes, tying the ends of the twine into little knots, and letting them hang down. She brushed a crease in the shoulder of the shirt, her hand trailing down to rest above his heart.

"You look very handsome," she said, just above a warm whisper, her hand still on his chest, feeling the quickening of his heartbeat. She pulled it off, clasping her hands together and smiling. "I'm headed to the gardens for a walk," she said, in her regular voice again, "if you'd care to join me."

"Y-yes," Theo gulped, trying to shake off the shivers that had run down his arms. "Give me just a moment?"

"Of course," Amair smiled, "I'll wait for you in the hall. I should check if anyone's seen Lupa. She does like to disappear every once in a while, and some of those times she has reappeared in the coolers gnawing on fish and completely ruining chef's plans for the week."

"Okay." Theo watched as the Princess turned, grabbing her book and the door, letting it close behind her quietly. He put his hands on his hips, staring at the spot where she had stood, letting out a puff of air that turned into a quiet chuckle. Theo rubbed his arms, brushing out the shivers and shocks still coursing through him.

"Oh boy," he muttered to himself with a grin, shaking his head once and heading to the door.

"Apologies, again, for… barging in, like that." Theo turned his head to look at her, leaning down closer.

"It's only fair," Theo whispered into her hair, "after the other day." A blush raced up her cheeks, and she pressed her lips together trying to suppress her smile as they passed a pair of guards. After they had passed, Amair looked up at Theo, but he was just smiling, looking forwards. She pulled her head back down, smiling, chewing the inside of her cheek, trying to keep her fingers from squeezing his arm.

Theo glanced down at her, watching her for a second, resisting the urge to reach over and sweep her hair out of her eyes, the stray thread on her shoulder. She took a little step closer to him.

"Care to walk the gardens with me?"

"I would go anywhere with you, Princess."

- CHAPTER XXXIX -

Amair was getting harder to find, pulled into meetings and party planning she constantly complained about and, when she could, disappearing with Arthur or Lenora to find the comforting weight of a sword.

"Who's this?" Theo asked, falling back into the little sofa with her as he finally spotted her one afternoon. She huffed a little laugh as the sofa bounced a little under her.

"Queen Sofira."

"Your…"

"Great…great…great…" she took a breath, "*great*-grandmother."

"Ah. The daughter of the two kings?"

"Well…technically a King and a Prince Consort."

"Of course."

She chuckled. "I come and sit with her…when I'm having a bad day, or I'm stressed or have a million pieces of paperwork to do…or dad entrusts me to lead a Council meeting. She was the first, first-born daughter in the Sovereign Skylock line."

"And only."

Amair nodded a little. "True."

"Her portrait is beautiful."

"It is. Always thought it was the most interesting. If you look in the corner of her portrait – there, just behind her – there's a pair of men's boots. She wanted a piece of her brother in the portrait with her. They were best friends."

"That's cute."

"Mhm." Amair smiled. "Layton always said he planned to share his portrait with me. I told him it was *his* portrait, but he could have his pick of my heels or my riding boots." Theo chuckled a little, peering at the blue eyes of the Queen. "I was completely enamoured with her when I was little. My dad showed me where all her diaries were kept in the Familial Library. I read every single word of them. And there are *dozens*. She wrote every thought, every decision, every moment of her days."

"What did you learn?"

"That she had a lot to say." Theo laughed. "But that she was my very opposite."

"Hm?"

"She loved to paint. And music. And she preferred to spend her days inside doing those things. I've found some of her art strewn throughout the castle. That was cool. Like a piece of her still here with me." She took a deep breath. "She was a great leader, though. And she inherited a country that was only one generation past the Keenian occupation. She got everything settled again."

Theo couldn't help but smile at the awed look on her face. He looked back up to the portrait, tipping his head a little. "So, what brought you here today?"

"Two-hundred-and-forty pages of Farm Start applications."

"Ouch."

"Mhm. I'm behind – had to meet with Mulayah and Ebberon to go over details for a few of the memorial pieces. Plus, every time I am asked to look at the blasted birthday planning book, I lose a brain cell. I love that I've been put in charge of the Farm program, and it's such a good and important program...but there's so much paperwork!" She laughed squeezing her eyes shut, leaning her head back. "So, I needed to get out of my study. And she's always a good support."

"Best listener?"

Amair snorted. "Toss-up between her and Lupa."

"Hey Ama, I–" Theo and Amair both stopped, glancing at each other as they noticed what he had said. "I'm sorry it just...it slipped out, I didn't even–"

"—it's okay," Amair smiled. "I liked it." She smiled softly, looking back up at the portrait as their hands brushed against each other.

- CHAPTER XXXX -

"Mom, I am *sure* there is someone much more qualified to plan my birthday than…" Amair glanced over the books, "*me.*"

"You have already shirked half the planning off to Lydia, and dumped another third of it onto Kylo," the Queen laughed, marking something on one of the pages. "The least you can do is make some of these final choices." Amair huffed as her mom looked back down at the planning book.

Amair shot a look over her mom's shoulder, catching Theo's eye as he scribbled on his notepad in the corner. He caught her stick her lip out as she forced a pout, and he bit his lip to keep from snorting.

"Amair," the Queen scolded, not looking up. "Guest list."

"Yes, mom." Theo chuckled, watching Amair flip through the heavy pages of the planning book, glancing at the pages she passed until she landed on the long guest list, every name elegantly written by the Queen.

He could spot Amair's edits in her messy cursive.

It was less than five minutes before Amair slammed the book closed, pouting again. "Mom, I can think of five things that I could be doing that are *ten* times more productive than this."

"You may not think so, Amair," the Queen, raised an eyebrow, "but state events are just as important as those Council meetings, documents, and training sessions."

"Finalizing guest lists and creating seating plans don't really *scream* royal duties." The Queen stood, the attendants snapping to attention and Theo jumping to his feet.

"You need to contribute to this party, Amair. Not only will Theo be covering it for the serial, it proves that you have the ability to make decisions. And believe me: seating arrangements can mean the difference between war, and peace." Amair bit her lip, nodding slightly.

"Kenaia will be coming by. I expect you to select the flowers and arrangements. And…I think they miss you…"

Amair sighed. "Yes, mom."

"Very good." She brushed her skirt, glancing around the parlour. "It's nice to see you, Theo. Hopefully this won't taint this week's serial."

"No, your majesty. And it's nice to see you as well." He noticed Amair roll her eyes sarcastically.

"We should have tea."

"I...would love that!"

"I'll have one of my ladies set it up. I will see you both later. Amair."

"Yes, mom?"

"Plans."

"Yes, mom." One of the attendants pulled open the door, the Queen nodding to her as she whisked out the door.

"Come on," Theo slid into the chair next to Amair, "it can't be that bad."

"I hate parties. And I hate planning them even more."

"You make plans on how to run a whole country."

"Not yet."

"Think of this as practice, then. Like your mom said...even the seating arrangement could mean war."

"Or peace."

"Or peace," Theo agreed, brushing a wayward hair off her shoulder. "And besides, I need something to write about this week and *Oighre extraordinaire plans her party* is the least bad headline I can come up with right now."

Amair laughed, bumping her shoulder against his, picking up a pen drawing an arrow next to one of the small drawings of a chair, checking off one of the names on the guest list.

"That's a start. Now...who's next?"

***

"Hey, Kenny."

"Hey, you," they grinned. "Her majesty asked me to bring the flower samples by."

"Ugh, Kenaia," Amair rolled her head, groaning. "No more party planning." She pulled on the word, Kenaia laughing as they unloaded the vases from a cart.

"One day you will be Queen and you can delegate...which I think is what her majesty is doing now." They both laughed, Amair reached to brush her fingers against one of the buds.

"Don't take my annoyance at the party as annoyance with flowers. These are beautiful, Ken."

"Dad said only the best for the Oighre Princess' eighteenth."

"Oh, come on," Amair rolled her eyes, "when have you ever used my title?"

"I mean, you are *of age* now," Kenaia snorted, dodging the balled-up sample napkin Amair tossed at their head. "Well, luckily your sword skills are better than your napkin skills, Princess."

"Kenaia!" Amair laughed, balling a second napkin, Kenaia grabbing her wrist before she could launch it.

"Okay, okay, *Amair*."

"Thank you."

"But, to be fair," Kenaia tipped their head, fixing a Skylock thistle, "you disappeared...after the accident. I haven't been so sure where I stood with you. Hard not to feel like just another staff member when you go a full season without seeing your best friend."

"Oh, Kenny." Amair glanced up, shifting her wrist to hold Kenny's hand. "I'm so sorry."

"I know. And so am I. I haven't had a chance to say that to you."

"Lydia had strict instructions to keep everyone away. How Denna slipped past her baffles me."

"I was in the crowd, the day they introduced you. You looked...very Queen-like."

"And then I went back to bed."

"You put the crown on again."

"Doing what I can."

"And succeeding, I'd say."

Amair blushed, looking back at the flowers. "You've clearly never seen me in a Council meeting."

"No, but I do know the Councillors." Kenaia pulled a light-yellow flower from one of the bouquets, handing it to the Princess. "I'd say they stand no chance against you."

Amair snorted, gently pressing her nose to the petals. "Alright. So, before my mom tracks me down and shoves a thistle down my *throat*," Kenaia laughed, moving one of the thistles back, "tell me about my options here."

"Well, *your highness*," Amair shot them a warning look, earning a laugh, "I've put together three different options–"

"–Kenny?"

Kenaia sighed, laughing as they looked away from the bouquets. "Yes, Princess?"

"Do you like what you do?"

"Well...my dad always said I could be whatever I want. You told me once you would pull any string needed to get me into university. And I still chose this. I like being in the garden, and the greenhouse. I like..." They pulled one of the plants that dripped like rain down the side of a chubby vase. "I like the beauty. And the calmness."

"You do have an eye for the beauty."

"And I'm good at it, Ama." They ran their hand over their short, sandy curls. "That's not why I decided to stay, to do this – and don't get me wrong, being there for my dad... helped the decision."

"Is...that a yes?"

Kenaia laughed. "How about you choose the flowers and figure it out."

"Saying 'do whichever you think is best' is the wrong answer, right?"

"*Yes*." Kenaia laughed, cocking their head. "If only so I can give Theo that soundbite he asked me for."

Amair chuckled, half-grumbling. "Well, we definitely need some thistles…purple *and* blue. And…you know those little blue wildflowers we used to have in the gardens?"

- CHAPTER XXXXI -

"Amair?"

"Yes?" she asked, not looking up from the page in her hand.

"I know it's late notice…you may have filled your rosters already, and I would totally understand…"

Amair lowered her book a little. "Theo?"

"Could I…I was wondering if I could invite my mom…to your birthday?"

Amair sat up straighter, dropping the page, grinning. "Oh! Oh, yes, please do! I want to meet the woman who raised *the Writer*." She looked confused suddenly. "Just your mom?"

"What?"

"I can make room for another parent, or…"

"Ah," Theo hung his head a little, sliding into the seat next to her. "No. I had a father, but he died when I was four."

"Oh…oh, Theo…" Amair reached out and held his hand. "I'm sorry—"

"—I was almost too young to remember him, aside from a few small memories here and there. It's not an issue. It's me and mom."

"She must miss you, hey?"

"She does. But she's proud, too."

"Okay…" Amair studied his face. He studied her long lashes as she looked down, thinking. "Your mother will sit with us. At the family's table."

"Oh, Amair, she doesn't have—"

"—no, but I'd like her to. It's decided." She squeezed his hand. "I'm so excited! But I have to go see one of the designers. The *centrepieces* for the celebrations are ready for approval."

"Oh, I'll come," Theo jumped up, offering her his elbow. She kept smiling, taking it, the messenger opening the door for them. "I want to let the readers know how you make decisions," he grinned, "from the smallest to the biggest."

"Well...I think this falls *somewhere* between those," she chuckled, bowing her head to a messenger. She had thought he would simply pass on his way, but he pulled a letter from inside his breast pocket. He said nothing and passed it to Amair. Theo glanced down, noting the dark wax – not a Skylock colour – but made out the edge of Amair's personal seal. She broke the seal, reading it, digesting the words slowly. Theo resisted the urge to read over her shoulder but spotted a name he recognized at the bottom.

Denna.

"I have to go," Amair said, quietly, setting her book on one of the tables. "Talk to the Queen, and have her send out an invite to your mother, she should be personally invited. We can send a messenger and a knight, to make everything official." She paused, looking into Theo's eyes. "I'll be back by the New Year."

"Wait," he jumped to his feet, "you're leaving?"

"For a few days." Her face was determined but he had spent months reading her and he could see what he thought was annoyance. "Keep me interesting until I'm back?"

Theo tried to hold in the sigh, nodding. "I promise." She raised a hand, hesitating as though she wanted to reach out to him, but just curtsied and whisked hurriedly from the room.

***

Theo cobbled together an article from old interviews, the end of it less eloquent than most of his writing had been. His mind was on the Princess, who he had seen sneaking out the courtyard the morning after the letter, under the cover of the morning haze.

A photo of Denna and Amair surfaced, whispering through the magazines, but Theo rushed to write it off as a scheduled visit for the Princess to see her best friend, and her people seemed to let the rumours die from there.

"Thank you for this," a voice said gently from the hallway outside the guest sitting room, making him jump and nearly drop his teacup. He turned, clutching the same edition of *High Lands* gossip magazine the Princess did, the fire casting a glow over her face. She stepped into the room, finding her way over to the chair next to his, the arms close enough their hands almost touched, her eyes still on the article. He looked down at his copy.

"This photo of you and Lady Raziel has taken quite the storm."

"Mh..." Amair tipped her head, wondering where the photographer had been hiding when she had flung herself into Denna's arms. "I think I may have loved her, once, you know." Amair smiled a little, blinking softly. "I've loved since, and it felt quite the same."

"It didn't work out, though?" Theo asked.

"Sometimes love is just love, and not meant to be more."

"Where were you?"

"Can't tell you."

"What were you doing?"

"Can't say."

He huffed, but there was a smile playing on his lips. "Well, was it a successful trip, at least?"

Amair smiled. "Denna was born to be a diplomat. She could have done it without me, but I think a face of a throne helped, a bit. She could have asked someone from Tunngas, or RiKoi, and had the same effect."

"And yet, she asked *you*."

Amair shrugged, tossing her copy of the magazine into the fireplace. "We make a good team."

Winter

- CHAPTER XXXXII -

Lydia fluffed the back of Amair's wide skirt, the hints of gold in the navy gown catching in the last bit of sunset.

"Lydia," Amair swatted at her, "it's the Feast of the New Year, you are *not* supposed to be working!" Amair looked over her shoulder, watching as Lydia kept fixing her. "You do know I'm going to wreck this as soon as the guests start arriving and I have to start moving?"

"Yes, well, I am big on," Lydia straightened finally, smoothing her own skirt, "first impressions."

"I adore you," Amair chuckled, brushing her fingers against Lydia's chin.

"Now. Smiles on," Lydia winked, backing away to stand with the other staff chattering higher up the stairs under the butler, Mr. MacDen's watchful eye. Amair took a deep breath, pushing the air out with puffed cheeks through puckered lips.

The King fixed his jacket, jumping down the steps to stand next to his daughter. "Here we go, sweet girl."

"Does it ever bother you having two huge celebrations back-to-back?"

"Feast of the New Year is small so that we can celebrate you after. Your arrival meant everything to us, Ama, *you* are the party. This is just family." He smiled. "A few friends."

"Right." She took another deep breath, and her father glanced down at her.

"Gets you used to company, too."

"Oh, *please.*"

"It's true. You find comfort in being alone, and that's fine. Just means we have to," he chuckled, "ease you into encounters. At least the ones that don't involve swords."

"Ha *ha*." Her father laughed as the first carriage pulled up.

"Though, Lady Denna writes me that you didn't require a sword in Forra."

Amair blushed, and glanced about them thought knowing the only person close enough to listen was Lydia, who had been a part of her quiet escape from the castle. "More to come, dad."

Amair bit her lip, bouncing as the next carriage pulled up, an attendant's hand already on the door's handle. A grinning face appeared as the door was pulled open, catching Amair's eye.

Without thinking, Amair grabbed her skirt and raced down the steps, barrelling into Denna as she stepped out of the carriage, arms already outstretched. They could hear the guests and staff behind them chuckling.

"You're home!" Amair exclaimed, holding her tight.

"You just saw me!"

"It's different!" Amair chuckled. "You're *home*."

"Well, I did make a quick stop. An early birthday gift, if you will"

"I–" Amair pulled back, trying to read Denna's face. Denna smirked, pushing back gently on Amair, leaning over. A second head popped out of the carriage, her thick, black-and-caramel twisted hair pulled into a low bun, warm smile catching Amair's eye. Amair gasped, a hand over her mouth, looking the young woman up and down.

"Shehada!" She shook her head, reaching a hand to help her down out of the carriage. "You're supposed to be at university."

"Denna made a convincing argument," she grinned, pulling Amair into a hug.

"Why...how?" Amair's eyes were wide and excited, holding Shehada's face as the two girls grinned.

"Well, we...we missed you...at Alanmas..." Shehada glanced down, biting her lip, the faces of the Lost Ones passing through all their minds.

Amair bit her lip, sucking in a short breath. "It was...we..."

"We know..." Denna nodded, brushing Amair's cheek. "But we wanted to be together for this."

"And I figured two extra days off wouldn't hurt anything."

"Oh my gods," Amair laughed, the three girls clutching to each other. Amair's mouth moved, looking for words, the other two giggling at the empty air.

"My ladies…we do need to move the carriage—"

"—oh, right." They jumped out of the way, picking up their skirts as they slowly made their way up the steps, the last two carriages pulling up.

"I'm glad you're here, Aunt Elena can't make it until the day before my birthday, I was worried I was going to be alone."

"Isn't Orlaith coming early with her father?"

"She's coming mostly to see Lenora, I think," Denna reminded with a grin.

"Fair enough," Shehada laughed, wrapping an arm around Amair, Denna doing the same.

"Dad…" Amair smiled at him, batting her eyelashes.

He chuckled, nodding. "Go. Be with your friends, the New Year guests will start congregating in the small ballroom soon. The staff should go in and start as well."

"Thank you, dad." The girls went back to giggling, heading up the pristine white stairs. Shehada fixed the floral, golden piece in her hair, shining as it caught the last light of day, the final light of a horrible year.

"So, the High King arrives the day after next," Amair told Denna, "will he…"

"The High King of Forra?" Shehada asked, raising an eyebrow.

"I…will explain after the feast," Amair assured her, Denna snorting. "Snacks and drinks in your room?"

"Fine by me!"

"Actually, if it's anything like last year, someone will be carrying Ama back to her chambers, so…perhaps sometime between now and your birthday, Ama?"

"Right. Maybe that."

Shehada snorted, nodding, conjuring up the image of Amair dancing on a table the year before.

"And yes, Ama," Denna assured. "He will be keeping his mouth shut."

"Thank you." She smiled, glancing up at the crows that had formed outside the doors of the grand ballroom. Amair could tell the drinking had started, cheers of merriment and hugging starting, two girls she noted as friends of Kenaia swinging each other around. "Hello, everyone!" Amair called, approaching the staff. "As the last light of this difficult year sets on the castle, make your way into the ballroom so we can welcome in the New Year together." Everyone cheered, following the three girls towards the door, the lights and golden decorations drawing the same awe as always. Amair grinned, listening to the guests gasp the same as they did every year. She could picture Mr. MacDen beaming as everyone admired the hard work.

The doors to the small ballroom opened, the tables adorned in the finest gold fixtures and tablecloths from the collections. Amair and her friends were the first through the doors and a sound popped, golden streamers floating down from the doorframe, showering over the guests who walked through, more gasps of excitement echoing into the room.

Amair's eyes landed on the tower of champagne glasses that swirled with golden glitter. "Do you think it makes it taste better?" Shehada whispered, the two girls giggling.

"I'm pretty sure I'm going to be drinking too many to care," Amair giggled.

"And I made quite certain," the Butler appeared next to them, "that there are glittering options without alcohol, too, so not to worry, Lady Raziel."

"Thank you, Mr. MacDen." He smiled, nodding, backing out of the way as Shehada grabbed the first glass of the champagne tower, passing a second to Amair. They clinked glasses, Denna reaching over and taking a dark, glittering glass, clinking with the other two.

"Happy New Year!" Amair exclaimed, everyone else in the room cheering, the three girls laughing as they sipped.

"May it be better than your last—"

"—and the best you've ever had!" Shehada finished for Denna, the three of them clinking again and chugging their glasses. Shehada wrapped her arm back around Amair, who took Denna's hand, leading them to seats near the King at the head of the centre table.

"Mhm," Amair nearly choked on her drink, setting it down too quickly, "there's Kenny!" She waved, trying to get Kenaia's attention, who broke into a grin as they sidestepped other staff to make their way to the head table.

"Ladies," they gave a dramatic bow, glitter falling off the top of their curls as they did so.

"Get over here and pull up a damn chair," Amair snorted, leaning back a little in her chair, Shehada kicking the chair out with her foot for Kenaia to sit with them. "Seen any of our other friends around?"

"Aramis was here, but he ended up with a migraine and wasn't in a festive mood. Gio went to spend the New Year with his parents on the farm."

"Where's your writer?" Shehada asked, raising an eyebrow, immediately starting to scan the crowd. "Screw our friends, *him* I want to meet—"

"Friends!" the King exclaimed, standing on his chair, everyone laughing at him as they found seats. Amair spotted her mom and brothers taking seats at the head of the next table, Jasper's hands waving as he whispered something excitedly.

"May I join you?" Theo whispered, making Amair jump and the others giggle.

"If you insist, *Sir Crawford*," Denna whispered, pushing out the chair in front of her with her foot. Shehada immediately sat forward with a less-than-conspicuous grin, Amair trying to kick her under the table.

"Friends!" the King called again as Theo sat, the rest of the crowd looking up at him. "Thank you for joining us for this special day," everyone cheered, "and remember that today, we are one, together, to celebrate, and all our staff have the day off – *including you*, Mr. MacDen, stop trying to work." Everyone laughed, looking over at the Butler who smiled sheepishly, stepping away from the curtain he was in the process of fixing. "There we go. This year…this year has been beyond difficult. Last year started with a hailstorm that wiped out the farms in the lower Hill province. But we saw everyone come together, including our neighbours in RiKoi, to rebuild damaged structures, reseed and a harvest was still possible.

"And of course…" As the King choked on his words, Denna immediately reached for Amair's hand under the table, squeezing as tight as she could. "We lost," the King's voice broke and there were sniffles around the room, "we lost four beloved children. The Lost Ones, Layton

Skylock, Johanna Moores, and Dylan Armada were amongst our greatest treasures and have been some of our hardest goodbyes.

"But our Amair," he turned so his gaze could fall on his daughter, "she rose out of the ashes of the tragedy and has done so with grace and all of you," he looked back out at the people, "have accepted her with so much grace. We could not be more grateful to those of you who have helped mould her into the young woman who has become your Oighre. This has been a hard year…but we have come through it. Together. I cannot find enough words to thank you for that.

"Now, please, serve yourselves, be merry, get to know each other, and most importantly…enjoy!"

Everyone cheered, heading towards the long buffet of golden plates, piled high with food. People stopped by the head of the centre table, shaking hands with the King, trying to curtsy to the Princess who just jumped up to hug everyone and wish them a Happy New Year. Denna and Shehada got up, leaving Amair to welcome the guests, chatting with one of the Chiefs' sons about sheep, disappearing around a corner to whisper something with Kenaia and another boy Theo did not recognize.

Denna set a plate full of luscious pastas and pastries in front of Amair, Shehada putting another glass of champagne down, Theo filling her water glass and tapping it with insistence.

Theo joined the girls as they chatted, chins starting to rest on hands as the night stretched out, listening to stories of Denna's diplomacy. Shehada's university life.

Her small crush on her early modern literature professor.

"He's cute!" Shehada defended as the girls giggled, Theo suppressing a grin behind his water glass, casually sliding a glass of water towards the very giggly Princess. "He's got this beard and I just wanna…touch it." Denna shrieked with laughter, covering her mouth with her hand as a few people looked over their shoulders at her. Amair caught Lydia smiling at their table, tipping her now-empty champagne glass at her attendant, who tipped hers back.

"You should talk to Kylo," Amair said, trying to catch her breath from laughing, "I plan to lobby to let him go to a regular university. He could use some first-hand experience. If he decides to, of course but…I think he will."

"You should have gone."

"Ah, well…I get to live vicariously through you," Amair assured Shehada, trying not to let her disappointment show on her face.

Denna swung her head to the Writer, tapping her glass against her lip. "What were your university days like, Theo?"

He shrugged. "I wish I could say they were brimming with fun, but really, I was quite boring…started in the program probably too young, was on the school paper, editor my final year."

"I can picture him showing up to parties with his pen in his pocket, just in case a story broke," Shehada giggled, Denna and Amair snorting with her. Shehada's cheeks flushed as her drinks started hitting her. He shrugged. "You're handsome, charming…your days must have had some mystery to them?"

"I wrote a lot — creative, and journalistic — and spent a lot of time sitting in my favourite room with these big windows so that I could enjoy the rain without ruining all my notebooks." The girls giggled, shrugging at the thought of Skylock's gloom.

"Did you love it, though?" Amair asked, her new glass of sparkling bubbles halfway to her mouth, eyes wide.

He smiled, wanting to reach for her hand under the table at the hope in her face. "I did…the learning. The friends. The professors. The libraries."

He noticed the soft pain pass her eyes.

"But…in a lot of ways…the castle is similar. Busy with people. Stuffed with books. Nooks and crannies to sit in for quiet days. Teachers…some of them meant for classrooms, but often those who surprise you with where and how and what they end up teaching you."

Amair smiled, glancing up at the people around them as she considered his words. The night went on and the party grew and shrunk again as everyone tired, the depleted drinks table catching up with everyone.

A few stable hands were slumped over the table snoring when the first of the guests made their way out the ballroom, stumbling back towards bedrooms and guest rooms.

The chatter had died down, the streamers in the air starting to settle on the ground. Amair grinned as Kylo supported a mostly-drunk Jasper, two of the cooks tossing a sleeping twin over their shoulders. Her grin softened, watching the King stand, stretching, and stride towards his wife, a warm, tired smile spreading across her face, the two of them wrapping each other into their arms. They walked in synch towards the door, bobbing their heads at the lingering guests.

"We should go too," Denna pressed her hands into the table, "lots of work to do in the next days." She glanced at Shehada. "You can stay in my room tonight."

"As long as you promise to open a window," Shehada yawned, the hints of red starting to show on her brown skin, "it's hot."

"That would be the six glasses of champagne coursing through you," Denna laughed, reaching a hand across to her friend. "Sure, we can open up the window."

"Goodnight you two," Amair smiled, both of them leaning over to kiss Amair's head, Shehada bumping her lip accidentally against the edge of the golden laurel wrapped around Amair's head. There were murmurs of '*To the New Year*' as they hugged, Shehada still rubbing her lip as Denna tugged her away, stumbling slightly over a chair with a sleeping kitchen hand. Amair sighed, picking herself up out of the chair, realizing Theo had disappeared. She shook her head, picking her way through the golden chaos left behind in the small ballroom, slipping out the half-open door.

She spotted Theo trying to catch her eye in the small corridor heading towards the bridge, her feet making their way towards him as though they had a mind of their own.

"Your highness," the Butler bowed as he spotted her. She slowed, eyes sliding away from Theo.

"You outdid yourself this year, Mr. MacDen," Amair curtsied to the Butler. "Thank you for tonight." Theo hung off to the side, hands behind his back as Amair thanked the Butler again, watching him bow to her.

"Goodnight, Princess."

Theo covered his mouth to keep from chuckling at the grin that burst across his face as soon as he had turned away from the Princess. They walked out of the ballroom, Lupa appearing at her side. The dog shook once and a puff of golden glitter erupted off her white fur.

"Well, that's over," Amair said, her voice quiet, turning to Theo. "I should go to bed. I have a long week coming. One down, one extremely major one to go."

"Soon the castle will be bursting at the seams with guests."

"Indeed…and I believe one of them will be *your* guest."

"She gets in tomorrow," Theo grinned, bouncing a little on his toes as they passed two guards who stood to attention. "She's going to lose her *mind*."

She sighed happily, still giddy from the many glasses of glittering champagne. "To the New Year, Theodore."

"To the New Year, Amair." He tucked a piece of hair behind her year, pulling a gold streamer from her shoulder. "See you when your birthday festivities begin." She bit her tongue, watching him step back into the dark, and disappear down the hall.

- CHAPTER XXXXIII -

"How on earth did they manage to clean up all the glitter in less than a day?" Theo asked, glancing about the corridor.

"The real secret is that it's probably clinging to every crevice and we'll be picking it out of couch cushions for months," Amair chuckled. Theo laughed, his eyes lingering where the wall met the floor to see if he could spot anything shining. "So, you ready?"

"For what?"

Amair's face was kind but her eyes were searching as she looked up at him. "To see her? For her to see you?"

"Definitely a change," he shrugged, looking down at her.

"A good one, hopefully?"

"Anything with you is good, Ama." She was looking up at him, a warm smile spreading across her face as they turned into the foyer, Theo's eyes lighting up at the woman being greeted at the door.

"Mama!" Theo called, dashing over the tiles towards her. She grinned, dropping her small bag and reaching her arms out.

"Teddy!" Theo wrapped his arms around his mom, towering over her.

"I missed you."

"I've missed you too." They pulled back, her grin turning into awe. "Theo! I can't believe I'm in the *castle*."

"And we can't believe it either," Amair grinned, slower in her approach than Theo had been. Theo's mother let go of him, pushing past him a little, her eyes wide.

"Princess!" She started to curtsy, but Amair stooped a little, trying to catch her eye and reaching a hand to her.

"There's no need," she smiled, shaking her head, holding the woman's hand and picking up her small piece of luggage.

"Princess Amair Skylock, may I present to you my mother, Annalise Crawford."

"Thank you for letting me come, Princess."

"Oh, if Theodore hadn't asked me, I would have been begging for you to come." Amair glanced at Theodore, warm smile pierced with the slightest, clever smirk. "I very much needed to meet you…the person who raised our Writer."

"Oh…well, I never imagined he would be here."

"I have a bit of time this week, before the festivities start. You'll have to tell me all about young Theo."

"Oh, I would love that."

"Good! I'll have one of my ladies arrange a tea, or maybe a luncheon." Amair smiled at the attendant that appeared behind the Crawfords. "I think your room is ready."

"It is, your highness."

"Come, let's get you settled in." Amair offered her hand to Annalise and she took it, leading her to the staircase.

"Hey, Ama," Theo whispered, brushing his fingers against her elbow. Amair glanced at him, looking back up the stairs, catching one of the attendant's eyes.

"Would you mind getting Mrs. Crawford settled into her room? I'll be up in just a moment."

"Of course, Princess," the attendant nodded, taking the small bag from Amair's hands and smiling kindly at Theo's mom, the two of them chatting as they headed up the stairs. Theo and Amair watched them go, disappearing around the bend in the stairs.

"I can't thank you enough. She's so excited," Theo grinned.

"I meant what I said, Theodore. I *really* wanted to meet her."

"Just…" He reached to her, cautiously, his fingers running down her arm, hesitating at her hand. "Thank you."

"You're welcome, Theo." She twisted, wrapping her fingers through his and squeezing. "Go, be with your mother. It's a party, we should all be with the people we love." She took a breath, steadying herself. "Make sure she really settles in. Our home is your home is hers."

Theo laughed. "I promise."

"And Theo?"

"Hm?"

"She can stay as long as you'd like."

- CHAPTER XXXXIV -

"So this is where you're hiding," Theo called, walking into the library and spotting the top of her braided updo. She sat a little taller so that she could look over the back of her tall chair at him.

"Just…needed a break."

"I could come back–"

"No…no, that's okay." She smiled, pulling her legs back as he came around the couch.

"I brought you something," Theo grinned, flopping down into the other chair, tossing something over into Amair's lap. She laughed, flipping the corner of her page and setting it on the table. Theo watched her untie the string and pull back the brown paper. Amair shrieked, but it turned into a laugh as she pulled the edges of the brown paper together again. "Happy birthday!"

"Theodore Crawford!" she scolded, trying not to laugh. "If my father saw this, he would have you hanged!"

"I thought they stopped hangings like three sovereigns ago?"

She threw the book at him and he caught it, both of them laughing. He thumbed through the pages, raising an eyebrow catching sight of a few of the more scandalous phrases.

"Where on earth did you even get this?" she laughed, reaching to snag it out of his hands.

"A woman was selling them in town when I popped down there to show mom the paper."

Amair shook her head pointing to the almost naked man on the cover, his heavily tattooed arms pulling open the back of a woman's corset, her skirt dropped to where her skin peeked out.

"Why this one, exactly?"

"You said you liked drama and romance!" She shook her head, but clutched it to her chest.

"I think 'thank you for thinking of me' is the best response I can muster at the moment."

"I'll take it."

"I'm going to have to hide this somewhere Lydia can't find it."

"Oh gods, she would kill me."

"Probably." He watched her nimble hands as she folded it back into the paper, creased and crinkled now, and tied the string back around it. She tucked it in next to her in the seat, lounging the way she did when she was calm. Theo watched her kick her feet around, trying to get comfortable again. "How is your mom?"

"She keeps getting lost," Theo snorted.

"Sounds like someone else I know."

"Must run in the family," Theo rolled his eyes. "I found her wandering across the bridge. She told me," he laughed, "she told me she had been looking for her room for over an hour." Amair giggled, tipping her head as she studied his face. "I also found her in the kitchens. Laughing and chatting with some of the cooks and hands. Helping them roll dough."

"I'll know where to check if I'm looking for her." She thought for a moment. "Her and Lisell would actually make great friends, I think."

"You think?"

"If she had reason to stay at the castle." Amair's eyes flitted up, watching Theo's face for a moment. They both shook their heads, blushing.

"She's um…she's really happy to be here, though."

"I'm glad…I'm sorry I haven't seen her much, things have been so busy, Lydia and I are taking meals together in my chambers."

"It's alright, I've been taking meals with her in the guest dining hall. Plus, that way I'm meeting some of your guests."

"Scoping any gossip yet?"

"Oh tons. I hear one of your childhood nicknames was peppertongue…"

Amair grinned at him, running her tongue over her upper lip but neither confirming or denying anything.

"So, are you excited for the ball?" Theo asked.

Amair sighed. "As excited as I can be," she folded her book over her finger, looking over at Theo. "First birthday without Layton."

"There's a lot of people here for you though."

"I know. I…I'm trying to remember that."

"So, when do the diplomats start arriving?"

"The invasion starts tomorrow afternoon." She sighed, looking away as she thought. "At least my chiefs are already here…I get to appear in front of the world with all my forces behind me."

"Will you greet them?"

"No. There's a welcome reception in the evening. I get to appear for the first time in my very best."

Ink & Crown:
The Princess Serial

by Sir Theodore Crawford

What's in a name? Names bear a lot of power for us Skylish people. We know better than to say them too loudly in the Grand Forest, for fear that the fae could get ahold of us. We take great care to name the next generations. We know that they connect our family lineage, and is why the bairns take on the name of a grandparent as part of their name, as an honour and memory. Our surnames often denote our Clan, our clan allegiances as septs.

For our Princess, there are many secrets to be held in her beautiful, admittedly uncommon name, for a Skylish Princess.

As the story goes, according to many sources who were present at the Oighre's birth, the Late Prince Layton was so excited for the arrival of his baby sister, he attempted to insist on breaking tradition to name her. Eventually overruled by the King's and Elected councils, word was sent of her birth to the aged and dying Adventuress Dowager Queen Daniella Skylock. One of her last acts from her sickbed in Tunngas was to pen the name of her granddaughter. She would pass just days later, before the name returned to Skylock. Severe smudging in the notecard would lead to its interpretation as *Amair*, and she took on *Daniella* in the tradition of honouring her late grandmother. It was not until the arrival of the then young Queen Nukila at the birth announcement that it was noted the Princess' name was meant to be *Annis*! With birth announcements already sent across the kingdom, the Princess' name stuck.

Pet names have come and gone with the years. I recently learned that she was called *peppertongue* by the other castle children growing up, as she was always armed with a comeback.

Her brother and the other Lost Ones called her their *weeun*, the youngest and smallest of their group, but forever one of them.

And of course, there is another name we all know her by: *Oighre*. By the Princess' admission, a promise, to her people, to be there for them. To fight for them. To serve them.

So: what's in a name? Everything we need to know, if we are willing to look. Now you know, before we kick off her birthday.

- Sir Theodore Crawford, Staff Writer, Special Liaison Reporter to The Palace, Man of Letters

- CHAPTER XXXXV -

Theo stood with the royal children looking down off the balcony at the crowd of people below, a mix of new and remaining guests, trunks and cases scattered around them. People stopped to shake hands and stare each other down as staff weaved through the political matches.

"I can't be the only one who finds it extremely random that all the realms *just so happen* to have a bachelor son your age?"

Jasper laughed, nodding furiously, Kylo laughing quietly next to him. Amair's laugh was quiet, far away as she studied the crowds below. The boys leaned against the railing, Amair resting a hand against it, her fingers perched as she kept herself held tall, chin up just a little. Theo glanced at her, his hands clasped together, smiling as Amair stood there, regal, even though none of the guests could see her.

"Here comes the cavalry," Jasper pointed as the twins ran in, weaving through the guests making their way towards their own targets.

"Oof, that's one hell of a welcome," Theo snorted, watching Evander casually stick his foot out and trip one of the boys, Alec wrapping his arm around another. They couldn't hear him, but they watched his mouth move fast, the boy's eyes a bit wide. And a bit scared.

"It's not like they're all Princes," Amair tipped her head a little, blue eyes darting around the crowd below them, trying to spot the young men being offered up to her like a wine tasting. "Forra's Prince Jaxon. Goes by Jax. Over…there, that's Prince Maximilian, of RiKoi. We've always just called him Mils. He's…kind. A bit of a flirt."

"That's an understatement," Jasper snorted.

"Hm. So two princes, two dukes, a son of some earl, and three lords, plus every eligible boy from the village."

"And a partridge in a pear tree," Kylo murmured, making Amair snort.

"And our very own Knight General's boy. Who came home from uni for this. And don't forget the Archduke of Keene's son," Jasper snickered, his sister shuddering slightly.

"Don't remind me." Amair rolled her eyes.

"Who—"

"—just," Amair interrupted Theo, taking a little breath, "a very horrible man and his very horrible son, and I don't know why our father continues to insist they be invited to things." Amair scrunched her mouth together.

"Maybe dad's hoping you'll get married and unite the Kingdoms," Kylo snickered.

"Not likely. Remember that time Layton nearly killed him?"

"What?" Theo asked, looking up at her as her brothers snorted.

"Another time," Amair waved Theo off.

"Maybe he's trying to make all the other candidates look better," Kylo tilted his head with Amair. She laughed, covering her mouth as she tried to stifle it, all of them jumping back from the railing as her laugh fluttered down towards the guests below.

"Do you actually know any of these guys?" Theo asked as they settled back against the rail. Amair shook her head, slowly at first and then quicker, her eyes wide, biting the inside of her lip.

"I've met Jax a couple times. And Novak, unfortunately. That's the uh, the Archduke's son. Mils and I are actually good friends. Or…we were… I keep meaning to send him a letter…I let any communication slide after Layton… Anyways, I'm sure others have been around at balls, and feasts, and festivals, and such. I may have even danced with some of them. But I've…always kept to myself." Theo's mouth twitched and he lowered his head, trying to avoid her seeing it. "But that is what this weekend is all about. Getting to know them. As allies. Or…" She let out a long breath as they watched as Evander ran under the arm of one of the young Lords, a valet trying to catch up. Amair sighed, turning her back against the rail, leaning back and steadying herself with her hands. "You'll be in the guest wing with most of them. Mom insisted on organizing the rooms by age. So all the *suitors* are near you. You'll have to get all the dirt on them and report back."

"Ooh, yeah, use those reporting skills!" Jasper exclaimed. Theo was shaking his head a little, trying to get the two to stop chattering about getting information on all these new boys.

"Stop," he murmured.

"Honestly," Amair shrugged, "I *must* be getting boring, you can refocus–"

"–Amair, stop!" Theo exclaimed, standing up.

Amair raised her eyebrows, studying Theo's sudden abrasiveness, how his sharp jaw tensed. Her brothers stood up off the railing, looking over Amair's shoulder at their friend. "Okay." He watched her eyes look him up and down. "Okay. Sorry." The two looked at each other, locking eyes, trying to say things without opening their mouths. Kylo and Jasper watched them, Kylo's eyebrow up, reading something behind what they were not saying.

"I have to go and get ready for the Welcome," Amair smoothed a hand down her dress. "You boys should too, mom wanted members of the household in our colours tonight. Your valets should all have them. And try and corral the twins to do the same. They listen to you more than anyone"

"They listen to *you* more than anyone," Kylo murmured.

"Suggestions on what I should w–"

"–our colours," she gave Theo a pointed look, raising an eyebrow at him. He glanced towards Jasper, surprised, but Jasper shrugged it off. "I'll see you all later."

"That was weird," Jasper said, cocking an eyebrow as Amair snuck down the secret staircase off the balcony. Theo watched her go, ignoring Kylo's eyes still boring holes into his soul.

- CHAPTER XXXXVI -

Theo did not want to be called a snob, and nothing in his life up until that night would have allowed him to think he ever could have used that word. He had left his room at the sound of the bell which Gaelen informed him was the call to the Welcome Ball, only to find himself corralled into the corridor, pushed and shoved by boys forced on Amair as potential suitors, and the annoyance and jealousy in his stomach made him feel very much like a snob.

He clutched his goblet, eyes scanning the lines of young men who talked like they knew each other but stood defensively, shoulders stiff and it took staring to notice his own stiff shoulders in his brilliantly Skylock blue jacket he had not worn since his knighting ceremony. His badge was pinned expertly to his chest and the buzz of conversation was becoming annoying. It was too much to make out a word, to pull a line of gossip or a quote for the article, but not enough to truly make out anything of substance anyway.

"She should be on her way," a voice said beside him. He turned a little, Denna smiling up at him, her headscarf the same shade of Skylock blue as his jacket.

"Lady Raziel," he bowed to her.

"Denna is fine, Theo." She glanced to the stairs. "Those of us who…" She looked for a word but the squint of her eyes at him warmed his cheek. "Those of us who care about the Oighre get a first name basis."

"Are you here alone as well, tonight?"

"That's the great benefit to being in Ama's world, Theo." Her tone was just a little bit scolding and *snob* rang in his ears again. "She's a force to be reckoned with. Once you have her," she glanced up at the stairs as the doors opened, one of the Criers stepping out, "you'll never be alone again." She patted his hand, turning her attention up top.

"Ladies and gentlemen," the Crier banged his staff at the top of the stairs, "introducing her royal highness, Oighre, Princess Amair Daniella Skylock." The heavy wooden doors at the top of the stairs were pulled open, Amair walking through them. Theo noticed her pull her hands apart, letting go of where she had been tugging on her fingers as she breathed a little taller.

She took a deep breath, leaning forward a little on the railing. "Welcome, to all of my guests, from the near and far. Thank you, so very much, for making the journey for the celebrations. Tonight marks the opening with the Welcome Ceremonies. My official portrait will be unveiled, marking the true beginning of my birthday, before the large festivities take place tomorrow. So: enjoy. Drink well. Thank you again. *Failte.*"

The crowd cheered, and Amair bobbed her head, catching the eyes of a few people as she looked around the ballroom. Arthur appeared at the top of the stairs. He reached a hand up to her, and Theo could see him murmuring something to her. She nodded slowly, wrapping her fingers around her knight's and letting him escort her down the curving staircase.

"The Princess will start the celebrations by sharing a dance with the Sovereign!" the Crier announced, and everyone swept away from the centre of the floor. The first plucks of Skylock's royal song whispered through the air, the twinkle of instruments close behind as the King appeared, grinning at his daughter. She walked into the misshapen circle that had been left for them, and curtsied deeply to her father, letting her head fall forward as she did, her tiara sparkling under the high ballroom lights. The King took a step forward to hold out his hand to her, helping her rise.

Amair raised a hand gracefully to his shoulder and took his other hand, letting him guide her into the first step.

Theo glanced around the circle as his leaders moved around the dance floor. Guests smiled, the mix of warm, excited smiles and the sadder, pained smiles watching their Sovereign and Oighre. He noticed the Queen, flanked by her two older sons, her hands clasped at her chest, swaying with the music as she smiled at her husband and daughter. Jasper's face held a pain behind his smile.

Theo blinked a few times, watching Amair and her father sway, the King leading as they twirled around the dance floor. The song started to change, and as it moved from the royal song to something with more lilt, Theo watched other couples in decadent dress step into the circle and join the dancing. Jasper stepped in with the Queen. It took a moment, but Theo realized they were the Chiefs and their partners, and the leaders of the other realms, dancing in celebration to kick off the night.

As King Niall and Princess Amair passed close to him he took a moment to look around the circle and though the air was filled with brilliant music, everyone looked like they were going to cry.

"Psst, Lydia!" Theo whispered, reaching for her.

"Sir Crawford." She raised an eyebrow, pulling her arm away from him.

"Everyone...why were so many people sad looking?"

"My lady has always shared her first dance with the Oighre. The...the late-Oighre." Her mouth twitched, frowning. "It's her first year without him."

"Oh...oh I...I." He sighed, losing his words.

"Historically, royal children share the first dance with the Sovereign, but from the time she was six, my lady requested to dance with her brother, and it stayed that way. The whole Kingdom knew they were friends above anything else."

He nodded, slowly. "Thanks, Lydia." Theo bobbed his head, tucking his hands behind his back as he started to turn away from her.

"Sir Crawford!"

Theo paused, looking at her over his half-turned shoulder. "Yes?"

"I...I may not like you very much..." She bit the side of her mouth, squinting at him slightly. "But...I think she would like to dance with you. So. Do that. Please."

Theo smirked. "Already planning to."

"Good." She turned away this time, linking arms with a boy he recognized from the stables. Theo spotted Amair talking with a short man, her eyes wide and exasperated. Theo laughed, ducking around attendants with trays held high, nearly tripping over one of the twins inexplicably sitting cross-legged in the middle of the crowd.

Their shoulders brushed together, Theo breathing in the soft floral smell of her shampoo. "You look incredible," he murmured to her as she jumped a little. The man next to her bowed, turning away.

Amair bit the inside of her cheek, trying to hold in her smirk and her blush, pushing against his shoulder. "Go. Mingle. People are dying to meet the Writer." Theo rolled his eyes, letting her push him into the crowd as it sucked her in the other direction.

"They can wait…" he whispered.

"I have people to say hello to," she reminded him. "While I wish this weekend were about friends…I have a duty."

He sighed. "Which is yet another reason I know you shall make an amazing Queen." She bobbed her head a little to him.

"Be sure not to let your mother get lost in the crowd."

"I promise."

She was swallowed back into the crowd, the son of an earl who had already introduced himself twice to Theo but was not memorable enough to be more than his father's title offering his arm to escort her through the crowd. Theo chided himself as he spent most of the night trying to spot the Princess, thankful that her friends cycled through to say hello, stopping and getting to know him.

Shehada and Denna stayed wrapped tightly onto each other, moving as a unit, Kenaia popping in and out every time they noticed a bouquet starting to droop. "You're in university?" Theo asked, his eyes finding Amair's head again as he drank from a mug of something sweet.

"Yes, in Torrent," Shehada smiled. "Studying Policy and Political Science."

"Wow!" That caught Theo's attention.

"I'm hoping to come back to the castle eventually…originally, I wanted to do something like policy…though now…" She hesitated. "I can see myself…supporting our future Queen." Theo opened his mouth to ask another question but was interrupted.

"Ladies and gentlemen," a voice called for attention, "Sir Ebberon Dovith, royal portraitist, presenting the Princess' first official portrait as

Oighre." Ebberon and his apprentice Mulayah stood with their hands behind their backs on either side of a covered frame, grinning out at everyone as gathered. The Crier's apprentice made his way through the crowd, cutting a path for Amair to follow him. Her walk was slow, nodding to the crowd who were growing in anticipation. Her eyes grazed Theo's before turning them to the artists. She smiled at Mulayah, who nodded their head to the Princess. Mulayah glanced at Ebberon, silently discussing something. Together they reached for the cover, lifting the dark fabric.

"Behold, your Princess," Ebberon called, the covering pulled aside.

All the air left Amair's chest.

Her soft smile radiated out of the portrait, seated in the Oighre's throne, hands folded in her lap, the Oighre's silvery band crown looking perfectly in place on her head. Every detail of the gown that hung around her echoed back in the portrait. Her eyes just slightly squinted like they were when she smiled but they were more than that here, peering back, inquisitive in a way, thinking.

It was what was behind her in the portrait that was drawing more attention.

Or more precisely, who.

Behind her throne, hands wrapped over the back, was Layton, with his regal, knowing smile that she missed so much, wearing an Oighre crown that matched hers.

And beside her chair, were Johanna, smiling with a sword at her hip, and Dylan, goofy smile and loose jacket intact.

Amair pressed her hand to her stomach, trying to catch her breath as a tear slipped down her cheek. Jasper and Theo broke through the crowd. Theo reached her first, just as people started to press up, trying to get a better look, a few gasps and exclamations ringing through the crowd as they all took it in. Theo's hand landed on Amair's waist, wrapping his fingers gently around her. She reached behind her, grabbing his arm, trying to make sure she didn't crumble to the floor. Somewhere off to the side, the King cleared his throat, thanking the painters for their beautiful work. His voice was tight, as though he was about to cry.

"Ama, are you okay?" Jasper whispered from beside Theo. She nodded ever so slightly, swallowing. Slowly, she looked from the portrait to

Mulayah and Ebberon. Amair took a little breath, her words tangling in her throat. Mulayah leaned forward as the Princess looked up at them.

"Thank you," she whispered, swallowing again. "Thank you," she said, louder. "It's perfect."

Mulayah stepped down, walking up to Amair, gently resting a hand on her shoulder. "You had asked for two portraits, but…you said something. That all four of you…you were a group. And the whole Kingdom knows that. We wanted one more chance for the four of you to be together. And this way," Mulayah looked over their shoulder, "you have a reminder that they're behind you. Supporting you. Always."

"I don't…I don't even know how to put this…this kind of thanks into words."

"There's no need, Princess," Ebberon smiled behind Mulayah. "This has been the most rewarding thing I have ever worked on. And I painted your grandparents' final portrait. This…this was better."

"Thank you. For as many times as you will hear it." Amair finally smiled, another tear rolling down her cheek.

"Ebberon!" the King called. The painter and his apprentice turned, disappearing into the crowd to see the King. Amair let go of Theo's arm, turning, catching her breath.

"Are you okay?" Theo asked, running a hand soothingly across the side of her head. Amair nodded as Theo's hand fell back down by his side.

"It…it caught me off guard. It's…it's more than I ever could have asked for." She looked down, Theo's fingers still gently wrapped around her waist. He cleared his throat, pulling them back but she smiled up at him.

"Amair!" someone called.

"I'll see you boys later." She glanced at Theo again, before turning into the crowd. Jasper looked up at Theo, raising an eyebrow.

"What?"

"Nothing." The Prince grinned. "I'm gonna find Kenaia, I promised them a drink on me."

"Are the drinks not…free?"

"Well, yes, but this one will be *handed* to them *by* me."

"Alrighty then." Jasper grinned wider, waving and disappearing into the crowd.

Theo stood in his spot, letting the party pass him by, the Princess suddenly missing from the ballroom. He tried to take a step towards the doors, wondering if she had gone for some air, his eyes wandering over her portrait again, when a voice stopped him.

"Teddy," his mom smiled, gently touching her fingers to his elbow. "You look quite dashing, in Skylock blue."

"Hi, mama." He stooped to kiss her cheek. "Are you having fun yet?"

"Oh, plenty. Some of the village ladies are just wonderful. And the Queen is something special, too."

"You met the Queen?" he exclaimed, his voice tightening a little.

"She found me, actually," his mother boasted. "Wanted to gush about you…everything you *have done for their family*." He could almost feel the pride radiating off of her as she squeezed his hand. "I think your da would be very proud of you."

"Son of a farmer making it to the palace?"

"No…*his* son, doing everything to achieve his dreams…and doing it in a way that makes other people's lives a little bit kinder." He watched her smile, the way her eyes crinkled that had always let him know he had come home. "That's all we ever wanted for you, my dear – kindness. And love."

Something in him warmed as he looked around the ballroom again and the annoyance melted away. The Princess reappeared on the stairs with Arthur and her Aunt Elena. Theo met Amair's eye, the two sharing a smile as she spoke softly to her knight and for a moment, it did not matter that the room was packed with suitors he could not remember the names of.

- CHAPTER XXXXVII -

It was rare that rain got in the way of anything in Skylock, but the torrential downpour had taken everyone by surprise, and all the activities that were supposed to have taken place had been cancelled, cooping everyone up together inside the castle. The pent-up energy that was supposed to have been spent on a hike or a ride on horses to give the Princess a break had turned into broken vases in the main hall and the sitting room as a wrestling match had broken out trying to win her favour.

Theo had snuck out at the first sign of trouble.

"Having fun yet?" Jasper laughed, watching Theo throw the dart at the board they had set up on an old music stand at the back of Jasper's study.

Theo shook his head, snorting. "I don't really know." He threw another dart, wincing as he missed the centre. "I'm glad to be *away* from the chaos of the guest wing…thanks for saving me."

"I had my own motives…any dirt on the roundup?"

"The roundup?"

"Yeah…what does one call a group of suitors? A roundup? A Colony? A…swarm?"

Theo tipped his head. "I was thinking more like a gaggle…"

"Ooh, that's good."

"You like that one?" The two of them laughed. As Jasper lined up for his next shot, there was a growing sound echoing somewhere down the hall.

The door flew open, Amair whisking inside and closing it firmly, pressing her back up against it. The boys stared at her, mouths poised with words they couldn't find as she caught her breath, Jasper still holding the dark. She looked up, jumping as she noticed them. She breathed heavily, head swinging between the two boys. "Can I hide here?"

"Uh…sure…" Jasper tipped his head. "You okay?"

"They will not leave me *alone*." She watched the confusion on the boys' face. "The *suitors?*"

"Oh!"

"Trying to *win your hand?*"

"Earning my blade is more like it," she huffed, sliding down the door. She blinked, tipping her head at the target. "I have absolutely no energy left to answer questions about *who I shall dance with at the birthday ball, why I chose the decor, what my favourite flowers are.* It hasn't even officially arrived yet, and I already want my birthday to be over." She grumbled something to herself that the boys couldn't make out. She finally looked up from her balled fists, looking down the office towards the target. "What…are you doing?"

"Used to play at the public house near my university, so I'm teaching him darts," Theo told her, walking over to grab the three out of the target.

"He's losing at darts," Jasper snorted, turning to glance at Theo. Something whizzed past them, making Jasper jump, the sound of something tearing into the target. The two young men whipped their heads around, one of Amair's throwing knives planted in the centre. They looked back at her, the pink skirt pulled up, the knife-strap on her calf missing one.

"I win," she smirked.

"Yeah," Theo sighed, laughing, walking over to pull her knife out, "you do."

- CHAPTER XXXXVIII -

She kept reciting the list she had been left, the names an annoyance, and yet the cadence was becoming a comfort to her growing anxiety. From the moment she had been ushered from her room she had been running through the suitors that were being lined up in front of her, ripe for the picking and yet she wanted none of them. Instead, they were just another list that she could go down to stop her brain from spinning.

"Prince Jaxon, first Prince of Forra." Amair peeked through a crack in the curtains, watching the winning smile of the Prince as he started down the stairs, the Crier quick to pick up the next announcement card. Theo noticed the Princess peeking out from her hiding spot, winking at her. She smiled, pulling away from the curtain and covering her mouth as she stifled a small giggle.

"Princess," Lydia hissed, picking her way along behind the curtains. "How did you even fit back here in that dress?"

"Years of practice." She shook her head a little. "What are you doing, I thought I told you to have *fun* at this?"

"*This* is fun."

"Lydia."

"When I didn't see you mingling with the guests, I had an inkling and I wanted to check on you!"

"Oh, Lydia, I'm fine—"

"—hush," Lydia shook her head, brushing a stray hair off Amair's face. "You are my masterpiece," Amair laughed a little, raising her chin as Lydia brushed at her cheek, "and I'm not letting you out there as anything less."

"Yes, ma'am." Amair smiled, letting Lydia primp her for the third time that day, giggling again as Lydia pulled open her clutch and pulled out Amair's lipstick.

"What would I do without you?" Amair laughed, Lydia grabbing her chin to keep her from moving.

"Run around barefoot with the hair of a Highlands witch." Lydia brushed Amair's collarbone, leaning back and inspecting her work. "Okay."

"Good. Now go," Amair pushed Lydia, "*enjoy* the party! Please." She grinned. "And dance with someone."

"I'm going, I'm going." Lydia smiled and picked her way back towards the entrance. Amair peeked back out the curtains, running a hand along the bodice of her dress, and focused on each breath, feeling the way her body pressed against the fabric and bones of the dress.

"It's fine. Everything's fine…" she whispered to herself, letting out one more breath, and pushed the heavy curtains open. "You're fine."

Theo's eyes fell on the Princess as she appeared, throwing open the curtains with enough flair to make the attendant near them jump. The Crier's eyes widened, fumbling with the card in his hand, the Princess' name mixing with whichever dignitary was in front of him. People turned from their conversations, slowly looking over at the Princess emerging from the side of the room, a quick look of annoyance passing over the Queen's face, settling into a smile as she looked over her daughter.

The light pink tulle looked like it had been draped across her torso and the white lace that peeked over her chest, light, puffy sleeves off her shoulders swallowing her arms, long, lacy cuffs wrapping over the tops of her hands. Her skirt floated out around her, whispering against the ground with every small move. Somewhere behind him he heard the Crier announcing her properly, title in full, but all Theo could focus on was the girl in that dress. Not the girl with the second most important title in the kingdom, not the girl he was writing about, just the girl, in front of him, in the dress that she had spent weeks looking forward to wearing.

'*Beautiful*' he mouthed when she was close enough to see and he caught her blush, mouthing a thank you back before she was captured into the crowd, a series of *happy birthdays* cascading around them.

***

She could not move out of his line of sight fast enough to get away, her mouth twitching as she set her shoulders, trying to remind herself how much power she truly held. "Hello, *Princess*." As always, it felt like a horrible word in his mouth.

"Novak."

"Quite the party." She could smell too much alcohol already on his breath and she tensed, wishing she had gone with her gut and tied a knife to her calf, even if the entire Council had warned against it.

"Only the best, for my guests."

She felt him look her up and down, his eyes lingering. "How far does that extend?"

"I'm leaving now, Novak," Amair rolled her eyes as the boy scowled, watching as she spun and let a crowd of people swallow her. Amair slinked towards the wall, finding her way out of the people and gulping the air. She smiled as Theo popped out of the crowd, appearing beside her.

"Hello, you."

"He's kind of gross, isn't he?" Theo scoffed.

"You're telling me," Amair snorted, glancing up at the Writer. "What do you care?"

"*Because*, Amair, if you weren't the Princess, I'd be pushing you against a wall to kiss you right now." He blinked a few times as Amair jarred, stopping, looking up at Theo, her blue eyes brighter than ever. Her mouth was open, and he braced for her to yell at him.

"I…" She glanced around them, seeing if anyone was listening. Her tight shoulders relaxed down ever so slightly, leaning in towards him. "I wouldn't object." Theo felt a little zap run down his body, looking down at her.

"I can't leave," she murmured. "I'm the Princess, the heir. Oighre." She tipped her head. "And it is…*my* birthday. I can't leave."

"I know," Theo nodded. Amair looked around them, trying to see if anyone was close by and ever so discreetly reached out to and squeezed his hand.

Later she mouthed, pulling her hand back. She took a deep breath, glancing at him one more time and turned away.

"Jax! Hi!"

Theo noticed the tiniest glance back at him as she said it, the corners of her mouth flicking up into a smirk just fast enough for him to see.

"Hopefully I am better company than Novak."

"The flies in the compost yards are better company than Novak," Amair spat, composing her face. "Apologies…that was unkind."

"It's your birthday," Jax laughed, "you can be unkind if you want to."

"I'm sorry I have not been around much."

"It's a difficult year, I understand." He turned to look her up and down. "Doesn't help that, from what I can tell…" He scanned the crowd next. "You have an army of potential suitors when someone else suits you better."

"Jax…I–"

"–it's alright. I have my eye on someone at home." He shrugged. "My gift is on the table, it's a quill."

"Thank you–"

"–you can write, you know. Us future rulers…it wouldn't hurt to stick together. There are more ways to unite kingdoms than just sending second, third, and fourth children to marry into them."

Out of the corner of her eye, Amair spotted Elena pushing people out of her way. "Thank you, Jax." Jax leaned over to kiss Amair's cheek gently and then bowed.

"Happy birthday, Princess."

"Bug," Elena pulled Amair out of reach of another suitor before he could grab her, pulling her out into the chilly air on one of the balconies.

"Auntie." Amair just leaned into Elena, letting her whole body sag forward a little as Elena wrapped her arms around her niece.

"How's it going?"

"Exhausted."

"Collateral damage of suitors on the prowl," Elena laughed, a warm sound that rumbled through her chest and onto Amair's. "Your dress is beautiful, no one in that room can keep their eyes off you."

"Mhm."

"I'll be staying an extra day before I head back to my mountaineering trip in Innisil, so we can go for a ride together, put out anything you need me to know."

"Thank you."

"Now," Elena stood her niece back onto her feet, fixing her dress, adjusting how she held her glass, and cupping her face, "go remind those fools why we Skylock women are better."

"Than?"

"Just," she kissed her niece's forehead, "better." She winked. "I love you, bug."

"I love you, too, Elena." Amair turned, taking a deep breath and as soon as she stepped through into the ballroom, a young man had already offered her an arm and a conversation starter. It was a whirlwind, and her list of names was barely keeping her head on straight, mixed in with the handful of answers to the same questions. Every time she tried to make a joke, the young men would hesitate before they laughed, and she resisted the urge to roll her eyes at them.

"May I have this dance?" Amair turned, her eyes scanning their fingers and their arm and up to their face. A relieved smile wiped across her face, reaching for Theo's hand.

"I would *love that*." He held her hand, leading her out to the dance floor as the music picked up into something bright, notes hitting the air with force.

"How's your night going?" he asked, spinning her on cue with everyone else on the floor.

"My feet hurt. There's been *a lot* of dancing."

"I would assume."

"I like pretty shoes, but pretty shoes do not always like me," she giggled, making Theo laugh. "I'm glad I finally get to dance with you," she grinned, squeezing his hand. "Have you danced much?"

"A couple with my mom. A couple of girls I think were about Kylo's age," he laughed as they swung around with a loud beat in the music, "they were daring each other to come over and ask me to dance, all adorable and giggly." Amair watched the way Theo's whole face smiled when he talked, "But once *one* of them had danced with me, they *all* wanted to dance with me."

"That's so sweet."

"Oh! And then your mom."

"My mom?"

"Yes, the Queen! She asked *me* to dance."

"How…was it?"

"Oh, lovely. She's a great dancer."

"Luckily," Amair looked down at their feet, "so are you, apparently."

"I've learned. But we chatted, about your siblings, mostly, and then I handed her off to Jasper."

"Who I *also* want a dance with."

Theo smiled, watching her face. "I may steal one more from you, before that."

Amair grinned, squinting a little, pulling slightly at his shoulder. "I wouldn't object."

He pressed a little more against her back, his face not shifting from the soft smile, but she noticed his eyes turning playful as he watched the dance floor past her head. "Good." Amair smiled, biting her lip and glancing down, again, focusing on her shoes as they danced. The music slowed, another melody taking over. Lighter, jumpy music filled the ballroom, everyone springing to attention for the next dance, bouncing and twisting their partners.

Amair laughed, and Theo broke into a huge grin as the two of them rushed to keep up with the guests dancing expertly all around them. One of the couples behind them nearly ran the Princess and Writer over, their jumping overtaking the two. They passed so close, Amair felt one of their elbows swipe across the back of her dress, making her laugh again. Amair and Theo managed their way through the dance until the quick paced music finally died out, taking deep breaths, Amair leaning over a little to laugh and catch her breath. Theo rubbed her back gently, trying to catch his own breath. Amair stood back up, hands clasped on forearms, laughing and balancing on each other. Amair blushed, pulling her hand back and placing it over her chest, looking down to check that her dress hadn't slipped.

"I should go find Jasper."

She did not move at first, still leaning into his hand.

Theo nodded a little. "Sure, sure."

"Thank you...for dancing."

"Anytime." He winked at her. She smiled, straightening her shoulders, and pulling on her skirts to weave through the guests.

"It's been a very long time since I've seen her like that," Kylo appeared beside Theo, sipping from a goblet. He looked up at Theo, swirling the glass in his hand. "You did that. Thank you."

"Uh…" Theo shook his head, letting the words roll around him as another song struck the first chord. "You…you're welcome?"

"I really mean it, Theo," Kylo was nodding a little. "You make her…warm again. You're special. Thank you." He tipped his head to the Writer, going to disappear into the crowd.

"You okay, bud?" Theo asked, stopping him in his tracks. Kylo's shoulders drooped a little.

"I…Nusiq…he was not able to come." He shrugged, glancing around at all the young men forced to make nice to each other. "Just…lonely, despite all these people."

"I'm always here. If you want a friend."

"I'll remember that." Theo looked around, in the sea of people on his own, now, wondering where everyone had disappeared off to.

He spotted Elena slipping out the main doors to the ballroom and without thinking, he followed her, slipping past guests partying and dancing and the few still talking politics. "Elena!"

She turned, the dim corridor lights flickering over her face. "Theodore."

"I haven't had a chance to see you."

"It's been busy…I've been an extra hand and…well, mostly keeping Amair from strangling someone."

"Quite a feat."

"It is."

"You haven't been bored, then?"

"Oh, never, here. This castle is just as much an adventure as anywhere else."

Theo paused, one of his hands in his pocket, rolling his pen around. "Why do you call her 'bug?'"

Elena grinned, tucking her hands behind herself and leaning her weight back as she considered him. "It's short for lightning bug. She always thought she was just a shadow." He noticed her eyes slip past him, watching the ballroom as something loud happened inside. "When she has always been the light."

Inside, Amair was finding a quiet moment on her own, slipping out onto a balcony for some fresh air when she spotted a quiet face. "Mrs. Crawford," Amair touched her shoulder gently. Theo's mother spun around, grinning warmly. She took Amair's hand from her shoulder, squeezing it.

"Princess."

Amair glanced around them, making sure no one was listening. "I don't mind if you stick to Amair."

"I hear that's what you let my son call you." She smirked. "I believe I overheard a nickname as well."

Amair blushed. "He's picked it up."

"You have that same...mischievous little smirk that he does," Theo's mom chuckled. "You made quite the entrance." Amair shrugged.

"I'm a Princess...gotta add a few dramatics now and then." Theo's mom laughed, caressing Amair's cheek.

"You are a sweet girl, Amair. With a lot of heart." Amair felt something in her flutter, biting the inside of her lip. "You're going to make a great Queen." Councillors and friends and her brothers kept telling her but no one outside the castle had actually said it yet. Her words brought tears to Amair's eyes.

"Princess," someone said behind them, making Amair pull her face away from Mrs. Crawford's hand. The attendant smiled cautiously, arms behind their back. "The King has asked you to say the farewell, for the night...he says it's time to get everything to wind down." Amair glanced towards the large clock, nodding, a hand still wrapped in Mrs. Crawford's.

"He would be right. Maybe that's why I feel like I'm going to vomit...the exhaustion is getting to me."

- CHAPTER XLIX -

The castle felt suffocated with movement as staff bustled about with cases and laundry and leftovers. Amair was being shuffled from meeting to meeting as fast as the King's staff could move her, taking her down back halls and secret staircases to keep the guests from spotting her. Theo spotted her at one point, raising a hand to wave to her and she smiled, waving back before one of the staff pushed a little on her back and pressed her into the next meeting room.

Theo sighed, turning and wandering down a hallway that was finally quiet, lined with reading rooms that were mostly empty, most everyone working or in some form of partying or packup. Theo peeked into each one, hoping to spot someone he knew or had met and could get to know – or better yet, steal a quote from. He rounded the corner to the edge of the Family Wing where the Children's Room was, the door open and a familiar face inside.

"How you doing?" Theo smiled at Kylo, falling back onto one of the couches in the Children's Room across from the middle Prince.

"Hoping when I turn sixteen come Spring, it can just be family, you, and my boyfriend." Kylo lowered his newspaper. "Why are you in love with her?"

"Wh-what?" Theo asked, eyes widening.

"Oh, come on. I could spot it a mile away. I have three older siblings – granted I was the first one to *get* a boyfriend and none of them have been all that interested in finding *anyone* to date. But I know the look. So. What did it?" They stared at each other for a second. "See, Jasper, he just wants the old Ama back. The twins just wish there was a bit of joy back. Our parents just need a crowned heir right now. The Kingdom sees her as an heir. I want Ama to come through this. But *you*. You didn't know her *before*."

"I…" Theo opened his mouth and closed it again, thinking, watching Kylo. "She's fierce. She knows her mind, and she has…this passion that bubbles in near everything she does. And she's strong and she doesn't care if she scares someone off, because if it's the interest of her people or the plans she has or needs to put into place…then that's what she will do. And despite all that, despite all her fierceness, and all the grief she has suffered…there's still something soft, under all of it."

Kylo smiled slowly, watching Theo's face as he talked. "Don't let her scare you off."

"You know…you're the second Skylock to tell me that." They both chuckled, Kylo flicking his paper to go back to his reading, handing the sections he had already read to Theo.

A knock came at the door, a messenger popping her head in. "Pardon my interruption." Her smile was kind, even if it was a little stiff.

"No worries," Kylo sat taller, "please, come in." She pushed in, silver message tray first, bowing to let Theo pick up the message with his name on it, Amair's unmistakable messy writing on the front.

"Duty calls?" Kylo asked, mouth quirking up, trying to pretend to read his paper instead of the notecard.

"Duty calls!"

***

"So, you've said goodbye to the last of your oh-so-lovely guests?"

"The last one has been pushed out the front door, I am back to my lovely, cosy bubble." Theo laughed, watching her tuck her hands behind her back as they walked up to the stone bridge.

"Do you…do you remember what you said to me at the ball?" she asked abruptly.

Theo turned his head sharply, raising an eyebrow. "I said a lot of things." Amair glared at him, playful, but annoyed. "Oh, I think it's coming back to me."

"I want that." She stopped walking, holding her hands in front of her in the way she always did, like she had to balance herself. A piece of hair escaped from her tight hairdo, the golden chestnut hair falling and catching in her eyelashes. Theo rubbed his chin, feeling the tiny bits of stubble coming through, looking down at Amair, standing there valiantly, shoulders back. He turned his head, looking down the quiet hallway, the little bit of light from the rising moon coming in through the arches of the bridge. He looked back at Amair, shaking his head a little, his grin less mischievous than usual, and finally took the step. He grabbed her, hands on her waist, pushing her back into the stone wall behind her.

Her hands were on his jaw, holding him close. Her lips were warm against his, even in the chill of the castle, of the corridor open to the outside. She moved a hand to the back of his neck, and he could feel her balancing on her toes, trying to reach up, to get closer to him. He held her tight, wrapping his fingers into her hair, one of the pins clattering on the ground.

Theo pulled his head back, holding Amair, hand still in her hair. She looked up at him, her eyes wide, excited, a tiny smudge of pink escaping off her lips. She opened her mouth to say something but closed it again, letting out the tiniest breath of a laugh. She settled back down on her feet, Theo ran a hand through her hair, down her cheek.

"Can we do that again?"

Theo smiled, wrapping his arms around her, putting a foot out and balancing himself as he dipped Amair, kissing her furiously as she held his face again. He brought her back to feet, the two standing there, holding each other.

Their heads whipped around as a noise echoed through the halls, a light appearing around the corner.

Amair turned back up to Theo. "You need to go," she whispered, their noses still touching.

Theo's eyebrows knit together. "Amair—"

"—no, no. It's okay." She smiled, cupping a hand against his cheek. "You need to go so I don't have to explain this just yet. Gossip spreads like glitter around here." She brushed a kiss to his chin. "Go. I'll find you tomorrow."

"Okay," Theo smiled, kissing her forehead. He let go of her reluctantly, walking briskly down the hall, ducking into a corridor.

"Your highness!" he heard someone exclaim. "It's late, you shouldn't be—"

"—apologies. It has been…a very eventful few days," Theo could hear the laugh behind her voice, "I just needed some time. To myself."

"Of course, m'lady. Understandable."

"Would the two of you mind walking me back to my quarters?"

"Absolutely, your highness."

Theo waited until Amair and the guards had disappeared around the corner, slinking backwards to find another way back to his room.

***

Amair waved and thanked the guards, pushing the door closed, turning and pressing her hand to her stomach.

Her lips still buzzed, feeling heavy.

Amair shook her head a little, pulling at her sleeves as she walked into her room, breathing in the fresh air coming in the open balcony doors. It was nice to walk into her room, having been forced to spend little time for the solace she liked in her quiet moments. She looked up as the sound of paper rustled against the floor. A small, folded scrap floated across the rug by her bed, catching it under her shoe. Pulling her skirt out to the side, she flipped the paper through her fingers, carefully pulling it open.

Messy ink ran across the paper.

I know what happened to your big brother

Amair's breath hitched in her chest. She clutched the scrap of paper in her hand, holding it into herself, gripping it, biting the inside of her lip so hard she tasted blood.

- CHAPTER L -

No work tomorrow after luncheon. I'm all yours. - A the note read, a little heart drawn on the bottom of the card. Theo smiled, slipping it between the pages of his notebook.

***

Theo laid on Amair's bed, resting on his stomach, his hand draped over her, sprawled out on her back, both their eyes half closed. One of her puffy, organza sleeves was bunched up, her shoulders bare where the low, off-the-shoulder sleeves draped down and he let his fingers run across her skin.

The sun shone bright through the rows of windows, lighting up her mostly white room, warming the couple as they laid quietly together. The doors to the smaller of her two balconies had been left open, the white curtains billowing in, a warm breeze and the smell of the gardens filling her room.

"Your hair is so pretty," Theo smiled, pressing his nose against her head, letting the faint smell of roses wash over him. She grinned, tossing her arm over him, playing with a loose thread on the back of his shirt.

Theo moved one of his hands across her face, through her hair, wrapping the dark strand around his fingers. "Witch child."

"Mhm."

"Any truth to that?" Theo teased, raising his chin off the bed a little to try and look at the dark hair looped over his fingers.

"Friends?" she grinned, her eyes half closed.

"I'm thinking your bed is a safe space."

"Good point," Amair laughed, letting her hand rest on Theo's back. "I don't know where it started. But y'know… No kids for five years, and suddenly there was a daughter. A photograph was published for my first birthday, and it was the first time I had really been seen and my hair had come in. I've heard theories flutter through the castle over the years. That my mother slept with a witch, that my father slept with a witch, that a witch cursed me, that a witch blessed me, that a witch blessed my parents to help them have a baby…I think my favourite is that I'm a changeling switched out by the fae." Theo chuckled, running his fingers through her hair. "They're just birthmarks, though. Like Kylo's freckles, or the twins' matching branches on their shoulders."

"Hm."

Amair turned her head all the way. Theo opened his eyes a little at the shift in the bed, smiling tiredly back at her. He untangled his hand from her hair, running it down her head to her neck, pulling himself over to her to kiss her softly. She rolled towards him, moving her hand she'd had on his back, when a loud knock sounded at the door. Amair sat up, leaning back on her hands, Theo rolling off the bed and trying not to yell as he thumped onto the ground.

"Your highness?"

"Ah...y-yes?" Amair called back, glancing at Theo.

"Your father has sent a message, may I come in?"

"I uh..." she fumbled, "I'm not decent!" Amair called back.

"Oh my...my apologies!"

Theo had to cover his mouth with his fist, trying not to snort.

Amair glared at him. "Yes um...can you slip it under the door?"

"Of course, Princess! He did say it was urgent!"

"Of course it is," she muttered. Amair pointed at the door, nodding at Theo with her chin. "Getting it now!"

"Have a great day, Princess!"

"You too!"

Theo snatched the small card tossed under the door, walking it back to Amair. She scanned it, falling back against the bed groaning, crossing an arm across her face.

"You alright?" Theo perched next to her.

"I have to go back to work," Amair pulled on the last word, falling back onto the bed, peeking out from under her arm at him. He smiled, trying not to look disappointed. Theo reached over, running his fingers down Amair's arm.

"When are they expecting you?"

"Twenty minutes." Theo smirked.

"Alright then," he leaned over her, wrapping an arm around her back. He snatched the card from her hand, tossing it across the room as she squealed. "I'll only take fifteen," he murmured, kissing her.

- CHAPTER LI -

His fingers buzzed when she was not around and it was the late night stops by her room, waiting for the guard change she had perfected that stopped the buzzing for just long enough to let them rest on her waist or her cheek as he held her.

He walked to her study one afternoon and felt the buzz running up his arm after not seeing her for a few days and slowed his walk, watching one of the King's aides step out the door. As the aide finally made it to the end of the corridor, he knocked at her study, looking in.

"Amair?"

"Hello, Theodore."

He laughed quietly, stepping into her office as she stretched in her chair. "Have you been to bed?"

"Uh…I'm not sure." She lowered the workbook a little, leaning all the way back over the armrest to look at him. "What day is it?"

He laughed again, settling in the chair across from her. "Next time *I'm* putting you to bed."

"Maybe you should." She smirked, still leaning back over the armrest. He felt himself blush but tried to shake it off.

He ran his fingers over her mahogany desk, knicks in the wood that told the stories of the royal children that had come before her. "Hey, so a request was sent to me."

"Oh yeah?" she asked, her eyes on her book.

"From the editor at the paper."

"Oh?"

"The serial has been picked up by papers in a couple other Kingdoms…"

"That's cool!"

"Yeah." He blushed. "Well, a journalist from Waiwhe has sent us a request to do a special interview with you to get some detail from you, explain some Skylock stuff…"

"Oh. Well…" She laid looking back at him, her book hanging from her hand above her head. "I'd probably have to talk to my father. And he'll probably make me talk to someone in the administration." She paused, watching her book slip a little in her fingers. "I don't see why not."

"Wow."

"What?"

"I'm…surprised at how easy that was. I had a speech. I know you don't love the press."

"It's growing on me." The way she raised her eyebrow made Theo bit his lip. "If you're really disappointed you could still give your rousing speech."

"No, no, I'll take the easy way out. Talk to whomever you need. No rush."

"Let's do something today," Amair grinned, sitting up, stretching in her chair again as she yawned.

"Maybe you should have a nap."

"Nah." She tapped her chin with her book, thinking. "Come with me. Let me show you one of my favourite spots."

"Whatever you wish, your highness."

***

He kept his hands on her, holding her hand, grabbing her hips, running after her flurry of skirts as she slinked through dusty castle corridors. She zipped around corners so fast that she nearly pulled him off balance, but used her momentum to pull her back in to him, spinning her back into his arms.

She shrieked a laugh, a sound he had never heard her make and it made him beam, wrapping his arms around her, holding her close as he kissed her.

Up a set of stairs she led and finally, as his ears popped a little he looked up at the sound of rain. "Welcome to my favourite place," she whispered, reaching up on her tiptoes to kiss his cheek. The space was small but warm from the fire flickering in the hearth. There was a pile of discarded blankets and pillows and a few boxes strewn about, a semi-forgotten storage room. They found a comfortable spot and sat quietly, watching the rain, gently enjoying the quiet peace.

"I always wanted my chambers to be up on this floor." Amair smiled, her head in Theo's lap, his shoes and jacket discarded off to the side. His tie pulled loose from Amair pulling him closer to her lips. "I wanted to watch the rain all day and all night." She sighed. "But they insisted I stay in the Family Wing."

"I get it. Easier to protect the family if they're all in one place."

"Wow, yeah, that was the reasoning I was given," she chuckled, leaning into his hand, the crackle of the fire warming them. "You slipped up, in the serial this week."

He stiffened. "What?"

Amair smirked, catching his eye. "You forgot my title. Called me Amair." He blinked once, before his eyes widened, horrified.

"I...I am so sorry–"

"–it's fine," she chuckled, reaching a hand up and gently rubbing her fingers against his cheek. "Humanizing, I think is what they keep saying about your writing. What's more human than a name?"

"Hm."

She smiled thoughtfully, eyes half closed. "If anyone makes a fuss, we can just say it was a misprint and they forgot to add my title on the printer." He ran his fingers up and down her arm, the constant bustle of the castle that always surrounded him not reaching them on the top floor. He had almost forgotten perfect quiet. He saw the small goosebumps along her skin, the smear of her lip colour from where he had kissed her, the flyaway curl that never quite found its way into her hairdo.

The humanity in the mystery.

"Layton used to catch me up here all the time. There was a while where they tried to ban us from coming up here, but no one really paid attention to the second born... He'd find me and come lay next to me, watch the rain, we'd just...sit in quiet." Theo looked up at the panels of the glass ceiling, the constant rain tapping against it in in a soothing rhythm.

"There's something...I don't know, comforting, about this room."

"It's all the natural light. It may be the grey light of Skylock, but it still makes you feel good."

"Having a beautiful girl in my lap probably helps." Theo glanced down, watching her smile. His fingers trailed up her arm, slowly climbing over her shoulder and up her neck. He felt her shiver as his finger dragged over her collarbone, gently over the soft skin at her throat. He pulled his thumb over her chin to find her lips, gently tracing the edge of her bottom lip. A sound whispered through her chest as she lifted her chin closer to his hand.

After a moment she settled again, turning her head, her eyes half closed and she sighed.

"You should rest."

"I'm okay."

"Rest," he brushed her cheek. "It's okay. We have all the time in the world."

- CHAPTER LII -

"Hey Amair?"

"Yeah, buddy?" Amair asked Evander, taking a bite of her breakfast, not glancing up from the letter in her hand.

"What's a threesome?" Everyone's eyes widened, Amair coughing as she choked on her croissant. Two of the attendants jumped, scurrying towards her but she waved them off, clearing her throat.

"I'm sorry," Amair swallowed hard, her voice scratching, "*what?*" She didn't dare turn her head to glance at her parents.

"*Ember Kids* magazine came today. One of the articles," Evander explained as Amair took a sip of the water an attendant handed her, "was that you had a threesome with Dylan and Layton." Amair sputtered the water, covering her mouth but it was too late. Jasper blinked, wiping at his chin.

"I…" Amair finally looked over at her parents, both of them holding spoons above their bowls of porridge, everyone waiting to hear Amair's response. "Where...who said this?" Amair glanced across the table at Theo, who just raised an eyebrow.

"In Ember Kids. I don't know, it said they had an inside source."

"Well it's very much not true," Amair shook her head a little, eyebrows raised high. She glanced at her parents again. "I *swear.*"

"I believe you, hon," the King sighed. "Rumours and gossip sell."

Amair glanced at Theo again, chewing the inside of her cheek. He smiled a little, trying to keep his composure, turning his head to the King and Queen.

"I unfortunately can't write every single thing that gets published about the Princess, but I will talk to some people and see if I can get this under control. Quickly."

"Thank you, Theodore," the Queen smiled, glancing back at her daughter. "Believe me, darling, rumours come and go. We'll try and get this one staunched." Theo could feel everyone's eyes going between him and Amair, the usual calmness of their mornings sucked out of the air.

"Wait! No one answered my question!" Evander pouted.

***

"Well…gag order on Princess in the press is gone," Amair murmured.

That evening, the moon passed over the window of Amair's sitting room, the fire blazing as giggles filled the room, mismatching chairs dragged in from Kylo's study across the hall. Amair laughed as her brothers and Theodore looked at the article in Evander's *Ember Kids* magazine, sipping the good whiskey Jasper had snagged from the King's study.

"Okay, but truth," Jasper asked, "did you ever sleep with Dylan?"

"No!" Amair exclaimed, giggly as the alcohol started to hit her.

"*Johanna?*"

"No!" Amair leaned back, giggling so hard Theo had to grab at the glass in her hand before her amber liquid sloshed out.

"Who *was* your first time?" Kylo asked absent-mindedly, to no one in particular, his head tipped to the side, twirling his glass.

Amair's eyes shot towards Theo, raising an eyebrow at him over the glass she held tightly. "I'm here as a friend, don't worry," he assured her, holding his hands up in front of him. He chuckled, watching her scrunch her lips, trying to be serious. He picked up his glass, shaking the ice as he watched the three siblings. Amair's narrowed eyes turned playful, glancing at Jasper.

"Don't give me that look," Jasper shot at her, but snorted, trying to hide behind his glass as he took a sip.

"What?" Kylo asked, swinging his head back and forth, trying to decipher whatever was happening between his siblings.

"She's making fun of me."

"For?"

"My first time was with Orlaith Torrent."

"Chief...Torrent's...daughter?"

"Mhm. In the corridor behind the kitchen, during the Alanmas Ball year before last."

"First Skylock kid to do it," Amair snorted.

"Isn't she...?" Kylo asked, looking bewildered.

"Yup!" his sister exclaimed, knocking her foot against their brother's ankle. "Started dating Lenora about two seasons later. Still happily in love." They laughed and Jasper shrugged, chuckling into his glass.

"Wait...how were you the first Skylock kid? You're...the middle child." Theo asked, glancing at the old portrait of all six kids on the mantle.

"Technically I think that's Kylo," Jasper shot back.

"*Technically*, it's both of you." Amair reminded, following his eyes. "And Layton wasn't into...sex. Or relationships, for that matter."

"Hm."

"Amair?"

"Mmm..." She bit her lip, smiling ever so slightly, not making eye contact with the three of them.

"I shared!" Jasper shouted.

"This is a safe space!" Kylo snickered. Her eyes flitted up to Theo who just smiled, tipping his glass towards her.

"Mmm...Johanna, Dylan, Layton, and I were on a Circle trip, we were out East...I think...I think we had to deal with something happening with one of the Chiefs. It was like...ten weeks before they died? Anyway, *Arthur* was dragged along, he was training with Johanna. And the two of us, the kiddos, were left in the room during one of the meetings.

"I was mad. *Steaming* mad. I hated...*hate* being left out of things. Especially with them. I did everything in my power to not be the little kid, and most of the time I wasn't. But sometimes... Anyway...Arthur came up to my room and we played *Ouron*."

"Wait...hold on..." Jasper raised an eyebrow, putting the pieces together, sitting forward in his chair. Theo slid his eyes to Jasper, drawing them back to Amair.

"One thing led to another..." Amair smirked, tipping her head back, taking a slow sip of her drink.

"How...how was it?" Kylo asked. Amair studied his face for a moment.

"Kind of uncomfortable." Amair rolled her eyes as Jasper snorted. "But...it was fff...fun. And...he was so kind. *Is* so kind, I said that like he die– like he had gone away." Jasper noticed her catch herself on the word, but tried to ignore it. "So...it was good, in that way. I don't know, it was my *only* time, so there's nothing really to compare it to." She couldn't help looking over at Theo, ripping her eyes away back to Kylo as soon as Theo had met them.

"But you guys...you guys are such good friends?"

"Yeah. We are. We both...we knew there was nothing really...*between* us. There's no hard feelings or anything. But it was...it was nice to feel safe and cared for, that first time."

"Hey, Theo," Jasper turned his head, almost cutting off his sister. "Your turn."

"Oh. Genevieve Gurtz. I was kind of nerdy but she thought that was *super* hot. I really played the...*sexy smart*, thing, my last year of high school." The three laughed.

"And..."

Theo smirked, swishing his glass. "I don't like to kiss and tell." Amair rolled her eyes at him but matched his smirk. Jasper turned his head, glancing at his sister as she was saying something to Theo quietly, her mouth not moving, but their eyes matched over their glasses. Jasper smiled, sipping his drink and watching whatever giddy happiness was in Amair's face.

Spring

- CHAPTER LIII -

Weeks passed quietly. Theo put out articles and when he was not writing and Amair was not studying or being dragged into meetings, they were wrapped in each other's arms, trying to quietly figure out exactly how they felt about each other. Amair felt something so wonderfully dangerous about falling in love with the person meant to be sharing every detail of her life. Jasper and Kylo knew and she was quite sure the twins had put it together. From her letters, even if she was however many realms away, she got the feeling her Aunt Elena had put it together as well.

There was some kind of peace, of normality coming back to the castle. Friends came and went, diplomats visiting, Amair managing to slip training with Lenora and Arthur into her schedule that seemed to be growing more and more busy by the day.

As they left behind the torrential downpours of winter and Kenaia filled every inch of the gardens and castle with new blooms, the castle was alight with energy again, people coming from every corner of the Kingdom to welcome in Spring with the next festival quickly approaching.

"Jasp," Amair smiled, skirts and Lupa's nails whispering down the hallway. Jasper looked up, smiling tightly, looking back out at the ring. Amair leaned onto the stone bannister next to him, smiling.

"Hey, Ama," he murmured, glancing at her.

"Making sure it all looks perfect?" she asked, looking at him.

"You know me. Keeping my eye on everything."

"I always knew you were the trustworthy one." She smiled, pulling at her fingers, turning her head out onto the grounds again.

"Are you competing tomorrow?"

"The one time of year I show my face." She snorted. "Well…"

"Different now."

"Yeah."

"I'm glad you're doing it."

"Me too."

"I wish I could compete."

Amair shrugged. "Do you want to?"

"I don't know. Everyone else gets their chance to show who they are. To prove themselves," Jasper muttered, staring down at the ring, stands being set up around it.

"Jasper, don't worry," Amair pressed her warm hand to his cheek. "You proved yourself to me long ago." Amair smiled kindly at her brother, fixing his hair, before turning and walking away. Jasper watched her brush down the hall, Lupa jogging up next to her, pressing into Amair's skirts. Amair and her dog disappeared around the corner, off the bridge, Jasper still standing there, looking out at the game grounds. He leaned his forearms onto the stone bannister, the moon lighting up the edges of the ring. Jasper took a deep breath, filling his lungs with chilly night air.

Amair clipped through the castle, her eyes falling on Lenora as she rounded the corner into the training grounds. "Princess."

"Lenny." She smiled, watching Lupa shoot past her to the Captain of the Guard who crouched to pat between her fluffy ears. "How are preparations?"

"The guards who are competing have spent the day practicing and are off for an early bed…mostly to stay out of the way of the arriving guests. I was just off to inspect the armoury tent, Moritz has tasked me with assuring everything is balanced, polished…"

"Could I join you? I haven't been down to the grounds, yet."

"Certainly," she pressed on her strong thighs to stand, offering the Princess her arm, "follow me."

"Has Orlaith arrived?" Amair asked with a smirk as they reached the stairs, glancing to the side, Lenora wearing a matching smirk.

"She's waiting in my quarters."

"Then we should do this quickly."

Lenora laughed, pushing on the door for Amair to step through, holding her arm to balance her as she pushed her heavy skirt through. "Pulling out every regal stop again?"

"That obvious?" Amair glanced down at herself, pouting a little. They both paused as they got up to the field filled with tents and people running from one to another, the flicker of light from torches as people reuniting with old friends from across the kingdom laughed and shrieked, making the two girls smile.

"Not obvious, per se," Lenora shook her head. The two girls watched the field, noise growing around them. "Merriment is returning," Lenora mused, laughing as she spotted two young men jumping up and down in an embrace. Amair managed a smile, flexing her free hand.

"I hope so," she whispered, feeling something deep in her chest squeezing. They walked through the tents, stopping to admire two women dancing a reel, arms locked together as they wheeled around each other in perfect step. As people spotted the Princess they stopped to bow drunkenly, making her laugh and bob her head in return.

"I love the Feast of Skylock…all the drums, and Skypipes…somehow, even despite the drunkenness, we remember our songs and stories."

Lenora and Amair finally reached the armour tent, tucked behind the duelling ring, the guard standing at attention as the girls walked in. The Princess released the Captain's arm, letting her pull out a white glove to inspect the armour and weapons waiting to be put to use in the morning.

"Is yours here?" Lenora asked.

"I bring my own down from the store," Amair told her, arms tucked behind her back as she tried to resist the urge to touch the row of perfectly reflective shields in all shapes. Lenora paused, watching Amair stare into the shields.

"Is anything the matter, Ama?"

"Just…trying to pull out my own merriment…"

Lenora glanced at the opening to the tent. "I'm almost done here…Orlaith can wait. Shall we have a drink and a dance?"

"I can't ask—"

"—you're not," Lenora replaced a cup of polish, tossing her glove aside and fixing the front of her jacket. She smiled. "I'm offering…to a friend. Not my future sovereign." She reached out a hand. Amair pushed out a breath and smiled, taking the hand. "You may not be able to reel in that dress but…I can certainly dance with you."

- CHAPTER LIII -

The sun was rising over the camp and the duelling ring on the morning of the festival. It peaked out from behind the trees, blanketing everything in pink hues as most of the castle was only just starting to stir. Amair crept through the corridors, fixing the armour Lydia had awoken early to help her into. She stepped carefully across the bridge, pausing to look down at the ring, each of the kingdom's flags whispering back and forth in the morning breeze.

Denna was there as Amair walked out of the castle into the field, already in her thick leather armour, the chain mail pinned as a high neck around her throat.

"Good morning, your highness," Denna smiled tiredly, stretched, a thermos next to her. "I brought coffee."

"Thank you."

"Figured a pick-me-up before anyone else has to see you…" She trailed off, raising an eyebrow and reaching up to adjust her headscarf. Amair raised an eyebrow, turning slowly.

"You don't need to be awake yet," she chided with a smile at Theo.

"Well, I knew someone would be up with the sun." He reached for her, hesitating as he glanced at Denna but Amair closed the gap between them, grabbing her gloved hand around his wrist and pulling him close.

"I'm going to warm up," she told him. "You can stay?"

"I'll pour the coffee."

He sat next to Denna, the two of them watching Amair walk out into the dewy grass, stretching each limb as she looked up into the stands and for a moment Theo watched her pause, staring up into the Sovereign's box. She stood, hands on her hips, shoulders back, brave. There was noise starting to fill the fields as cooks and dancers and attendants found their stations and it broke her concentration, wandering back in to where Denna and Theo had made their way to their feet, more alert, the sun starting to warm the grounds.

"You should sit with my family, Theo," Amair offered. "Best vantage point…perfect for a story." He nodded bowing slightly to Denna who bobbed her head in reply.

Theo slowed as he walked past, grabbing her hand and letting his fingers linger just long enough for the buzz to run up both their arms. "Show 'em what you're made of." He paused, checking to see if anyone was looking and stooping to kiss her forehead, then her cheek. He glanced at her head. "I'd be more comfortable if you had a helmet on."

"You and my mother both." She shrugged. "I'll be fine."

"You don't need it, but good luck."

"He's cute," Denna whispered, bumping her elbow against Amair's with a grin. Amair grinned, glancing up at Theo's retreating back. "Does he write poetry? I think you've earned a sonnet or two…" Amair snorted this time, as Jasper walked in.

"Good morning," Amair was still laughing, and second layer joined it as she took in his slightly rumpled look.

"I don't do mornings," he shrugged. "But for the Oighre, I will do mornings."

"I appreciate it," she laughed, reaching out one of her hands to fix a section of Jasper's hair, as Denna wrapped her sword around her hips.

"You'll do great out there," Jasper assured her.

Amair turned towards the ring, the stands starting to fill up, everyone dressed in their clan tartans. "I know." She spotted her competitor walking in from the other side of the ring, wondering who was standing there having given him his pep talk. "This is what I'm good at."

"Give it up for everyone's favourite hero, Princess Amair Skylock!" The crowd cheered, Amair's eyebrows tight, taking a deep breath. She glanced back to Jasper and Denna, the two of them shooting her a thumbs up. There was a tear in Amair's eye and for a second she could only picture Layton and Johanna standing beyond them, doing the same year after year as she rose from rookie to champion. Amair finally smiled, stepping out and waving into the stands, glancing to the side as Ebruc swung his sword in his hand a few times. She resisted the urge to roll her eyes.

"Her royal highness insists that even as Oighre, there are no hold backs in her match. What do you say to that, folks?" the Crier's apprentice yelled, met with applause. Amair tipped her head side to side, stretching out her arms. Finally, she turned away from the edge of the ring, facing Ebruc, and pulled out her sword. She twirled the hilt in her hand, feeling its weight against her palm. She looked up to the Sovereign's booth, where her parents sat hand in hand, her mother's hand over her mouth. Theo stood behind Amair's empty throne, smiling, pen and paper in hand.

"If you lose," she muttered to herself, "everyone gets to read about it on Sunday." She shook her head, twirling her sword again, eyeing Ebruc. He grinned at her, making a show of raising his sword to inspect it. She watched as he flexed his arms, waving to random people in the stands, jumping like he was warming himself up. Amair just stood, taking stock of her limbs, the tip of her sword planted into the dirt, both hands on top of the hilt. She felt the breeze that ran over her.

"Competitors, to the ready!" the Crier called, the crowd cheering so loudly Amair could barely hear him. Ebruc and Amair walked up to each other, and he bowed, a deep, long bow, grinning as he did so. Amair raised her chin to look down her nose at him, but bobbed her head in reply. He stood, reaching out his arm so they could clasp each other, holding just below the elbows.

"Good luck, Princess," Ebruc said through his teeth, still grinning out towards the crowds.

"And to you, Sir." They let go of each other, taking a few steps back. Amair's world quieted, blocking out the noise of the crowd, even if she could see the citizens jumping in their seats. She watched Ebruc's smug face, still grinning, holding his sword out. She glanced to his hand, noting a tremble in his wrist. Amair smirked, looking back up at Ebruc's eyes, squinting a little, the two watching each other as the world moved like strips of colour around them.

"Go!" she heard the Crier's voice pierce through her mind, garbled as she slowly came back to reality, Ebruc's sword slicing through the air towards her head. She smiled, blocking it quickly, their eyes meeting again as he brought his face too close to hers and she could smell the liquor he must have poured in his coffee.

"They're only letting you do this cause you're the *Princess*," he snarled, his annoying little grin still plastered on his face. Amair let him pull back and took advantage of his momentum, swinging and hitting him hard in the shoulder. He cried out, as she turned and hit him again, this time across the back. He grunted, pulling his sword around with an angry growl, blocked by Amair's sword easily. She could feel the annoyance radiating off him. He tried to push down against her, trying to bring his full height over her and she grinned. She pushed her sword up into his, watching as his wrist twisted back. She narrowed her eyes, watching as he gritted his teeth.

Suddenly he cried out, Amair feeling his sword drop onto the grass between them. Ebruc's eyes widened, just as Amair swung, catching her arm against his breastbone, sending him flying backwards. She winced when his head snapped back against the ground and he laid there for a second. She could hear the crowd counting, and she stood, gripping her sword, waiting. As they called out *ten*, the crowd went wild, one of the ring attendants rushing to hold up Amair's arm, the Crier yelling to announce the winner.

Amair glanced back across the field as one of the nurses splinted her opponent's wrist. She looked down at her feet, taking a deep breath. She slipped out the back to sneak back up into the royal box. Denna waved from where she was chatting with Kenaia in the front row, flipping another thumbs up and Amair laughed, returning the thumbs up.

Amair turned, raising her eyebrows as the crowd erupted with an ear-splitting cheer again. She looked around the ring, trying to figure out what had caught everyone's attention. Her eyes finally landed on a face carrying the same fear it had the first time she had placed a sword in his hands.

"Oh, he's gonna die," she said to no one, shaking her head a little as she stared at Jasper, walking into the ring in full trial gear. An attendant took Amair's helmet and she thanked him, turning with her hands on her hips.

"Out next champion!" the Crier exclaimed, a little too much amusement in his voice for Amair's liking. She glanced at Jasper again, hanging her head as Vaughnessan, the middle son of Chief Torrent, walked into the ring. He raised his sword high, his strong arms flexing and rippling in the glimpses of Skylock sun. Amair looked up as Theo and the King scurried up next to her, all of them pressed into the wooden rail. She crossed her arms in front of her as she watched Vaughnessan slice through the air a few times, warming up.

"What is your brother doing?" the King shook his head, looking down at Amair. Amair smiled tightly, a hand on her hip, letting out a short breath.

"Proving himself, I think."

"He's gonna die."

"Probably."

"Chief Torrent!" the King exclaimed, turning to try to find the other champion's father.

"If he dies," Theo tipped his chin, "would it be disrespectful to put this in the serial?"

"Nope."

"Thank gods," Theo laughed, pulling out his pen.

"Champions, to the ready!"

"Oh dear gods," Amair heard the Queen whisper behind her. They watched as the boys' swords clashed against each other, Queen Kier letting out a scream as Vaughnessan threw the first strike, Jasper narrowly slipping away from the bite of the blade.

"Mom, where are the twins?" Her mom didn't say anything, staring as the swords slicing through the air. "Mom!"

"They were seeing the sheep races." Her mother's voice seemed far away, watching the two boys fighting down in the ring.

The tip of Vaugnessan's sword clipped the slit in Jasper's helmet and he reeled, turning, putting a hand in front of his face. Kier screamed again, lunging towards the edge of their box.

"Do not!" Amair warned her mother, grabbing both her arms, jerking her back. "If you distract him, he will not recover. Let him be." Niall pulled his wife into his arms, the Skylocks and Theodore watching, the rest of the visitors on the edge of their seats as another clang of swords echoed across the grounds.

"I can't watch!" the Queen exclaimed, her dress rustling as she turned to bury her face in her husband's chest.

"My lady—"

"—shh," Amair hushed the attendant holding her dress bag, her eyes trained on her brother as he ducked under another strike from his opponent's sword.

Every sound on the plain dissipated the second Jasper whipped back around and put his foot on Vaugnessan's back, pushing into his unbalance, Vaughnessan fell to the ground, hitting the grass hard enough Amair winced when his chin clapped against the ground. Jasper quickly dropped his knees onto Vaugnessan's back, holding his sword to the back of the young man's neck.

"And that's ten!" the Crier exclaimed, waving the light blue flag, "Jasper Skylock wins the match!"

The crowd erupted in applause, a few people whistling, yelling Jasper's name. Amair smiled as she watched Jasper break into a huge grin, getting up off the Torrent boy, offering his hand to help him to his feet. Vaugnessan laughed a little, taking it and letting Jasper help him up, clapping Jasper on the back. One of the game attendants walked into the ring, bowing slightly to Jasper who bowed back. The games attendant grabbed Jasper's hand and lifted it high into the air, the crowd cheering again. Amair shook her head at the look on Jasper's face as he walked out of the ring, Skylock citizens reaching out to pat him on the back, people still calling out to their Prince.

"You're an idiot," Amair called to him as he stood under the Sovereign platform to bow to them, surrounded by people wanting to congratulate him.

His face fell a little, "I—"

"—and I am very proud of you." Jasper broke into an even bigger grin than before. "Mom's gonna kill you, though," Amair laughed, turning to her attendant to let her help her down off the steps. She glanced behind her at Jasper's face as their mother turned out from their father's chest, already raising a hand and pointing down at him. Amair couldn't hear her over the roar of the crowd as two more champions walked into the ring, but she was pretty sure she could picture what she was saying.

Amair and the attendant weaved through the crowds, a few people reaching out to shake Amair's hand.

"Amair!"

"Domiko," Amair smiled at the familiar face. "Hi."

"How are you? You looked great out there."

"Thank you!" Amair glanced at the attendant. "Domiko, I'll be right back, I just need to change."

"Oh, of course. I'll be around here, if you have some time after."

"Absolutely, I'll see you shortly." Domiko bowed his head to her, and gave her one more smile before she turned away, ducking into the Skylock Family tent.

Lydia waved to Amair as the attendant walked her into the large dressing tent. One of the attendants was already pulling on Amair's armour by the time they got to Lydia, who waved the others away. She carefully removed each piece of Amair's leather, inspecting each one, finding only a singular new scratch on her shoulder pad.

"No one stands a chance against you," Lydia smiled, pulling off her chest piece, putting it aside as Amair pulled off her linen top.

"I got lucky."

Lydia grabbed Amair's face with one hand. "Luck has nothing to do with it." She released the Princess, grabbing her blue corset. "Pants, off." Amair shimmied out of them, watching the attendants around them scurry back and forth, grabbing pieces and passing things off in a flurry.

"We should do petticoats first," Lydia murmured to herself. Amair raised her arms, stepped as she was told, watched Lydia and one of the other attendants fluff out the dress, stood taller as the light top was tied into place over the soft white shirt, puffy sleeves poking through the velvet vest's arms.

Lydia pulled Amair's sheath onto her back, letting Amair throw her sword back into it. She shrugged a few times, pushing the sword into its comfortable spot. "Good?" Lydia asked. Amair nodded, smiling into the mirror. "Still don't know what to think about your sword and this beautiful, *traditional dress*." She pouted a little, pinning the light blue tartan shawl to Amair's shoulder, fixing the silver brooch with Amair's crest on it, tucking part of it into the back of her skirt, hiding it under the vest.

"It's who I am," Amair winked at her as she draped the fabric carefully. "I promise only to fight someone in it if provoked."

"You will give me an aneurysm, I swear to the gods." Amair laughed, jumping off the small box.

"Your brother is a fierce warrior," an attendant along the side mentioned, shaking out Amair's pants.

"He had a good trainer," Lydia smirked behind Amair, fixing her tartan. Amair just smiled, raising her arms to let Lydia fluff out the tulle sleeves. Lydia dropped Amair's shoes, steadying her arms as she picked up the layers of tulle, finding her feet and slipping them on, one of the attendants swooping down to tie them around her ankles.

"Well, that should do it," Lydia patted Amair's shoulder. "Go remind them why the Skylocks run this kingdom," she called after the Princess, watching her swish out of the tent.

"You are quite the sight, Princess," Domiko smiled, offering Amair his arm. "Kingdom Tartan, not your clan's."

"The only thing the Skylock Clan Tartan is used for is a few pillows in my father's study. This is a sign of impartiality."

"Jasper was great out there today," Domiko grinned, and she guessed he was thinking of the young man in the ring. "You must be proud."

"Very." Amair grinned. "I taught him how to use that sword."

"Warrior brother of the warrior Queen—"

"—I'm not Queen," Amair reminded firmly, side-eyeing him.

"Oh. Of course. I didn't…I didn't mean—"

"—it's alright," Amair dropped her gaze to the bottom of her dress.

"So," she heard the shift in Domiko's voice, the tug of gossip that always followed him, "have you heard that the Emperor of Keene believes there is another land across the sea?"

"Great, and if there is, he should *leave it be*." Amair snorted, glancing at Domiko. "He can barely run his own realm. Maybe he should focus on that before invading and terrorizing yet another…or perhaps he is already forgetting history."

Domiko started to laugh but looked around him, seeing if anyone was listening. "There's been a rumour."

"There have been many rumours in my years in this court."

"That tensions are brewing—"

"—Domiko," Amair stopped, turning to him, "I am not the little girl you remember," she threatened coolly, "I cannot discuss rumours with the son of a War Chief."

Domiko swallowed a little, nodding slowly. "Yes, your highness."

She softened her warning eyes, turning and letting him continue escorting her across the grounds. They waved to people who passed, children running by, tripping over their feet and squealing with laughter. Amair looked up to one of the bridges, noticing the extra guards, keeping their watchful eye above the festivities.

"So…excited for the feast?"

"Am I ever," Amair laughed, the touch of tension finally falling away. "Food, music, all six Chiefs *and* War Chiefs yelling at each other across my feasting hall? It's the best part of the year."

"Weren't they here for your birthday?"

"Everyone tends to be on their good behaviour for the Oighre's birthday party."

"Good point."

"And only your father was here representing the War Chiefs side of things."

"Ah, so we're in for a *real* treat this time."

"You know it!" Amair laughed, noticing her brother talking excitedly with Kenaia.

"Jasper!"

"Ama!" he exclaimed, grinning, patting Kenaia's shoulder and jogging over to his sister.

Domiko glanced at the Princess. "I'll take my leave of you, Princess. See you tonight?"

"Tonight," she bowed her head to him, eyes on her brother. Domiko paused, leaning over and kissing Amair's cheek.

"Enjoy the Games, Princess."

Jasper pulled her into a tight hug. Amair smiled, pulling back and patting his cheek, swiping at the blood drying on his cheekbone. "What did mom say?"

"That she's happy I'm alive."

"Oh. Hm." Amair raised an eyebrow. "That's it?"

"And that if I ever tried something like that again I wouldn't be."

"Ah. That sounds more like our mother."

"Have you seen Theo?"

"I had to change, I thought I left him with mom and dad?"

"Mm, he wasn't there when mom was talking to me."

"Smart boy, get out of the line of disaster."

"Yeah, yeah," Jasper laughed, rolling his eyes.

"Did you need him?"

Jasper smiled brighter. "Not particularly just…finding friends. It's the Feast of Skylock, we're meant to be enjoying ourselves."

"Understandable. Now go, dress. I should not be the only Skylock child wearing tartan. And send Theo if you find him."

"Yes, ma'am." Jasper pretended to salute her, laughing, ambling in the direction Amair had arrived from. Amair chuckled to herself, shaking her head a little, watching him stop, turning back to her.

"Thank you."

"For what?"

"Teaching me." Amair smiled, nodding.

"Of course, love. Now," she pointed, "go. Change."

Jasper laughed, in a way that she wasn't used to. "I'll be right back."

"Ama," Kenaia smiled, Amair glancing after Domiko. "You were wonderful, as always. Champion of Skylock."

"It was nothing."

"I found something that made me think of you." Kenaia opened their satchel, fetching a tin and pulling something from it. "There," they smiled, fixing a blue thistle under the old brooch holding Amair's tartan in place, "a reminder to your people that you, dear Oighre," they brushed a hand over Amair's shoulder, "are a warrior. As sharp and beautiful as our national symbol."

Amair glanced from the thistle, up to Kenaia's sharp green eyes. She did not have anything to say, but bowed her head a little to them. "Thank you, Kenny."

"Now…I'm going to go and try the axe throwing." They winked. "Still looking for my weapon of choice…just in case."

Amair laughed, waving as they headed off. She felt someone behind her but it was an immediate comfort. She turned, smiling up at Theo. "Hello, you."

"Hello, Ama." He bowed a little, reaching for her hand. "After that display…well, I feel I am not worthy."

"You've already been at the end of my sword," she laughed, "you survived it."

"I pity those who do not." He offered her his arm. "What should we see first? Now that Jasper has cleared himself."

"I have duties, as Oighre, today…" She laughed, spotting someone thrown down in the wrestling match. "I want to stop and watch the dancers, though. The clans do much more dancing than we do here." She paused, thinking of her words, bobbing her head automatically as people stopped to bow to her. "I'm very proud of Jasper."

"As am I."

"He never would have done that a year ago…it may have crossed his mind, but I doubt he had the confidence to go through with it."

"You bring out the good in people."

They stopped at the animal pens, Amair unable to help herself from leaning down to pet the variety of animals. "I'm surprised how much it reminds me of the games back home…" Theo admitted, glancing down at her as she placed a baby goat back into the pen, watching it bleat. "I figured there would be some…crazy, royal element here."

"The Skylocks were just another clan before they were chosen to be the Sovereign clan," Amair shrugged. "Today…though we aren't meant to show any kind of favour, and we do a lot of the funding and organizing…I feel much more like an equal."

"You ready for tonight?"

Amair sighed. "Every time I have to do something without my brother, I simultaneously feel like I'm honouring him and losing a piece of him…so…we shall see…"

- CHAPTER LIV -

As the sun set, the goblets filled.

"Theodore," Amair smiled, glancing out the window at the dark sky, "this is Domiko MacLine, first son of War Chief Flora."

"Nice to meet you!" Theo reached a hand to Domiko, who grabbed him into a hug. Theo's eyes widened, glancing down at Amair as he was gripped tightly. *'Super drunk'* Amair mouthed, chuckling. She pressed a hand to Domiko's back, coaxing him off Theo.

"You should find your table, Dom," she suggested, rubbing his back, holding him as he swayed a bit. "Dinner and the show will begin soon."

"Right," he hiccupped. Amair laughed, catching an attendant's eye who had to bite their lip to keep from laughing as they walked over.

"Could you bring Sir MacLine to the Flora table?"

"Of course, my lady." The attendant bowed a little, a tiny snicker escaping as they wrapped a supportive arm around Domiko.

"Untillllll next timeeeeeee, Princessssssss!" Domiko exclaimed, giggling a little as he was half-dragged away.

"Ah, the fun, drunk, debauchery of the clan reunions," Amair laughed and Theo cautiously wrapped an arm around her. "We should find our seats, too."

"Certainly."

"We should do this more often."

"Oh, I'm so in," Theo snorted.

"I'm surprised they put you in Skylock tartan," she mused as Theo navigated through the increasingly drunk group of Skylish people.

"Gaelen was worried it wouldn't be proper to have me in Glenn tartan if I was sitting at the Family table." He laughed. "Then he spent two days fretting that I was supposed to be sitting at the Glenn table, so he had a Glenn tartan delivered, and checked three times with the Queen on where I would be sitting – news flash, it was the Family table...all three times."

"Aw, poor Gaelen," she laughed, bowing to her father as they reached their table. "He cares so much."

"He just knows me making a fool of myself reflects on you."

"And him," she reminded him as he pulled her large, high backed chair out, letting her settle, pulling her tartan back to keep from sitting on it.

"Ama," her father grinned, patting her head.

"Papa," she chuckled, watching him leaning slightly to one side, dropping into his throne. "Having fun?"

"Pleased to say I can still," he pointed at her, blinking a few times, "beat Glasslight in a chugging contest."

"That's wonderful, dad...you did it against all the chiefs, didn't you?"

"It's the Feast of Skylock, it's only fair to keep no favouritism."

Amair tried not to laugh, hearing Theo snorting as he sat beside her. "Should I..." She caught her breath, trying not to laugh. "Should I make the announcement, dad?"

"Maybe that's...." he leaned onto his hand, looking far away, fiddling with his beard, "a good idea."

"Yeah," she patted his shoulder, collecting her skirts, Theo pulling her chair back out as she stood, "thought so." She glanced down at Theo, who winked at her. She held a hand out to him, earning a slightly confused look, and shook her hand until he took it. Leaning onto him, she bundled her skirt and stepped up onto the chair, making sure she was balanced. Theo's eyes widened, feeling her hand on the top of his head as she pushed up to her feet. He instinctively reached out, holding her strong calf, keeping her steady. She let go of her skirt, clasping her hands in front of herself as she looked around at the people, clearing her throat.

"Hello everyone!" It was sung back to her, the sound of chairs creaking as they turned to look at her, the joyful music still playing. "Seeing as you have all managed to get my level-headed father piss drunk," the crowd laughed, a few cheering, raising their glasses in toasts, making Amair laugh, "I have taken on the very important role of welcoming you officially to the Feast of Skylock!" She yelled the last word, earning more bellowing from the crowd, a few of them knocking their hands against the table. "Not that any of you will end up remembering this in the morning." They all laughed. "This is my first time giving a speech like this – to all of you, all my support, and it means the world to me that you would lend an ear…it will not be the last time you hear my voice, and I…I am glad the first time you hear me is on such an amazingly joyous occasion. Thank you very much for being here, celebrating the very important day where we all got over ourselves and figured out how to cooperate," she glanced up, smirking, "most of the time."

Theo laughed, watching the mayhem around them as the clan tables rattled with all the excitement, grinning at Amair soaking up the energy. "Thank you for bringing all your best products for this feast…including the ones that have been *distilled* and *brewed*," she glanced at the many glasses filled with brilliantly coloured alcohols that were immediately raised high. "This feast is about celebrating what it means to be Skylish and to me…that is coming together no matter who you are, where you have come from, and celebrating that in this moment, on this day, you feel like one of us. And I believe everyone who wants to be one of us shall be. Today, people of so many backgrounds came together to celebrate the old traditions, and the old language was heard on so many lips, but we celebrate something even more important in my eyes: possibility. Possibility of what may be. Thank you, for accepting me as a part of that possibility." She licked her lips.

"Well without further ado…if only to soak up your drink…let the Feast begin!" They cheered again, the music rising with the energy, the doors around the room flying open as dozens of servers streamed in, arms piled with plates.

Amair smiled, nodding once as she watched the first plates set down, turning to jump off her chair. Her body lurched to one side, tripping on the edge of her skirt, eyes widening as she fell to the side. She felt her body moving through the air, her ears ringing, but was swooped suddenly to one side. As strong arms wrapped around her, she blinked, looking up at a grinning Theo, hair falling slightly into his face.

"Still falling for me?"

"My hero, she laughed. "Good to know I have someone to catch me."

"Always," he whispered, his thumb rubbing small circles on her arm. She bit her lip, eyes widening as she heard people clapping. Looking over her shoulder, she watched the crowd cheering drunkenly, laughing as she waved to them. Theo helped her to her feet as attendants set plates down in front of them.

"Skylock: land of *hearty* meals," he laughed, looking over his plate filled with colourful potatoes, meats, a small, round pie, everything smothered in brown sauce.

"Yeah..." Amair laughed, moving things around her plate with her fork. "Oh! Look! A vegetable!" She stabbed it, pulling back a thin, blue carrot. Theo laughed, searching his plate and coming out with an orange carrot.

"Ah good, a vitamin," he laughed, the two of them tapping their carrots together like glasses. He watched Amair's eyes scanning over the crowd as she ate, digging into her small pie, both of them cheering quietly to find green vegetables smothered in more sauce tumble out of it.

"Traditional Skylock meals..." She glanced over at Theo. "I think I'll be requesting salads for both meals tomorrow."

"Good thing we figured out how to grow literally anything more than potatoes–"

"–and carrots–"

"–and carrots here," he chuckled. "I concur, salads for the rest of the week." Amair leaned forward as something thumped on their table, spotting Evander sleeping next to his small dessert plate, Alec stealing his berry crumble.

"Ah, the first one to go."

"And he's not even drinking."

"Yeah, starting to wonder how long my dad's gonna last," she whispered to Theo, both of them turning to look at the King half slumped onto the Queen's shoulder.

"What about you?"

"I'm a bit better at...pacing myself."

"Oh yeah?"

"Mhm," she smirked.

"Wanna get out of here?"

"Staff staircase straight to my room?"

"Sounds like a plan," he whispered, taking her hand under the table. Amair leaned over onto the table, grimacing as bright purple berry juice splashed onto the front of her dress, looking down the table.

"Jasper!" She couldn't help the giggle as Theo squeezed her thigh. "You're in charge!"

"What?" he called back, but Amair was already out of her chair, foolishly wiping at the berry stain on her velvet vest, a dribble running down her throat. She pushed on the hidden door just outside the ballroom, and Theo pushed her into the stone wall as the door swung shut. His hands wrapped tightly on her waist, kissing her neck, making her jump as his tongue brushed over berry juice, an arm wrapping around her waist as he leaned her close to him.

"We have an early morning," she whispered, holding him tighter.

"Then make the most of the moment."

Ink & Crown: The Princess Serial

by Sir Theodore Crawford

The Princess participated, for the seventh year in a row, in the Skylock Games to kick off the Feast of Skylock. As she stepped into the ring, she swiftly reminded the cheering crowd why she remains the Champion of Skylock, taking out her opponent, Ebruc Hill in the Duel Ring in less than three minutes.

The surprise of the morning came when Prince Jasper, age sixteen, took to the ring. Allegedly trained by his sister since he was old enough to hold up a sword (which a castlesource puts at about age twelve), she made sure he "knew just enough to keep him from dying if he ever did something stupid" and tended to focus more on his ability to throw a punch than to swing a sword. Whatever training she did give seems to have done the trick, though, because after signing up in secret, he appeared in the Duel Ring, much to the shock of his sister and the rest of the royal family. As the King and Queen held each other, the Princess and the rest of the crowd were on the edge of their seats as they watched the Prince battle Sir Vaughnessan Torrent.

And to nearly everyone's surprise, the Prince did not just survive: he won his match - and a scolding from his mother.

Princess Amair made her way to the Royal Tent and

emerged free of her armour to don a gown in Skylock's colours with a Skylock Vest, draped in a Skylock Tartan. Never one to let a dress slow her down, she dragged me all across the grounds to watch the heavyweight championships, which she got the honour of opening by throwing the first Cliffstone - with an arm strong enough to make the target a little difficult to reach. She notes that she would have participated in other events but "was banned from the archery events, and the knife throwing two years ago after beating everyone too many times." The Princess and I also stopped to award top prizes to livestock, chickens, and produce larger than I have ever seen, and to watch the sheep dog events, which her dog Lupa very much wanted to run in and join. She dropped the starting point for the Sky Ball game between the team of Clan people and the Castle Team. We also caught up with the Twin Princes as they competed in one of the children's event, the Sheep Races. Prince Alec fell off his sheep in the first three meters, but Prince Evander made up for it by placing second.

As the games closed, we proceeded to the Feast. The Princess kept her National Dress, and we indulged in hearty, traditional Skylish foods and drinks. The Princess may be more well known for her abilities in the duelling ring than with her words, but she impressed everyone with her opening speech, welcoming the guests to the Feast and reflecting on what they have come through and what was ahead. With the feast officially opened, this writer believes the healing that begun with the New Year can truly begin to be solidified...and perhaps that is what coming together is truly about. Not the awards and medals, nor the silly poems we try to recall from childhood memorization books, but the reuniting with old friends we see but once a year, and the reminder that we are all one beautiful people, working for one beautiful thing.

Happy Feast of Skylock, everyone.

- Sir Theodore Crawford, Staff Writer, Special Liaison Reporter to The Palace, Man of Letters

- CHAPTER LV -

Theo was nervous, walking down the hall with the visiting journalist. The pounding headache of his hangover was not helping.

"Princess Amair," Theo bowed to her, noticing her wink at him, "may I introduce Mr. Laek Arvenium, Foreign Affairs Reporter at the Blue Times, in Waiwhe."

"Oh, I'm Foreign Affairs now," Amair laughed, reaching a hand to the reporter. "It's nice to meet you."

"And you, Princess," he bowed, kissing her hand. "It was either that or popular culture, and I think you have far surpassed that. You are going to be Queen, after all."

"You make a good point, sir."

"I brought a gift, for you, with me. From the whole staff at my paper."

"Oh, you didn't have to—" He placed a small box in her hands and she blushed, thanking him. She pulled on the orange bow, passing it to Theo as she popped open the brown box.

"Oh, Mr. Arvenium," she whispered, pulling a silver chain with a small, off-white pendant on it. "It's beautiful..."

"It's hand carved from a mango seed. One of the ladies who helps clean our office makes them, so we commissioned one. It has the symbol of Endra, your patron saint, on it."

"Theo, help me?" She passed the bracelet to him, holding her wrist out as he helped with the clasp. He noticed the visiting reporter smiling at the two of them, eyes flicking between the Writer and the Princess.

"This is incredible, thank you. And to all your paper, and the lady who carved it...what's her name? Maybe we can put it out with our weekly dress round up..."

"Her name is Manny, your highness. Manny Jexell."

"Theo–"

"–writing it down," he smiled, notebook in hand.

"Wonderful. Well, Mr. Arvenium, shall we sit?" She gestured towards the table, walking slowly.

"Yes, that would be lovely."

"I had an attendant bring my favourite tea up."

"I'll pour," he smiled.

"Oh, you're a guest, you don't have–"

He picked up the tea pot, setting out the cups and she chuckled as she sat. "In Waiwhe, the guest always pours the tea. Gratitude is best poured out – not in words, but in action."

"Well. Thank you. And I agree…though I'm surprised a writer would say so."

He chuckled as he set the pot down, reaching for his notebook. Amair smiled to herself, thinking of Theo doing the same so many time and in some ways it made her more comfortable.

She still wanted to either run and hide, or vomit on the table.

"So. The Princess Amair serial has been picked up in three other Kingdoms. How does that feel?" the foreign reporter asked. Amair gulped a little, glancing over at Theo lounging on the window seat.

"I…a little strange. It's been um…a little weird, being the centre of attention. I have always been…a good background actor."

"And yet, people knew who you were."

"I'm a royal, the only daughter of a great King…of course people knew of me."

"Why do *you* think the serial has garnered so much popularity?"

"Do you mean outside Skylock?"

"Outside, and in."

Amair tipped her head as she thought, pulling slightly on her fingers. "It's a nice...easy look, inside the castle, I think." She shrugged. "People are often...bombarded, with bad news. This is...lighter, in some ways."

"I have a quote here, from a woman in Waiwhe, may I read it to you?"

"Certainly."

"Alright, she said to me, 'This girl will be a Queen. She won't be *my* Queen, but knowing her makes even me connected to Skylock.' And a young man I met yesterday at my inn here, in the royal village, told me, 'We love her, and it's so nice to actually get to know the person who will lead you.'"

Amair was blushing, glancing over at Theo on the window seat. "Well...I'm glad, it was meant to...introduce me in some ways, it does feel like I'm talking with my people...Theodore has crafted some beautiful articles, so I'm sure that helps."

"Does it make you miss your brother?"

Amair sucked in, biting her cheek. "Y..." She looked down, the grey light catching a few of the sparkles on her purple dress. "It does." She forced a chuckle. "I like to think he's reading them, though. I've um...I've left a copy of each article at his grave." Theo raised an eyebrow. "The Lost Ones liked to read to each other so...I can kind of picture the way they used to...to sit around, Johanna cross legged in front of the fireplace, Dylan and Layton lounging in chairs as they read. So, I uh...I like to think that's what they're doing."

The reporter smiled sadly, nodding as he wrote something down. "What is something Theo has not yet published about you that people should know?"

"I don't know, he's been pretty good at getting inside my head." The visiting reporter chuckled as Amair thought. "Does a funny story work?"

"Absolutely!"

"I once accidentally set the Children's Room on fire."

"How on earth did you manage that?" Theo blurted, glancing at Laek.

"I was practicing my archery...and proceeded to break a candle stick and light the carpet on fire." She looked over at Theo. "My aim hasn't always been as good as it is now..." He raised an eyebrow, nodding slowly. "Anyway, you can still see the scorch marks on the rug in there. I freaked out and ran *out* of the room, tracked down Dylan – because I knew Layton and Johanna would scold me – and we put it out. Acted like nothing had happened...I was...I don't know, *maybe* six? Dylan and I never told anyone.

I can...I can probably release him from this one secret." Theo watched her face falter, shaking her head sharply as she put her pleasant smile back in place.

"Any other secrets?"

She lifted her chin, smirking, but there was a warning in it. "You got this week's secret."

"Fair enough." She tipped her head a little, watching him scribble into his notepad, his writing quick and choppy, unlike Theo's long, elegant strokes.

"Oh, and last thing. We've been getting reprints, which is wonderful, but we have been hearing and getting letters that some people aren't quite getting all of the words, since we publish in one language, but some...traditional words are kept because of their significance."

"You're talking about *Oighre*? Right?" The salt-and-pepper haired man nodded encouragingly. "It just means heir, in our old language. We speak the language of the Land, after...the Great Chaos, but um...we've tried to hold on and revive the old language. Some words have stuck. I've been learning it my whole life, I'm close to fluent, but yeah...Oighre translates directly to heir. And we use it for heir to the sovereign throne. Different words are used for the heirs to the clans. But yes, heir to the sovereign throne but um... I'd say it's more than that. Oighre is a promise to my people that I am learning all I can to be ready for the sovereign throne."

"And that's you?"

"And that's me."

"And are you proud? To be...*Oighre*?" His garbling of the word didn't faze her, but the question hit her. Theo noticed her still completely, lips open. She looked down, pulling her eyes away from the visiting reporter and down into her hands, where they had been folded in her lap. She gripped them together, her nails digging into the back. Theo swung his legs down from the window ledge, sitting up, hands on the edge of the pillow. He opened his mouth, ready to intervene, when she looked back up finally.

"Becoming Oighre was terrifying. It was...it was not my fate, it was not the Kingdom's fate. Layton, my brother, he was incredible." Her blue eyes, with the remarkable dark birthmark in one, shone under what Theo tried to decipher to be tears or something deeper. "But the past few months...I've learned so much. I love my people."

"So?"

Whatever tears had been in her eyes, it was just fire now. "I am so, *so* proud to be Skylock's Oighre."

- CHAPTER LVI -

"Prince Jasper, Prince Kylo?" a castle messenger called from the door.

"Yeah?" they both called.

"I have summons from the Oighre."

"What?" Jasper looked over at Kylo who reflected the confusion on Jasper's face. "Has she really stooped to *summoning* us–"

"–please, take the summons and you can follow me." The boys got up, opening the crisp envelopes with Amair's messy calligraphy on the front. They pulled out matching cards, someone else's cleaner calligraphy requesting their presence. Kylo turned his over a few times.

"There's no room here?" he said, confused, reading. "I don't think there's even a wing"

The messenger smiled. "That is where I come in."

"Ah…"

"Just…follow me, your highnesses."

Kylo looked up at Jasper, running a hand over his curls. "Lead the way," his big brother nodded.

"Very good." The messenger turned, tucking his letter tray under his arm, and walked down the hall. With one last look at each other, Jasper grabbed his tie off the chair and walked along behind the messenger.

"Where are we?" Kylo whispered as they ducked through a short doorway neither of the boys had ever noticed before, turning down a new corridor.

"No idea," Jasper whispered back. They both looked at the messenger's back, expecting him to pipe up, but he was quiet. Jasper was shaking his head a little, looking around the corridor. The castle they knew – the brilliant corridors lined with windows and paintings and arches – melted away and dark, stony walls replaced them, candles lining them. Kylo looked up into the shorter ceilings, trying to make out something carved into the dark stone.

"We're here," the messenger announced as they approached the end of the unusual corridor. A door was there, unlike any of the other doors in the castle. The messenger knocked, three sharp knocks.

"That's not the castle kno–" The door swung open and Kylo cut himself off, reaching over to grab Jasper's wrist, holding tight.

"Go ahead boys." The messenger grinned. "And congratulations." They were more confused now, but Jasper led his brother into the room full of warm light. He had to duck a little through the short door.

"Hey, you two," Amair smiled inside, standing at a circular table. Jasper looked around, his eyes falling on friends, some the boys had not seen since before The Lost Ones' funeral. Everyone looked a little confused as they leaned back against the tall backs of their chairs.

"Now can you tell us what's going on?" Arthur asked, looking up at Amair. She smiled. The door closed tightly, everyone turning their heads to glance at it, and swinging back to look at the Princess.

"Thank you for coming everyone," Amair smiled, standing tall, her eyes crinkling. "I know you probably aren't sure where we are right now.

"Welcome to the old wing. From the original castle." She walked around the table, looking at each person slowly. "This room was where the first Skylock King met with his six closest friends, and they built our Kingdom.

"Welcome to my Inner Circle." Jasper's eyes widened, a smile creeping onto his lips. He glanced across the table at Denna, a matching smile on her lips "Every heir finds their inner circle as they prepare themselves to be sovereign. My closest advisors, plus my knight, who will eventually become Knight General. When I am crowned, you will be the castle's side of the Council, along with the Chiefs and elected Council people."

Amair's face was soft as she thought through her words. "I was in my brother's Inner Circle. So luckily, for what feels the first time, I actually kind of know what we do here.

"But this is *my* Inner Circle. Not my brother's. I have agonized over who is meant to be here. Because you are here to be…confidantes. Anything that happens in this room, or someday in the Council room, it stays here. You are my advisors. You help me make the big decisions. But more importantly, the ones that seem small. Because every decision we make will affect *my* people. Who are now *our* people.

"I have this whole…speech, thing, prepared, about why I picked each of you. I know…I know almost all of you know each other, I just…"

"Go ahead, Ama," Kenaia laughed.

"Okay, okay. So, my darling brothers. Jasper, because he seems to be the only person willing to yell at me when I need it. And Kylo…for his mind and his kindness.

"Shehada, the girl who made me feel beautiful every day…who had the courage to leave the comfort of the castle for her own adventure at university, and one of the kindest, and *smartest*, people I know.

"Denna, who slaps sense into me whenever I need it, and has the diplomatic poise that every other ambassador craves.

"Kenaia…Kenny…the person who ran through the woods with me and showed me the power of not following the rules, and somehow always manages to find the beauty in everything…in everyone.

"Gio. Layton's friend. Strong hands, stronger mind. Never lets anything get in his way. The only other person I know who has the experience of an inner circle. Who told me I was doing a good job, whenever I felt behind. Who wears his disability with pride.

"And Aramis. The *almost*-Knight," everyone chuckled, "who realized there were other things waiting for him. The boy who may know the castle better than anyone, since he's worked just about *every* position within its walls.

"And my dear Arthur. Who is always ready to protect me, no matter what that means. My knight in shining armour, who misses The Lose Ones just as much as I do. Who has been gentle with me, and given me some of my best scars.

"Thick or thin. I trust you all. With every ounce of me. Now I need you to help me shake things up."

Ink & Crown:
The Princess Serial

by Sir Theodore Crawford

Princess Amair has taken another important step in securing her position as Skylock's Oighre. Late last night, word arrived that the Princess had chosen her Inner Circle, and the announcement papers have been distributed throughout the palace. The main members of the Oighre's Inner Circle work as advisers, along with their personal Knight who will someday serve as Knight General. The Circle will also soon begin training under the current Elected and Sovereign Councils. After the Oighre's coronation as Sovereign, the members of the Inner Circle will be sworn in as the new Sovereign's Council. Without further ado, the new Inner Circle.

Lady Denna Raziel

Lady Denna is no stranger to anyone in Skylock. Lady Raziel was raised in the palace, the daughter of an economist and a tailor. She and AMair have been close as they grew up together. Lady Raziel is currently serving as a diplomat, on assignment to Forra. She will continue in her posting for the time being, travelling back and forth to support the Oighre.

Lady Shehada Westfall

Lady Shehada grew up in Glenn Province, and moved to the castle with a family friend when she was fourteen, getting a job at castle. She was initially a room server, but after meeting the Princess, joined her attendants team and was Lead Attendant , confidante, and friend to the Princess after just a few months. Lady Shehada left the castle last year and is currrently pursuing a Policy and Political Science degree at Torrent University. She will travel back and forth to support the Oighre.

Serd Kenaia Marksmun

Serd Kenaia grew up in the castle. They are the child of Head Gardener Lazaran Marksmun. They are currently training in the gardens as a florist and garden tender.

Sir Aramis Diabolyn

Sir Aramis moved to the castle from Glasslight Province to train to be a Knight. After failing out of the training program, he chose to stay at the palace, filling various roles and befriending many staff, and also the Princess.

Sir Gio Valence

Gio was raised on a farm just outside the Royal Village. He lost his leg in an accident at the age of seven. He was friends with the late Prince Layton and served in his

Circle with the Princess. Sir Gio splits his time between specialty training with the palace guard, and helping on his parents farm.

Sir Arthur Moores

My fellow Skylish people will recognize the Moores name. Sir Arthur was raised in the palace, son of a Knight Trainer and a Chef, and the younger brother of The Late Lady Johanna Moores, a Lost One. The Late Lady Johanna held the same role previously, serving the late Prince Layton. As a longtime friend of the Oighre, Sir Arthur has been training for many years, and is considered her most valued protector.

The Princes Jasper and Kylo have also joined her Circle.

I know all of you will help me in welcoming the new Inner Circle of Skylock. As these bright, young minds move into their new roles supporting our Oighre, they will serve a crucial role in creating the future of our realm. The Princess has been unable to comment on her selection process, but as soon as I am able, her take will be coming to you all.

May the gods guide and protect them all.

- Sir Theodore Crawford, Staff Writer, Special Liaison Reporter to The Palace, Man of Letters

- CHAPTER LVII -

The moon was shining from behind a shroud of clouds passing fat across the skies. Amair crushed the note in her hand that had been hidden in a book since her birthday. The second note sat pressed against it, the ink no doubt running in her sweating palm.

Amair pulled her hood up, shielding herself from the late night wind whipping at her and the eyes of a delivery carriage passing on the road.

She turned as something scraped behind her, only for a hand to wrap around her throat, and a sack pulled down over her head.

***

"Has anyone seen Amair?" Theo asked, popping his head into the boys' room.

"Nope," Jasper shrugged from behind his book.

"Did you check her room?" Alec asked. Theo raised an eyebrow, snorting.

"No, I skipped that step and came straight to you dorks," he shot back, making the twins laugh.

"In or out?" Kylo asked, hunched over a schoolbook, tapping the end of his pencil furiously against the pages. Theo glanced at Jasper, who nodded encouragingly.

"I guess Amair can wait," Theo grinned, catching the ball that Alec threw his way, stepping into the boys' room.

They spent the afternoon chatting, laughing. Kylo was stressing, reviewing his notes, having promised Amair to challenge his science test to better focus on his politics now that he had joined the circle.

"His foul mood," Jasper whispered, "is also because he's trying to power through a bunch of stuff. We got word that Nusiq is finally supposed to be coming for a visit and he doesn't want to have to spend the whole time doing homework."

The day passed quietly and Theo finally slipped out of the room before dinner to change. He noticed Lupa curled in front of Amair's door, nose sitting against the slit under the door. Theo knelt down next to the dog, running his hand over her fluffy fur.

"Did she lock you out bubba?" Theo scratched under Lupa's chin. The dog whined a little, leaning into Theo's hand as he scratched behind her ear. Theo glanced at the door again, patting Lupa's head one more time. "I'm sure she'll let you in soon." Lupa gave him one last forlorn look, pressing her eyes together in that way that she did, like she knew what you'd said, and turned to put her nose back against Amair's door. Theo watched her door a second longer, turning and walking away.

***

"Your majesty," a knight knelt next to the King. Theo looked up from his breakfast, watching the two whisper furiously together.

"Are you sure?" Theo heard the King ask sombrely.

"Yes, sir," the knight whispered hoarsely.

"Thank you, you can go." The knight nodded, standing to bow a little, and rushing out the side door.

"Darnan?" the King called to one of the servers, who ran over. "Could you fetch Knight General Ephenezer?"

"Of course, your majesty." The server bowed a little and raced for the door.

"Dad—"

"—not now Jasper," his father raised a hand, silencing him. Theo and Jasper shared a look as the King ushered one of the guards at the door over, the two of them turning to watch the urgent movement of their lips. The Queen leaned forwards, her shoulders tightening under her shawl. The doors swung open and Theo noticed Evander jump, bumping the table, liquid in all the goblets shaking.

Moritz strode in, his eyes locked on the King. Theo stretched, trying to catch the look on the Knight General's face but he moved too fast. He bowed hurriedly to the King and Queen, rushing over to kneel beside the

King's throne. The boys watched as the adults whispered, talking fast. The King shook his hand, the Queen clutching at her chest.

"I'll be back with more, sir," Ephenezer finally said aloud, getting up. He looked over at the concern imbedded on the faces of the Writer and the Princes, and sighed. "You should probably keep them informed, your majesties." Ephenezer bobbed his head to the boys, leaving as quickly as he had arrived. The King sighed, and looked around at everyone. He put a hand on his chest and for a moment, Theo though he looked like he may pass out.

"Amair is missing."

His ears rang.

Theo jumped out of his chair and it screeched, tipping into an attendant's hands. He heard Jasper call his name, but it didn't register.

"What do you mean missing?" Jasper asked, but Theo turned a corner, hand on his stomach, struggling to breathe as he stumbled through the corridor. He found himself in front of a long line of darkening windows, and fell back into the wall, his vision blurring.

"Good gods, Theo, breathe, man!" Jasper exclaimed, suddenly next to him, gripping his shoulders.

"I wasn't…I wasn't with her, I left her alone…I…I was with you and the boys…" Theo had a hand on his chest, trying to ground himself.

"Theo! They think she was taken last night! It wouldn't have mattered!"

"But we wouldn't have taken so long to know—"

"—Theodore!" Jasper was almost yelling, holding tight on to the back of his neck, "you can't help her like this!"

"I'm a writer, she needs more than that—"

"—no." Jasper shook his head. "We will get her out of this." Theo's eyes were wide, staring at Jasper, who stared back, soft yet determined.

"What do we do?"

Theo was suddenly reminded that Jasper was a Skylock, trained by his sister, a look passing through his eyes that scared him. "Follow me. The circle's not just about politics."

- CHAPTER LVIII -

Jasper pointe, "You know Arthur." The young knight reached out to grasp arms with Theo, acknowledging Jasper.

"And…you're going to help us get Amair?"

"She is my future Queen…but she's my best friend first." Arthur was nodding furiously. "Of course I'm going to get her."

"We're coming with you."

"We?" Arthur and Theo asked simultaneously, equally shocked, glancing at each other before staring at Jasper.

"Well I'm not staying behind," Jasper shook his head. "And Theo, it's time for your first adventure."

"I…"

"You're in love with an Oighre." He smiled. "Specifically, *this* Oighre. Adventure is part of the deal."

"And suicide rescue missions?"

"A typical weekday," Jasper snorted. "And besides, it's not like we're going in alone." He rolled his eyes, looking back at Arthur, who was trying to keep his face soft, placid.

"Of course not, your highness."

"You use my title, and I will have you flogged."

"Do you have that power?"

"No."

Arthur grinned, tossing black leather pants at Theo. "I have assembled three of my most trusted knights. And pulled…a few guards." Arthur smirked.

"Lenora?"

"She is among them, your highness." Jasper rolled his eyes again, but nodded.

"Good." Jasper fixed a sword to Theo's hips. "Lenora is the youngest person to be Head of the Guard."

"I think I met her, a while back…" Theodore nodded, trying to recall her face.

"She should be on duty at the castle, protecting the family but…"

"We need her," Arthur finished for him. "She's a farm girl from the far province. Daughter of immigrants. Maybe she should be your next exposé."

"Only if he doesn't start kissing this one," Jasper teased.

"This hardly seems like a time for teasing, Jasper," Theo snapped.

"Have you met my sister? You could be walking her to the gallows, and she would be making fun of the executioner." The boys quieted, their ears ringing at the word gallows. "She's too valuable alive."

"Right." Theo nodded as Jasper helped set his hood. "Right."

"Are we ready," Jasper looked to the young knight, "Sir Arthur?"

"We are."

"Horses?"

"As far as we can."

"Then let's go. It's a long ride."

Theo followed the boys through a passage, emerging in a small courtyard, horses and tall figures lined up in the middle. There were no other noises, no stirring in the dark of the night. Even the castle had fallen eerily quiet. As Theo looked up he could see all the candles flickering in the Council room, the shadows of Councillors passing back and forth, hands moving frantically, and he tried to imagine the panicked words they were sharing.

Lenora was wrapping a thick scarf around her neck, the pale blue of the Skylock Kingdom bright against her smooth, dark skin.

"At least you sneak out with guards along," Theo muttered.

"What's that?" Jasper asked, pulling on his reins to still his horse.

"Nothing."

"You two done telling stories?" Lenora asked, a hand on her hip as she walked her horse past them.

"We're coming, we're *coming*!" Jasper rolled his eyes, kicking his horse. "We're late, let's go."

"Can you be late to a rescue mission?" Arthur asked as they rode through the gates of the castle.

- CHAPTER LIX -

Amair blinked a few times rubbing her forehead as light fell on her eyes. Her head rolled to one side and then, suddenly, she was scrambling, trying to find her feet. She looked around the room, large and stark, a table and mirror on one side, doors on two of the walls. There were no windows, the only light from a large lamp above her head.

She couldn't remember how she had gotten there.

Amair spun around, trying to remember what had happened, the feeling of bouncing around in a wagon still printed on her skin. She glanced down at the purple marks on her wrists, angry red spots from where she had strained against ropes. She had moved too fast, her head pounding suddenly.

She rolled her wrists, looking around at the beige, fading wallpaper, trying to orient herself. Her eyes flicked between the two doors, running the choices in her mind. With a deep breath, she scuffled across the floor, and reached for one of the doors.

The door flew open and she stumbled back as a young woman was shoved into the room, two Keenian Guards barging in. "Hello, *Princess,*" one of them jeered, bearing down on her. She straightened, feeling something tug at her shoulder, trying to ignore the warm pain, and stood her ground.

"What the fuck am I doing here?"

"That's not very ladylike."

"Do I look like I care right now?" The two of them glared at each other, and out of the corner of her eye Amair could see the young woman getting up, brushing at her dress. "You will *tell me* where I am before I castrate you!"

"Keene knows better than to pass off a weapon to you."

"Funny that you think I'd need a weapon." He blanched momentarily, but regained himself.

"You are now under the rule of Prince Novak–"

"–seriously? He couldn't rule a Kingdom of mice."

"*You are now under the rule of Prince Novak of Keene,*" the guard repeated, making Amair roll her eyes, "and this girl will prepare you for him."

"You will not serve me up on a platter to Novak Jameson."

"You will be prepared for him."

"No."

"Or face dire consequences."

"Then kill me."

"He said you would say that." The Keenian guards nodded, looking to his colleague, who nodded back and snatched the young woman. "We were also told you respond better like this." The guard gripped the woman tightly, her eyes wide as he lifted a knife to her throat. "One wrong move, and you will have her blood on your hands." Amair narrowed her eyes as her hands balled into fists, watching the fear in the young woman's dark green eyes. With a huff, Amair stepped back, and the Keenian's arm unfurled from the girl.

"Agatha," the guard didn't take his eyes from Amair, "if she causes any trouble, ring the bell." One of the guards disappeared out the door, reappearing to lay a gown on the floor. "He is expecting her in an hour."

"Yes, sir," the young woman nodded, head bowed. The guards didn't move, watching the Princess.

"If you expect me to put that dress on, you better move it, because I am thinking through options on how to *strangle you with it,*" Amair said, her voice deep and warning. The guards shared one more look, and made their way back out of the room. Amair bolted towards them, trying to pull the door back as they closed it. She heaved on the handle, but it didn't budge.

"It's no use, miss…er…your highness… Most doors in the manor are locked by the guards from the outside." Amair shook her head, feeling her hands ball into fists again, trying to push back against the panic that was still pulling at her chest.

"Are you alright?" Amair asked, her eyes on the dress in a pile. "That guard pushed you in here pretty hard."

"I'm fine, miss. Not the first time they've been pushy."

"I'm sorry."

"No need, miss."

"Still," Amair sighed, finally looking up at her. "What's your name?"

"Agatha."

"You work here?"

"I...yes, I'm...I'm an enslaved, miss. Uh...your high–"

"–what do you mean?"

"I serve Keene...I don't..." The girl glanced around.

"Where are you from?" Amair asked gently as Agatha pulled the rough cloak off her shoulders.

"Here, your highness. Keene. My grandparents were taken from their village in Forra when the Keenian Knights tried to burn it to the ground, and they were brought here, as were others. And some from RiKoi, and from..." She trailed off, her eyes travelling up and down Amair who didn't need to hear the last word to know the girl wanted to say *Skylock*. The Princess knew the old stories.

"But they...pay you?"

"No, your highness." Agatha pressed gently on Amair's shoulders, encouraging her to sit in the chair by the mirror. Amair turned her head, trying to look back at the girl. She stilled as Agatha picked up a brush, pulling on a section of Amair's hair. Amair could see how she studied her hair, her eyes darting back and forth as she planned the style in her mind. The two of them were silent, Amair watching as Agatha worked, moving from her hair to her face, running soft brushes over her skin.

Agatha fixed one of the pins in Amair's hair and cautiously reached for her hand, helping her out of the chair and standing her in front of the mirror. She pulled the chair away, undoing the clasps on Amair's nightgown, pulling layers away. Agatha kept her eyes away as she picked up the pieces of the gown, wrapping the corset around her and starting to lace it. Amair tried to picture Lydia flitting around her bedroom at home, finding the pieces of her outfits, her soft words and the rain pattering against her window.

There was a blur of deep red, Agatha zipping around, doing up underskirts, adjusting the corset, helping Amair step into the gown. It took all of Agatha's strength to lift the heavy gown up to Amair's shoulders, doing up what felt like a hundred buttons down the back, a high neck that felt more like a collar.

Amair looked down, brushing her fingertips across the rough layer of red tulle, dozens of layers beneath it, short sleeves anchoring her shoulders in place.

"I must go, miss." Amair looked down, watching her fingertips.

"Okay."

"I'm sorry—"

"—no, no Agatha," Amair took a deep breath. "I understand. I don't want to keep you."

"Don't fight him, your highness." Amair looked up, horrified, clenching her hands around the dress. "The other girls say it's easier that way." Amair's jaw was open as she watched Agatha slip out the door, closing it behind her. She looked back into the mirror, gripping her fists so tightly one of her nails broke the skin on her palm. She winced, holding up her palm to check the tiny injury, watching a drop of blood roll off it and land in the layers of red fabric.

Amair felt her chest tightening, glancing down at herself as she was escorted out one door and she tried to eye the hallway, but the large Keenian guards blocked her view, nearly chucking her into a room, through a heavier door.

She looked around and jumped as she heard the door click shut. The room was doused in shades of reds, the bedspread and every piece of décor, the books all wrapped in a reddish-brown leather. The books were heavy looking and something in her picked at her brain, wondering if Novak had ever actually read them. There were no photos, nothing else personal, just drapes and fabrics trying to make the room feel whole. She waited, trying to take stock of the space.

The door was opened again, the sound of heavy boots scuffling into the room. It took her a moment to turn but she finally managed it, watching the slimy boy she had spent every ball avoiding walk into his bedroom.

"Amy Skylock," Novak grinned, wrapping his fingers around the arms of the chair, built to look like his grandfather's throne.

"It's Amair," she seethed, but Amair couldn't stop staring at the crown on Novak's head. It was Layton's. The one that had gone missing shortly before his death. "You've been called into my throne room to be tried for injustice against the ruler."

"Throne room? Novak, this is your *bedroom*, in a manor your father sent you to so he could get away from you."

He ignored her, the grin still on his face but she could see him cracking. "I have brought you here to right those injustices."

"You're enjoying this aren't you?" she asked, her eyebrow raised in annoyance. "And? How do you plan to do that? Hm? I can take you, Novak, no matter what ridiculous outfit you put me in–"

"–by taking your hand in marriage."

The way he said it hung on Amair's shoulders. "You horrible, re*pugnant* boy."

"Watch your tone, girl." Amair twitched, her throat burning.

"You sit up there like a Prince, but you, Novak, are nothing of the sort," she snapped. Novak's grin faltered as he rose out of the chair, gliding across the floor towards her. She noticed his hands gripping into fists, relaxing, and doing it again. She kept on in her momentum. "You wear a crown you have no right to. You sit in that chair playing dress up. You know nothing of honour. Of sacrifice. Of love for anything aside from yourself." Amair's lip curled back. "You are a traitor to your own Kingdom." Novak raised a hand and she braced herself to be slapped, but he ran his fingers across Amair's back. She fought her body to keep from shuddering, trying to stand her ground. Her stomach churned.

His hand suddenly snaked around her, pulling her body back, tight against his. "You are here now, Amair."

She glanced down, watching his fingers trail across her stomach, thankful for the layers of corset and fabric protecting her from his touch. She could feel his breath on the back of her ear as he leaned towards her. Out of the corner of her eye she could see him in the mirror. She could see how close he stood to her, creasing into the skirt.

He raised his hand, up one of the bones of the corset, and Amair sucked in a breath. The second he opened his mouth to chuckle, she threw her elbow backwards into his stomach, ripping his hand off her and twisting, pulling a shriek from his lips. Amair heard him stumble backwards, cursing the dress for limiting her movement as she tried to rush away from him. Her hand reached for the heavy book she had seen on a stool. She could hear him barrelling back towards her, and turned, both hands clutching the book, swinging. She felt the book connect with the side of his skull, the impact radiating back through her arms. He stopped, his hand inches from her shoulder, a dumb look on his face. Amair didn't move, book still raised from where her swing had ended, the two staring at each other. Novak's arms dropped, his eyes rolling, and crumpled to the floor. Amair dropped the book, wincing as it landed on Novak's nose, and stepped back, pulling all her skirts out of his reach. She panted, the fear coursing through her a second longer.

She picked one of the books from the shelf and stared down at Novak. She bent and pulled the crown from his head, eyeing the Skylock crest stamped inside it. Without thinking, she knocked the book against Novak's nose.

"That one's for Layton," she muttered. She pulled her heavy skirt across the floor and with a deep breath tried the door handle.

It was unlocked.

She pulled the heavy black door open a crack and there was no one stationed in front of it. She had no weapon but in that moment she would have been happy to make a run for it but peeking further out, there were guards walking the edge of the hallway. She sighed pulling the door closed. Grabbing one of the books from Novak's shelf, she found a place to sit, pulling her legs crossed under the skirt, opening the book, praying someone was coming to help her.

- CHAPTER LX -

"Jasper has to be the one to go in," Arthur murmured. "You've been here before, haven't you?"

"Ah...a million years ago, back when it was an ambassador's waypoint, before the Archduke got tired of Novak's douchery."

"Well, it's some advantage over the rest of us. You go in with Theo, find your sister, and get out."

"Move quietly," Lenora whispered, creeping back up to the group. "We'll keep watch out here." Theo and Jasper nodded, sharing a look.

"And plan our way out."

"Here. They aren't perfect, but the laundry had some Keene servants' clothes, from some old event," Knight Madson tossed two jackets at the boys. "You'll be a little less noticeable."

"But don't get cocky," Lenora warned, eyes on Jasper. "We need to get in and get out as fast as we can if we want to avoid an all-out war. I counted at least seven Keenian guards, and that was just what I could see from the lookout point."

"We'll be careful," Jasper promised, helping Theo with the buttons on his jacket. The jackets were long enough to obscure the swords attached to each of Jasper's hips. Madson fastened one around Theo, fluffing the jacket to keep them hidden. "You ready?"

Theo whistled out a breath. "As I'll ever be."

"Yeah," Jasper let out a deep breath. He gripped Arthur's hand. "Amair would be charging into this without a hint of panic, right?"

"She'd be panicking, alright," Arthur told him solemnly. "She'd just be doing it anyways." With that, they snuck around the side of the wall, and slipped in the little staff door.

***

"Try this one!" Theo hissed, beckoning Jasper. The tall black door stood out from the rest of the wooden ones, feeling sleek and cool against his hand.

"It's unlocked," Jasper whispered, his hand already turning the handle. Theo tightened his grip on the hilt of the sword he did not know how to use, and nodded at Jasper. The Prince pushed on the door and it squeaked as it swung open into the dim room.

"Wh…what?" Theo and Jasper looked around, and found Amair woth her legs tucked under herself.

"You're here!" Amair smiled with relief, throwing the book aside.

"What are you wearing?" Jasper asked as Amair ran across the room, throwing her arms around Theo, holding him tight, the huge skirt nearly enveloping his legs.

"Wait…" She pulled her head back, holding his face. "Why did they bring you?"

"Ask *him*," he nodded towards Jasper.

"Is it just the two of you?" Her eyebrows went further up.

"No, what…happened here?" Jasper asked, leaning to look into the room.

Amair looked back at the Keenian prince splayed out on the floor, her head tipped a little bit. "I knew I couldn't make it out of here on my own. But, I knew I could take *him* out." Her lip curled a little. "One hand on my waist and he didn't stand a chance."

"He touched you?" Theo exclaimed, holding her arms.

"I'm fine," she waved him off. "He ran his hands over me twice and I whacked him really hard in the head." She suddenly furrowed her brow. "We should probably be getting out of here right?"

"Right, yeah, we probably should."

"Yeah, I overheard something about midnight," she glanced at the clock, "which by my calculation is in about twenty minutes, so can we—"

"—go, yeah, yeah, we should go," Jasper nodded, pulling off the servant's jacket. "Brought you something." He passed her the extra sword on his hip, shrugging off the back sheath and letting her get settled.

"This is a feeling I missed," she shrugged a little, trying to get the sword to sit flat against her, stuck in the skirt.

"Ready?" Theo asked, bouncing on the balls of his feet, looking over his shoulder and then down at Novak.

"Yeah. Let's get out of here."

"Wait, one sec," Amair turned, grabbing one of the leather belts from the open wardrobe, pulling it around her waist, looping it through her late brother's crown and fastening the clasp. "Okay. Now we can go." Theo pulled on Amair's arm, helping her push the whole skirt out of the doorway.

They heard the clinking of armour before the shadows of men hurrying down the hall appeared on the wall, sauntering slowly.

"Other way," Jasper exclaimed, spinning. The other two nodded, turning and hustling down the hall, Amair trying to push past the twenty pounds the dress added.

"Sounds like they found your rescue party," Jasper shook his head as he glanced over his shoulder, shouting in the hall behind them.

"Setting the place on fire would be a bad plan, right?" Amair glanced over her shoulder as the first guard's face came into view. Jasper burst through the door at the end of the hall, a winding staircase in front of them. Without hesitating, they took off down them.

"Probably. We're trying to *avoid* an act of war right now."

"Does you breaking in just cancel out them kidnapping me?" Amair mused, picking up as much of the skirt in her arms as she could and hustling down the winding stairs.

"That's a really good question for *after* the break in is successful."

"Let's hope those guys don't have a crossbow with them," Theo murmured, looking back up the staircase. "Any idea where this goes?"

"Not a clue."

"Fantastic." Theo shook his head, a door with a torch beside it finally appearing.

"Alright, now's when we start praying," Amair told them, both the boys nodding as Jasper ran full force into the door.

"Sorry, haven't we been doing that the whole time?"

It popped open and they took in the sight of the dark courtyard, torches around the edge. The sound of swords clashing and people yelling filled their ears as Keenian Knights and the Skylock rescue party battled.

"Theo!" Knight Marvin yelled, barrelling towards them. "You're coming with me, we're getting horses."

"I guess that means we're helping," Jasper muttered.

"Uh-huh," Amair nodded at her brother as she pulled the sword from her back, watching Theo disappear around the side of the manor. She blocked a Guard's sword aiming for her brother's head, whacking her hilt back against the guard's face so hard he crumpled backwards.

"Thanks for that."

"Be safe."

Jasper nodded. "I'll see you on the other side." Amair turned as a guard let out a scream, running towards her as Jasper disappeared from her sight. "Now why would you announce yourself like that – I mean thank you but come *on*, you cannot be that dumb?" Her sword glided through the air, and she stiffened as it pierced through the guard's armour.

Amair turned, kicking a short guard running towards her in the stomach, whacking the back of his head with the flat of her sword. She looked up only to whip her head around as she heard Lenora scream. A Keenian guard gripped the neck of Lenora's armour, tearing her from her saddle, another leering in on her as she was dropped to the ground, one running up behind her. A Keenian guard swung their sword at Amair, almost catching her. She jumped back, her large skirt barely moving around her. She gritted her teeth, feeling her sword slice through an arm as the guard screamed, dropping and gripping the wrist that once held his sword.

"I'm sorry!" Amair turned to try and run and help Lenora, another Keenian guard clashing swords with her, knocking the wind out of her chest. Amair turned her head, eyes wide, watching a Keenian guard grip Lenora's hair to pull her head sideways, pushing her to her knees as she shouted in pain.

"Unhand her!" Amair screamed, looking back at the Keenian guard with a sword crossed on hers. She pulled her sword back, just enough to make the guard stumble, and took the opportunity to pierce a gap in the armour on his leg. "I'm sorry," she murmured as the guard squirmed on the ground, clutching his knee. She took a deep breath and picked up her skirt, running as fast as the layers of fabric would let her, pushing her sword through the shoulder blades of one of the guards. Lenora jumped to her feet, spinning on her heel and kneed him in the chin.

"Don't touch my hair," she snapped, as the guard stilled. Amair passed Lenora her sword back, Lenora spinning the hilt in her hand once and putting her helmet back on.

"You okay?" Amair asked, reaching to pull her skirts aside.

"Yeah, yeah. I'm okay." She looked around the courtyard. "Where are Theodore and Marvin?"

"They aren't back yet."

"We really need those horses." Lenora shook her head, her eyes flicking to where another half-dozen Keenian guard barrelled into the courtyard, yelling at the top of their lungs. Amair tensed as she heard swords clash, knowing at least two guards would be coming for her and Lenora. Lenora looked Amair up and down, readying herself for the next attack. "We're not getting you out of here in *that*," she motioned to the dress, "on foot."

"You go find your horse," Amair turned, clashing swords with a Keenian guard. "You go find *your* horse and see if we can get out of here."

"Amair—"

"—go!" Amair insisted, pushing her knight. "My orders." Lenora shook her head but whipped her sword through two of the guards, avoiding a third sword and running towards the gates.

"Amair! Keenian Knights coming in!" Jasper called, running up close, kicking a Keenian guard's feet out from under him and kicking him in the head.

"Of course they are," Amair muttered, eyeing the group barrelling in. "We have to get out of here!" Amair wiped at her forehead, blowing at the hair that was falling into her eyes. "This place is gonna be showered with arrows in minutes."

"Their Guard's down here, they—"

"—have you known the Keenians to spare *anyone*?" Amair asked, raising an eyebrow.

"Good point," Jasper conceded, turning instinctively and shoving the tip of his sword through a guard barrelling down on him. The siblings stood back-to-back, taking on as many as they could

"Amair Skylock!" someone's voice boomed through the courtyard. Amair and Jasper looked up, finding Novak standing at the top of the wall, gripping the stones, lit up by the torch right next to him, blood around his nose.

"I really wish I had an arrow right now," Amair rolled her eyes, squinting, slowly pointing at him. "Right between the eyebrows…"

"Amair! Jasper! Let's go!" Lenora's voice flew through the courtyard, galloping as horses rushed through, whinnying in fear. Jasper expertly grabbed one, pulling himself up onto the bare back.

"Jasper, I'll never get this dress up behind you."

"Amair—"

"—go, Jasp," Amair waved him off, picking up her skirt. "I'll get one and catch up. Go!" Amair glanced to the side and shook her head, sighing angrily. "And get Theo," she snapped, noticing the Writer on a brown horse almost entirely surrounded by Keenian guards and Knights. Jasper nodded, turning and galloping through the men in red, more of them starting to appear from what felt like nowhere. They dove out of the way, trying not to get crushed by Jasper's horse. She watched him grab the reins of Theo's horse, the two boys galloping over the Keenians.

"Amair!" she heard Arthur call, and nodded at the gates. She noticed a horse in knight's garb running, nickering. She threw her sword into the sheath on her back, picking up as much of the skirts as she could, running towards the horse. It didn't slow, but she reached up to grab the saddle horn, trying to run alongside it, narrowly missing an arrow fired towards her. With a deep breath, she pulled a foot up and managed to throw herself onto the horse, the dress billowing.

"Come on buddy. Faster…please…" she murmured, getting her feet into the stirrups. She felt something hit her and cried out, curling slightly as a pain vibrated through her body. She pushed the pain away, leaning over on the horse and riding through the gates, the Skylock party galloping with her, Lenora and Marvin ahead of her, Theo and Jasper falling in line ahead of her, Arthur and Madson coming in behind them. They could still hear the noise of the castle behind them, people hollering, the sound of horses behind them.

"Ride hard, Theo!" Amair pressed, all of the Skylock party leaning forward, horses galloping as fast as they would go. "Don't look back!" He didn't. He turned to look at her, though, determined face, hair and dress wild in the wind rushing past them. Shouting in the distance behind them.

They rode through the first peak of sunlight, dawn starting to appear on the horizon, stuck behind the mountains as they put Keene behind them. Lenora veered them off onto a skinny trail leading into the forest.

"We're back into ally territory," she told them. Everyone nodded tiredly, Arthur glancing over his shoulder.

"Ally territory, but they could still be coming for us."

"For her," Marvin murmured, taking off his helmet, his eyes trailing over to Amair, her horse almost engulfed by all the red fabric.

"Wow, don't I feel popular," she muttered. Amair rubbed her brow. "What are we gonna tell the Council?"

"Forget the Council, what are you gonna tell *dad*?"

"Definitely not that Novak put his slimy hands on me." She noticed Theo shift on his horse, his shoulders tensing. Amair tapped her feet against her horse's side, clucking her tongue to trot up to Theo, just behind Lenora. She smiled at him cautiously, shifting her reins to one hand and reaching out to him. He smiled a little, reaching out to hold it, squeezing her.

"I srt of thought it would be you we'd be rescuing from a kidnapping someday." When he didn't reply, her tentative smile faltered. "I'm sorry."

"It's fine, we—"

"—I mean," she tightened her grip on his fingers, "about Novak."

"My love, that is *not* on you."

"I know. But talking about it. I saw you tense."

"Because I want to *kill him* Amair."

"I get that. I'm guessing Jasper is in the same boat. But it's okay. I'm okay. We're okay." Theo smiled again, nodding.

"I wish I could kiss you right now."

Amair smirked, leaning over and grabbing the front of his shirt, pressing her lips to his. He carefully took a hand off his reins, touching her cheek. "Thought you'd never ask."

"There's a stream!" Lenora called over her shoulder, and Amair sat back on her horse, looking to where Lenora pointed. "We should get some water."

"I'll water the horses," Marvin offered.

"I'll keep watch," Madson told them, turning his horses around and going back down the trail a little. The rest of them slid off their horses, stretching as their feet hit the ground. Amair cringed as Jasper cracked his neck.

"My lady," Lenora bowed a little, reaching her hand up to the Princess who chuckled, taking it.

"Why thank you, Captain," Amair laughed a little, coughing. "Whew, can't wait to get out of this dress."

"No kidding. Can you even move?"

"No…" Amair looked down at herself, the skirt moving with the wind. "I think that was kind of the point." Lenora picked a leaf off the sleeve.

"I'm sorry I couldn't protect you."

Amair smiled sadly, shaking her head, reaching out to grip Lenora's hand. "I snuck out, Lenny. I got a note, and *I* made a decision."

"The castle grounds are *my* responsibility."

"And I went against protocol. If anything, you should be *angry* at me. You are *allowed* to be angry at me, we've been friends too long for you to just treat me like your future sovereign." She took a deep breath. "Thank you, for risking your life for me, Captain. You mean more to me than you know."

Lenora nodded a little, her face still distraught, squeezing Amair's hand. "Go get some water. Clean up. We still have quite the ride ahead of us."

"Yeah," Amair nodded, running her hand across her skirt. "Fun fact, this dress is also ridiculously warm." She adjusted the side. "Damn, and poky, this is the worst constructed corset I have ever worn."

"Yeah, not surprised." The team fanned out, giving themselves space to stretch their legs and clean up. Amair walked down to the stream, letting the edges of her dress drift into the water. The tulle looked like blood tugged along by the stream. She shuffled her feet into the chilly water, soaking through the slippers they had put her in in Keene. She tilted her head back, cool sun trying to break through the clouds. She breathed in, the musty air of the manor finally leaving her lungs. She could hear Lenora and Arthur and Theo laughing somewhere further up the bank.

Theo looked over just in time to watch Amair buckle over, her knees giving way as she crumpled into the stream.

"Oh my gods!" he yelled, dropping the saddle bag picking his way over to her, eyes following him.

"Amair!" they all exclaimed, running towards her, trying not to trip in the brush and over the stones. She twisted in pain, her hands on her side, Theo's legs suddenly cold as he knelt in the water, wrapping his arms around Amair, holding her in his lap. He went to move the hair out of her face, recoiling his hand when he realized it was covered in bright blood. He shifted her torso in his lap, trying not to gasp at the blood soaking into his pants and his other hand.

"Amair," Jasper bit his tongue seeing the blood smeared on Theo's hands and onto his shirt as Amair tried to hold onto him.

"I'm okay."

"You're really not," Lenora told her.

"What happened?" Jasper demanded.

"I think someone threw something at me on the way out." She writhed a little. "Maybe a spear? Or a big dagger?"

"Do you feel anything Theo?"

Amair tried to bite back a scream as Theo tried to find where the blood was coming from. The knights turned away as Amair screamed, Theo whispering apologies over and over, his voice straining more every second, trying not to cry. "I can't feel anything through this damn dress, but there's no hilt or anything sticking out."

"You guys are making so much noise–" Madson whispered harshly, stopping short on the path when he saw the blood on Theo and Jasper's hands, reaching for his sword. "What happened?"

"She got hurt at the castle."

"Wh…"

"We have to get back to *our* castle." Amair's face twisted, lifting her head. "We can't do anything for me out here. I think the corset took some of the blow."

"Can you ride?"

"I made it this far."

"Sure, but the adrenaline will have worn off."

"How did we miss this?" Jasper asked,

"The dress. It's red. And there's like nine layers of fabric on the bodice."

"I'm so sorry," Theo held her

"We need to go. And avoid being seen."

"That's gonna be kind of hard given that you're wearing a gigantic *red* dress."

"We have to."

"She's right, you guys," Lenora seconded, her hands in her hair.

"I know she is," Jasper huffed, annoyed. "Do we have any…any bandages?"

"There's an extra shirt in my bag," Marvin offered.

"Oh, me too!" Arthur nodded.

"Grab them, I'll try and staunch some of this blood." Jasper dropped his voice to a whisper. "Can you ride?" he cupped Amair's face.

"I don't have a choice."

Jasper shook his head but looked up at the knights. "Tear the shirts into strips, Try for about three inches thick." Amair could hear the tearing of fabric, Theo and Lenora helping her stand, each strip being wrapped around her torso, fastened into little knots. Theo looked away, trying not to listen to the ragged breaths coming from Amair's lips.

"There, that should hold," Lenora nodded, testing the bandages already starting to show the first signs of blood. Theo and Jasper were shaking their heads.

"You two go get on your horses," Arthur offered, reaching for Amair.

"No, she needs—"

"—go," Arthur took Amair from Theo. "I've got her." He cupped her face as he helped her sit again, wrapping his arms around her. It was tender, soft as he tried not to grip her but to hold her close. "Hey you," he whispered, kissing her hair.

"Hey."

"You're gonna be fine. We've got you."

"My…knight in shining armour," she laughed, gasping a little as she shifted.

"Let's get you up onto your horse," he whispered, seeing Marvin rush up, trying to steady the horse that was no doubt soaking up the anxiety of the crowd. Lenora steadied the horse from the top of hers, Arthur helping Amair to her feet, pulling the heavy dress along. With Marvin's help, Lenora reaching across to pull her up and Theo and Jasper having to look away, Amair pulled herself up, more of the colour draining from her face.

"Hey," he gripped her leg as she managed to sit on the horse, leaning forward in pain. "You and I made a pact...remember? At the funeral?"

"You and me," she nodded, trying to breathe evenly, "in it forever."

"Against the world." He wiped hurriedly at a tear that was running down his cheek, not wanting to scare her. "You hold on...for me, kay?"

"Arthur and Ama. I remember." She nodded, gripping her reins, trying to sit as tall as the dress and her pain would allow. "Let's do this."

- CHAPTER LXI -

"We're almost home, we're almost there!" Amair's head bounced, hanging forward, but she tried to nod, gripping the reins as tight as her tired hands would let her. "Hang on Amair!"

It felt like they had been riding forever, tucked into forests and side trails, avoiding the Forran villages to keep from prying eyes and gossip, Amair insisting they had to control the narrative. The landscape had been rough, full of rugged tree roots of the Grand Forest but it changed slowly, from the grand forest into the beautiful Skylock Highlands.

The horses tore through the hills, chunks of the green grass churning up. Finally, the castle showed on the horizon. "We're almost home!"

Lenora led them through the Second Wood, around near the cliffs, everyone's eyes glued to Amair. Arthur and Jasper kept to the outside, scanning the area for any townspeople, but their eyes always came full circle back to their Princess. Lenora led them straight through a back entrance, into the back of the stables. Everyone slid off their horses, Amair still splayed out on her horse.

"Theo, go tell the doctor what's happened," Arthur told him.

"I—"

"—go!"

"I'll be right back, Ama." He looked over at her lying on the horse, the knights swarming around her to help, and turned to run into the castle. Madson and Lenora reached up, helping slide Amair off the horse, catching her and dragging her skirts down with her.

"Run and fetch the King and Queen," Lenora whispered to Marvin, helping Jasper hold Amair up. "We'll meet them at the hospital wing."

"Give her to me," Arthur reached for her.

"Arthur–"

"–Lenny, for the love of gods, please."

Lenora sighed, untangling Amair's arm from her neck and draping it over Arthur's, his arm gentle but supportive, immediately covered in more blood.

"Please, get me out of this dress," Amair murmured, her eyes drooping as they carried her across the employee courtyard, easing her through the door. She smiled, the warmth of the kitchens gripping her. "Mhm."

"You okay?" Jasper demanded, looking her up and down, thankful for how few people were there in that moment.

"I'm home."

Jasper smiled a little at her, he and Arthur racing down the hallway as fast as Amair's injury would let them move, Lenora behind them trying to pick up as much of the dress as she could to make moving the Princess easier.

"They're coming for her!" Theo yelled, running down the hallway. Sound filled the space behind him as he reached out to hold Amair's hand.

Nurses filled the space and Jasper reluctantly stepped away, but Arthur kept a protective arm around her.

"Sir Arthur," the doctor coaxed, her silky hair in a twist, keeping it all out of her eyes, "you've gotten her this far."

He was still hesitating, holding her but finally released, keeping hold of her hand as she was swept up onto the rolling bed, walking alongside her until they reached the sterile hospital wing.

"Only two of you can stay now."

"Theo and Jasper should stay," Lenora nodded, patting Amair's shoulder and starting to back out of the wing. Arthur looked down, his hands trembling. He dropped to his knees, gripping Amair's hand.

"You do not get to die on me too."

"Against the world," she said with a gasp. His mouth trembled, barely making it back to his feet, and Lenora reached for him. Theo turned his head just enough to see Arthur collapse in tears on the other side of the doors as they swung shut.

"Don't ruin the dress!" Jasper exclaimed suddenly, pointing to the nurse with the scissors in her hand.

Theo's head snapped back to them. "No, please, by *all means*, destroy the dress," he countered.

"*Do not* ruin the dress," Jasper pressed, glaring slightly at Theo. Theo looked at him confused, looking back down at Amair. She was looking past him to Jasper, her half-closed eyes just as confused as Theo. The siblings stared at each other, no words, just watching. She sighed, through gritted teeth, reaching up to hold Theo's hand.

"Okay. Let's get it off."

"My lady–"

"–just," Amair raised her other hand, silencing the doctor, "get me up and we can get it off."

"I'll do it," Theo looked up at the doctor before she said anything.

"I'll help," Jasper said, looking at Theo instead of the doctor.

"Are…are you…my lady–"

"–they're okay, doctor. Just give us a few minutes."

"Yes, my lady." The doctor gathered her medical staff, scurrying to the other side of the hospital wing. One of the nurses rolled a divider around the bed, blocking out some of the natural light and the view of others.

"Come on, Amair," Jasper said, leaning over to help her sit, pulling her off the bed as she yelped in pain. Theo looked away, pushing back tears. Jasper wrapped his sister's arms around his neck, helping her stand, holding her up as she leaned her head into his chest, forcing her breaths.

"Bandages first," Theo told her, undoing Jasper's little knots and pulling the blood-soaked strips of cloth off her torso. He brushed her loose hair off the back of her neck, undoing the tie and slowly pulling the ribbon out of its loops, each row of the ribbon coming out with less blood as he worked up her back.

Jasper whispered something in Amair's ear as he helped hold her up, so quiet Theo couldn't even hear the outline of the whisper. Amair raised her head a little when her brother pulled his lips back, and she nodded ever so slightly. Theo sighed, moving her hair again that had trailed back down, and started undoing the clips, having to pull the dress together across Amair's wound to get them undone. By the time he got all the silver hooks open, pulling open the organza fabric, her back and black corset showing, Amair's knees buckled, falling further into Jasper's arms.

"One more layer, Ama, we're almost there," Theo assured her but she didn't reply. He undid the ribbon on the corset as fast as he could, pulling it open. Amair instinctively took a deep breath the ill fitted corset had kept in. Theo pulled the two sides of the corset apart, the sleeveless linen undershirt almost entirely drenched in blood. He fought bile at the back of his throat

"Get it off her," Jasper instructed, transferring Amair to her side so that Theo could pull one side of the short sleeves off her, managing to get the other side off her and pull all the red fabric down to the ground. Jasper eased Amair back onto the bed, the open corset held in place.

"Doctor! We're good!" Jasper yelled, the medical staff appearing and dragging the divider out of their way. The two boys stared at Amair, incredibly pale, the black corset not helping.

"Alright you guys, let's get her to the theatre and get her cleaned up!" the doctor instructed her staff, three of the nurses descending on Amair and getting the bed set up to be rolled away. The doctor glanced at the boys, blood covering their hands and arms, caked across Theo's legs and stomach. "You two should go shower. Get the blood off." She turned to walk away. "Before any of the papers see you." The doctor stopped, turning and pointing at Theo. "Writer?"

He raised his hands defensively. "Under wraps, I swear."

Amair tried to catch her breath, looking up at her brother. "If I die—"

"—you're not going to die," he assured her.

"Bury me with Layton." Jasper opened his mouth but choked on his words. "You'd be a good King, Jasper." Her eyes fluttered closed as her hand slid off the bed.

"Wait," Amair croaked, the staff ignoring her. "Wait!" she managed to say louder. They looked down, still moving around her. "Theo, kiss me." Theo kneeled next to her bed, reaching to hold her cheeks. "Just one more time." He fought back tears, pressing his lips to hers, trying not to think about the bloody fingerprints he left.

"Okay, we *have* to go." The doctor ushered the medical staff forwards, and Theo's arms fell to his sides as the bed was wheeled away.

"What was that?" Theo demanded as all the medical staff disappeared.

"Destroying a royal wedding dress is considered an act *of war*! *This*? This is a Keenian wedding dress," Jasper explained, his voice low. He bent down, trying to gather all the red fabric into his arms. Theo watched him struggle for a second, finally rolling his eyes and kneeling to help pick it all up. They counted, standing up at the same time, and carefully made their way towards the exit. Jasper stopped at the window, glancing around, making sure it was empty. He pushed the door open with his shoulder, the boys making their way through. Theo could feel the blood seeping out of where he held on to the fabric, squishing between his fingers. He squeezed his eyes closed, trying to shut the thoughts out of his mind.

Jasper led Theo up to a dumbwaiter, not saying anything. He dropped his half, Theo leaning suddenly as the full weight of the heavy dress pulled him forward, waiting until Jasper had gotten the door open and crawled in. Theo pushed his half of the dress onto Jasper's lap, crawling in and leaning into the wall, enough room to sit straight, his legs straight out in front of him. He pulled the dress out of the hallway, hauling it up inch by inch to settle it on his lap. Jasper kicked the door closed. They sat, panting a little for a second before Jasper took a deep breath, twisting to grab the rope and pull the dumbwaiter slowly.

It felt like forever by the time they reached the level they were looking for, coming out of the basements into the upper levels of the castle. Theo noticed the *Family Wing* sign on the inside of the dumbwaiter door. Theo pushed it open with his foot, him and Jasper pushing slowly sliding out of the cramped space one by one, the dress flopping onto the floor.

"Where is everyone?" Theo asked as he jumped out of the dumbwaiter.

"They probably just got to the hospital wing," Jasper explained, picking up the dress.

"Your highness!" a young man in a Crier's hat exclaimed, almost dropping his papers.

"Open this door, please."

"Yes, of course your highness." The Crier ran in front of them, throwing open the doors to Jasper's study, pushing them closed as the boys and the dress stumbled in.

"There are clothes hangers in that cupboard," Jasper instructed, motioning with his head to a chestnut wardrobe beside his desk. Theo dropped the dress, rushing to throw the wardrobe open and grab one of the hangers as Jasper found his way to the bodice of the dress, trying to shake out the heavy garment. Jasper helped Theo pull it onto the hanger, letting Theo tie the ribbon together in a loose knot. The two of them lifted the hanger onto the edge of a cabinet near the window. Satisfied it would stay, they took a step back and just stared at the bright red dress, the blood starting to dry and pulling the fabric together, some of the beads missing from broken threads. Jasper crossed his arms in front of himself, the same way Amair protectively held herself when she was nervous.

"I'm moving you into the Family Wing," Jasper told Theo, not taking his eyes off the dress. Theo nodded, not moving his eyes from the dress either.

"What are we going to do with this?"

Jasper shook his head, shrugging. "The King will decide."

"I'll show you to one of the family guest suites. You can shower there. I'll send for your valet and he and your men can move your things by the time you're done."

"Alright." They didn't look at each other, finally managing to pull their eyes away and walk back into the fire.

A speck of blood dripped off the hem of the dress, staining the light blue carpet.

- CHAPTER LXII -

Theo let the hot water rush across his face, his eyes squeezed shut as drops rolled down his eyelids and across his lips.

He turned, the hot water pounding against his back. He finally got the courage to open his eyes, looking down at the dried blood on his arms, streaked where water droplets ran down his skin, red dripping off the tips of his fingers. He watched the red water rush past his feet, swirling around the drain, the marble tiles of the shower floor washed in red. He felt panic rise in his chest, leaning a hand against the glass shower door, a handprint in the steam covered glass, drops rolling down under it. He waited for the panic to stuff itself back down, but it turned into tears, salty tears rushing down his face, disappearing with the hot water. He ran his hands up his face and back through his hair, feeling the grain of dried blood there too. He remembered how many times he had run his hands through his floppy hair, each finger dragging more of her blood into it. He barely noticed the quiet sobs escaping his chest.

Theo didn't move, water padding against his skin, hanging his head. He glanced to the side, a new bar of soap unwrapped on the wooden soap dish, a real flower stuck on the top.

He glanced down again, blood still noticeable across his skin, still noticeable on the tiles, despite all the hot water. He sighed, sending water droplets flying, and picked up the bar of soap.

Theo walked out of the bathroom, steam still filling his lungs, tying the heavy robe he had found around him, looking around the bedroom. The bedspread was different, black with silver embroidery instead of the light blue of the guest wing. Large bedposts held a matching canopy high above, heavy looking black curtain tied to each of the high posts. His books lined the shelves of a large, sleek bookcase. "Theodore," Gaelen grinned, hanging up the jacket in his hands. "Welcome to your new home."

"You…you moved everything that quickly?"

"There are nearly two hundred maintenance staff in the castle," the valet chuckled. "We work fast."

"That's an understatement."

"Prince Jasper has said if there is anything you want to change, you most certainly can. To make it more like home."

"It's fine."

"Seriously…anything you need."

"Right."

"Are you…are you alright, sir?"

"Hm?"

"We…the news has made its way through the staff." Theo looked over, raising an eyebrow. "Our oath to this family means we won't say anything. Don't worry. But…you were there. I think you…you care for her. Deeply, from what I have seen." Gaelen rubbed his hands together. "You must be feeling…some very unhappy thoughts."

Theo bit his lip.

"They just…took her. And held…" Theo gulped, disgust twisting his lips and his nose. "And kept her. Touched her. And then almost killed her. She could have died. It was the *boning* in a damn *corset* that saved her life." Theo shook his head, leaning into his hands on his knees.

"You helped save her, Theo," Gaelen reminded him. "You got her out. Hold on to that."

"Have you heard? Is she…is she alright?"

"No news, yet. It will likely be another few hours, if there was any damage. You could rest, sleep after what you went through–"

"–no. No. Please find me a clean suit and have one of the attendants come and help me clean up. I'd like to go be with her family."

"I believe they may be becoming your family, too." Theo looked down, a sad smile touching his lips.

"They might be."

He glanced around the room. "Maybe…I…I'm not a huge fan of black could we…could we find something warmer?"

Gaelen smiled a little. "It would be my pleasure. For now, let's find you that suit…and perhaps a cup of tea."

***

Theo walked into the waiting room, adjusting the sleeve of his grey suit jacket. He patted Kylo's shoulder where he leaned into his hands. He jumped, looking up at Theo. "How are you?" Theo asked, hovering over Kylo.

"Nusiq is still coming. I was going to tell him not to but…figured…" Tears jumped to his eyes. "Ama would want me to have him with me. With the family."

"Good. Good, you should have all your people around you right now."

Kylo nodded, leaning back into his hands.

"Theodore!" the King stood, reaching a hand out to him. Theo took it, bowing a little.

"Your majesty."

"Thank you for coming." Theo stood up, the King still holding his hand. "My son has moved you into the Family Wing." Theo wasn't sure if it was a question or not.

"Y…yes, your majesty."

"I think…from what I hear…what I know…you can call me Niall." Theo smiled, surprised, but nodded.

"If you wish." The King let go of him and Theo turned, the Queen reaching up to pull him into a hug.

"Thank you." She kissed Theo's cheek. "For getting her home." She pulled away from him, tipping her head. "And loving her."

Theo sat, Alec wrapping his hands around Theo's arm, leaning against him, and Theo could see him shuddering with tears.

People came and went. Councillors handing out documents to the King as the kingdom continued to operate around a tragedy. Denna and Kenaia who had been the first people Arthur and Lenora had run to with the story, stopping in and hoping for updates, their chests tightening when there was no news to pass on. Denna's eyes lingered on Theo, watching him wrapped in one of the twins, the valiant comfort as the royal family tried desperately to keep it together and keep the news from spreading too far.

He was grateful to an old attendant who stepped in with a tray of steaming cups of coffee and cocoa, letting everyone take their pick. "We're all praying for her, downstairs," Theo heard the attendant tell the King quietly. The King gasped a sob, leaning further into the Queen but nodded his thanks. "Princess Amair is strong…we believe in her." The attendant bowed carefully over the tray before turning to leave.

Alec and Evander both ended up asleep in Theo's lap as he sipped his coffee, rubbing his eyes, still no sign of Jasper as the minutes ticked by agonizingly slowly. The kitchen delivered a tray of food but no one had the energy or appetite to eat anything.

It felt like an eternity before the doors to the waiting room swung open, the doctor striding in, shoulders hunched and tired. The King and Queen jumped to their feet, Kylo reaching for his mom's elbow. Theo woke up Evander, getting him and Alec on their feet.

"Is she dead?" the Queen asked, her voice breaking, clutching her husband.

"No, no, your majesty. The corset saved her life." The doctor shook her head, almost in disbelief. "By Endra's grace, no major organs were pierced. Lots of blood and her tissue was a mess, but there was almost no major damage. She has stitches but should be back in her fighting form soon." The Queen let out a noise that almost sounded like a scream, turning into a gasp, the King and Kylo supporting her in a hug. Jasper burst through the door, head sweeping back and forth between his family and the doctor.

"Is she dead?"

"She's very much alive," the doctor smiled, and Jasper gasped, leaning over to rest on his knees, letting out a shuddered breath.

"Thank gods," Theo heard him murmur and managed to smile at him, despite wanting to demand where he had been.

"Go be with your brother," Theo told the twins, sending them over to Jasper, watching them wrap him into a hug.

"Can we see her?"

"Sure." The doctor glanced at Theo. "Family only–"

"–he is family," the royals said together. Theo raised his eyebrows, but took the Queen's hand when she offered it, letting himself be pulled into the hospital wing with them.

"Amair!" Alec exclaimed, spotting her as the doors opened. He broke away from the group, running towards her as she smiled tiredly.

"Hey buddy," she smiled, squirming a little to get one of her arms around him. Evander held her other hand, kneeling next to the hospital bed.

"My darling girl." The King sat, planting his hand just above Evander's. "Thank gods you're alive."

"Thank those boys," Amair smiled past her father, catching Jasper's eye.

"How are you feeling?" the Queen asked, sitting on the bed next to her.

"Not too badly. I'm…I don't know, it hurts."

"You scared us, Ama." Her father moved her hair out of her eyes. "Going missing. Then the boys sending word they had just *gone after you*. Suddenly hearing you were in surgery for an injury." He shook his head. "After everything we…"

"I know, daddy…" Amair's face fell. "When do we tell the Council?"

"I will tell them you're safe. We will meet with them once you've recovered some, give you a few days to recuperate before you lead the charge on what we do next." Theo and Jasper noticed Amair grimace a little.

"The dress?" Amair asked, looking at her brother.

"Hanging in my study," he nodded, his arms crossed over his chest.

"What dress?" the King asked.

"That's…a long story," Amair tried to smile but it faltered.

"I'll explain it," Jasper assured her. "What I can. You can fill in the blanks later."

"Come, my boys." The Queen pulled at the twins, glancing at her husband. "You too, Niall. Let's give Amair and Theodore some time together."

"Theo." The Queen pulled him aside as the boys said goodnight. "We are going to go have a quiet dinner in my sitting room. I'll make sure supper is sent to your room. But you stay with her as long as you need…you both need."

"Thank you, your majesty."

"If you're calling my husband Niall, I feel that you can probably call me Kier."

"Yes, ma'am."

"Although everyone here just calls me mom." She winked, turning to grab the twins. Kylo and Jasper leaned over to kiss Amair's forehead, Jasper rubbing her cheek and Kylo holding her in a hug just a little longer, whispering something to her. Theo waited, watching the royal family disappear out the door, their chatter bubbling just outside. Theo smiled, pulling off his jacket, laying it across the back of the chair.

"You got all the blood off," she smiled, patting the bed next to her before he could sit.

"I did," he smiled, taking her hands and kissing them.

"Good."

"Your brother moved me into the Family Wing. One of the guest rooms."

She grinned a little. "Not a guest room if you're there. Now it's Theo's Suite." She ran her hand up and down his forearm. "How far is it from mine?"

"Right around the corner."

"Next to the twins?"

"Mhmm."

"Darn," she smiled, squeezing his arm, "he did that on purpose. I can't possibly sneak over there without waking Evander."

"Were you planning to be sneaking?"

Amair laughed, tired and strained. "It crossed my mind." They were quiet, holding each other.

"How do you feel? Really?" he asked, squeezing her fingers.

"Mhm," she shifted, tears rolling down her cheeks, "I wanna say okay but…the numbness is starting to wear off and…everything hurts and my head is spinning but…I'm warm again. I was so cold, for a while. Like the ice rivers we would dare each other to jump in in Tunngas, but…worse, somehow." She wiped at her tears. "So…better. Can only get better, I hope."

He brushed his fingers over her cheek, brushing at the wayward tears, relieved at how her skin looked pink again, instead of the grey that had set in when they had returned to the castle. "You look human, again."

"Yeah, the trolls will be disappointed."

"I was just thinking less ghost-like."

"Ouch."

"How is that worse than trolls?"

"Trolls are cute."

"And ghosts aren't?"

"Hard to be cute when you're *dead*."

"I'll remember that." Amair chuckled, head tipping a little bit.

"Can you lay with me? Just for a few moments?"

Theo paused, studying her for a moment, but smiled. "Of course." She scooted to the side as best she could, giving him room to lay on his side and wrap an arm around her, above where he could see the outline of the bandages. She picked up his hand, raising it to her lips and kissing the tips of his fingers.

"Even in a hospital gown you are the most beautiful girl," Theo murmured into her ear, pressing a kiss just below it.

"Kiss me," she murmured, turning her head, letting go of his hand to let him cup her cheeks. "Kiss me, and don't let there be a last one."

"You scared me Amair," Theo whispered, tears streaming down his cheeks suddenly, "asking me that." Amair fumbled her hand, reaching for him, grabbing his elbow and squeezing.

"I couldn't go in there without it." He kissed her, his tears wetting their lips, some of them falling onto Amair's cheeks as he held her.

"They move me back to my room in the morning."

"I'll be there every day."

"Is this going to affect your serial?" Theo laughed, pressing his forehead against hers.

"I think yes. But the people know you now, anyways." He grinned. "Besides. I may have found a new subject."

"Yeah?" she smiled, leaning back onto the pillow.

"Yeah," Theo shifted, snaking his arm behind her, letting her rest into him. "Lenora seems pretty fascinating."

Amair smiled, but it faltered after a second. "You're not in my circle but…will you deliver something, for me?"

"Anything for you, my darling."

"You'll need a pen and paper. They need to know all the pieces."

"It can wait—"

"—it can't," she shook her head, wincing as she tried to sit up. "They need to know." Theo chewed on his lip, nodding finally, reaching for the pen he had shoved into his pocket out of habit.

He swung his legs off the bed. "Let me find a notecard."

Her face was stony but determined as she recounted every brutal detail and Theo tried to keep his journalist's hat on. His hand slowed as her words brought them back to the castle.

"I would have to give up the paper," he murmured, looping the last letter and waving the third notecard to dry the ink. Amair turned her head, her eyes searching his face.

"I would never ask you to." She shook her head with as much force as she could muster. "But…being a reporter…could be…more difficult. You would likely have to monitor what you wrote about from inside the castle walls. Going beyond the safety of them causes other…issues." She tried to shrug. "It's up to you. More things to think about…this relationship is in your hands. Loving a royal…not just any royal, but the heir, the future Sovereign…it can be rather difficult." Her eyes were heavy now.

"You should sleep," he whispered, leaning over to kiss her forehead. "I love you Ama." She mumbled two words in reply, her head slumping to one side as the next wave of exhaustion finally caught up with her.

Theo snuck out of the hospital wing, picking his way through the basement hallways, finally finding the staircase he recognized as the one he'd been led down. He tried to keep the questions about his future out of his head, figuring out what he could possibly write about in the serial that week that was deep enough to honour what Amair had been through, without tipping off the kingdom.

He had to stop at the foyer, letting go of the bannister and walking across the foyer to the door. It was night time again and exhaustion was starting to take over his body.

"Teddy!" a voice called behind him.

"Oh, Kylo," Theo smiled.

"How is she?"

"Sleeping, at last. On her own, this time."

"Will you," Kylo tugged at his hands, "walk through the garden with me?"

"Uh," Theo looked the boy up and down, "I can. Of course. I would like that. Are you…are you alright?"

"It's Amair's favourite place. To walk. And think. She says she has seen spirits and fae there. I don't…I don't know, it just feels like a good place to be. Her place." Kylo's eyes widened. "Unless you're too tired. I understand—"

"—I would love to walk the garden." Theo followed Kylo towards the other door, the young Prince motioning to the guard to open it. The guard bowed a little, turning to push the door open, and the boys moved out into the chilly night.

"Jasper said they took her to try and marry her off to Novak," Kylo mused, his hands clasped behind his back.

"Yes."

"I said we should burn the dress and to fuck with if we go to war or not."

"What will happen to it?"

"They're packing it to send to the Emperor of Keene."

"What will that do?"

"Father's hoping it will call out Novak, if the Emperor doesn't know."

"How could he—"

"—the place you were at isn't actually the castle. It was Novak's. His father, the Archduke doesn't even live there." Kylo snorted. "Even he can't stand to be around his little beetle of a son."

"Why not send it to his father? The Archduke?"

"The Emperor is Novak's grandfather. Novak's uncle is Grand Duke, heir to the crown, not the Archduke. The Archduchy is a position of…convenience, to brush him off to the side. But he *and* Novak must act at the wishes of the emperor and the heir. Like…Jasper and I, to Amair and our father."

"So…if the Emperor did not know?"

"I'm not sure. Amair will have to talk to the Inner Circle in the next day or so. I think if he didn't, something will happen to Novak.

Maybe...exile? That'd be cool." Theo laughed at the expression that passed Kylo's face. "Then I'd just sick the twins on him and that mess would be dealt with."

"And if the Emperor *did* know?"

Kylo sighed. "That, *I* don't know." But Theo could hear the secret in his voice.

"Kylo?"

"I can't say for sure. It's not...a one size fits all type of situation."

"Kylo—"

"—all I know is that I remember a tutor trying to explain something like this to Jasper a while ago..." he looked up at Theo. "He said it led to a war."

"Lovely."

"Our Kingdom hasn't seen a war...since the Great Chaos, like a hundred years ago. And we have allies...more allies than Keene, I think. But the Keenians, they're known to be...vicious. They have mandatory service, make their citizens do things."

Theo nodded. "So, no matter what..."

"No matter what, I only see hurt. For *someone* involved." Theo and Kylo were quiet the rest of the way around the garden.

- CHAPTER LXIII -

The castle was quiet. Every tap of a raindrop seemed too loud, every scuffle of the staff's feet jarring. Everyone sat, waiting for news as the Princess was quietly moved back to her room and though the doctor assured the royal family it was about recovering in her comforts, Theo had a sneaking suspicion it was more about Amair being less than a model patient.

Theo tapped on the Princess' door with his shoe, rocking on the balls of his feet. The door pulled open, Lydia's face falling a little as she took him in. "Sir Crawford."

"Miss Lydia. Is she awake?"

"No."

"Ah. Well, I'll just drop her breakfast inside."

"Well, I can take—" Theo pulled the silver tray back as her hands came out the door. Lydia huffed, the two staring each other down before she finally gave in and pulled open the door. All the curtains were open, letting the first light of day come in.

Theo raised an eyebrow. "I thought she was sleeping."

Lydia pursed her lips. "The day the Princess has a normal sleep schedule will be the day she is dead."

"Mmhm..."

"Just let him in, Lydia" Amair's voice called from inside. Lydia rolled her eyes a little, opening the door the rest of the way and stepping to let him in.

"Good morning, darling."

"Good morning." She smiled, resting on her back, peeking one eye open. "Leave the tray and come hold me." Theo smiled, the tray clinking a little against her desk and settled carefully next to her on her bed.

"What are you putting in this week's article?" Amair asked, eyes resting.

"I was thinking 'A View Inside The Princess' Bedcham–'" He noticed the murderous look Lydia shot him from across the room. "I'm sure I have an old interview I never used."

"Mhm." She pulled a hand out from under her covers, cracking one eye open. Theo laughed as Amair tapped her hand against her bed, glancing at his arm with her open eye. Glancing at Lydia again who had disappeared into Amair's closet, he reached over to take her cold hand in both of his.

"Part of me wishes I could crawl up next to you," he whispered, bringing her fingertips to his lips.

"You aren't the only one." She shifted, opening both eyes. "I am still freezing."

"I will knit you warmer socks!"

Amair laughed. "Perfect–" She paused, tipping her head. "You knit?"

"Ah...sort of."

Amair snorted, squeezing his hands. "How are you going to occupy your time?"

"I was planning on having Gaelen drag my desk in here and–"

"–absolutely not," Lydia called, making both of them laugh.

"No, but I think I'd like to spend some more time with your brothers."

"I like that idea. And...maybe my mom?"

"If she'll have me."

"I'll ask her." She tipped her head. "Could you do me a favour?"

"Anything, anytime."

"Instead of me, could you do a couple short interviews with my Circle, for the serial? I know something was published introducing them a while ago but..."

"I would love to."

"You're amazing."

"I try my best." They smiled at each other for a moment.

Amair's eyes flicked over, glancing back to Theo and dropping her voice, "Can she see us?"

"I don't think so," he whispered back. She reached over, wrapping her finger into his collar and pulling him down to kiss her. Theo grinned against her lips, slipping a hand behind her head.

"You should go so Lydia can stop pretending to be folding something." She smirked, pulling back.

"And you should eat." He ran his fingers down her cheek as he stood up straight. "Get your strength back. I get the feeling you're going to need it…" Amair nodded. "Alright, Lydia, I'm leaving!" Theo called, hearing the shuffling in the closet slow.

"Thank the gods," they heard her call. Theo chuckled as he waved to Amair, backing slowly to her door to keep his eyes on her just a little bit longer, and letting himself out into the hallway.

It was a pretty morning, turning into a pretty afternoon, grey light casting off the dew as the rain finally paused after days. Theo walked slowly, thinking through each step, the buzz having returned to his fingers and it was somehow more persistent, as though knowing why he could not hold her made it worse.

"Theodore!"

He glanced up from his book, smiling as the Prince ran down the hall, pulling someone along with him. "Good morning, Kylo."

"I wanted you to meet Prince Nusiq, of Tunngas."

Theodore grinned, glancing at the raven-haired boy, bowing to him. "I've heard quite a lot about you, Prince Nusiq – have you just arrived?"

"This morning, I've just been moved into a guest suite in the Family Wing. I've read your serial!" The boy bobbed his head back. "And heard about you in our letter. And you don't have to bow, I'm, like, barely a royal."

"More royal than I." Theo winked, both the boys giggling, Nusiq slipping his hand into Kylo's. "I'm glad you're here, though. To be with our prince."

"So am I."

"And so am I," Kylo agreed, squeezing Nusiq's hand. "We're off to say hello to Ama...have you seen her today?"

"Just now, under Lydia's watchful eye. I brought her breakfast."

Kylo laughed, slipping his arm around Nusiq, pulling him closer. "She warms up eventually, I swear."

"Here's hoping."

"Best bet is sneaking in at evening guard change." Kylo winked this time, and Theo's eyes widened a little. "Just saying."

"Not that we'd know," Nusiq added, his eyes sliding between Kylo and Theo.

"Oh, of course not." Kylo bit his lip. "See you later, Theodore."

"See you both later?"

"I'm not going anywhere," Nusiq grinned as Kylo pulled him around to walk down the hall.

***

"How long is Nusiq staying?" Theo asked, running his fingers over her cheek, a fire crackling to try and get her warm.

"My father sent a letter to Queen Nukila, asking permission to keep Nusiq here." Amair smiled, watching their interlaced fingers. "He's the second son of the heir to a matriarchal throne...he plays no big role in their court, it makes sense to have him with us. And Kylo, he's...happier, when he's here. It's hard being the middle child, especially in this family. Jasper and I work so much...I think he gets lonely, even if we try to keep him close to us."

"And I mean, he's young."

"So young..." Amair murmured.

"He's allowed to be giddy, and in love."

"I think Tunngas is going to send Nusiq's head tutor, so they can do their schooling together, too." She sighed. "I thought I was so grown up, when I was their age. Somehow, I feel younger now than I ever did." She snorted, shaking her head. "Doesn't help that the Council treats me as the little girl they knew."

"You were stabbed, I think that will change some perceptions."

"Perhaps..."

***

The days dragged on, Councillors slipping in and out to check on Amair, Theo trying to work around them and keep more rumours from flying. He had been trying to memorize the names of the Councillors with little success. They would sit quietly together, hands folded as she slept and he let the time pass reading to her, the librarians quietly passing along what they assured were her favourite books.

On the fourth day of her bed rest, he snuck in an early copy of a Liza Belgrade novel he had found. Amair had squealed with laughter, sitting and listening to him read all the scandalous details, her laughter floating out into the hallway. Staff paused, smiling, listening to a sound they had not heard in so long. As their day together ended, the book slipped under his jacket he pulled the door open to find Lydia standing there, trying to hide the smile on her face. She rearranged her face quickly, looking him up and down with a satisfied sniff.

On the fifth day of her bed rest, another scandalous novel tucked into his satchel, Theo reached for Amair's door to find it already open a crack, voices inside. "Why were you out there?" he raised an eyebrow, recognizing the Queen's voice.

"Mama," Amair sighed over the crackling of her fireplace. Theo peeked in the crack in the door, the Queen perched on Amair's bed, her back to the door so he couldn't see their faces. "After my birthday I found a note, I…I didn't know the handwriting. It said they knew what happened to Layton." The Queen inhaled sharply. "I got a second note, that night, asking me to meet in the exterior courtyard and they would tell me what they knew."

"And they grabbed you."

"I…" Amair sniffled a little. "I should have known better, but I had to know, I–"

"–it's okay, Ama."

Theo pressed his lips together, letting go of the door handle and letting Amair cry without an audience.

***

"Are you still in bed?" Theo joked, leaning against her bedpost.

"Just one, *one* more day," Amair groaned, hitting the bed beside her.

"And then," he kissed her hand, "I will hold you tight again."

"I mean…" she grinned, "what difference does a day make?"

"Whatever difference the doctor thought it would." He kissed her forehead. "I will see you *tomorrow*." He laughed as she grumbled, slipping out the door into the hall.

"How is she this evening?" he heard Lydia ask behind him. He spun and bowed slightly.

"Well, she doesn't like being in bed," Theo chuckled, Lydia already with an eyebrow raised and her eyes narrowed. "I'm pretty sure she'd even take a Council meeting right about now." Lydia nodded, looking partially amused. Theo nodded at her, turning and finding his way down the hall.

"Theodore!" Lydia called after him. He slowed, turning to raise an eyebrow at her. She pursed her lips, tipping her head back a little. Finally, she shrugged. "You're not terrible." She twisted, disappearing down one of the corridors. Theo blinked a couple times, a laugh bubbling out as he shook his head and went the other way.

***

It was late, the last night alone and Theo desperately just wanted to find his way back to his new room in the Family Wing so he could sleep until they could all say she was more or less okay again. He rounded a corner, the sun setting gently into the Highlands.

"Theo!" His name echoed gently around him and he looked up. It had been only over a week and yet it felt like an eternity since he had heard the specific lilt of her feet, always halfway to a run even in her perfectly cobbled, heeled shoes.

A smile spread across his face slowly, Amair's silhouette filling out as his eyes adjusted to the light coming in the window. "She's up!" Theo breathed, grinning, bounding down the hall towards her. Amair smiled, picking up the skirt on her linen dress, kicking off her shoes and running down the hallway towards Theo.

She winced as she crashed into him, arms reaching out to hold him, but she ignored the warm pain that bubbled through her side. Theo's hand was on the back of her head, holding her as her arms gripped tightly around his neck. The cool light slipping through the clouds fell over them as Theo stood there, holding her.

He ran his fingers across the back of her hair, taking in the way her body felt next to his. Memorising every inch of how she felt in his arms.

"Don't let go," she murmured against him, pulling her arms a little tighter. "Not yet." Theo felt his cheeks flush warm, smiling as he buried his nose further into her hair. He pushed the noise of the castle out of his mind, existing, for a perfect moment, with her.

"I've got you."

- CHAPTER LXIV -

Amair walked back into her room after her first breakfast, stretching with a wince but for the first time in over a week, her body felt like hers again, feet moving across the floor. She paced around her room, the traces of her sickbed already starting to disappear but she paused, staring into her wardrobe.

"Lydia?"

"Yes, my lady?" She glanced at the Princess. "What's wrong?" Amair turned her head, raising her eyebrows at the concern on the woman's face.

"I need every red dress taken out of this closet. Please." The woman's face changed, less concerned and more sad.

"Of course, my lady." Lydia nodded, reaching out to touch her fingers to Amair's arm.

"Lydia?"

"Yes, my lady?"

"Do you," Amair choked a little bit, a sob strangled, "do you feel trapped here?"

"My lady?"

"Do you feel...trapped? Forced. Any..."

"My lady...where is this coming from?"

"Keene..." Amair shook her head, a tear slipping down her cheek. "They have slaves, Lydia. They went into Forra, and RiKoi, and Elira, and..." She could not bring herself to say Skylock. "And kidnapped people from their homes and...they scare them into staying in the castle. And they've been there for generations, so it's not like they can just make their way back to their people." Another sob escaped her lips.

"My lady, come here." Lydia squeezed her hand, pulling her towards the settee, helping her sit, gathering some of her big skirt out of the way. "My lady, I chose this work. We all did. We were not born into it. We didn't get brought here. We weren't coerced. We replied to a listing. You gave me a home, and colleagues that I love. And I do well in this job. I like this job. And if, someday, I want to do another job, or go to university, or I decide to move to another district and have an adventure and take after my lady," she smiled, squeezing Amair's hands, "I have no fear that I can." Amair cried and smiled at the same time, leaning her head against Lydia. "I live in a country that provides a home, and a farm if we want it, and medical care, and education. If I…want to pursue a masters someday, working for the castle means it's paid for. I love you, Princess." The two of them wrapped their arms around each other. "I am so glad we got you back."

Lydia touched her chin gently for a moment, the two sitting with one another. "Now," Lydia brushed a piece of hair from Amair's face, "let's get you dressed. You have the Councillors to parry with."

***

"My first major act as Oighre *cannot* be *a war*!" Amair clasped her hands together behind her head, looking up as she paced. She stopped abruptly, turning her head to glare at Theo. "That does not leave this room, Theodore."

"Hey, there is no pen in these hands," Theo exclaimed, raising his hands in defence, fingers wide.

She pointed, twirling one of her fingers. "Yeah, that doesn't always mean those little writing wheels aren't…whirring."

"I'm here supporting you." He lifted his chin a little. "Not as the Writer." Something picked at the back of his brain as he said it, but he tried to ignore the feeling. He wasn't sure if she'd heard him, just continuing to pace back and forth.

"You need to calm down, Amair."

"Yeah, cause saying that is gonna help," Amair scoffed at her brother. "I chose the wrong day not to put on the big dresses." Jasper and Theo glanced at the mustard-yellow linen dress coming to Amair's shins.

"There's probably enough time for you to change before the meeting—"

"—no," she shook her head, pacing again. "No, I'm just in regular undergarments, it would take hours to get myself together, and anything against the bandages still hurts like nothing else…I'm still putting that off."

"Okay then." Jasper and Theo shared a look, and Amair went back to pacing.

"I…I am not ready to be making these decisions. I've been heir for all of like, two minutes. I'm not even Queen." She paused. "Can I tell them that? That I'm not even Queen?"

"Don't think that would fly," Theo shook his head. Amair finally stopped pacing, leaning against a stand that he recalled once seeing a fancy vase on.

"I think I'm gonna be sick."

Theo furrowed his brow, watching her. "You survived being kidnapped, knocked a man unconscious, and then literally fought your way out."

"And saved Theo's dumb ass in the process," Jasper snickered.

"Yeah, that too," Theo laughed.

They managed to make her chuckle but they all went dead silent as the doors clicked open and Moritz slipped out, someone's holler slipping out with him. He was in his casual armour, his sword at his hip, and his eyes trailed over the teenagers. Theo caught him gulp and try to stiffen. "Princess," he said, bowing his head a little. Amair swallowed hard. "King and Council are ready for you."

Amair looked at her brother, looked at Theo. "It's time," she murmured.

"It's time," Jasper nodded. He got up to kiss his sister's forehead, walking over to wait at the door. Theo got up, holding her hand and kissing her knuckles.

"You'll be fine."

Moritz stared at her a second longer, acting before he thought and reaching out to squeeze her shoulder. They looked up into each other's eyes, steady looks. He squeezed a bit tighter, nodding, and turned to knock twice on the door.

The doors seemed to shudder before they opened with a *whoosh*, chaos inside the Council room that the King tried to quell as heads turned to inspect the Princess. She ran her hands nervously down the sides of her dress, straightening her shoulders.

"Princess Amair. Please, do come in." Jasper, Kylo, and Theo stood behind her, watching her walk slowly inside, her yellow dress stark against the pale Council room as the light of day shone in the side windows, a long table in the middle stuffed with people who all looked as though they wanted tear each other apart, though a few looked as though they wanted to cry. Amair turned her head just enough for them to catch a glimpse of the fear she was trying to hide, as two room attendants pulled the Council room doors closed.

***

Jasper paced. Then Theo. The only person too nervous to stand was Kylo, sitting with his knees bouncing watching the two older boys pace back and forth in front of the door. The doors rattled at one point, making Jasper jump, whipping his head towards the others, wondering what had been thrown.

It was minutes to twilight when Moritz opened the doors again, the Council exiting first, dishevelled and annoyed. Moritz paused, his eyes on the King and Amair when they were the last to file out into the hall. The rest of the King's aides had gathered at the edge of the hall, watching, balancing on the edge of some imaginary line of what could come.

"How'd it go?" Theo asked as Jasper called, "What happened?"

Amair took a deep breath, her bottom lip trembling ever so slightly. She opened her mouth and closed it again. The King walked up behind her, and Amair looked down at her shoes, staring down intently as he placed a hand on her shoulder.

The King's face was stone cold. "We're going to war."

Gasps and hushed cries whispered through the aides. Theo felt eyes flicking onto his and the pen in his pocket suddenly felt very heavy. "Go, be with your families, the Council and my staff will begin preparing an announcement immediately. I must go and send word to the Chiefs and War Chiefs. Get some rest, everyone." As if for emphasis, though Theo suspected it was all just starting to hit him, the King rubbed his eyes, turning down the hall to head for the Family Wing.

Moritz paused as the others peeled out of the hall, stooping to give Amair a one-armed hug, shaking his head a little, before turning to follow the King.

"Should have burned the dress when we had the chance," Theo growled, Amair already taking off in the opposite direction.

"What *happened?*" Jasper demanded, pulling Theo after him. Kylo ran to catch up with them, all of them trying to keep up with Amair clipping down the hallway.

"Yeah, so I thought the plan was to *not* go to war."

"Ugh, Kylo–"

"–Amair!"

"We didn't send the declaration!" Amair exclaimed, the yellow skirt swishing around her legs. She looked around, walking straight through the door beside them. The three boys glanced at each other, turning to follow her.

"*We* didn't send the declaration." She put her hands on her hips, looking up and trying to blink back tears. "*They* did. It was waiting for me, on the table when I walked into the Council room."

"When–"

"–I'm going out the night after next to try and solve this." She pressed her lips together but they could all see them trembling, a tiny speck of blood on her linen dress, her eyes meeting Theo's. "I didn't want this. But I love my people…if I can't talk my way out of it…then you can bet I am going down fighting."

- CHAPTER LXV -

Holding Amair the night of the Council meeting as she had broken into a panic had nearly ended him. She was exhausted, sitting at her desk trying to organize her people and correspondence to prepare for the impending meeting with their greatest enemy and something about it had finally dug into the cracks she had worked so hard to hide and split her open.

If Theo could have picked up a sword, training or not, and killed every last person who had gotten her to that point, he would have. But as she had wrapped herself into the safety of his arms, he had known where he was needed. He held her as the moon had risen high, her breathing finally slowing from the panicked gasps to something that was almost like a normal rate.

He woke up, alone, in her bed. Her side was already cold, and someone had tucked him in. As he blinked, he could see the intricate designs on her canopy, and Lydia fussing with a pail of fresh laundry in the corner of the room. He could smell the castle's laundry soap wafting through the room as the comfort of Skylock's grey morning streamed through Amair's gauzy curtains. As he sat up, trying to wipe the exhaustion from his eyes, he could see Lydia wiping at her face and realized she was wiping at tears. The two locked eyes and stared at each other, not saying anything, but somehow acknowledging the growing fear they were both feeling.

Theo rushed back to his room to change before heading off to find Amair, with the help of a maintenance worker who pointed him in the direction of the armoury. The castle seemed to have split down the middle, half preparing for the ride out, half bustling about with tasks Theo could not put together.

"Arthur!" Theo called, spotting him directing knights in the back foyer. "What are they doing?"

"Preparing for the ride out," Arthur said, not looking up from his list.

"No…the others."

Arthur paused, gripping his pen a little tighter. "Preparing for a war." He turned away from Theo, making it clear he had nothing more to say.

Theo gulped, going on his way.

He pushed open the door to the armoury, a warm fire behind a table with basic smithing tools the first thing to greet him. The main keep was lined with sharp swords, brilliantly decorated and he wondered how many people had stepped through the door looking for a solution or a show of power. He kept on through a second door, blinking at Amair's leg up on a stool, fastening a buckle on her boot. Theo looked her up and down, eyes falling on the row of knives on the side of her.

"What?" Amair asked sharply, stretching her arms in the long, heavy-looking jacket, a belt-like strap tight around her waist.

"Nothing."

She raised an eyebrow, tightening the strap one more time, dropping to fix the holster of knives on her thigh. "I'll be done soon…you can wait in the main store." She bobbed her head, turning to pull something else off the wall.

Theo bowed slightly, stepping back out of the smaller room. He walked past the rows of weapons, gulping at the sharp blades, and the weapons he would not even know how to start picking up.

A voice startled him, "What's your weapon?"

Theo glanced back at the aging man, his sparse white hair pulled back into a low pony, glasses set on his nose. He had a black apron on, and Theo spotted a hint of soot or polish in his white goatee.

"Uh…a pen, usually," Theo shook his head, looking back across the rows of weapons, the Armoury Keep studying him.

"Which is why *you* won't be going," Amair said as she walked briskly into the main keep, a sword attached to her back.

"Amair–" She ran her hand down the side of his face as she stepped up to him, resting it on his jaw, the sound of the door opening behind him.

She stood on her toes, gently pressing her nose against his. "You'll be okay."

"Amair!" he cried, two guards taking his arm from her.

"Kylo," Amair looked over Theo's shoulder to where her brother came in. "You keep Theo safe." She smiled sadly at him, looking back to Theo.

"I can help–"

"You," she touched Theo's side, "have helped. You have made me ready for this. I am so much stronger. And you can help here, Writer." She turned her head to the guards. "Lock him in his room if he tries to follow. Guards at the door, and under the window."

"Amair!"

"I love you, Theodore." Theo stared at her, mouth wide at the words that passed her lips for the first time.

"Amair!" But she wasn't listening anymore, Jasper helping whisk her down the hallway. Theo fought against the guards, demanding they release him.

"I'm so sorry, Sir Crawford," one of them said, keeping his grip on Theo's arm but laying a hand on his back. "I'm so sorry." They dragged Theo from the room as he fought against their strong grip, already feeling the bruises where they were trying to keep hold of him, one of the guards still trying to console him. At the end of the hall, Amair glanced over her shoulder once, her eyes on Theo, forcing a smile. A tear escaped from the corner of her eye, and she turned the corner, Theo's calls for her fading into the back.

"He helped save you, Amair."

"Barely," she scoffed, but Jasper noted the pain in her voice.

"He could come."

"No, because if *he* is there," Amair looked up at her brother, her voice cracking slightly, "*he* will be the only thing I am thinking about. And I can't have that." She laughed crudely. "Besides. Someone's gonna need to write my eulogy."

"Don't."

"Luckily this family has backups and extra heirs."

"Amair!"

"Come on, Jasper." She looked up at him, the blue in her eyes gleaming, the brown in her eye almost looking black as she glared up at him. "Keene doesn't do mercy. And we don't exactly have an upper hand, here."

Jasper glared at her. "We have you."

She shook her head. "Just another broken heir."

Jasper sighed. "We should go."

"Yeah." She shoved a knife into each of her boots. "Let's go."

"How do you move with all that hardware?"

"Practice," she shrugged, as they turned into a staircase to the courtyard.

Arthur caught her arm as they walked into the yard, the anxious horses trying to be held in place by even more anxious stable hands. "Hey, you and your brother okay?" Arthur asked.

"Fine."

"He's shooting daggers into your back with his eyes."

She rolled his eyes. "He's mad at me."

"You told him we didn't send the dec–"

"–oh, of course I did." She shrugged. "He doesn't like my *attitude*."

"Well, I figured he'd have gotten used to it by now, I mean the rest of us ha–"

"–Arthur."

"Don't pull the Princess card."

"No, I'm pulling the 'I will stab you' card."

"Can't. Need all the hands we can get for the battlefield. So! Why's he mad?"

She looked down, fiddling with something on her saddle. "I just…I said a few things, and I think they got to him. Sometimes…sometimes I forget that he went through losing Layton too. And that…I don't know if my brothers can survive losing another sibling."

"You're more than just another sibling, Ama. You know that."

"And I'm covering my deep, deep fear, the only way I know how."

"Riders! At the ready!" Amair heard Moritz's voice as he and the King walked into the cobbled courtyard.

"Time to go," Amair murmured, looking up at the castle one more time. *I'm coming back,* she promised herself.

- CHAPTER LXVI -

The words in the declaration kept ringing in her ears, the Councillors' insistences and reminders still weighing on her. She gripped the reins of her horse, her hips sore as she sat back in her worn saddle, glancing back and forth at the others trotting ahead of her. Three of the four Skylock knights they had been allowed to bring with them had gone ahead to set up the tent in a neutral corridor Denna had convinced the Forran King to establish for the meeting between Keene and Skylock.

"Chin up, Ama," Arthur murmured, falling back as the top of the two flags came into view just beyond the edge of the next hill. She snapped a glare at him. He turned to meet her eye, adjusting his knight's scarf. "Don't let them see the crown slip."

Her eyes softened, sitting a little taller in her saddle as they started the descent into the corridor, coils of smoke from two small fire pits trailing into the sky.

The three longest serving Councillors, Vyron, McRuun, and Avelenn, were the first to the tent, greeted by the Skylock knights. Amair slowed her horse, watching each of the elected slide off theirs, leaning their heads together to whisper. She narrowed her eyes, tightening her hand on her reins again and clucking her horse up, galloping down the hill as the rain that had been threatening started to spit.

She pulled Elleban to a halt, letting one of the Knights grab her reins as she slid off, her long coat whipping back in the wind as Arthur rushed to catch up with her.

She paused outside the tent, hand raised to let herself in but pictured her family and friends waiting for her at the castle. Her mom trying to stay strong but silently weeping in her study. Theo pacing, locked in his room to keep him safe, yelling at the door, demanding to be let out. Kylo's head bent with Nusiq's, ready to go for cover, each tucking their favourite book under their arms. The twins, with no idea what was happening, but trembling in the anxiety that was growing around them. Her Circle waiting for instructions.

She took a deep breath, remembering who she was there for, and stepped inside.

"Princess." The Councillors stood abruptly as she walked in, flanked by her Arthur and for a moment, she felt more regal than she ever had. Jasper turned, hands gripping the back of the chair.

"Your majesty!" a knight called, racing into the tent, "your highness…" Amair and the King stood taller. The knight swallowed hard. "They…they're here." Everyone's eyes went to the crack in the tent's opening, trying to calm their breathing.

Amair swallowed hard, her fingers dancing over the hilt of her sword. "Let's go squash a bug."

Jasper leaned towards Arthur. "I was thinking more *slay a dragon.*"

***

"Novak."

"Amair." A sour grin spread across his face. Amair stared at him in disgust.

"It's *your highness,* to you."

Novak's mouth twitched.

"The grown-ups are talking, Novak." The Archduke waved his hand to his son. "Go sit in the tent."

"Father—"

"King Niall." The Keenian Emperor bowed his head slightly as he strode out of the black tent, his eldest son the Grand Duke just behind him.

"Emperor Omnan." Amair watched her father bob his head. "Grand Duke Mevelon."

"Novak?" the Emperor raised an eyebrow, as though noticing him for the first time. "What are you doing here? Go sit in the tent," the Emperor instructed. Novak huffed, turning to walk away.

"Princess Amair." The Grand Duke bowed, deeper than Amair had expected. He tried to reach for her hand, but she yanked it away, listening to Arthur and Moritz behind her step forward threateningly.

"So, let's talk about why we are all here—"

"—because you went ahead and declared war on us," Arthur said, Moritz grabbing his arm and shaking his head.

The Keenian *tsked* with his tongue. "You broke into my grandson's home and murdered seven of my guards, and two of my knights."

Amair's glare turned incredulous. "Your oh-so-darling grandson kidnapped me."

"The adults are—"

"—I am as much the heir to my Kingdom as your eldest is to his, you will address me as such," Amair warned. Jasper glanced at Amair, trying not to beam with pride. The Emperor and Amair stared each other down. It was he who turned away first.

"Niall—"

"—my daughter's right, Omnan. It's her story."

"Fine. Fine." The Emperor looked at her again, unable to meet her eye. "What happened?"

"Novak—"

"—*Prince* Novak."

Amair's mouth tightened, taking a slow breath. "Prince Novak lured me out of the castle with claims he knew what killed my brother. He dragged me back to his pretty little palace. Where I was introduced to your *slaves*, the stolen generations. And he put me—"

"—in my late wife's wedding dress." Amair paled, putting his words together. "Yes, that part I was informed of."

"And he ran his hands all over me."

Jasper's mouth twitched but neither of the men in front of them stirred.

"So, you and your friends proceeded to knock him out and killed seven guards and two knights in return."

"Well, I didn't see you coming to my rescue," Amair fired back.

"Alright," Mevelon stopped them. "This isn't productive. Clearly Novak screwed up. It is absolutely not the first time."

Amair put a hand on her hip. "I'm glad you agree with me."

"But…" the Grand Duke continued.

"My least favourite word," Amair muttered.

"We still need payment for the lives lost. An eye for an eye."

"Makes the whole world blind," Amair finished, glaring.

"There are…*other* options, but I'm sure you and your Council know that." Mevelon raised an eyebrow. "Take some time to think. Discuss." The Skylocks watched as they turned and walked back down the hill towards the rows of their men.

"We aren't finished, Emperor!" Amair hollered, her face hardening. The men stopped, turning to her again.

"What, *girl?*"

Amair paused, hating how he tried to make the word out to be a weapon. "The other option?"

Mevelon smiled slyly. It almost reminded her of Theo. The thought made her sick. "I'm sure you are figuring it out."

"And if we don't agree?"

"My army is larger, and ready to mobilize." The Emperor raised his chin. "You won't stand a chance." They turned back towards their tent. "We await your answer."

***

"Mevelon offered up a way to settle this between the Kingdoms." Amair looked up at the Councilman. "They have an heir. A single heir." Amair opened her mouth, but nothing came out. "And we have a female heir–"

"–that is *out of the question*," the King bellowed, slamming a fist on the table. Amair and Jasper jumped, glancing at each other across the table, Amair trying to keep her composure. "He is *forty* and she is *a child*. And she is already *in love*." Amair smiled a little, but flattened it down again.

"Not to mention inheriting *our* throne – do you really want to go handing Skylock over to them? Build their empire? That's how they'll see it?" Jasper added.

"What about a trade?" Councillor McRuun asked, his voice always on the edge of nerves. "A life for a life for the men you killed–"

"–saving my life!"

"Or another girl in her place?"

"I am not," Amair stood so fast the makeshift throne behind her toppled to the ground, "sending an innocent to be slaughtered or feasted on. In fact, I would almost rather marry the asshole."

"Amair!" Jasper exclaimed.

"Oh, Novak, not Mevelon." She waved him off.

"No!" Jasper and the King bellowed at the same time.

"Is there anything we can even *counter* with your majesty?" Councillor Vyron crossed his arms over his chest. "We came here to negotiate peace, are we not even considering the possibilities?"

"*They* didn't come here for peace," Arthur seethed, Moritz grabbing for him again, trying to remind him of his place but he pulled away. Amair raising her hand silenced him.

"Arthur's right…Keene knew we wouldn't…*couldn't* take a marriage offer. I'm not ready to just…hand over my Kingdom to their empire."

Amair looked around the room, her eyes falling on every one of the Councillors individually. There were tears pricking at her eyes, her sword suddenly feeling heavier than it ever had. She turned her head to look at the King sitting back in his makeshift throne, his hands folded in front of him as he contemplated.

"Daddy…"

"I was raised in a time of peace…" he said quietly, staring at the table and the Councillors jumped to listen. "I tried to raise my children for peace…" The King had tears in his eyes as he looked at his daughter. "Do you think they had anything to do with our Lost Ones?"

Amair looked down at her feet, shaking her head at first but it turned into a nod. "I can't say for certain."

"But?"

"But…I have my suspicions."

The King's eyes ran slowly over the faces at the table. He stood, knocking a fist on the rough wood once. "If they want to come after us…then damn them.

"Let them taste the wrath of Endra's people scorned."

***

Jasper dragged the massive bag he had insisted on hauling along with them, red tulle exploding out the top of it and people on both sides knew what it was. He dropped it on the centre line between the two tents, the

Keenians bursting from their tents as their knights informed them of what was happening.

Amair stood behind the boys, the Councillors and the Skylock knights behind her, all watching, ready. Her Oighre crown was in place and she managed to sneak a glance at Mevelon's pinched features as he watched Jasper rip open the bag to expose more of the tulle and fabric that had almost been her prison and her death sentence.

Arthur passed him a matchbox, letting Jasper light one, and, with his eyes up on Novak, tossed it into the tulle. It took a moment for the fabric to catch, but as it did, the Keenians turned to watch.

The Emperor's eyes flipped up from the growing flames. "This is war."

Before the King could snarl a return, Amair's steady voice said, "It always was."

- CHAPTER LXVII -

The Skylocks did not move as the flames climbed high and finally burnt down, the rain finally coming in a downpour. The Keenian royals and their knights took off on their dark horses, sending in boys in tattered clothes to take down their black tent.

"Knight Macklin?"

"Yes, Princess?" He stepped forward slightly.

"Please cross the boundary and help them." She looked them up and down. "They aren't more than children…" she muttered. He bowed but did not move at first.

"Moritz, I want a Knight posted every ten feet of our border, all the way along," she forced the words out as fast as the thoughts came, "and coordinate with Forra to aid them in patrol of their land as well, I want an extra cohort stationed in every province ready to help the Clan armies. Send a message to RiKoi…" She turned to find her knights, and family, and Councillors staring at her, eyes bright and focused. "What?"

"You are not the Oighre we planned for," the King told her, pulling off his gloves, and she started to look down. Her father's smile was warm, rain gathering on his brow. "But you have more than proven that you are the Oighre we need."

Amair looked up, her eyes wide. Her father dropped his gloves, the sound of his sword *zinging* as he pulled it out and knelt, planting the tip of the blade in front of him. His fingers wrapped around the hilt, and he bowed his head towards his daughter. Amair stood there, shocked. Slowly, the Knights followed his lead, pulling out their swords and kneeling to her,

Arthur joining with a knowing grin. Moritz stepped forward with the King to kneel with him and Amair nearly fell over in shock as the Councillors knelt, a hand crossed over their chests. She looked over at Jasper, who grinned, crossing an arm over his chest and kneeling with the Knights.

"Long live the Oighre," said Moritz. The rest echoed him. The words rattled in Amair's bones and she stood taller, feeling the rain beating against her back and shoulders. She flexed her fingers and finally bowed at the hips back to them. "Long live the Oighre!"

***

"Open the gate! They've returned!" Amair's horse restlessly stepped back and forth under her as the noise of the castle gates opened slowly, the guard all standing at attention in rows in the main courtyard.

"Long live the Oighre!"

"Long live the Oighre!" echoed across the crowd, some of the townspeople gathering at the edges of the knights escorting the royal family back.

"Word travels fast," Jasper murmured.

"That's what happens when you send word ahead," Arthur reminded.

"We're going to war and somehow I'm the spectacle," Amair muttered.

"You're their saving grace," Arthur shrugged.

"How mad do you think Theo is?" she asked, trying to acknowledge each of the guards she passed. She had a hand on her hips, trying to keep her attention on the crowd, reminding herself to keep breathing.

"You were doing what you thought was best."

"So really mad?"

"Probably."

She took a deep breath, her cheeks hot as Elleban's first hoof passed through the gates, Skylish people screamed and waved, their words still leaving goosebumps on her skin. She looked up, the castle ahead of her, behind the droves of people who had gathered, many coming in from the small communities and farms beyond the royal village.

She could see a figure standing in one of the windows, arms crossed, waiting.

Theo.

***

"You don't get to say that and then send me to my room," Theo's voice was harsher than she had ever heard it as he walked into Amair's room. Amair hung her head, hands folded in front of her, bracing herself for worse.

Theo lifted her face, cupping her cheeks and putting his forehead to hers. "I love you too." Amair smiled, standing on her toes and pushing her forehead back against Theo's, threading her fingers into his hair. "Thank you," his voice was just above a whisper, "for coming back to me."

"I was always planning to come back to you."

"You should have seen her out there. She was amazing, Theo," Jasper grinned, leaning against the doorway. "Actually, it was all quite civilized."

"Nothing about war is civilized," Amair shot back in a warning tone as Jasper stepped in.

"You're gonna want to go out and get statements on it for the paper. The whole Kingdom should know about this." He glanced out Amair's window, a crowd still lingering. "Though I think they may already."

"What happened?"

Amair tipped her head a little. "It was a war or marry the Emperor's creepy son as options, so…yeah, we might have made it worse."

"How do you get worse than a war *they* declared?"

"We set the dress on fire."

Theo glanced at Jasper. "*The* dress?"

"Turns out," Amair sat on her bed, rubbing her hands nervously along her leges, "it was the Emperor's late wife's wedding dress."

"Again, how does this not all come back on Novak?"

"He's an heir to a broken throne."

"How is he an heir?"

"Long story." Amair shrugged. "Jasper, can you leave us, please?" Amair asked, not turning her eyes from Theo.

Jasper was quiet for a moment, eyes swinging between the silently quarrelling couple, nodding slowly. "Anything you need, Ama?"

Her eyes did not leave Theo's, "Please gather the Circle notecards, I have to call everyone home." Jasper bowed, walking out the door. He turned, mouthing '*Good luck*' to Theo before disappearing out of the room.

"Please don't do that again. I felt like a child."

"That…was not my intention, although if it makes you feel better, none of the children were locked in their room." He glared at her a little but she seemed unphased. "I could not function the way I needed to if you were slipping into my head, Theo."

He understood.

Of course he did. He had spent the two days yanking on the door, demanding updates and on the brink of a panic, wondering where she was and what she was doing. "Can you tell me what happened, then? While you were there?"

She chewed on her lip, looking down for a moment and he spotted something cross over her face. "I have a lot of work to do Theo…There's a war coming, now…" His heart sank, feeling her start to push. "But…if you want to come just…sit with me? As I find time between tasks we can…just talk. Like…like when you first got here?"

He sighed, grateful. "I'd like that." She nodded, turning to grab her shawl from her bed but he caught her hand, pulling her to him and she managed to crack a smile. "I'm proud of you, Ama," he whispered. Without thinking, she grabbed his tie, and pulled him in for a kiss.

- CHAPTER LXVIII -

Gaelen cracked the door open to Theo's bedroom, and Theo could hear murmuring as he read an excerpt from one of the encyclopaedias he had snuck from the reference library. *The Art of the Sword.*

"Sir?"

"Yeah?"

"Papers, from her royal highness' office. She sent a note too," he held it up, "she's in meetings all day, her Inner Circle arrives on the morrow and is preparing, she will not have time to sit for an interview, but had something pulled to offer anyways as thoughts. Notes for your serial, I believe."

"Oh, you can just leave them on the table?"

"Of course, Sir."

"And would you mind just...leaving dinner at the door? It's..." Theo glanced towards the door. "It's been...crowded."

"Of course, sir. I'll tell the family you are feeling under the weather." Gaelen bowed, and disappeared through the hidden staff door. It clicked closed, and Theo was alone.

There was too much energy in the castle, more Knights and trainees arriving, friends and family of the royal family and Councillors and extra political advisors coming in from all over the Kingdom to support the royal family as everyone dove into planning. Theo recognized some from other feasts and festivals and yet despite the gravity of their invitations, somehow they still had time to stop and ask the Writer for gossip. Hiding in his room felt easier, especially with Amair surrounded by a new kind of wall as she threw herself into her work.

Theo finally slithered off the window seat, running his fingers over the edge of the metal dinner tray. He stopped, pulling his hand back, noticing the pages filled with Amair's messy handwriting in the rose ink she always had on her desk, a line of ink smudged along the side.

Layton once told me that to be King was to be there for your people before anything else.

I think he was nine when he sat in on his first Council meeting? He was fifteen when he built his inner circle. I was eleven but he still brought me into the circle. Almost everything I have learned I learned from those meetings. I learned from him.

My brother was not a warrior. He was strong. He was incredibly smart and cunning. He loved to sit and dissect policy. He enjoyed the debate. And the challenge.

I, on the other hand, was the warrior. People forget that. Or overlook it, sometimes. I come across as quiet. Which, sure, I am. I have always happily smiled, and lived my life behind the scenes. Because I <u>was</u> behind the scenes. The second child. That was the whole idea. I wanted to get on my horse and put a sword on my back and follow in my grandmother's and my aunt's footsteps to see this world. I trained with the guard. I wasn't reading policy and history books; I was reading fiction and drama and memoires. I wanted to be Layton's right hand. I could be the warrior that he wasn't. He could be the politician I didn't want to be.

I had a dream a few months ago. I was riding through thick brush in Forra. I could feel the comforting weight of my sword on my back. And a messenger would ride up to me, calling my name, saying that I had been summoned to the castle for an emergency circle meeting.

I would go home and hug my brothers. Johanna and Dylan would be there to welcome me. And then when we had vanquished whatever problem had arisen that time, I could turn around and ride for the other coast.

That was my dream.

Before they became The Late Ones. I hate that line. Something ~~seems~~ is so unfinished, about it.

But I am putting myself aside. I love my people. I always have.

I am not going to be King.

<u>*I am going to be Queen.*</u>

Theo ran his fingers over the ripped edges of the page, furrowing his brow at where they had been torn from a book. He turned back to the first page, finding a date at the top of it.

It was dated from three days after Layton's funeral, nearly two full seasons ago.

He ran his hands over what he realized were old diary pages. He could picture Amair curled in one of her secret nooks, a coffee cooling by her side, trying to fight back tears. He read over the last lines again, and again, finally having to put the papers down to stop himself from reading the letters into incomprehension. He paced beside the table, picking pieces of roasted potatoes off the tray.

He called for an attendant who helped him dress quickly. He ran into the washroom and splashed water on his face, rubbing the tired eyes and looking at himself in the mirror again.

He remembered the day he had sat on the second floor, and the way Amair laughed.

It wasn't her.

Then thought about the way his pen had felt in his hand on the day of his first case.

Amair wasn't pulling away.

Then about Amair holding his hand when they had danced at her birthday.

He was.

***

"Your highness?" an attendant knocked on the door of Amair's study. Theo stood behind him, hands behind his back, the pages folded carefully behind his back.

"Let him in, Richard."

"Of course." The attendant bowed, stepping out of the way.

"You pulled these out of a journal?" Theo asked, holding up the pages as soon as the door clicked shut. Amair nodded, casting her eyes back to her papers.

"Yeah, I figured some inner thoughts on something silly and frivolous might be a breath of air for everyone right about now."

"What are you talking about?"

She paused, looking up from her papers. "What are *you* talking about?" she asked, eyebrows knit together. He slowly slid the pages towards Amair, watching her pick them up curiously. She read over the first one, flipping it over in her hand and sucking in her cheeks.

"I'm going to kill my brother," she muttered, turning the pages over in her hands. She set them on her desk, folding her hands and leaning her chin over. "I sent Jasper to find something silly and *appropriate* to give you."

"You just…casually sent him to your journal?" Theo asked, pulling out the chair facing her desk, sitting and leaning forward.

Amair set the papers aside, matching Theo as she leaned forward. "My brother knows things that aren't even in those journals. Some things, writer, cannot be written down."

Theo nodded slowly, processing. "Can I ask you a follow up question?"

Amair closed the folder on her desk, giving the Writer her full attention. "Of course."

"You…you still do all those things you mentioned in this." He pointed to the papers.

"Mhm."

"You…you go out and train with the knights and the guards. You fought in the festival."

"I did."

"You still read dramas. Liza Berelli novels."

"I do."

"You still sneak out to the market."

"That is top secret and off the record," she smiled a little, "but yes."

"But you said you were ready to give it up."

"Because I *was*. In a heartbeat. And I did." She shrugged. "For about two weeks, after I got out of bed."

"What happened?"

She sighed a little, her eyes getting distant as she looked off to the side. But it wasn't sadness or anger. She looked content. "Denna happened. She…forcefully reminded me who I was. Am.

"Layton…his whole identity was being Oighre. He was *raised* to be Oighre. And not because it was forced on him, I mean yes, he was born into it, but it just happened. He is…he *was* like Kylo, he really understood all the history and policy stuff. And he *loved* it.

"At first, when Layton died, and I was crowned as Oighre, I threw my whole self into it…I thought I had to *become* Layton. It didn't help that we had lost him and the whole Kingdom was grieving. And honestly, the Council and the administration pushed that too. I was *ready* to leave everything I knew and wanted and loved behind.

"It wasn't until I found *Layton's* journals that I started to figure it out. He had nearly a decade of notes and thoughts about himself, and being heir and future King. He did not start ready. He did not start good at this. He made mistakes. He had his strengths, his weaknesses.

"I…am the best heir, and will be the best Sovereign, if I am able to be me. I learned how to…fold in the things I loved to be a part of my days. I *am* the Oighre. I studied the history, learned the policies, attended the meetings.

"But I…I put away my work so I could read fiction. I take days that are only for me. I have a schedule to try and keep it from taking over my life before I am *actually* the Sovereign. I go riding. I make the guards practice with me. I run through the woods, and I spend time with my brothers. I…" she grinned, "sometimes go see the village. I…sit in the garden with my papers, so I can be outside. I've built my Circle with people I love and trust to make sure I am surrounded by good people, always. I fell in love…" She looked into Theo's wide eyes. "I learned to balance." She got up, walking around her desk and leaning back on it, putting a hand on Theo's shoulder.

"I love my people, Theo. I figured things out for them. All of this…making you angry, putting everything on the line…it's for their futures. Not mine." She looked over his shoulder. "It's getting late. You should go, I have to do my check in with my Circle," she said, handing the pages back to him.

"Okay." He reached for the door handle. "Amair?" he asked, the door half open.

"Yes?"

"Can I publish this?"

"You know the things that are off the record." Amair raised her chin, walking back around her desk. "I trust you."

"Ama?"

She tried to bury the tiny sigh. "Yes, Theodore?"

He paused, thinking through his words, studying her and it was as though he was seeing her for the first time again. He felt his cheeks flush, smiling. "You're my people."

"I'm sorry?"

He glanced at the pages in his hand. "I…you're *my* people."

It took her a moment, but she smiled. "I love you too, Theo."

- CHAPTER LXIX -

Dear Senator Ona,

You may not remember me. Relations between Skylock and Waiwhe have been interesting, if not to say strained *for as long as I can remember, and we did not have a chance to host you or any of your representatives at my birthday this year. My name is Princess Amair Daniella Skylock, and I have been Oighre of Skylock for nearly a year, since the tragic death of my late brother. Him, you knew. He saw potential for relationships between Skylock and Waiwhe to grow.*

I hope that these relationships can build throughout my time, and, eventually, throughout my rule.

I wish I could say I was only reaching out to grow our relationship, but alas, I must start our acquaintance under more dire circumstances. I need your help. My people, and others, have grown tired of Keene's bullying. They treat their own people as slaves, whether it be the stolen or the citizens. They have spent years stealing people, traditions, language, and land, thinking they can do so without consequence. After the younger heir, Prince Novak, kidnapped and attempted to force my hand in marriage, violating the Old Laws of Land, the Keenian Emperor forced our hand and declared war on Skylock.

I will admit that I am a swordswoman. But I wanted peace. I never wanted this.

Waiwhe are negotiators, I know, but there are further tales or your power. There are great tales of your mounted warriors, and the strength of your spears. I am writing, hoping that you will join us. Keene mandates that every man in Keene, and to the edge of their Empire, must serve in their army. There is a very good chance that we will be wiped out. We are already beginning work with our allies, but having the Waiwhen on our side would give us the potential to actually turn the tides.

I plead with you today to lend us your hand in defeating this enemy, before any more innocent lives are destroyed.

With great admiration,
Princess Amair Daniella Skylock

"Aramis," Amair stood up from the Inner circle table, catching the eye of the white-haired boy. He looked up from where he was laughing with Arthur and Kenaia, clearing his throat.

"Yes, your high—" She glared at him and he rolled his eyes with a laugh. "Yes, Amair?"

"You've been in the administrative staff?

"Twice, now."

Kenaia snorted and he elbowed them.

"You have some writing skill, and I don't want to burden Theo. Could you read something for me?"

"What is it?" he asked, already reaching.

"A letter...to the Waiwhen Senate..."

"Oh...oh boy."

"We need...well...all the help we can get."

Aramis nodded, unfolding the page, Amair's writing assembled into something slightly less chaotic than usual, at the very least legible this time.

"It's well written." He tipped his head. "You sound strong, but kind. Not so full of admiration that you let go of your power."

"Do you think it will work?"

Shehada raised a hand. "Have they ever lent aid before?"

"No."

Aramis smiled sadly, handing her back the letter. "Then we should all start praying it does it."

- CHAPTER LXX -

"Denna!"

"Hey, you!" She grinned as Theo slid to a stop in front of her. He started to reach a hand out before he remembered, pulling it back and bobbing his head to her instead.

"How are things?"

"Balancing this conference, and my actual job, and the circle–"

"Yeah, how can she do this? She's literally preparing for a war."

Denna shrugged. "Her people are still relying on her…sometimes that just means for some normalcy. Beacon of hope."

"Hm…fair. And the rest of your life?"

"The High King has finally started to pass some of the duties off to his son," she laughed, "so my life has been made at least the tiniest bit less difficult."

"Do you think you'll ever come back to working in the castle?"

"To be fair, I never worked in the castle." The grinned, the two of them turning a corner. "It's tough, being in and out. Right now, I'm mainly here, with the Circle, but in many ways, Forra still needs me so…we'll find the best solution. New diplomats will graduate from the program at the end of Summer and we could potentially start training someone to replace me, and then I will come home permanently."

"Knowing her, she's probably already designing them in her head."

"Good point, I should probably remind her my favourite colour is pink."

"Hello you!" Amair exclaimed, turning the corner in front of them, smiling warmly. "That, I will never forget. Aramis, on the other hand, changes favourite colours faster than he can change castle jobs, so we may have to choose something *neutral* for him."

"Or just put him in charge of decor," Denna laughed as Amair walked up, kissing her best friend's cheek. "Meeting done?"

"Yeah, I'm actually headed to the North Room to play cards with the twins for a little while." She shrugged, lacing arms with Denna, the three of them continuing down the hall. "I think they're feeling a little..."

"Neglected? Left out? Overlooked?"

"D, All of the above," Amair laughed, glancing up at Theo. "Care to join us?"

"You wrecked me the last time we played cards, but I'll come watch."

"At least you weren't playing for money," Denna laughed, "you should have seen the way she wiped through visitors when we were kids."

"Quite the welcome."

"Layton and Johanna thought it was hilarious."

"Not Dylan?"

"No, because somehow, he kept playing her, convinced he would win that time." Denna bumped her shoulder. "She's always been too smart for us."

"Just lucky, I think."

"Whatever you say–"

"–Ama!" a high voice interrupted Denna, peeking out a door just ahead of them. "Come on you–"

"–promised," she finished for Alec. "I found friends, they wanted to join us."

"*No,* we want to play with you!" Evander's head popped out below his twin's, pouting.

"And you *shall,*" she grinned slyly, "I even promise not to let you win."

"We will win," Alec said confidently.

"We've been practicing!" Evander added.

"Can you...practice at cards?" Denna asked, her eyebrow up as she smirked. The twins pulled out of the way as their sister and her friends walked into the North Room, waves that seemed to move painted intricately across the walls.

"I've been here how many weeks, and I'm still discovering new rooms?" Theo laughed.

"I've lived here eighteen years and I'm still discovering new rooms." Denna squinted, glancing over at the twins taking a seat on the floor. "They, on the other hand, probably have this place mapped."

"Don't tell them about our map!" Evander exclaimed as his head snapped up. "It's a secret!"

"What if one of them falls into the hands of a spy?"

"Or is a spy?"

"You two are ridiculous," Amair laughed, tossing her lavender skirt as she sat on the ground next to them, tucking her legs up under herself.

"Care for a drink, Denna?" Theo asked, dragging one of the armchairs over.

"Something...sweet?" she smiled, taking a seat, fixing her skirt, watching Amair mess with Evander's hair as he laughed, and Alec passed out cards for whatever game they had chosen. Denna kept her eyes on them as Theo handed her a glass.

"You were there, weren't you?" Theo asked, sitting in the chair next to her.

"Hm?" Denna didn't turn her head away from the royal children laughing over the game.

"When Layton died." Denna turned her head, her dark eyes wide, and then squinting a little at Theo. "Were you there?"

"No, not right at first, I...I had just started my posting," she looked down into her tea, "but...I was there, in the aftermath." She looked back at Amair, her face sad as she sighed.

- CHAPTER LXXI -

Denna walked through the mossy garden, the beautiful, tall grasses of Forra in every shade of green she could imagine. She ran a hand along them, letting the texture of each stem linger on her fingertips, the sound of birds and bugs ringing in the cool morning.

"Lady Raziel!" she heard someone bellow behind her.

Denna spun, squinting into the sun, as two people on horseback rushed down the lane. She tried to make them out as someone called out her name again. She took a step back, tripping and pulling on her skirt, trying to keep from falling into the plants as the horses pulled to a stop. Denna looked back up, noticing the Skylock crest immediately, and two Knights slipped onto the soft ground.

"What on earth…can I help you?" Denna asked, raising an eyebrow as the knights pulled off their helmets, adjusting their scarves.

"Lady Raziel." The first one bowed his head a little. "We're here to bring you home. Immediately."

"I'm working. On behalf of the Sovereign. *I have a meeting in twenty minutes, I cannot just leave—"*

"—Lady Raziel," he put his hands up, stopping her, "this is a Callback. It is non-negotiable." The word flashed through Denna's mind.

"Has something happened?" she demanded, standing a little taller.

"You just…you must come. We can't say—"

"—I'm not going anywhere until you do."

"Lady Raziel," the second Knight piped in, holding her helmet tight to her chest. "We are also here on behalf of the Sovereign. With orders." The Knight raised her chin. "Now, I will toss you over my shoulder if you don't come." Denna took a deep breath, pursing her lips.

"Alright. Alright, fine."

"Thank you. You can ride with me, m'lady."

"Fine." Denna picked up her skirt as the other Knight mounted his horse. The second threw herself up on her dark horse, offering her hand and helping Denna pull herself up, adjusting her headscarf and her skirt.

"My things are still in the guest wing—"

"—the castle is arranging everything's return. The Callback Protocol has been put in place." Denna noticed the look the two exchanged, lifting their helmets over their heads.

"Alright, what in the name of the gods happened?" Denna demanded. The Knights clucked at their horses, bringing them up to a brisk walk.

"There's…there's been a death, my lady," the Knight on the other horse told her.

"Oh my God," she whispered. "Wh-who?"

"I'm sorry, my lady," the Knight she had her arms wrapped around said, shaking her head. "That is more than I should have said." The royal family's faces flashed through Denna's mind, the King's valent smile at the forefront.

***

"Aramis!" Denna called, rushing down the hall towards the boy with blonde curls. He turned, eyes widening and calling to her, running forwards. The two slid to a stop, Denna crossing her arms over herself. "What's happening?"

"I have no idea…the whole staff was told to stop their work; we're being called into the grand ballroom. I — wait, I thought you were in Forra?"

Denna nodded, biting her cheek. "I was. The…the Callback Protocol has been put in place." Denna straightened when Lenora appeared beside her, her dark eyes wide, adjusting her uniform scarf over and over.

"Lenora!" Aramis shook his head. "Do you have any idea what's going on?"

"I was just told to bring the class inside." She looked down at Denna. "You must know, you're in the diplomatic corps—"

"—no, the Knights who retrieved me said they couldn't say anything." Denna's eyes widened this time. "Have you seen the Family?"

"No," Lenora's voice was barely above a whisper. A chill ran down Denna's spine, a tear inadvertently slipping down her cheek and Aramis immediately offered her his pocket square. She nodded at him, choking on words, dabbing at her eyes and chewing on the inside of her cheek. More of the staff started to congregate, everyone wearing the same worried expression, all of them trying to mask it. One of the other diplomats passed, waving a little at Denna. She just bobbed her head at him, holding herself and staring blankly into the little circle she formed with Aramis and Lenora.

Denna looked up as the doors to the ballroom creaked open, the Crier walking out, wringing his hands.

"Friends, please," he gulped a little, his usually steady voice faltering, "come in. Find a seat." Denna glanced up at Lenora, watching as she took a deep breath, and walked into the quiet stream of people pushing through the doors. Denna took a deep breath, glancing at Aramis this time, and the two of them pushed forwards to follow.

Lenora found three seats at the front, pulling Denna out of the crowd to follow her. The three of them sat, looking around at solemn faces, hundreds of staff trying to find space.

"Do you see any of the family's attendants?" Denna whispered. Lenora sat a little taller in her seat.

"I can't...oh wait," she raised an eyebrow, pointing at the side of the room as they noticed Lydia and some of the family's staff, the King's administrative staff and a few others, holding each other and crying.

"This is bad," Aramis murmured to himself, looking back again to the front as the Crier walked up to the front.

The room fell so silent Denna could hear the candles high above. They all watched as the Crier fixed his uniform, forcing himself into limp composure.

"At one o'clock the night before last, two Knights discovered Prince Layton's royal carriage. Princess Amair and her parents rode out and they found Prince Layton, Lady Johanna, and Sir Dylan...dead from their injuries."

All of the air left Denna's chest and a few members of staff shrieked. "An investigation into the accident has begun. The news is being released to the Kingdom and the rest of Land as we speak, which is why the Callback was put in place – we wanted you all to be the firsts to hear, and to hear it from us. The King regrets that he is not here to pass this news on personally, but he is attending to his family now.

"The state funeral for His Royal Highness will be held in two days' time, and it has been decided that Lady Johanna and Sir Dylan will be interred with him. You are all welcome at the ceremony, or we will give you leave to attend one of the local memorials. It is a great loss, to all of us. Prince Layton," they heard him sniffle, "is...was a good man.

"The day after the funeral, Her Royal Highness Princess Amair will be crowned as Oighre, making her the heir to the Skylock Throne." Whispers passed through the crowd, Amair's name whispered back and forth, and Denna's eyes widened. "The family is asking for quiet and space as they process everything that has happened, and as they prepare for the changes ahead of them. If anyone would like to pass any thoughts on to the *family, department supervisors can collect them and bring them to the Sovereign offices, one of the administrators will be putting them into albums to pass on to the family for when they are ready. The number of staff who may interact with the family has been tightened and absolutely no extra personnel is to enter the Family Wing without strict instruction."*

***

"Oh my god," Aramis shook his head, fingers on his mouth as he tried to keep breathing steadily, staring forward into nothing.

"I'll...I'll send a letter to Shehada," Denna murmured. "She should be here."

"Yeah...yeah, good idea."

Lenora glanced at Denna. "I know we were told to give them space but...."

"Oh, fuck space," Denna shook her head, Aramis and Lenora raising their eyebrows, wondering if they had ever heard a cuss leave her mouth, "I'm going to find Ama. She'll see me if she likes it or not."

"Leave it to the diplomat to be oh so diplomatic," Aramis shook his head, managing the smallest hint of a smile.

"Of any of us, I'm sure she'll see you. It was always you and Jo..." Lenora trailed off, looking down, shaking her head. "She was my first..." she whispered. Aramis reached over, squeezing her shoulder. "Gods, poor Arthur."

"All of them...we um..." Aramis swallowed hard. "We should organize some kind of...gift, or something."

"What do you get parents who just lost their child?"

"What about Dylan's moms?" Lenora had tears in her eyes suddenly. "He...he was all they had and...he was their whole world, I don't..." Denna reached over and squeezed her hand.

"Right now just keep our lost ones and their families in your thoughts. That's all we can do until we know more."

***

"Princess?" Denna was quiet as she pushed the door open.

"You don't call me that," she heard Amair's voice. "You've never called me that."

"Things are different—"

"—no. I am Amair. You are Denna." Denna walked further into the room, spotting Amair's legs dangling off a chair. The room was starting to fill with noise, people gathering in the courtyard and main driveway below.

"I don't know if I can do this Denna…" Amair wrapped her arms tighter around herself. She looked up, her eyes red and puffy. Denna stared at her, squinting a little, suddenly slamming her hand on the table.

"Well, you don't really have a choice."

"Denn—"

"—you are Amair Skylock. My best *friend. I have never seen you step back from a challenge. Even the ones that were ridiculously dangerous…especially* the ones that were *ridiculously dangerous. This isn't. This isn't dangerous."*

"This is politics! Of course it is!"

Denna opened her mouth but closed it again, shrugging. "Touché."

"It's a Kingdom*!" Amair went on. "With millions of people to take care of."*

"And they aren't asking you to start ruling tomorrow!" Denna pulled on her flowing sleeve, not pulling her eyes from Amair. "This is a crown to let your people know they can count on you. That there are plans to train you. That you will not abandon them."

"But it is not my crown!"

"It is*, though, Amair. Alan of Rin brought the prophecy that the Skylocks would rule for a thousand prosperous years. I hate to break it to you, but we are only three hundred years in. Hate to break it to you, but you are a Skylock."*

"You know what I mean," Amair muttered.

"I do." Denna sighed, finally pulling her eyes away, glancing out the window. "But Amair," she turned her head back, peering at her intently, "you have to do this."

"I don't know how*!"*

"You do though," Denna cupped Amair's cheeks in her hands. "You have watched for years, Ama. You are a product of the shadows— you are yourself, but you got to be more. You are right, Amair — you were not raised to be Oighre, never planned to be Queen. But that gives you something no Skylock Sovereign has ever had — a chance to know yourself without the weight of a title looming."

"Denna…what if they don't want me?"

"They will Amair. They do.*" She took a deep breath, the sound of the growing crowd outside echoing through the room. "And there are many of us who have your back."*

"Princess?" queried a timid voice at the door. Amair took a deep breath, her eyes on Denna, who nodded at her.

"Come in!" Amair called.

"Are you ready, Princess?" an attendant asked, the door opening slowly.

"I…" Amair gulped. "Yes." She pushed her shoulders back, standing a little taller. "Yes." She forced the confidence through her teeth.

"Very good." The attendant nodded, pointing a leading hand towards the door.

'Stay,' she mouthed to Denna, who nodded, holding her hands over her mouth as a sob pushed against her chest, the royal family and King's Council filing into the room.

The doors to the balcony pulled open, the sound of trumpets whispering into the cheering crowd. But there was another sound: sobbing. Amair took a deep breath, stepping past the doors, a new roar as the crowd watched her, waving as she plastered on a half-smile. Denna watched from the room, the Queen next to her, hearing the shuffle of feet behind her. Denna glanced over her shoulder, stony-faced Jasper and Kylo standing next to each other in the doorway.

'Twins?' Denna mouthed to Jasper. He averted his eyes, shaking his head a little.

Amair's blue dress floated in the wind, the King walking out next to her. Denna could see the red splotches across his nose, his eyes red from crying. Amair hesitated as the box with the Oighre crown was pulled open and presented to the King, everyone collectively holding their breath as he stared down at it, his bottom lip trembling. With shaking hands, he picked up the thick band-crown, tiny Oighre symbols carved every few inches into the metal. Amair knelt onto the damp, concrete balcony, feeling the wet soaking through her dress onto her knees, pulling the tears out all over again. She felt the weight of the crown rest on her head, and her shoulders.

The High Priest and Priestess stepped past the King. The Priestess made a sign with her hand over Amair's head, mouthing something, the wind blowing the billowing sleeves of her green robes around Amair's head, blocking her tears from the audience. The Priest took one of Amair's hands, pressing something into it that Denna couldn't see, watching another sob rock across the Princess' chest. The Priest and Priestess took Amair's hands and helped her to her feet, turning her to face the crowd, the King matching her stance, forcing their shoulders back.

"Your oighre!" he called as the Priest and Priestess raised Amair's hands, a new wave of cheering and sobbing rising out of the crowd. Amair set her jaw, forcing back her trembling lip as she managed to wave, keeping her one hand in a fist at her side.

To the dismay of the crowd, Amair stepped back, turning away from the people as she walked back into the castle, a chilly breeze running through the room. Her shoulders hunched back over as she looked over her family, eyes hesitating at Denna.

"Oh, darling," the Queen tried to smile, stepping forwards and tucking a loose strand of Amair's hand behind her ear, *"you were..."* she sniffled, *"you were wonderful."*

Amair didn't meet her mom's eye, looking at Denna as the tears started to stream down her cheeks. *"I'm going to bed."* She finally opened her clenched fist, letting *something fall to the ground as she brushed from the room. Denna pressed her lips together, leaning down to pick up the small object.*

A Skylock coin.

With Amair's portrait on the heir's side.

"Long live the Oighre," Denna whispered to herself—

"Oh, Denna!" Amair exclaimed, rolling over and pushing up to her feet, interrupting her story.

"Hey, love," Denna smiled.

"I didn't even notice the time, we should be going!" She slipped an arm through Denna's, smiling.

"Mhm, I didn't even notice the time."

"Where are you two off to?" Theo leaned back on the chaise.

"To meet a group of political science students from across the country. They're here for a few days, there are a couple seminars, some speaking contests…a few others. Anyway, they put their names in with their unis a few months ago, and the unis each chose…I think ten? Ten students? Anyway, today's the launch. There's a luncheon with the Sovereign and the Oighre, and I am dragging Denna along as my backup. Plus, she's one of our best diplomats. Plus, she makes me look good." Amair glanced up, thinking. "And a Circle member. So," Amair shrugged a little, smiling, "she's a good role model."

"You'll have lots of people to track down and get quotes from," Denna laughed, "for the serial."

"Ah, smart. Have fun you two!"

"Thank you, Theo!" the two of them said in unison, giggling a little and turning to head down the hall.

"How are you, today?" Denna asked, glancing over, noticing the wavering edge of Amair's smile.

"We are still going to war, and I am off to tell a dozen wonderful young women that their futures are going to be about creating good."

"You're doing a good job," Denna said quietly, flexing her arm, squeezing Amair. "These girls will see that."

"Remind me of that when I have actually *given* them a future."

- 335 -

Summer

- CHAPTER LXXII -

"We're going to RiKoi."

"Need a vacation?" Aramis snorted. Summer had brought little relief from the Skylock rain but with everyone working to prepare for the impending war, the few warm days could not even be celebrated with a picnic.

"I would after the year she's had," Kenaia agreed. Amair tossed a letter onto the table in the Circle room, and Shehada was the one to carefully pick it up.

"They've asked us to come." Shehada looked up from the letter, passing it to Kenaia. Kenaia smirked.

"No, Princess. They've asked *you*."

"It's a bad idea."

"Which…part?" Amair asked, squinting at her brother. "They want the terror to end! Jasper…our Kingdom has barely escaped the clutches of war, but Tunngas may be willing to help. Innisil may even join."

"Innisil won't help, and you know it. Nor will Waiwhe."

She bit the inside of her cheek but shrugged. "Then we figure it out!"

"Amair, we have stirred the pot enough–"

"–have we, Jasper? Have we stirred the pot so much we can turn an eye to *slavery*? To…the dozens of other atrocities we are just…sitting by and watching? While Keene is breathing down our necks? The necks of our allies?" He opened his mouth but closed it again.

"How would we do it?" Denna asked.

"I don't know. They aren't exactly forthcoming in this letter. I want to go see them. I want to hear what they're thinking. What they have in mind."

"Alright," Gio nodded. "I'm with you."

"So am I," Shehada agreed. "*If* your father consents."

Amair grimaced. "That might be a little more difficult."

***

"Hi, daddy…"

"Oh, don't *hi daddy*," Jasper snapped, brushing past her into their father's study. Amair glared at his back as she stepped in, the King's staff immediately scurrying out to avoid the line of fire.

"We've been…offered a chance to get some…help. Possibly."

"I'm sorry?" Her father's eyes were wide.

"I think RiKoi wants to help—"

"When did you talk to RiKoi?" her father shouted, so loud Jasper noticed one of the attendants flinch.

"They sent me a letter."

"*You?*"

Amair's mouth twitched. "Apparently they know I'm the only one in this family with enough courage to stand up to bullies."

"Amair, watch yourself."

"What are you gonna do? Tell me I've been a *bad Oighre* when I didn't even want the role in the first place? Send me to my room without supper?" She raised her chin, glaring at them. "You want me to rule? Here I am."

"Ama—"

"—Amair." The King raised his eyebrows at the force behind her voice.

"I'm not some little girl. Everyone knows it. I am stronger than anyone you know. For so many reasons. I'm taking my Circle to RiKoi. If you have to, think of it as a social visit. I *will* be hearing them out, and, if I feel like it's necessary, I will be making whatever deal I need to."

"Well, this is probably my fault for raising a strong headed girl," the King muttered.

"This is a chance to get ourselves more help which I don't know if you have noticed, we need."

"I don't want more people putting themselves at risk—"

"—they've offered!" she shouted. "We have *all* felt the effects of Keene. What they've done. What they've taken." Her cheeks were flushed with anger and in how warm the King had been keeping his study.

The King contemplated her words. "I thought you said you didn't want your first major act as Oighre to be a war."

She shook her head, letting out an annoyed laugh, her lips curling. "Well, three men took that choice away from me, didn't they?" Jasper flinched at her words, looking down at his shoes. "So, it's too late now." Amair raised her chin. "So…do we go with your blessing? Or are we sneaking out the back door?"

- CHAPTER LXXIII -

The King looked on as Amair and her Circle, with Theo and a half dozen attendants in tow, tacked up their horses and a carriage stuffed to the brim with cases.

Denna walked out into the small courtyard, fixing her riding gloves, her eyes first spotting Amair and Theo pressed together in a corner, exchanging quiet words. He tucked a loose strand of hair behind Amair's ear. It made Denna smile, her eyes sliding amongst other members of the Circle as they checked off whatever mental lists they had prepared for themselves. Denna slid up next to the King, observing with him.

"She's a force to be reckoned with," she said quietly as Amair walked back to her horse.

"She didn't need this…"

"She's more ready than you give her credit for…she's quite the diplomat." Denna bit her lip, not looking up at the King. "I would know."

"Would you?"

"It's probably time I mention I broke the Diplomat's code and asked Ama to come to my aid."

The King's ears pricked at that, looking down at the young woman. "When was this?"

"Do you recall her and Arthur disappearing for a few days, shortly before her birthday? I believe a photo was spread of our reunion in Forra…"

"She told me it was a friendly getaway…"

The corners of Denna's mouth quirked into a knowing smile, tucking her hands behind her back as she finally met the King's eye. "She stopped the Forran High King from marching on Keene."

"Amair did?"

"Nothing I or the King or either or the Queens or any of their advisors were saying was helping. I wanted to bring someone in and…something about her has always…" Denna took a deep breath. She did not have the words for the feeling. "I knew she was the right person. We kept it secret, I wanted to avoid an all-out war. She was there less than a day, your majesty."

"And?"

Denna's knowing smile grew, adjusting her headscarf and taking a step forward. "You have nothing to worry about in RiKoi. She's as good a diplomat as she is a warrior. The fates may be cruel but somehow…I think Ama may actually have been born for this."

The King watched the young travelling party mount their horses, three of his children breaking protocol despite the Queen's screaming they could not all go together. Kylo passed Amair an extra tie for her to tie down her sleeping mat on the back of her saddle, before the Princess turned to catch her father's eye.

"You feel good?"

"I never feel good," she admitted. "But I feel ready. And that is enough."

***

It took half a week to get to RiKoi, and another two days to travel through the rolling fields that seemed to go on for miles, straight into the horizon. They camped when they could, everyone taking shifts to keep watch. The closer they got to the castle, the warmer the air got.

"Have you been here before?" Theo asked, turning his head to her.

"Many, many years ago. I remember being so amazed by the wheat fields in particular…" she turned her head a little to study the fields that surrounded them, "something in that golden colour."

"I'm not surprised," Theo smiled, looking around. "Ama?"

"Hm?"

"What are we? While we're here?"

"Friends." She slid her eyes back to him. "Unless you want to be more. I know rumours of our friendship are…spreading."

Theo raised an eyebrow. "Will you explain who I am to the RiKoi?"

"I've told you what we are is up to you, Theodore. I'm a Princess. Being with me is a big responsibility." She raised her chin, looking back out at the wheat fields around them, waving to a group of young girls poking their heads out among the plants. "You tell me what I should say."

Theo thought for a second. "Don't tell them right at first but…maybe let them know."

"Sounds good to me." She smiled at him once more, as the castle appeared ahead of them. "Here we go."

They followed the path that started to widen from just a cut in the fields to a proper path, still almost mixed in with the golden fields, to the main gates of the RiKoi castle, lines of guards and staff prepared and waiting for them.

"Princess!" the young man exclaimed, waving. Amair grinned, slipping off her horse and waving back to him.

"Mils!" She smiled, wrapping her arms around his neck, the two of them holding each other for a second.

"You are even more beautiful than the last time I saw you."

"Stop," she smiled, blushing a little. He offered her his arm

"Maximilian, do you remember Sir Theodore Crawford?"

"The Writer?"

"And…" Amair smirked at Theo. "Friend."

"Welcome to RiKoi," the Prince bowed to Theo.

"Thank you for having us, your highness." Theo bowed back. Mils ran his hand over his short, coiled hair, smiling at the party.

"We have a big dinner tonight. No politics, just friends. And food. And dancing." Maximilian was beaming. "And tomorrow, we can get into why you are here."

"Okay, but…politics do have to happen…"

"Oh, I know. We all know…that's why we wanted you here."

"Then thank you, Mils," Amair squeezed her friend's arm. "My questions can wait."

"I can't have the Skylock Oighre here without wining and dining her."

"Oh, by the way: do you have someone who could help me dress? I didn't bring my ladies with me."

"Absolutely. I'll ask my aunt to loan you someone."

"Oh, she shouldn't have to–"

"–I insist," the Prince assured her.

"Well, thank you." Amair bowed her head to him.

"Alright! I will show you all to your chambers, and dinner will arrive soon."

"Lead the way!" Amair smiled, the circle and their travelling companions falling in line behind her.

***

"And I have put you here," the housekeeper pointed for Amair, "and Sir Crawford just next door, here." Amair looked up at Mils, an eyebrow raised.

"I figured it out pretty easily," he whispered to her, winking.

"You always were too smart for your own good."

"I was determined to keep up with *you*." Amair laughed, patting his arm. He cleared his throat, standing tall and looking around the Skylock party. "Change. Relax. Explore. The ball starts in two hours."

"We'll see you in a bit!" Maximilian smiled, bowing, and turning with a small wave.

"Maybe telling RiKoi is already off the table," Theo chuckled

"Don't worry. Mils is…discreet…sort of." Theo reached out, squeezing her hand. The two glanced at each other, smiling. "I think I'm going to have a nap…there is a pain that has been blossoming in my head, and this heat is not helping."

"I'm going to explore…are we here…officially?" Theo asked. He raised a pen in explanation.

"How do those just always seem to appear from thin air with you?" Amair laughed. "Yes, we are…though…we are mostly just visiting friends. For now, at least."

"What comes after friends?" he asked, raising an eyebrow.

She took a deep breath, thinking. "Allies, hopefully."

- CHAPTER LXXIV -

Amair swept down the hall, watching herself as she brushed out a wrinkle in her warm yellow skirt.

"Amair!" She looked up, hearing her name, smiling at the Prince walking towards her, his crown slightly askew. "You look beautiful," Mils grinned, touching the layers of tulle on the short, flowing sleeves.

"Thank you," she smiled softly, letting him kiss her knuckles. "I figured if you're wining and dining us, the least I could do would be honour the RiKoi colours."

"It's too bad your heart has been claimed," Mils winked, "you are quite a vision in yellow."

"Maximilian!" Amair laughed.

"What?" She rolled her eyes, turning to look out over the crowd in bright and pale gowns and suits.

"Not nearly as beautiful as the women of your court." She spread her hands out on the bannister, smiling down into the sea of colourful outfits. "I have *always* loved how bright your parties are."

"We break out the best for our Skylock friends." She glanced to the side, Shehada helping Denna with one of the pins on her deep green headscarf, Aramis and Kenaia pressed arm to arm. Amair squinted, watching the way the two of their heads moved together as they talked quietly.

"That's the last of us."

"Then here we go," Mils grinned, bobbing his head at one of the staff near the door.

Trumpets sounded, the crowd parting down the middle as one of the Criers took his stand at the top of the stairs. Amair stood shoulder to shoulder with Maximilian, tucking her hands behind herself. Jasper nudged her ever so slightly and she brought them back, forcing herself not to dig her nails into her palms. Theo watched as she pushed her shoulders back, raising her chin, the stance she took when she was readying herself for a ball or a fight.

"The King!" was all the Crier called into the crowd. The doors opened, the King walking in, waving as people clapped. He smiled, spotting his son and the visiting Princess, striding down the stairs towards them and offering his hand to her. She took it and he bent to her.

"Welcome to RiKoi, Princess Amair." He stood, his expression warm. "Thank you so much for coming."

"Thank you for having us."

"We have much to discuss."

"We do."

"On the morrow, though." He smiled, putting a hand on his son's shoulder, their wide, kind smiles a matching set. "Tonight, we shall feast."

Amair hesitated a moment, but gave in with a smile and a nod. "I have no problem with that."

"Dinner is served, then!" The King smiled, offering Amair his arm. She took it, glancing at her party, winking at Theo. The music started, guests chattering again, pointing at the Skylock visitors. Theo managed to smile at them, watching as the people in bright colours found seats.

"She's in her element," Theo murmured to Jasper, watching Amair juggle chatting quietly with the King and waving elegantly at guests.

"She does seem to be getting very good at this, hey?" Jasper smiled at his sister's back. "She's proud of you."

"Oh yeah?"

"It's not easy joining this family. This life. Theo smiled, watching Amair's back, nearly drowning in pale yellow tulle as the RiKoi Prince pulled out a chair for her near the head of the table, just beside the King. "And you've done it beautifully."

***

Amair and Mils laughed, arms wrapped around each other, holding tight as they twirled around the dance floor. Music filled the room, the large band grinning out at the crowd of dancers jumping and twirling. The long, colourful skirts brushed across the floor as feet moved in quick steps, laughter bubbling out with the music.

Theo sipped his brilliantly blue drink that warmed his mouth, watching Amair's wide eyes as Mils danced her around the floor. Her hand was wrapped around his neck, holding on as they spun, stopping to laugh every few moments, fluffing her skirt and turning to whisper and laugh with other guests.

Aramis walked up, Mils nodding and laughing as he passed Amair off to him. She grinned, wrapping into him, raising their elbows and joining the spinning chaos.

Mils pushed his way out of the crowd, plopping down next to Theo. "You two look like you're having fun," Theo laughed, handing a glass of water, Mils chugging it down.

"Oh, she's so fun." Mils laughed, motioning to an attendant for another glass as he caught his breath, swiping at his forehead. They watched Amair and Aramis link hands with another couple, spinning in a circle with the rest of the crowd, looking over their shoulders to try and keep up with all of the moves. Theo tipped his head.

"I don't know if I've ever seen her like this."

"I have," Mils smirked, his eyes glinting, but there was something warm behind it. "She was a going concern, keeping us all on our toes. The fun, the party. The mischief, too…that's why her and Dylan got on so well."

"I heard you kissed her once."

"If *I* remember correctly, she kissed me," he laughed. "One way or the other, it was a good first kiss." Theo glanced to the side, looking past him at Jasper and Arthur with their heads together, murmuring at the next table. "Maybe in another life we would have been good together."

"Not anymore?"

"Well, aside from the fact that she's fallen head over for you," Mils shot him a playful grin, "heirs can't marry each other."

"Why?"

Mils shrugged. "It's an old law, I think. I'm sure if we fell madly in love both our parents would go to the ends of the Land to make it work. I think it's just a way to keep the Kingdoms separate, not have to worry about joining and breaking kingdoms."

"No need for an Empire," Theo murmured.

Mils' face faltered for a second but he recovered. "Exactly," he laughed. "We all know how Land's last empire project went."

"Good thing there's no way for their heir to marry ours," Theo raised an eyebrow, looking back to watch her dance, her yellow dress twinkling under the rows of warm lights and candles. The music slowed, a few members of the band switching out. Aramis grabbed Amair's hand, leading her out of the crowd, spotting Theo and Mils, and heading towards them.

"Hi!" Amair grinned, grabbing the glass of water Theo had just picked up, ignoring him raise his eyebrows and watch her chug it.

"Tired yet?" Mils laughed, grabbing her hand as she tripped on the edge of her dress, laughing.

"No, I want to dance some more!" She plopped the glass on the table, getting her feet settled under her.

"Are you drunk?" Theo asked.

"Nope." She smiled, scrunching her nose at him, spinning on her heel as her eyes locked on Jasper, bee-lining for him and reaching a hand out as another brilliant song echoed into the ballroom. She grabbed her brother's hands, dragging onto the floor as he laughed, grabbing her waist and spinning her around. Theo laughed, clinking his glass against Mils' as they leaned back in their chairs and watched. Theo could not help but feel mesmerized by the smile on her face as she was spun around, letting go. He finally got out of his seat, setting his glass down, and crossed the floor towards her, slipping past flying limbs and jumping dancers.

The song slowed for just a moment and it was long enough for her to turn and spot him as he reached a hand towards her. "My turn," he said, sly grin on his face. She smirked, curtsying, and took his hand.

- CHAPTER LXXV -

Amair tucked her hands behind her back, humming a song from the party the night before. Early daylight streamed down the long hall as she looked up at the tall portrait of the woman in blue. She looked into her dark brown eyes, that seemed to watch her back.

"Saying hello to my mom?" she heard Maximilian's voice behind her. She turned her head ever so slightly, looking back up at the painting.

Amair smiled, Mils matching her stance next to her. "She was so beautiful."

"She was." Mils smiled. She could see him turn his head to study her but she kept her eyes on the woman with the beautiful hair.

"Do you know much about her?"

"No. Dad's always started to cry when she gets brought up." He glanced at the *Queen Coralie* plaque under the painting. "I've never seen your hair down," he mused.

"I usually put it up...hard to wield a sword or stare menacingly at a Council-member with it down." Mils snorted. "But I didn't want to bother your maids. I'll have Shehada throw it up for me later, if it becomes cumbersome."

They were quiet for a moment, watching the light cross up the painting.

"So much loss," Amair murmured.

"Hm?"

"Oh just...thinking. Of all the people that have been lost. That we've lost. Whether I knew them..." she swallowed hard, "directly or through others."

"You and I both know that kind of pain."

"It's true. And Theodore...he lost his father as a boy."

"It's hard to lose a parent."

"I can't even imagine."

"But losing mom so young...I can barely remember her. For you...I can't imagine seeing–"

"–loss is not a contest," Amair shook her head. She smiled sadly at Maximilian, tipping her head a little.

"What's going through that pretty head of yours?"

Her mouth twitched, looking back up at the portrait. She was quiet for a second and Mils watched her think. "Something is coming, Mils. I..." She took a deep breath, her eyes reflecting the blue of the late Queen's dress. "I think we're going to lose more people. I could have done something that *might* have stopped it," she looked down, "but...I honestly don't think it would have helped."

Mils let out a breath, nodding a little, looking up at the portrait of his mother. "My mother left me a letter. I read it when I turned fourteen. She knew she was dying before it happened. But she said something that has always stuck with me."

"What was that?"

"When the ground feels like it is falling out underneath you...find someone to hold you on their shoulders." The young royals turned their heads, looking into each other's eyes. "I would hold you up until the end of days."

"That...has nothing to do with what I–"

"–it does, though," Mils nodded a little, his eyes intense. "Because I think you're right Amair." He didn't pull his eyes away from her. "I think there is a lot of loss coming. Skylock has a war coming."

She turned in surprise at the boy who had once been nothing but foolishness and practical jokes. "You know?"

"Of course I do. And you need people you can trust by your side. And I plan to be there."

They were quiet again. But Amair nodded, ever so slightly, her eyes intense, the brown birthmark in her blue eyes looking darker than usual. "I may have to hold you to that."

- CHAPTER LXXVI -

"I forgot how warm it can get here," Amair murmured, tugging at the bodice of her dress. "Kind of missing my linen dresses right about now."

"Do you want to change?" Mils asked, stopping his pacing, hands still rubbing against each other.

"No, no." She took a deep breath. "This is about to be the most important thing I've done since becoming Oighre. Or the biggest. Or…the biggest I can talk about." Amair shook her head. "This dress gives me confidence."

"You are perfect," Mils murmured his encouragement, wrapping a hand over her waist, Theo eyeing his fingers. "And my father already thinks the world of you, Princess."

"Thank you for arranging this in the fields." She looked up at her friend. "It feels…comfortable, somehow. Despite the fact that I'm *sweating*."

"Closest thing RiKoi has to the splendour of your gardens."

"A different beauty entirely." She shook out her hands. "It's warm here. The colours…they make you *feel* warm."

"Warm and sweaty?" Mils laughed.

"But also…warm…inside?" She shrugged, wringing her hands again. "Layton used to like that. Feeling warm inside. You're never…*fully* warm, in Skylock. You're either wet or chilly. There's a reason we eat a lot of potatoes. And wear lots of big socks." Mils laughed as her nervous words floated from her mouth.

"Here comes my dad."

"No vomiting…" she muttered to herself, straightening her shoulders. "King Devinray!"

Amair walked through the field, the wheat bowing under her skirt and the King's cloak, her arms folded behind her back as she looked up to the King. They insisted on their parties staying behind as they walked, speaking quietly. The King kept his head low, listening intently as the Princess talked. He nodded, and Theo tried to make out what she was saying by how the King moved his head.

He guessed the tides were changing when the King turned his head away from Amair, his eyes closed, looking as though he may be sick.

Theo, Jasper, and Mils shielded their eyes from the sun, peering out into the wheat fields, Amair and the King just a speck on the horizon, walking through the plants, stalks flattening under her heavy skirts. No one said anything, the RiKan and Skylish watching their royals.

They could see the two turn to each other, Amair folding her hands on top of her skirts, the movement of her mouth just barely visible. The King was nodding furiously. He stuck out his hand and she hesitated but took it, the two holding forearms, a quiet understanding between them. They nodded, pulling their arms back, continuing down the field.

Amair looked down at the party, pointing at Jasper and beckoning him forward as the King pointed for his son. The two boys shared a look, taking the first step together.

"They know about the stolen citizens," Amair told Jasper.

"Of course we do." But Maximilian didn't seem to, whipping his head towards his father. "My great-grandfather saw it happening."

"So did ours…" Amair murmured, glancing at Jasper.

"But he never did anything about it. He couldn't, at the time, and Keene is so powerful, going to war would…it would destroy RiKoi. We can't do it."

Amair tapped her fingers together, thinking. "I was told I can't make any promises."

"But I can. You have us, Princess."

She swallowed hard, Jasper holding a sigh, knowing what was coming. "We're doing this. Together."

"And what about you?" Mils asked, raising an eyebrow.

"I'm sorry?"

"Will you be at the battle? Champion of Skylock–"

"–the Oighre can't go charging into battle–" Amair held up her hand, silencing Jasper.

They were all silent for a minute, her mouth open, thinking. "I've never been known to back down from a fight." The King smiled. Jasper tried to keep his face flat, watching as Amair clasped arms with the King again, and then the Prince.

"We have to get home, your majesty. I think…I have a lot of planning and convincing to do."

"Yes. Yes. There's a war coming."

Jasper watched as Amair gulped. "Yes," she nodded so slowly it was almost in slow motion. "There is."

"And because of that we are going to need help." Amair glanced at her party.

"You're right…I can send word to Tunngas. I also have a contact in Innisil…I doubt anything will come of it, but–"

"–we can try. I'll reach out to Forra…I've…I've already sent a letter to Waiwhe." She nodded to herself, eyes flicking towards Maximilian. "I want to bring Prince Mils with us."

"What?"

"He can help me," Amair looked up to the King, "your personal link, right into my study. And…well…I think I could use all the support I can access." The King looked from Amair to his son, taking a deep breath. Mils looked at Amair, trying to catch her eye but she wouldn't look at him.

"Maximilian?" the King finally asked.

"Yes?"

"Are you willing?" Theo watched as Mils stood a little taller, in the same way Amair always did.

"Absolutely."

"Then you will ride out with them. Come, everyone. Let's go back to the castle and we can prepare you to go."

"Can someone send a messenger to my father?" Amair asked. The King nodded to one of his aides, who rushed towards one of the horses on the edge of the field.

"My son can stay until things are settled, or until we all decide it makes more sense for him to be working from RiKoi. He'll be eighteen soon, taking on responsibilities in our Kingdom—"

"—I understand, your majesty." She raised her chin. Amair looked over her shoulder, Gio and Aramis standing taller, wiping the sweat from their foreheads as she caught their eyes.

"Start getting us ready. We're going home."

- CHAPTER LXXVII -

They wasted no time upon returning to Skylock. Prince Maximilian was introduced to the Council, with a letter from his father announcing the official tie between the two kingdoms. A second, smaller desk was moved into Amair's study and she moved Maximilian in with her, the two of them working in tandem. They talked around each other, pacing back and forth, nearly wearing her carpet.

They both talked with their hands, nearly whacking one another whenever their paths crossed too close. It was like watching a production being staged, with guest actors whenever one of her Circle members popped in with a task or a question. It started to seem as though Mils and Amair were matching the amount of work the Councillors were putting in.

Theo brought tea into the study every afternoon, finding the two of them pacing, or their heads bowed together in confusion over a desk, or yelling at each other. He would sit quietly in one of the chairs in the corner, smiling with a pen in his hand as he watched the two young heirs work and, despite their clashing, always having something to show for it.

One afternoon he walked in to find her study empty. He left the tea tray on the edge of the extra desk and went to look for her, determined to get the little piece of time he had with her in all the turmoil.

Theo found Amair sitting in the photograph gallery. He passed through it nearly every day, a new photo catching him off guard every once in a while but it rarely caught his attention anymore. He watched her stare at the section of the wall that had caught his eye all that time ago, her likeness hidden in the background of all her brother's photos. A close up of her laughing with Johanna, Jo's arm slung over her shoulders, both of them in leather jackets, looking prepped for the training grounds. Just beyond it was a new photo, slightly larger and it stood out in the chaos of frames, the official portrait of her with her circle. They were so young, and yet so determined.

"Hi," he whispered, kissing her temple as he wrapped his arms around her. She breathed back into him, staring up into the photographs.

"Hey."

"What are you thinking?"

"Just…grieving a life I thought I was going to have." She breathed slowly. "A girl I was."

"Who are you now?" he whispered into her ear, feeling her shiver in his embrace.

"Amair." Her breathing was measured but he could feel her heart beating fast under his hand. "Oighre Princess of Skylock." She raised her chin. "And no one is taking this Kingdom from me."

- CHAPTER LXXVIII -

Amair's heels snapped menacingly against the stone floor of the Skylock castle as she turned into a skinny hallway. "*What* is going on in here?" she demanded, Jasper and Mils turning their heads as she stormed into the room, Theo a few paces behind her.

"*He* keeps trying–"

"–nah!" She pointed a warning finger at her brother. "There will be no more yelling." Jasper huffed, glaring at Mils. "Now, if someone would like to *calmly* explain to me why the entirety of this floor's staff needs ear plugs, and the junior staff are cowering in corners, it would be *very much appreciated*." Both of the young men were silent, refusing to look at Amair or each other. "I would *love* to miss my afternoon meeting. I will stand here as long as it takes."

"He keeps getting *in* everything."

"Getting...in?" Amair glanced at Mils, his arms still crossed, looking away.

"Yes!" Jasper's voice started to raise, a warning look from his sister bringing it back down. "The libraries, the Family Wing, your study! He's fucking everywhere!"

"Jasper Alistair Skylock," Amair blinked a few times at him, mouth agape, "*Prince* Maximilian is here as a guest, more importantly, *my* guest, not to mention a great friend, and important ally. He is here trying to make *my* life easier, so that we can try and squash a *war*!" Her voice rose this time, both boys averting their eyes again, Jasper flinching at the word. "If I have to separate the two of you, I will do so without hesitation. This is a very large castle, I am certain I can find somewhere to stick you both. Now, will there be any other problems?" They muttered, still turned away from each other. "*Will* there be any other problems?"

"No!"

"Good. You are to see each other at meals, and after that, I will ask that you avoid each other, Mils…you may see me in my study, but please leave Jasper to the Family Wing, you can use anywhere else in the castle. Both of you…please make this easy on all of us, and don't make me assign guards to you.

"Maximilian, you may go, I need a moment with my brother."

"Yes, your highness." Mils bowed, glancing at Jasper who didn't look back at him. Amair nodded as he passed, slipping out the door of the Lineage Library. She turned angry eyes back on Jasper, her icy stare sending a shiver through him. He bit his tongue, trying to match her glare.

"What in the name of the gods *is wrong with you?*"

"You're not my mother!"

"No! I'm worse. I am your Oighre, and currently, a really *pissed* off one. What has gotten *into* you?"

"Him! He's so…I don't even know."

"I thought you liked Maximilian?"

"I…I don't know. He's never spent *weeks* here. Never been allowed in…in with the family."

"Oh, Jasper…" She hung her head, hands on her hips. "Okay. No more yelling. What are you feeling?"

"Annoyed."

"At him? Or at me?"

Jasper gulped. "I…I don't know."

"Uh huh." Amair sighed, and Jasper couldn't interpret the look passing over her face. "I want you to stay away from him for the rest of the week."

"But he—"

"—is a guest," she reiterated, the warning look once again replacing whatever had softened her. "Stay away from him. I have loads of work to get through this week, I do not have time to deal with you, and unless you want *Kenaia and Shehada* mediating this, you will keep your distance. I am free at the end of the week, and we will work on a truce." She sighed, beckoning Theo with her head. "Mils is a good man, Jasper. If you let him, he could be a good friend."

"Doubtful."

"Then a steady acquaintance, at the very least. If nothing else, do this for me. And right now...for our Kingdom."

Jasper didn't catch her eye as Theo wrapped an arm around her waist, the two of them leaving her brother leaning against the large black table.

***

"Maximilian Abes."

"Your highness—"

"—oh, don't 'your highness' me, Mils." Amair raised an eyebrow, her lips pursed, making Mils gulp. "What the fuck?"

"Look—"

"—shush." She shook her head curtly. "I've already yelled at him, it is your turn now."

"*He* started the yelling—"

"—so you, what, started yelling back?"

"Maybe."

"I do not believe you to be that stupid." She watched Mils sigh, shrug, toying with the edge of his cravat. "You have been known to push people's buttons. Especially when it comes to my brothers."

"What happened between me and Layton was resolved *years ago.*"

"Yeah, and do you remember *who* got you to resolve it?" He pursed his lips. "The two of you will be friends, if it *kills me*, because there is a very real chance that he is going to end up Oighre if this *war* goes to *shit.*"

"Amair!"

"Shut up and listen to me. He is a good boy, he is going to be a *great* man, and I need you to show him what an heir should be. It is time both of you started to grow up."

"With due respect—"

"—no. Despite your boyish shenanigans that I have watched for years, you are a good man, even if at times I am the only one who knows it." She stood as tall as she could, staring into his dark eyes. "I need you to be his friend. I need you to *step up*, now, Mils. As a friend. And an ally."

"I am not an heir like you are, Amair, not in the same way, I have...no power."

"But you are *an heir*. I have not been Oighre for very long…but if I can teach you anything, it is that you need people. You, and Jasper, are both my people. Now, I need my people to *get along*."

"You're right."

She smirked. "I often am." Mils laughed, reaching and brushing a stray hair, fingers gently touching her cheek.

"I'm sorry. I didn't…something just…I don't know, snapped, I guess. I wasn't the one pushing buttons. Or…not the only one."

She watched him for a second, thinking, shaking it off. "I honestly don't give a shit at this point what happened, or who started it. *I* ended it. I have *one day* that I don't have to work, a day I would normally be spending with my friends, or my very under-appreciated boyfriend, but instead, I will be sitting *the two of you* down, and you will not be leaving my study, until I am satisfied that you are, at the very least, friendly."

"How friendly are we thinking? You and the Writer kind of friendly, or–" She glared at him and he laughed.

"Wow, wait, I *get* it now, Jasper is in the right, you truly are an ass."

"And you love me anyways."

"Surprisingly." She took a breath, somewhat relieved but still on edge, looking out the window at the rain. "We're all at the end of our ropes, here. Everything is just tension, and if you nick it too hard, everything will come apart, and we can't have that, right now. Please…help me out here."

Mils nodded, slowly. "Of course, your highness." He bowed his head.

- CHAPTER LXXIX -

Your Royal Highness,

It is true that we admired your brother, and his single visit here not many weeks before his death convinced us he would make a great King. If you are his sister and learned from his strong footsteps, we believe you could, someday, be a great Queen.

But we cannot help you.

Waiwhe is a peaceful nation, our armies are meant to protect ourselves and do not leave our borders.

Should you need mediators, we are open.

But we will not raise our spears for you.

Wishing you all the best,

Senator Ona, Speaker

Amair growled, crumpling the page, launching it at the wall. Part of her went cold, the heat of bile countering it at the back of her throat. She looked out the window at the knights training in the grass, a few of them laughing as they were taken down.

Part of her felt the doom building in her stomach.

- CHAPTER LXXX -

"I want the boys moved somewhere safe," Amair shook her head. "They can't be anywhere near whatever war is coming."

"Then neither can you," Jasper shot back. "You must be kept safe as well."

"Jasper," the King warned.

Amair glared at her brother. "I'm the Oighre, Jasper."

"Even more reason to keep you safe!"

"I have a responsibility to keep all of *them* safe."

"Did you ever see our brother rushing off to war?"

"He went to *treaty talks* and died." Amair shook her head again, hands on her hips, not looking up at him. They both glanced over at their father, who sat extremely still on his throne, pensive. The King's eyes swung between his two children, but he said nothing.

"Both of you, stop," the King instructed, turning to his daughter. "What has brought this about? The plan was to keep them in the castle." Amair threw the crumpled letter at her dad.

"The Waiwhens won't help." Her father raised an eyebrow, sighing, glancing at Jasper, who was fuming. "They need to be somewhere *safe*."

"We're down a very brutal force. I appealed to morals, to their respect of Layton. Nothing."

"And where would we *go*?" Jasper demanded.

"I don't know, Jasper, this world is pretty freaking huge!"

"Alright, that is enough you two. Jasper, Amair and I have to meet with the Council and the War Chiefs."

"Great. My favourite."

"Hush, Amair. Jasper, go sit with your mother and your brothers in her chambers. We have our final Council meeting before the ride out." The King stood and the kids stood a little taller, shoulders back, still not lifting their eyes to make eye contact with anyone. "Let's go, Amair."

Amair lowered her head, following after the King into the hallway.

They walked quietly down the hall, hands tucked behind their backs and anyone who passed would know they were related, the same way of walking, and of holding themselves and their secrets in.

She saw Theo walking down the hall towards them.

"Dad…can I…could I catch up in a minute…" The King sighed but there was the smallest glint in his eye.

"Go ahead…I'll tell the Council you got caught with Circle business."

Theo bowed to the King as he passed, waiting to hear his footsteps retreat around a corner. Amair grabbed Theo's hand, pulling him into the closest room. He stumbled, trying to follow and she immediately wrapped her arms around him, burying her face in his chest.

"I miss you."

"I'm always here, Ama."

"It's different, now," she whispered.

"I think it was hope," Theo told her. "That look."

"What?"

"That look, in King Niall's eye." He looked over her head, kissing her forehead and folding around her once again. "It was hope."

"I have battle plans to review…did you know wars have supply orders? I feel like I'm running a shop, not preparing to fight for the lives of my people."

"You're doing wonderfully, I'm sure." He kissed her forehead again, looking down on her. "Care for an escort?"

"Always," she whispered, expecting him to offer his arm. He leaned down, scooping her up into his arms and her laugh echoed around the corridor as he carried her towards her meeting. "As your Princess," she told him, running her fingers gently along his jaw, "I decree you always take me to my meetings like this."

He kissed her nose. "Promise. I will be at your side for every meeting, and you will arrive in style to every one."

- CHAPTER LXXXI -

Amair stood, holding her shawl tight as she thought. He could see the tears in her eyes, the wind drying them as fast as they slipped onto her cheeks. "You okay?" Theo rubbed her arm, leaning over to try and gather what she was thinking. She stared out into the sea, wind whipping around them, waves crashing far below at the bottom of the cliffs.

He saw her face change, eyes widening. "We need to get back to the castle." She turned, lifting her heavy skirt, trying to hold on to her shawl at the same time. Theo looked out into the mist, trying to figure out what he was missing, turning and running to catch up.

***

"The Isle," Amair called to her father as she burst through the door of the office, the royal advisor sitting with him taking the papers he let go of as she tried to catch her breath.

"What…about it?"

"The old monastery is there." Amair brushed her shawl off her shoulders, Theo grabbing it as the wet wool fell to the ground. "It's safe. Almost no one knows about it." Her father stared at her, thinking for a second. "The caretakers have their home there. Priests, Priestesses. They would look after our boys." The King nodded slowly.

"Alright. I'll make arrangements."

Amair nodded, curtsying and turning out the door. Theo followed her, her shawl still bundled in his arms. "Amair, what is going on?"

She turned, pushing the shawl from his arms and holding them, stretching her fingers and holding him again. "The monastery is on the front side of the Isle of Ilona. The High Priests and Priestesses of Alan. Skylock Kings and Queens have been buried there for generations. There's a small old church and a rectory. And a graveyard. All built out of stone found deep in the mountains. A few spiritualists live there, in the rectory, along with two caretakers who oversee the care of the rectory, and the church, and the graveyard. It's not much. But no one knows of it." She looked up at Theo, sighing. "It's safe." She placed a hand on his cheek, her fingers cold against his skin.

"You'll send us there."

"Isn't it better than being locked in your room?"

"And you?"

She paused, trying to smile. "You know."

"Ama…"

"I'll need you there, Theo. To take care of my brothers. To watch them. Hold them…the poor twins. They've never been away from home. From me. From our parents. Mom will never go…not with us riding to the battlefield."

"I can't leave you," he ran his hand through her hair.

"Please, Theodore," her voice was just above a whisper, her voice warm. "*This* is what I need from you." She looked down, her eyes half closed. "I can't lead, I can't go to this war worrying about you. About you, and Jasper, and Kylo, and Alec, and Evander."

"Amair—"

"—and *if* anything happens…Jasper will need a strong, steady voice on his side."

"Amair!"

She sighed, pushing the breath out harshly. "What?"

"Will you marry me?"

Amair stared up at Theo, her eyes wide, her mouth open. He could see a million words run through her brain at once. After a minute, she smacked him on the arm.

"Ow—"

"What would your mother say if this is how you proposed?" she exclaimed.

"Amair—"

"—I'm walking out of here to plan a war…"

"I know." He brushed his hand over her head. "If anything happens to you…I want this tie to you."

"Theo…a royal engagement is a big deal, it's something huge, it's…."

"You don't even have to say yes. Just…that it's something you want. When this is all over that we do do it."

"Of course I want that. I've said that."

"Then hold on to that."

"So you'll go with my brothers?"

"I will."

"Theo?"

"Yeah?"

"Kiss me." Theo smiled, holding her cheeks, leaning over as she rose onto her toes, kissing her with all the fervour the idea of leaving her gave him. She held him, pushing her mouth against his, her fingers dug into his sides.

"You should pack," she whispered against his lips. "We only have a few days…"

"Can you just let me hold you for a minute?"

And she did.

- CHAPTER LXXXII -

It was a hundred stairs down to the water's edge. Theo counted every single one, trying to focus as the wind whipped up off the sea. Fog had rolled in, caressing their skin and joined with the water that lapped at his boots as they approached the boat at the water's edge. He helped the priest, their ferryman to the Isle of Ilona, load the few cargo items, their two shared cases, into the small boat.

He felt like he was being watched.

Theo looked over to find Amair in a flowing grey gown, the pale swaths of fabric carrying in the wind, looking ethereal, blending in with the fog and mist coming off the angry water.

The twins ran over to Amair, throwing their arms around her, hugging her tightly. He couldn't hear her, but she stooped, murmuring something to them. They nodded, Alec squeezing Amair's hand, nodding once, solemnly.

"Please don't die," everyone heard Evander say to her, a sob squeezing the last word.

"I don't think this is war attire," Theo murmured, pulling on one of the strips of fabric of her sleeves.

Amair forced a smile, glancing at the ground. "I'm changing at the camp."

"Right."

"The Council thinks having Skylock keep me in their minds as their Princess is better than having me an equal among warriors."

"I will always think of you as a warrior." She smiled a little.

"Sometimes, sovereignty is just about image. About hope," she murmured. Theo slipped two fingers under her chin, begging her quietly to look up at him. She gave in, looking into his eyes. The wind ripped one of the pins out of her hair, the strands of dark hair whipping back, mixed in with the gold, and Theo tried to commit the way she looked to memory.

"Please come back to me."

She didn't say anything, reaching up and cupping a cold hand against his cheek. "I plan to do my very best."

"I love you, Amair." She smiled, letting out a breath that almost sounded more like relief.

"And I love you, Theodore." She let her hand linger on the back of his neck, gently rubbing her fingers through his hair.

"Sir Crawford!" the young priest called. "We should be off."

"The Princess should be off, too," a Knight reminded them.

"I know," Amair shot back. She kissed Theo again, and the two backed away from each other. Jasper helped Theo step into the boat, then Nusiq and Kylo.

She chewed on the inside of her cheek, watching as two Knights helped push the boat off into the swirling grey water. They watched as the young priest, one of the few with the intuition to navigate the waters to Ilona, pulled on the oars.

"Take care of them!" she yelled, her lip and voice trembling as her words carried out by the wind. Theo nodded, feeling Kylo grab his hand as the fog wrapped around their boat.

"Your highness..."

"I'm coming." She nodded, fingers brushing her mouth. "I'm coming." With one last look at Theo's face disappearing into the mist, she turned towards the staircase.

Theo gripped the edge of the seat on the boat, the mist wrapping itself around him and the boys. Nusiq and Kylo each held one of the twins, Jasper staring ahead, anger still written across his features. They all jumped as it seemed that something moved in the mist, but the young priest at the front of the boat, arm outstretched with a lamp, seemed unphased.

Theo tried to take a deep breath, pushing the images building in his mind away. Amair would be fine. She had to be.

***

"I've sent down everything you'll need, your highness…except this." The armourer bowed to her slightly, raising a blade in a belt sheath. Amair recognized the slight wearing on the black leather handle, the jewelled end of the hilt.

"Kaymran–"

"–Princess. Your brother would want you to have this." Amair took a deep breath as the two stared at each other and Amair finally broke her gaze away, nodding. It was Layton's dirk, a long dagger that he had always worn ceremoniously, but twiddled nervously with the handle.

"Hey, Amair," Aramis and Shehada smiled, peeking into the room.

"Come in, come in," Kaymran beckoned them, tightening the belt with Layton's dirk around Amair's waist, over her silvery dress.

"How do you feel?" Shehada asked, looking Amair up and down.

"The weight of a kingdom," Amair muttered, glancing down at herself. Shehada smiled a little, her lips taught as she forced it through her fear. "You are doing as instructed?"

"Denna and Kenaia have set up, ready to strike if needed. We and the staff will stay in the tunnels as long as we can, so we can leave, if necessary."

"Hopefully, the war will not make it this far."

"But if it does," Aramis smiled, squeezing Amair's hand, "we are ready to defend your castle. Your people."

Amair nodded, glancing back at herself in the mirror. "Shehada… can we speak, for a moment?" The girls glanced at Aramis, who smiled, bobbing his head.

"I'll wait outside, Shehada."

"I will be there momentarily."

Kaymran disappeared into the back room, Aramis sneaking back out the door quietly. Amair glanced at her reflection in the wall of shields for a moment, before looking back at her friend.

"You are to take on the Circle passing, and train my brother if anything happens to me."

"Ama…"

"I love you. I love you, and I trust you. Denna…I don't know if she would be able to handle it. She could…the job part. But…with…what it would mean…"

"I know what you're saying, Princess."

"Take care of them."

Shehada nodded, her lip quivering, pulling Amair into a hug. "You're going to be fine," she whispered to the Princess. "I know you are." Amair hugged her back, but she was not as sure. She pulled back a little.

"I have to go see Mils…he needs his instructions next."

"I won't wish you luck."

Amair laughed hoarsely. "Good." It took everything she had to turn and walk out of the armoury, her hand brushing up and down the blade attached at her waist.

***

"Maximilian."

"You don't call me that," he whispered, turning away from the window to look at her. "You always call me–"

"–Mils," she corrected, trying to smile. "We're leaving."

"My turn for…what sage advice? Some kind of special Oighre spell of protection? He was trying to be sarcastic, but his voice was hopeful.

"If only." She reached out, carefully taking his hand. "Show my brothers what it means to be a great King."

"Amair–"

"–if something happens."

"It won't"

"It *could*."

His jaw quivered.

"And um…look out for my mom. If anything makes it this far…she's not a warrior."

Mils was nodding, staring at her. He pulled her to him. "Be safe," he whispered, holding her tight. "Is that even something I can say to a warrior?"

"No," Amair gasped, trying to push back her tears. "But it's something you can say to me."

***

"Lenora!" Amair called, passing her reins to one of the knights, asking him to wait for her.

"Princess…" Lenora forced herself to smile, the two girls clasping arms.

"I trust you with my home. My mom. Prince Maximilian. My Circle. And every other person who lives here."

"Amair—"

"—please, Lenora."

Lenora sighed, looking the Princess up and down. "The guard will not let you down, Princess." Amair nodded.

"I know." She squeezed her fingers just slightly tighter around Lenora's arm, the two staring into each other's eyes. The Knights glanced over to them, watching the girls hold each other. Amair looked young, with her hair down, the wind having finally toppled her loose bun.

For a moment, everyone remembered that they were still very much little girls.

"You need to go."

"I know."

"Are…are you afraid?"

Amair was surprised by the question and without thinking. "Yes." She nodded. She shook her hair a little, taking a deep breath, blinking back tears. "I'd be a fool not to be." She bit her lip. "But I'm doing this anyway."

- CHAPTER LXXXIII -

She could see hundreds of soldiers in the distance, trying to squint to make out the uniforms of their allies. The fur sashes of the Tunngas. The perfectly woven, strong breastplates of the RiKoi. The Forran metal that reflected back slick, rainbow shades. All there to help her cause. She felt her dress whispering around her in the wind and felt out of place amongst the growing crowd of warriors.

She passed clan warriors helping, RiKans turning to help Skylock knights adjust their scarves. Everyone paused to bow to her, a sense of pride and hope in them that did not quite pass onto her. She felt like she was going to throw up.

Amair rode up to the huge blue tent, pulling her horse to a stop and throwing her legs down before the horse had barely slowed. A Knight stood taller, recognizing the Princess.

"Your highness!" He helped slow her horse. "They're all waiting inside."

"I'm sure they are," she muttered. "Who are they?"

"Queen Nukila couldn't make it," he said quietly, "but Devinray, and King Extrin came in place of the High King of Forra. Your father, one of his advisors, and the whole of the Elected Council."

She grumbled something to herself. "Fantastic."

"Princess!" A few voices rose, greeting her, King Devinray breaking past the royals and ambassadors and advisors gathered around the table.

"My son?" he asked.

She touched his arm carefully, nodding encouragingly. "Safe, in the castle, with my mother, along with most of my Circle." He pulled her into a hug. "I couldn't have gotten through this without him."

She passed him to the bag of armour one of the RiKoi knights hauled in for her, and the visiting royals and their advisors watched her toss pieces of armour from the bag Kaymran had provided, deciding on her favourites, turning to Arthur, not having to ask for help.

"Amair…" the King murmured, seeing the leather armour protecting her arms, a light metal breast plate and chainmail around her throat, "that's not going to…protect you much…"

"Yeah, well," she glanced at her father, "I can't move in much else."

"Princess…" The Tunngas General bit her lip. "Let the warriors head out first. Please…you can swoop in for the victory."

"I'm not here for *swooping*." She pulled at the tie holding the metal armour on her legs, letting it fall to the ground, tinkling as she shook out her legs in their dark brown leather pants. She looked around the room at the worried faces.

"I um…I need a moment. Arthur? Help me with this? Out…outside?"

"Yes, your highness." He followed her out into the wind, watching her turn, a hand on her stomach as she tried to calm herself, the sound of the Keenian army in the distance.

"I keep wondering if this would be happening if Layton were alive."

"What?"

"I keep wondering what he would say. He would tell me this is ridiculous. To stop trying to barrel into things."

"And that is why, despite every cord of fate, you will be the greatest Queen."

It was her turn to look up in surprise. "What?"

"You are putting yourself on the line for people. Your people…and others." He raised his chin, valiant as he looked at her. "You said something to me, once, when we were shoved away during a meeting. Sometimes…change can't be clean. You know how and when to make that choice."

"I didn't plan for it to come to this."

"No…and that is why it is the right path, now." She took a deep breath, catching his eyes.

"Keenians!" a RiKoi soldier yelled, the sound of a horn falling over the hill. "On the horizon!"

"That's go time."

"That's go time…" she whispered, closing her eyes for a second, feeling her heartbeat quicken. She stepped back into the tent, looking over everyone. *Go time.*

***

Amair sat on her horse, a hand on her hip as she looked out into the edge of the trees where Forra met Keene.

"Are you ready?" Arthur murmured. Amair took a deep breath, holding her reins.

"Can I ever be?" She turned her head, the two of them looking steadily at each other. "But I have to be."

"Amair…"

"For my people. For RiKoi's. Forra's. And any further damage they want to inflict."

"Your highness!" someone yelled behind them, both the teenagers turning to look at the War Chief running across dirt.

"War Chief Hill," she acknowledged as he slowed, his eyes glancing at the Princess' horse that stepped restlessly under her.

"The Chiefs and I have made our lists, checked all of your troops, and our allies. RiKoi is ready. The Tunngas warriors are ready. Forra is with us." The War Chief stuck his shoulders back, but Amair saw the little twitch of his jaw.

"The King?"

"Staying put. At the camp, with King Devinray, and others. He keeps insisting that he could be here, though."

"I know *you* cannot take my word above his but…if I order two of your warriors to keep him there by any means," she looked down at him, "can they do it?"

He swallowed hard, but nodded. "Yes, your highness."

"If anything goes wrong today, Skylock, this coalition…any future heir…will need his leadership."

"Then…we are ready."

"We're ready," she murmured to herself.

War Chief Glasslight walked up on the other side of her, a mace in his hands. "Any rousing speech for the troops?"

Amair bit the inside of her lip. "I can tell them that they are strong, that they are in the favour of the gods…nothing I say will prepare them even more for what we might face."

"But they believe in you, Princess."

"I'm just a human…I don't bring any magical powers beyond my years of training."

"*Princess.*"

"Ama," Arthur whispered beside her. She grabbed Arthur's wrist for a second, steadying herself, and looked to the two War Chiefs. "Fall in line." He nodded and she let go of Arthur, turning to the two commanders. She pulled Elleban around, watching as he shook out his black mane as she looked out, realizing just how many fighters stood behind her. Her eyes trailed over them, watching people in all the different uniforms stood together, mingling, whispering, standing shoulder to shoulder. Her knights and the clan warriors standing with Forran soldiers, with RiKoi and Tunngas warriors helping fix small pieces on their uniforms and armour.

Amair sighed, raising her chin slightly, a hush falling over them all as she nodded once. "I look out at all of you," she called, hoping as many people as possible could hear her, "and I feel a sliver of hope. That this can have a good ending." She took a deep breath, nodding once more at them. "Let's give 'em hell!" It was quiet for a moment, and she felt her chest squeeze. There were no more words in her chest because mostly, she wanted to cry.

They cheered.

It was a cross of cheering and a battle cry, hurrahing and raising weapons, the sound of drums and Skypipes somewhere near the back, rumbling deep into the earth and through her bones. She smiled, tight and pained, but hopeful.

She glanced down at the leaders and War Chiefs next to her. "Give the order, gentlemen." They nodded and one of them raised the white horn, and Amair focused on the Skylark carved into its side. The shrill noise rang over the field, over the border, and the cries of the warriors behind her rattled through Amair's bones. She took a deep breath, pulling her sword from her back.

"For our people!"

"For our people!" they echoed, and the first of the Skylock warriors thundered down the hill towards the border.

"For *my* people," she whispered, pulling her sword from her back.

The sound of the first swords clashing was worse than a scream.

- CHAPTER LXXXIV -

The hints of the third evening swept over the valley, sending long shadows across the fighting troops. Amair ducked, hand brushing the grass beneath her, trying not to cower as she felt a sword slice through the air above her. She grabbed a knife from her calf, stabbing the man's knee, knocking him in the mouth with her elbow as he sank to the ground. He raised his sword, pain and anger in his eyes, Amair crushing his wrist into the ground with the heel of her boot. She winced at the scream he let out, rolling into the dirt as he cried out.

She bit her tongue, the weight of the screams crushing down on her chest. The rain that fell from the sky felt hot against her sweaty skin, and yet barely registered as it fell around her. She watched people she had once called friends fall, arrows and armour littering the valley.

She couldn't remember what day it was.

How many times it had been dark.

Which direction was home.

She shielded her eyes, looking up the green hill, gagging at the red starting to stain it. Without thinking, she raised an elbow, hitting someone in the mouth, flipping her arm around to dig her sword, the scream falling away with a crack of thunder above her. She pulled it back, trying not to picture the person sinking to their knees behind her, looking at the blood on her sword.

Amair looked around, her sword barely held up in her hand, her hand on her forehead, tears running down the dirt on her cheeks. She looked at the bodies of the RiKoi and Skylock soldiers scattered around her, a tight scream escaping at the bloodied face of a boy younger than she was, followed by a sob. "What have we done…"

She flipped a hand around, knifing a Keenian knight running up behind her, forever impressed by how many of them gave themselves away with rousing battle cries.

"Amair." She turned, a young man with dirt streaked across his face looking at her. "Princess…you shouldn't be here…" His voice was familiar. Tired, but familiar.

"Domiko…" She whispered in horror, climbing across a line of bodies and reaching for him, letting him partially collapse into her arms.

"This is…" He gasped and when she pulled one of her hands away, it was streaked in blood but she had to wonder if it was his, or hers, or someone else's entirely. "This is no place for our future Queen."

"Where else would you find the Champion of Skylock?" she asked, managing a smile. She stood them both up, wrapping his arm around her shoulders and started dragging him.

"You should leave me here…get out…" He coughed. "Get out while you still can."

His words made her run cold but she pushed it away, focusing on her blood pumping through her, insisting on keeping herself warm. Alive. "I'm not running away from this."

"We need our Oighre—"

"—good thing I have four more brothers—"

"—no," he rasped as she dragged him over a hill, trying to remember which way were the Skylock tents, wanting to bring Domiko back to something like home. "We need *you*, Amair."

There was the cold again.

"I'm here, Domiko. Doing what I can."

She dropped Domiko, turning to fight two Keenians running up to them, dropping low to grab the dagger from Domiko's hip. She turned in quick succession as she avoided blades, leaning back enough that the two Keenians crossed each other. In their confusion, she took her chance to take them out, scooping Domiko up again and trying to walk faster.

"We're getting you help Dom…and then I'm fighting for my kingdom. No matter what."

- CHAPTER LXXXV -

"Somebody help!" Amair screamed, nearly dropping the dirty, bloodied Domiko as she walked into the infirmary tent. Two nurses turned, arms reached for the boy. The beds were already lined with fighters in Forran, RiKoi, and Tunngas uniforms, and she spotted nearly every Skylock clan tartan around the room. "Help," she gasped as she felt Domiko's weight lifted from her shoulders.

"We have him, Princess," the nurse assured her. "here, let me look at you—"

"—I'm fine." She pushed away from the nurse. "I have to go… we're…" She stopped herself from saying *dying*. "They need me."

"Ama," Moritz's voice stopped her in her tracks as she left the infirmary tent. She pressed her lips together in annoyances, glaring at him.

"I have to go," she said, sword partially raised.

"King and Council, and visitors, are requesting your presence."

She shook her head, biting her tongue angrily, but bowed mockingly. "Lead the way."

"You may want to sheath—"

"—they want to see the warrior," she flipped her sword in her hand, "then the warrior is who they are going to get."

She wondered how bad she looked, suddenly, as she walked into the tent and various levels of shock passed over royal and noble faces. "Ama…" the King whispered.

"I'm a little busy," she snapped, wiping her brow.

***

"We need to consider surrendering."

"No."

"They're killing us, Amair. Isn't it better to survive this and—"

"—you're ready to give in, three days into one battle?"

"We were ill prepared," Councillor Vyron said, his chin lifted, flexing his hand.

"We weren't. We knew what was coming. It's why we have allies." The other royals nodded solemnly at their acknowledgement. Amair's eyes slid back to the Councillors. "If you have no stomach for this, I can have a Knight escort you home."

"It is…troublesome, that we seem to be making no advances," Councillor Edmund added, glancing at Vyron. Genevieve and Avelenn, the women on the Elected Council, glanced between their Council counterparts and the Princess.

"We are running out of options," Vyron was nodding, "soon there will be no options left."

Amair met Arthur's eyes, both of them straining against their mounting anger.

"Unless you're willing to send a marriage declaration to their heir—"

"—no," King Niall and King Devinray said adamantly. Amair's mind wandered as bickering started, throwing an arm over her head half in defeat, picturing Domiko sitting alone in the infirmary, wondering if she could rush out of the tent and find War Chief Flora to sit with his son, try to force Domiko to be okay.

"Backup heirs…" she whispered to herself, remembering their conversation. "Oh my gods…" She stopped suddenly, turning back to the table, her eyes wide. Her arms slid off her head, her dirty hair popping out of her tight, braided hairdo. "I have an idea."

"Please, do tell, Princess," Vyron raised an eyebrow, his face sour.

"Watch how you speak to her," Arthur warned him.

"Arthur," Amair looked to her knight, ignoring the Councillor. "Do you think we could infiltrate their camp?"

"I don't…depends?" He glanced at Moritz. "Maybe quietly, the two of us…around the back somehow…why?"

Amair raised an eyebrow, suddenly smug. "We need to kidnap their heir."

"What?"

She turned to her dad. "It's only just come to me now. One of the laws of Land. You harm an heir in any way, their end must be ten times worse. We've never enforced the rule, because, well, I can't think of any heir coming anywhere near harm, except perhaps outside a duelling ring. But Novak caused harm. To me. Physical and emotional." Amair noticed Arthur grimace as she talked. "If we get ahold of him, and get in front of the Emperor and that horrid Mevelon, I am almost sure they'll concede. It's a show of force that would actually throw them off guard, and risk their whole damn Empire."

Vyron was crossing his arms. "Why would they care—"

"—Mevelon isn't married," she reminded the Councillor. "That's why he was so absolutely disgusting to me. Until he is, and has produced a legitimate heir by the Emperor's standard, next in line for the throne is—"

"—Novak," Moritz murmured, nodding.

Amair grinned. "Novak. They have to protect him. He's in line, and we're all hoping Mevelon stays single, and childless. So they have to protect the heir. Whether they actually like him, or not.

"Plus, I might get to hold a knife to Novak's throat for added flair, and I for one am really looking forward to that."

"Amair," her father chastised.

"What? You're all thinking the same thing. Except, maybe Councilman Vyron."

Moritz stood, clapping his hands together. "Alright. Alright, let's go kidnap an heir." He flexed his hands. "And hopefully…stem the tide of this war."

- CHAPTER LXXXVI -

"Could you please fetch Sir Novak?" the young girl asked the Keenian Knights. They looked her up and down, one of them looking suspicious, the other grinning. "Please, hurry. I've been sent by the Emperor as a gift to his grandson for bringing us so close to the Skylock Kingdom."

"We didn't hear of this," the one Keenian Knights said cautiously.

"Does he often inform the army of hired girls?" The guards glanced at each other, one of them shrugging.

"Wait here." They turned off to the camp, leaving the girl standing amongst the trees.

"Thank you, Adonna," Amair whispered, smiling, creeping out from the trees. The young knight undid her cloak, handing it off to the heir, the girls wearing matching grins.

Arthur and Amair, with two knights disguised as Keenian peasants in tow, found Novak's tent, away from the rest of the Keenian camp. Their plan had been hatched quickly, and Amair was sending a silent prayer that everything worked out.

"I should go…keep helping the effort at the front…"

"Of course. Hopefully, it won't be much longer."

"Good luck, Princess."

"Of course. Go. Thank you."

Amair handed the cloak to the shortest of the knights that had followed her into the crowded hillside, trees towering around them, blocking out the sun. "You both ready? Clear on the plan?" Arthur nodded, the Knight wearing the cloak turning to obscure himself from view. Amair and Arthur tucked themselves behind the trees. Amair pressed her hands back, feeling the bark against her fingertips, trying to keep herself in the moment.

"Why hello there," she heard Novak's voice fill the woods.

She could barely believe how naïve he was.

"I hear I got a lovely little...gift." Amair could picture him, running his hand over the cloak, the Skylock Knight trying to stay perfectly still under his hands. Amair glanced over, tipping her chin at Arthur leading them. He nodded ever so slightly, pulling down the visor on his helmet, and raised his hand. Go time.

Amair stepped out of her hiding place, staring down Novak. It took him a second to process, looking past the knight, his eyes landing on Amair's. The knight didn't move, watching Amair. She closed her hand into a fist, putting two fingers back out, tight together. Do it.

Novak opened his mouth to yell, or to goad her, she wasn't sure. In the blink of an eye, the short knight had whipped around, wrapping his gloved hand over Novak's mouth and turning to wrap his other arm around Novak's neck. Novak screamed in the knight's hand, gripping their arm and trying to pull himself free. Amair walked towards them, just close enough for Novak's flailing arms to miss hitting her.

She didn't say anything, staring Novak down, chin up. Novak's eyes rolled back as he finally collapsed into the knight's arms.

"Got him," Arthur murmured, his voice laced with venom.

"We aren't done yet. Bind him" Amair knelt next to Novak as one of the knights pulled a tie from her belt, tying Novak's hands behind his back, glaring down at him. "Payback's a bitch," Amair murmured harshly. She stood back up, climbing the hill, Arthur and the knight hauling Novak behind her.

They found a Forran and two RiKoi fighters along the way who quietly helped point them along to the Keenian planning tent, keeping their weapons and eyes drawn. They set the Keenian Prince down, observing for a moment.

Arthur grabbed Amair's wrist, the two of them flattening themselves against the large boulder. Arthur looked across at troops lining themselves around the tent. There were people yelling inside the dark-sided tent, but she could not tell if it was in celebration or anger.

They watched, out of sight, a moment longer, for the signal they had set up. Their knight carried Novak to the door, nodding to Amair as she grabbed hold of the young man's collar. He was starting to wake, still groggy from being knocked out. A Forran and a RiKoi fighter positioned themselves, waiting for her.

She nodded.

They pushed in.

Amair pushed the groggy Novak in front of her to his knees, his arms bound behind his back.

"Emperor Omnan." Amair's voice was cold. Amair stood on the sole of one of his boots, digging him into place. She held Layton's dirk by her side, her shoulders back, the cool, midnight breeze sweeping through her loose hair, seeming to press into her cheek for a moment. She reached out, gripping Novak's hair and pulling his head back a little. He groaned into the gag, struggling against Amair's fingers, trying to pull away, but she held tight, digging her foot further into his. She didn't move the dagger.

"What is this?" the Emperor demanded, looking down at Amair and his grandson, motioning to the Keenian guards but before they could move on her, Tunngas and Clan warriors ripped through the side of the tent with a horrible, angry yowl, each grabbing a guard.

"You appear to have forgotten the ancient laws of Land, Emperor."

"Don't cite the old laws to me, girl."

"And yet you ignore them. You ask for an avenging of lives. Of harm. And yet here we stand, on opposing sides of a war *you* declared—"

"—that you could have ended."

"No. That was no fair deal. Apparently I do have to remind you that the laws of Land — not my Kingdom, not your farce of an Empire, but this whole world — clearly state that should any type of harm come to an heir, physically *or otherwise*, that harm shall be retaliated ten-fold." She raised her chin even further, glaring back at the Emperor. He said nothing. Mevelon turned his head between his father and Amair, his eyes wide, shocked. Amair raised the long dagger to the side of Novak's neck. "Novak broke the laws of Land when he kidnapped an heir. She thought the next words through, rolling them over her tongue. And I have reason to believe he was involved in the death of my brother."

A few of the clan warriors around them tried to hide their shock but it was difficult to do. Mevelon raised his eyebrows, the shock clear in the way his mouth twisted. The Emperor didn't stir, though. Amair pressed her blade slightly closer to Novak's neck, a sliver of blood appearing on the edge of the silver blade. "And now, you have befallen me as well, Emperor. This war has done unimaginable harm. Physical...*and otherwise.*"

"Father, he is next in the line of succession, we need–"

The Emperor hushed his eldest son. "Your father raised a strong heir."

"He did," Amair said curtly. "And he raised a strong daughter who had to take his place."

The Emperor sighed, hands on his hips. Finally, he bowed, hands splayed out. "Your royal highness," he hissed the title bitterly, "please have mercy on a future heir of Keene."

Amair's anger had yet to burn through. "I should be asking you for ten men to suffer the way he made me. Four generations ago, Novak *and* the Archduke would have been tortured as repentance." Amair stepped further onto Novak's foot and he yelped into the gag. "But I will be merciful." She took the pressure off his foot, loosening her fingers ever so slightly. "You can take Novak. Unharmed, which I think if you check the catalogue of my wounds any and all Keenians have inflicted at the manor, and the past four days, is more than generous. He is to be placed on house arrest and not be allowed to return to his personal manor." She took a deep breath. "And you will take your army, and you will cease the fighting immediately. You or any Keenian Knight found outside your borders after twelve hours, will be taken to our dungeons. Their fate decided later."

The Emperor chewed on the inside of his cheek, thinking, not taking his eyes off Amair, his mouth pursed in an ugly way. "I accept your terms."

"Good." Amair let go of the boy's hair, picking up her foot, placing it between Novak's shoulder blades and pushing him towards the grass, no hands to stop his fall, landing with an oof. "You, Novak Keene, are not brave. You have filthied your family name."

He twisted to glare at her as her words pushed through him.

Amair's eyes ran over the Keenian royals once more, the various levels of shock and anger, the Archduke cowering in a chair in the corner as a Keenian Knight dragged his son over to untie. "Send word this battle is over," she said, her voice slow and metered, not breaking her eyes from Omnan's. "Take a Red Jacket with you as collateral." She started to turn. "It's time we go home…I'll have a treaty drawn up, enough damage has been done this time—"

"Amair!" she heard one of her men yell, but the name was torn, slipping past her ears. A few of them gasped. She didn't turn, barely even raising her eyes and instead her hand without thinking, grabbing the knife from the air before it even had a chance to clip her ear.

The allied warriors and soldiers stared at her wide eyed, a few with their jaws dropped. One of the RiKoi looked past her, watching Novak, Mevelon, and Vermil's eyes wide, staring at Amair's back. She turned to look over her shoulder a little, her body slowly turning with it. She squinted at the three men standing paces from her, her hand still up by her head, thick lines of blood rolling down her wrist.

"Forget a treaty…" It came out a low growl, steady and threatening. "I would suggest running, now." The Archduke and Mevelon turned, two of their men following as they ran. Novak studied Amair's face for a moment. The world slowed as they watched each other. Amair dropped her hand, still holding the knife, blood dripping off her fingers into the dirt. Novak nodded a few times, turning and running after his father and uncle.

Amair and the troops behind her watched them for a second.

"Rawri?" Amair called over her shoulder to the Tunngas general.

"Yes, your highness?"

"See that they return to Keene."

"Are…are you sure, your highness?" The soul splitting screech of a retreat horn echoed over the valley, terrified screams following it, the clashing of swords melting into the tinker of weapons hitting the ground.

Amair took a deep breath. "*Sure*…no. We know where they're scurrying off to, though. And they've taken a serious blow, to their troops…and their egos, which I believe they value more than their people, so I doubt we will be seeing them anytime soon. I'll put my people in place as soon as I can."

"Should I…have something written…"

"—I don't think I could bring myself to sign a treaty today anyways," she admitted. "And I don't think this war is over."

He bowed his head. "Alright, your highness."

Out of the corner of his eye, Arthur watched the general grin, turning and beckoning three men and a woman to follow. They raised their spears, bowing their heads slightly at Amair, and headed in the direction the Keenians had fled to.

Behind her, warriors started tossing things in the air and cheering.

"Ama!" Arthur exclaimed, pushing through two tall men, reaching for her. "Here, let me help." He grabbed her arm gently, raising it as she nodded, her mind feeling far away. Arthur helped Amair pull her fingers and palm back off the sharp blade, blood gushing out of her hand, spilling onto the grass.

"Ow! Ow, ow, *ow!*"

"Gods," Arthur muttered to himself. He pulled off his glove, trying to use his hand wrap to clear some of the blood, trying not to flinch at the deep gashes on Amair's hand. She watched him work, watching the perfectly sliced lines ooze blood.

"That was incredibly dumb," he murmured, pulling off his scarf as she mumbled *ow* again, "catching the knife." He focused on the feeling of the threads against his skin as he wrapped the heavy garment around her hand as tightly as its bulk would let him. "But oh *gods* was it cool." Amair chuckled, flinching as something in her hand squeezed and then burned. "The look on Mevelon's face when you caught it…" He looked the Princess in the eye, smiling, holding her wrapped hand in both of his. "It reminded me why I'm so ready to follow you."

"Princess!"

"Chief Torrent." Amair nodded to him as he scurried down the hill.

"News reached us that…that it's over?"

"For the time being, at least. A few of the Tunngas warriors have gone to keep an eye on the Keenian royals scurrying back to their lair."

"Well, *I* am fetching *our* royal. I volunteered to come bring you back. There is a lot of discussion to be had."

"Alright." She took a deep breath, unsure if the tingling pain in her hand or the relief forced it out of her lungs. "Lead the way…the past few days have me…kind of turned around."

"Of course," Torrent offered her an arm, but she shook her head, holding her injured hand to her chest, her other hand instinctively still resting on her sword. "If you thought you came home a hero the last time, just wait until they all hear of this!" Arthur heard the Chief exclaim as he walked away, Amair's eyes on the ground.

She glanced back, looking for him. "Arthur? Are you coming?"

He raised an eyebrow, but scurried up the hill behind them. Amair kept her eyes on the bodies of the fallen as they made their way back to the Forran side of the border.

"So…can we go home now?"

"Your highness…before we do…" Chief Torrent caught her arm, turning to look into her eyes and she felt her heart break with the creases that formed under his eyes. "You should know…Domiko didn't make it."

She bit her lip, reaching backwards with her free hand, hoping Arthur was close enough to grab as she nodded slowly, the last piece of hope cracking a little. "It's time to go home," she whispered, her voice strained, days of being awake, the costs of every life around her grabbing hold of her shoulders suddenly. "Send our fastest rider back to the castle, get a message across to the Isle…I want Theo and my brothers to meet us once we have parted ways with our allies…" She shook her head, Arthur wondering if she was about to collapse, her hand pressed further into her chest as though she was physically holding her heart together. "We need to go home."

- CHAPTER LXXXVII -

Amair grinned, the boats rushing up onto the rocks, pulled further onto shore by guards. The boys jumped over the side, stretching arms and necks, taking in the sight of home. Amair jumped off the last step, dropping her shield.

"Theodore!" Amair exclaimed, tossing her sword aside, running for him. He smiled tiredly, stretching out his arms to her, catching her in a tight hug.

"Thank the gods you're alive," he murmured into her loose hair, his nose pressed against her head. They held each other, Amair's brothers watching, smiling softly, Jasper's arm around Kylo. She pulled back, opening her mouth to say something but Theo said, "We need to talk." Her face faltered a little, but she nodded, a hand on his cheek.

"As soon as we're back in the castle. I wanted to meet you but…my work is not done, yet."

"It can wait a bit."

"Okay." She forced herself to smile, nodding a little, even as the pit in her stomach grew. She turned to her brothers, grinning, pulling the twins into the tightest hug her arms, still tired, could manage. She finally let herself cry. She let go of them as she threw her arms around Kylo, the two of them holding each other, tears streaming down.

"You okay?" Jasper murmured to Theo, an eyebrow raised. Theo nodded a little, not looking at Jasper, and walked towards the stairs. Amair put her arms around the twins, all of them following Theo towards the long stairs, making the journey back up them. Jasper glanced behind himself at his sister, smiling in a way he had missed, but felt something growing in the pit of his stomach.

"How's...how's everyone else?" Jasper asked, and Amair glanced over her shoulder quickly, stumbling a little on the stairs.

"Um...we lost a lot of people..." She took a deep breath, watching her feet for a moment, letting go of the twins and letting them go ahead as the stairs narrowed. "RiKoi and Forra...they were hit hard." She gulped, thinking of the young boy's dead eyes staring up at her and she wiped at a tear that escaped. "Mom and dad, they're fine. Keene didn't make it off the battleground. We fought hard. Arthur survived, though spent nearly an hour getting stitches on his arm. Mils is fine. He didn't even make it to the battle."

"Did you send him to his *room?*" Alec laughed in front of them.

"He agreed to stay home and protect mom."

"Oh..." the twins stopped laughing, looking behind them at their sister, eyebrows knitting together.

They made it to the top of the stairs, emerging onto the castle grounds. Nusiq leaned over, whispering something to the twins, one of them jumping up and down. The twins took off running towards the castle, Nusiq barrelling after them, all three of them yelling, waving at the grounds staff and all of them hollered back excitedly.

Amair, Jasper, Kylo, and Theo stood, watching them run, taking in the sight of the castle as chilly wind off the ocean whipped at their backs. Amair crossed her arms over her chest, the energy of the castle feeling almost visible. They could hear at least two attendants singing folk songs somewhere nearby.

"Are you injured?" Jasper exclaimed.

"No. No, not really. Some bruises and a few cuts. Mostly from falling and other dumb injuries. I fell and tore a pair of pants open on a rock. Got caught in the cross hairs in one spot...got a pretty bad stabbing by a misplaced spear."

"Ouch."

"Oh and I...may have grabbed a knife from...mid-air..."

Both her brothers looked at her, eyebrows raised, but she waved them off. "There's time for that later. There are people with much worse," Amair murmured, shaking her head.

"But we won."

"We did...for now…with a cost."

"They went in knowing that."

"I know...but still. A part of me hoped we wouldn't lose anything. Life or limb."

"But it's over?"

"No. There's a lot of work ahead of us…I'm exhausted, so it may have to start tomorrow."

Kylo wrapped his arm around Amair's waist, resting his chin on her shoulder. "We've got you now."

She smiled. "Let's go home."

- CHAPTER LXXXVIII -

They walked into the library, Amair turning to smile across the table from Theo, opening her mouth–

"I can't do this, Amair." Amair's face fell, looking into Theo's eyes, her mouth still open. It took her a moment, processing the words he said.

"Oh."

"When we were there? At the Abbey? I couldn't…I couldn't stop thinking about you. Every moment you were all I could think about, as I watched the boys play. I was driving myself crazy." Amair nodded a little, tears streaming down her cheeks. "I can't do this."

Amair nodded a little, her lip quivering. "I…I understand."

"Amair…I'm sorry–"

"–no. I said I would let you out." Amair stepped back. "This is me letting you out, Sir Crawford."

"Amair–"

"–can I ask one question?"

"Yes…Princess."

She tried not to shudder as her name disappeared from his lips.

"What happened…to before?"

"I…can't be him."

"I…I have things to attend to. You can stay as long as you need. To pack, and…and make arrangements." She looked down at her feet, pulling on her fingers. "Take whatever you need. Food. Any of your clothes, all of them…if you want. Ask the stable for a horse they'll…" she cleared her throat, trying not to cry, "they'll provide you one."

"Your highness—"

She stepped back as he stepped towards her. "—just…let the guard know when you are leaving, so they can inform me. And…leave quietly. Don't…tell the boys. It's…easier. If I tell them. Afterwards."

"Okay, but your highness—"

"—safe travels, Sir Crawford." Amair turned, bursting out the door, closing it behind her as the tears finally spilled in entirety, a hand flying to her mouth to try to stifle her sobs, leaning against the tall white door. Her shoulders hunched, leaning her head down as her tears rolled down her cheeks.

Inside the library, Theo's head hung, tears dripping off his chin, chewing the inside of his cheek. After a few moments, he peeked his head out the door. The hallway was empty, Amair already rushed away to find her peace.

- CHAPTER LXXXIX -

"Your highness?" the guard called from the door. She didn't turn in her chair, the guard coughing uncomfortably. "He…Sir Crawford has left, your highness."

"Thank you," she murmured, still not turning. The guard watched the back of the chair for a moment, finally bowing his head and taking a step back, closing the door. She heard it close and looked up, the light of the grey day trickling in the library window. She pulled her feet out from under herself, heading for the door. She walked quickly, quietly, down the hall, glancing into the empty guest corridor. She stuck to the walls, slipping out the door onto the wide balcony, the misting rain clinging to her hair and her eyelashes. She could see the dark brown horse, Theo with a thick bag across his back, ambling just outside the castle gates, headed for the forests. Footsteps sounded on the balcony behind her, Jasper and Kylo leaning onto the bannister.

"He's gone?"

"He is," Amair breathed, not looking at Jasper, her eyes on the Writer's back.

"He'll…he'll be back…right? He has to come back…" Kylo murmured. Amair shook her head, pulling her shawl tight around herself, her arms crossed.

"No, Kylo. He's gone." She lifted her chin, the three of them watching the young man who had become their best friend. At the edge of the woods, Theo's horse stopped, pulling on the reins as he sat for a second. Slowly, Theo looked back over his shoulder.

He could make out the outline of Amair on the balcony. He watched her for a second, the two of them completely still in the moment, the distance between them closing as they watched the other. She shifted, pulling on her shawl again. He swallowed hard.

Finally, Theo turned his head, hunched his shoulders, and let the fog pull him away.

Amair watched one more moment before she turned away from the window. The battle was over. But she knew the war was still coming for them.

She had work to do.

Guard are asking all Skylos to stay aware of their surroundings, but that the actual threat to Skylock for retaliation remains extremely low.

- Andreya Renberg, Public Safety

A note on Ink & Crown: the Princess Serial

Reporter *Sir Theodore Crawford* has made the difficult decision to leave the castle and this paper. We thank him for his service and the castle has requested no replacement be sent.
This marks the end of the series on *Her Royal Highness Oighre Princess Amir Skylock*.
We apologize for the abrupt ending, and thank you for following along over the past seasons.

- *Jacobus Trint, Editor in Chief, Skyline Chronicle*

Famous Singer returning to Skylock

After her cross-Land tour, Skylock's beloved *Ohrra Verrante* will be returning to her family home in Glasslight Province. The singer's tour was set to begin on the seventh of Autumn, however due to tragedy that befell Skylock two days before, *Verrante* and her management team agreed that it should be postponed until healing had begun in the Kingdom. The tour took up at the end of Autumn, and *Verrante* was quickly invited to perform at the palace. *Verrante* is thankful for the tour and her 'incredible fans', but is pleased to be at home and begin her rest and recovery before she focuses on a new project.

- *Bailey McDermey, Arts*

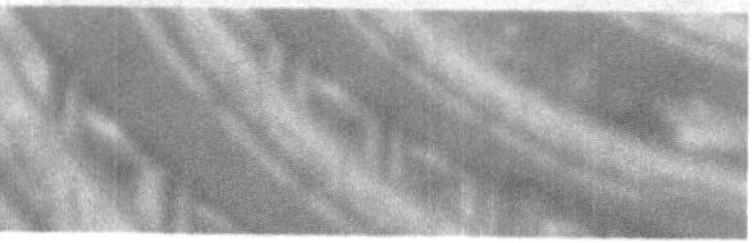

The End *for now*

- 399 -

Turn the page for an early sneak peek at
the next instalment in Amair's path to the crown

- 401 -

- CHAPTER I -

"Prisoner!"

"Catch him!"

"He's escaping!"

"Prisoner! In the castle!" Torrence heard the voices of the palace guard echoing behind him, jumping the last step of the dark staircase, bursting through the door at the end. His vision went white, almost stumbling back into the stairs, his heel slipping back over the edge. He blinked, hard, tripping forwards. It took a moment, turning a corner blindly, the room starting to materialize.

"Your highness!" Torrence heard the guards come to a screeching halt behind him. He looked over his shoulder, watching them come to a stop. He looked back where he thought freedom was, nearly careening into a young woman. He tried to stop, sliding on the slick floors, stopping close enough to feel her warm skin. Her eyebrows were raised as she looked up at him, shocked but steady despite almost being run over.

He looked around at the pale walls, lined with paintings on one side, tall windows along the other. Torrence suddenly realized he must have run into the palace instead out through the stables.

"What's…going on?" she asked cautiously, pulling her gaze away from Torrence as she closed her book, looking past him at the guards.

"A prisoner has escaped!"

"Yes, I gathered that much from the *yelling*."

"Yes...right…"

She sighed, glancing around at everyone. "What's his charge?" the Princess asked, looking Torrence up and down.

"Treason, my lady."

"No it's not!" Torrence spun, glaring at the guard.

"My lady—" She held up a finger, not turning her eyes from Torrence, and the guard quieted. Torrence watched as the Princess studied him, her lips pulled together, thinking.

"Leave him with me."

All the guards' eyes widened. "Your highness—" one of them exclaimed and she hushed them again.

"We'll be fine." The Princess glanced at the guard, their eyes steady as the Princess raised an eyebrow. Torrence noticed the way they shone, and part of him wanted to turn and run back to the guards as she eyed him mischievously. "Trust me."

EXTRAS

- 405 -

- ANNEX 1: SOVEREIGN TREE -

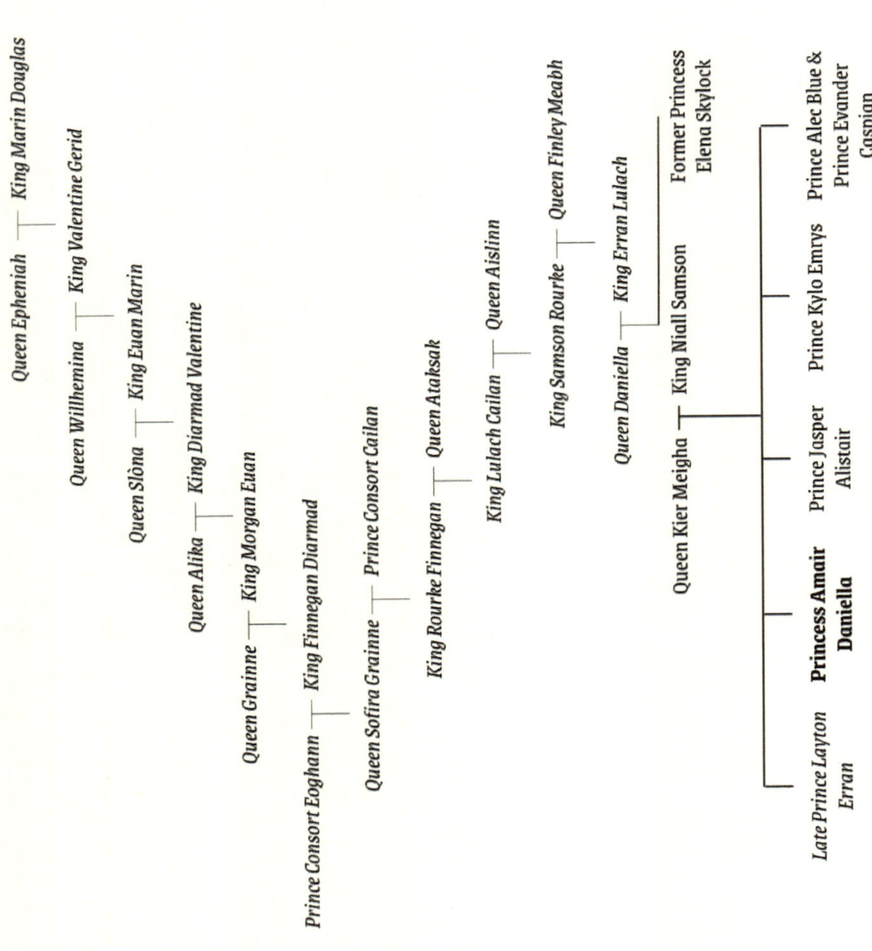

- ANNEX 2: DEITIES -

Sitwell (Sit-well, he/him), Deity King, God of Peace

Basigàn (Bah-zee-gan, she/her), Deity Queen, Goddess of Death/Life Cycle

Latarix (Lat-ar-ix, he/him), God of Day

Naticca (Na-ticc-a, she/her), Goddess of Fields, Farmers, and Harvest

Taleass (Tah-lee-ass, he/him), God of Rain and Water

Eula (Oi-la, she/her), Goddess of Birds

Seilleans (Shey-llans, they/them), Deity of Insects

Quinnm'on (Quinn-mey-on, she/her), Goddess of Wisdom and Education

Fluran (Floo-ran, he/him), God of Flowers

Ygraine (Ee-grain, she/her), Goddess of Children and Birth

MacCoreyog (Mac-corey-yog, he/him), God of Love

Endra (En-dra, she/her), Goddess of Skies, Patron of Skylock

Caradoidhcte (Cara-doid-chey, he/him), God of Night

Sloane (Sloane, she/her), Goddess of Warriors

Athdar (Ath-dar, he/him), God of Forests and Trees

Gavalia (Gah-vah-lea, he/her), Goddess of Labourers

Noabhail (No-avail, he/him), God of Messengers, Travellers, and Adventurers

Slàna (Shlana, she/her), Goddess of Medicine and Doctors

Bograyne (Bo-grain, he/him), God of Animals

Teagha (Tay-a, they/them), Deity of Homes and Families

Seannaiphe (Shawn-eph-ay, he/him), God of Merchants

Rowenea (Row-anaya, they/them), Deity of Music and Art

- ANNEX 3: THE 7 REALMS -

Skylock
Where the land touches the sky | Symbol: Skylark
Ruled by the Sovereign Clan, first amongst friends. The Sovereign King or Queen works in tandem with the Sovereign's Council of close advisors, the Chiefs and War Chiefs of the Six Clans, and the Elected Council. Second in command is the Oighre, the heir to the throne.
Known for their rainy weather, hearty root vegetables, some fishing, and vast highlands and lochs

Forra
Where the trees obscure forever | Symbol: Rabbit
Ruled by High King and the King, with some input from the heir, the First Prince.
Known for their beautiful greenery, wood and pulp industry, and the Grand Forest

RiKoi
Born of fire and grace | Symbol: Wheat bushel
Ruled by a King and Queen. The heir begins their training the season past their eighteenth birthday.
Known for their wheat and sunflower fields, their beautiful, healthy farm animals, and beautiful rolling hills that still bear some scars of the great fire of old.

Keene
Empire of chaos | Symbol: Snake
Ruled by an Emperor after Keene attempted to expand and absorb the other realms, left now only with one – Avira, the Sand realm they have held onto. Under the Emperor is the Grand Duke, and any other sons become Archdukes. The Grand Duke's first son would become Prince, unless he has none. In that case, it would be the son of the eldest Archduke to become Prince.
Known for their hedges and deep cut paths, cast over skies and ragged land that reflects a century of exploiting the limited raw materials within it, and their brutality.

Waiwhe
Republic of salted air | Symbol: Octopus
Overseen by a Senate made up of twenty-six senators representing
thirteen districts. Senators are elected every three years. Once elected,
one amongst them is chosen as the Speaker of the Senate to oversee
proceedings of the chamber.
Known for their fish, citrus and other fruits, nuts, glass, and the
beautiful beaches and blue waters that make up the realm.

Innisil
Kingdom in the clouds | Symbol: Mountain sheep
Split down the middle as the Eastern and Western Provinces, both
halves ruled by a respective King and Queen, who live in a connected
castle that straddles the border to maintain peace.
Known for their beautiful mountains that stretch high into the sky,
and the mining for metals and gems they produce.

Tunngas
Queendom of warm hearts | Symbol: Snow owl
Ruled by a Queen, the Grand Princess, and the Second Princess, along
with their Court of Mothers, chosen to represent each town.
Known for ice fields and snowy mountains, ice islands to the south,
hot springs high in the mountains, and their export of fish and glass
and ice fruits.

- ABOUT THE AUTHOR -

Tegwyn Skye is a writer who cannot claim one genre as her own, finding a love of writing in fantasy, contemporary fiction, and dystopian genres. Born and raised in northern Alberta, Canada, Tegwyn Skye can't decide what part of Canada feels like home. She spent her high school years on Vancouver Island, and moved to Ottawa, Ontario, to pursue a degree in History and Political Science, and has recently found herself back on the Island. She started university as a business student, but quickly realized it was absolutely not the type of things she wanted to be learning – and since switching, she has become a big advocate of making mistakes and finding your path at your own pace. She has worked in restaurants, hotels, tourism, government, and is now pursuing work in secondary education. All the while, writing stayed her beloved, passion project on the side. Her two favourite things in the whole world are her black cats Isaac and Sybil.

Outside of writing and education, Tegwyn Skye's great loves include dance, reading every fantasy and dystopian book she can get her hands on, rock climbing and boxing, singing along badly to musicals, and being outside. One of her biggest goals in life is to visit every province and territory in Canada, every national park, and as many strange and cool restaurants as she possibly can. She is looking forward to exploring more genres as she takes a quick break from Amair's story. She can also be found in the poetry section, with four poetry books that helped get her through her depression and growth.

She can be found on most social medias at **@TSC_WIP**, on Goodreads at **T.S. Curtis**, and on her beloved website and blog **tscurtis.com**.

- ACKNOWLEDGEMENTS -

When I wrote my first poetry book, the list of people I wanted to thank and acknowledge and send my love and gratitude to was longer than a good chunk of the poems. By the time I wrote my third poetry book, I mentioned how that third collection did not carry the same burden to acknowledge because it had gotten to the point where there were a few very specific people who made it happen.

Well, with this being my first novel – much larger, much longer, much, *much* harder (both in terms of the density of the physical thing, but also in trying to write it) – the burden is back and tenfold. Publishing works on your own as a self-published author is extremely, incredibly difficult. You don't have one person in your corner who can definitively tell you you're doing great, that you're meeting the goals you need to, that you're on the right path. There's no one with the inside secrets the traditional publishing world provides you. A lot of the time, it feels like the only person you have to rely on, is yourself. You have to become your own cheerleader.

So, while some might see it as selfish, I want to thank myself, first. Every version of myself that has taken part in the creation of this novel, from the twelve-year-old girl scribbling story ideas in the margins of her classroom notebooks who first came up with Amair and Theo, to the girl I was when I first opened the document at the start of NaNoWriMo in 2020, to the young woman writing this now with a completed manuscript in front of her. I am the writer, the editor, the designer, the illustrator. I was the person who had my own back when I felt the need to throw the manuscript out the window. I have kept my head up as I jumped headfirst into the rough world of what it means to publish. Poetry collections are one thing; a novel, somehow, is a whole other beast.

Now that I have taken the moment of grace I needed, on to the others!

This book absolutely, one-hundred-and-twelve-percent would not have been possible without Monica, Chelsey, and Srishti. From dealing with my absolute meltdowns and mental breakdowns and the chaos that is…just…me…I cannot thank you enough. For answering the dozens of questions, replying to probably thousands of Snapchats and Facebook messages, to propping me up when I need it, you have been the best people to have in my corner.

To Ndeye, who continued to lament that she did not have a copy of a novel with my name on it and a very large part of the reason I somehow managed to convince myself to survive this horrific process of trying to actually *finish* a novel.

To Zach, who was my voice of reason, and my best friend. I wish a Zach to every person – the kind of friend who is there when you need, who you connected with without reason or intent, and has instead become a member of your family.

To Celeste, who is no longer part of my world, but read the very first version of this story what feels like a million years ago now, when we were barely more than little girls cowering in hidden corners of the school yard with our notebooks swapping stories and poems and heartaches and stolen moments. The very first person to believe in me, my identity, and my words.

To Adrian, my writer friend, who felt like a cheerleader outside my main circle when I felt like I was failing or floundering, and we could celebrate the tiny wins, and the big wins together even if we have never actually met.

To Reane. Write your stories, darling. The world is waiting for you, and it does not matter who you are, or where you come from: you deserve to be heard.

To new friends, like Mica, who on more than one occasion kicked my butt into gear and reminded me what it meant to be creative – but also what it meant to take a step back and breathe.

To A, whom this story was once written for, and probably doesn't remember me. But I remember you.

And to my mom, Krysta. My first teacher, and my biggest supporter. She may not always understand me, may not completely grasp the intense need to write down the stories that have taken over my mind, but she supported me nonetheless. The first person to buy my books and my art. The first person to remind me to keep trying. And, with all the amazingness of the teacher and former English major that she is, my trusted editor, and the person to thank for there being almost zero typos and grammatical errors.

Thank you all of you for being My People.

And to you, reader, if you have made this far. The fact that you have spent this much of your life with Amair, Theo, and I means the world to me, and I hope you will come back for more when we have breathed, and the next part of our story is ready.

- 415 -